POLYSTOM

Also by Adam Roberts in Gollancz:

Salt
On
Stone

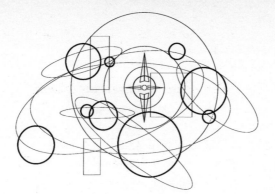

POLYSTOM

ADAM
ROBERTS

GOLLANCZ

LONDON

First published in Great Britain in 2003 by
Gollancz
an imprint of the Orion Publishing Group Ltd.
Orion House, 5 Upper Saint Martin's Lane, London WC2H 9EA

A CIP catalogue record for this book is
available from the British Library

ISBN 0 575 07178 8 (cased)
ISBN 0 575 07179 6 (trade paperback)

Typeset at The Spartan Press Ltd,
Lymington, Hants

Printed in Great Britain by Clays Ltd, St Ives plc

It is also calculated that at an altitude not exceeding the hundredth part of the earth's diameter – that is, not exceeding eighty miles – the rarefaction would be so excessive that animal life could in no manner be sustained . . . But in point of fact, an ascension being made to any given altitude, the ponderable quantity of air surmounted in any farther ascension, is by no means in proportion to the addition height ascended, but in a *ratio* constantly decreasing. It is therefore evident that, ascend as high as we may, we cannot literally speaking, arrive at a limit beyond which *no* atmosphere is to be found. It *must exist*, I argued . . . It appeared to me evidently a rare atmosphere extending from the sun outwards, beyond the orbit of Venus at least, and I believed indefinitely farther, pervading the entire regions of our planetary system, condensed into what we call atmosphere at the planets themselves.

Poe, '*Hans Pfaall*'

We know that the dead are powerful rulers; but we may perhaps be surprised when we learn that they are treated as enemies.

Freud, *Totem and Taboo* II.3.c

Characters

Old *Polystom*
His partner, *Egregos*

Young *Polystom*, his son
Beeswing, young Polystom's wife

Cleonicles, Old Polystom's brother and young Polystom's uncle
Parleon, his butler
Nestor, a servant of young Polystom
Elena, an aunt of Polystom's
Sophanes and *Stetrus*, military officers

ONE

Polystom

A Love Story

[first leaf]

Polystom climbed into his biplane one morning, having made up his mind to fly to the moon. It had come to him upon waking, the sudden whim to visit his uncle Cleonicles – the great Scientist Cleonicles, none other – in his mansion on the moon. It so happened that Cleonicles, the revered old man, the great scientist, had only three days of life left to him. Polystom knew nothing of this, of course, any more than did Cleonicles himself. Our lives are so densely filled with the atomic particles of existence, perception, memory, that taken together they accumulate into a sort of haze, and this prevents us from seeing very far into the future. Not knowing that his uncle was mere days from a violent death, Polystom was happy as he dressed. War was an impossibly distant blur on the horizon, nothing more.

It was a dim morning, yellow clouds reducing the sun's tack-head of light to a bleary focus of brightness. Far to the west, sunlight reflecting from the silvery rocks of the Neon Mountains seems artificially bright, throwing sharp black shadows long across the airfield. But apart from the silver-grey mistiness in the air the morning was good. Stom particularly liked the smell of the ground warming, a kind of acidic, gravelly, earthy smell. Like newly washed hair. He stopped and scratched his skull. The airfield reached flat to the line of trees, and then the forest swept away, before him, encircling the estate, reaching up and covering the hills in the middle distance. Beyond those hills the Neon Mountains rose in spectacular triangles and wedges of pure light. Look away, look up, and there was the deeply thrilling purple emptiness of the sky. Today, Stom thought to himself, it will be my sky.

. . .
[*three lines missing*]
. . . up the steps, the la[dder, and] into the cockpit. His leather

3

[helmet] was here, where the servants had placed it, and he fitted it over his head, snapping the goggles into place. It required only a sharp action of his thumb down on the contact to start the propellers. A choked-sounding series of barks, and then the engine thrummed, a rising arc of sound, grumble to moan, screech, whine and the plane rolling and jogging over the turf. A hop into the air, jar the ground and up again. The propellers catching in the air like a comb snagging a tangle of hair, and pulling – pulling Stom upwards, his spirit lifting in tandem with his body. He knew of no other sensation that came close to this. The thrill of lifting upwards.

He was up.

He circled, flew back over his own airfield, tipping the plane to one side to take in the view of the oblong runway, the sheds at the far end, and over to his house, its Γ-shaped magnificence (eighty rooms! As his co-father had boasted, many times – nearly twice as big as Cousin Hera's!). Then over that and there was nothing but woodland beneath him, trees and trees and away to the left the swordblade flash of sunlight on the water.

The controls were sluggish, the wings still dew-soaked, and lift was elusive, but as Stom eased the stick back and flew a gentle upward spiral, they started to dry. Soon the whole biplane was humming. The fabric on its wings was drying and shrinking in the overblow of air, singing slightly, a high-pitched wail just audible over the rush of the wind. Stom wedged the fingers of his left-hand glove under his thigh, pulling the hand free, nude; he reached out with his free hand and touched the nearest of the wires that linked lower wing to upper wing in a crisscross of Xs. Twanged, it thrummed like a guitar string. He slipped the hand back into its glove.

He banked, and looked down upon his home. This time the house was a mere comma, his own extensive woods a bent stretch of dark green. Mostly he saw the snout of the Middenstead sea where it rounded in innumerable coves on the border of his estate. The water looked shining but depthless, a range of textures from smooth-lit to pewter-dappled white-grey. Another circle and spiral upwards through the air and the wood had reduced to a curled finger, and the whole of the Middenstead could be seen: sausage-shaped, nestling in amongst the perfect miniature details of mountains, splotches of forest, stamp-sized squares of cultivated land.

One last look. Goodbye! I leave my world behind.

That morning, as Nestor had brought him his breakfast on a tray, he had said *Nestor, I think I shall visit Cleonicles today.* Nestor had only said *Very good,* with that blank look in his eyes so characteristic of servants, and had held the tray out towards him. But once the idea was in Stom's mind it was as if he were possessed by it. He hadn't so much as touched his breakfast, had bounced out of bed. *My silk underclothes, Nestor, if I'm to be flying today. Very good, sir, immediately. Tell the mechanics to prepare the biplane. Which one, sir? The* Pterodactyl. *My favourite!*

The plane is sprightlier now; Stom pulls back the long stick and sweeps upwards again, singing tunelessly in the sheer delight of it, an approximate operatic aria, except that he has no ear for music at all. Up and into the clarity of the blue sky. Surrendering himself to the great oceanic upper depths of the sky, up, up, up. *Ortheen,* he sings, *orthe-e-e-en keleu-e-e-es, heeto dendron fai-ai-ai-ainetai!* He remembers the words, but not the tune. When he next looks down he can see half a hemisphere, the whole of his estate and half a dozen other ones, the Middenstead and the Farrenstead seas, the scaly-looking chain of mountains stretching far to the west. The horizon still seems, by that strange trick of perception known to fliers and mountaineers, to be on a level with him, giving the panorama a weird, concave appearance, as if everything Stom owns is located in the base of a gigantic bowl. But an hour flying higher and the world has flipped round, bellied out. Now he can see the curve of the planet, the perfect arc marking off the browns and greens and blues of his world from the blue-purple of interplanetary space. One last look down, but now he couldn't even pick out the three-hundred-mile-length of the Middenstead sea amongst the variegated textures of the world below him.

The sun was still misty, a fingernail-sized smudge of brightness; the moon, forty times the diameter of the sun, glowed in the reflected light. Stom hauled his plane round, still singing, and positioned his nose straight at the heart of his destination. He pressed the engine-pedal down, and slipped the catch across it with his toe. The engines roared, heaved, and the plane started pulling towards the pock-marked green of the moon.

The interplanetary air was weirdly thin, breathable of course but not relishable. Some fashionable newsbook opinion pieces made great claims for the purity of it, even to the point of suggesting merely breathing it as a treatment for various ailments. But it always made Stom feel slightly headachy. Nothing too serious, but enough to take the edge off the experience. As air it was never quite enough for him, made his lungs labour in an asthmatic manner. It was extremely cold, of course. He buttoned up his Zunft flying jacket and pressed the button that warmed the heating coil in its back. The cold, unpleasant, started to recede, although his sinuses still stung with chill.

But he did love the view. Up here the sky was not the darker blue a ground-dweller saw; it was a rarefied, purified air, a delicate violet-blue, the colour of methylated-spirits. He could stare into the depths for hours at an end. It was almost a process of meditation.

For ten minutes, as his plane pulled away from the world and towards the moon, Stom busied himself. He undid his harness, and rustled around in the compartment under his seat. His servants had provided him with some food, two flasks of drink (one alcoholic, one not), extra layers of clothing should the cold prove unusually sharp, some books to read. Polystom liked to read poetry, and his servants knew this fact. They also packed a medical basket, including painkillers, and Stom reached for this first. He took out two lenticular pills, and washed them down with one of his flasks of drink. What was it? Some fruit whisky or other. Blackberry whisky, possibly. It didn't really matter.

The plane droned on.

The flight was necessarily lengthy, but Stom wasn't in any sort of hurry. He stood up in the cockpit and turned to face the rear of the plane. This brought him within reach of the storage compartment, and this he opened, drawing out of it a thin bundle as long as a man's height. Resting this upright in the cockpit, Polystom killed the engine and waited for the propellers to slow and stop. Coasting through the violet depths of interplanetary sky Stom's plane would fly onwards, losing speed in small but inevitable increments until the gravitational tug of his world ceased and eventually reversed his trajectory. But Stom didn't wait for this; he clambered out of the cockpit and lay over the warm engine casing, pulling free two bolt-catches and unfixing the propeller. This, hot from use, he removed and, turning, shoved it back into the cockpit. He had to wriggle backwards a little to retrieve the parcel, but then he easily untied it, unfolded the bent-up blades once, twice, three times, clicking each component into place. Finally, manoeuvring the enormous spindly thing easily enough in the miniature gravity, he slotted it into place and pushed the bolt-catches home.

Back in the cockpit he folded up the regular props and pushed them into the storage compartment. Then he gunned the engine to life again, and the vast arcs of the high-sky props spun round. Too fragile for use in the thicker air closer to ground, these interplanetary propellers pulled the plane harder through the ethereal medium that occupied the spaces between worlds. It was a long journey; too long to travel the whole way on take-off-landing props. There was a kick, jerking Stom against the back of his seat, as his plane roared onwards. Up up up!

For a while Stom listened with pleasure to the rapid whish-whish of the propellers, the contented purr of the engine. The speed rose, until he was travelling three times the speed the smaller blades could manage, five times, ten. Then he fine-tuned the direction, positioning the plane a little more precisely so that it was angled at the very heart of the moon. Already the great globe seemed closer. Dusty green and greys on the patched surface swelled minutely before him.

Polystom retrieved the bottle. He ate one of the sandwiches and moistened his throat between bites. Then he finished the blackberry whisky, and lolled in the cockpit for an hour or more, staring out at the blue-violet depths of interplanetary sky. Being cradled in the near-nothingness of space drunk was a peculiar pleasure. Eventually Stom dozed, hushed by the rushing of the air around him.

He woke thirsty, and drank some water. Then he ate another sandwich. With these physical needs addressed, he looked around. The moon directly ahead was conspicuously larger; more detail visible on the cracked and cratered green of its surface. Stom swivelled, kneeling on his seat to give himself a better view of the world he had left behind. His world, the world of Enting, was receding slowly behind him. Most of its arc was visible; clouds draped the mosaic fineness of the ground in intermittent shreds. The stretch of the hemisphere-crossing Great Ocean gleamed dark-blue, with strands of cloud gathered like folds in clothing, or like the ripples in sand at low tide, covering half its surface.

Stom turned again, and played with the engine, gunning it,

dethrottling. He pulled to the left, to the right, to check respon-siveness. It was so delightful, the way it responded, the way it fitted together, every component working in mechanical harmony with every other one. It sang in Polystom's heart.

He refixed the throttle fully out, settled back in his seat, dozed again. On waking he scanned the sky in all directions; left and right, up and down, before and behind. Away to the fore and several miles below he picked out the shape of a balloon-boat, pen-shaped, bringing in some cargo from another world. Strictly speaking, planes were supposed to give balloon-boats a wide berth, but Stom disregarded the rule; of course it didn't apply to him. He flipped off the catch and heaved the stick forward. The plane tipped forward, and within ten minutes the finger-sized balloon-boat was as big as a cathedral. A half-mile-long dark-green bladder of attenuated gas and storage com-partments, piled above and below with towers to which were ap-pended rank upon rank of mighty propellers. The passenger cabin, as big the south wing of Stom's own house, looked like a slug upon a giant marrow, nestling underneath. Polystom flew over the structure, coming close enough to see a steep-jack clinging to one engine carrying out some repair or other, and then circled round to sweep under it, where he could make out the faces of passengers in the observation globe. He waved, half-frantic with the excitement, but nobody returned the gesture.

These two vessels, tiny biplane and giant balloon-boat, in the violet sky between earth and moon, and nothing else. Stom circled for a while, until he finally provoked a response from the pilot, a blue-uniformed figure just visible in the wide porthole at the front of the command cabin. As Stom flew across the balloon-boat's line of flight for the fourth time the miniature figure of the captain flapped his arm angrily, waving him away. Stom cheerily waved back, and then pulled the stick towards his body and flew up, over the vessel's back, and away. He repositioned his plane so that it was aimed once more at the centre of the moon and flew straight on.

He saw little else on his flight, and took to reading one of his books. Once, several hours later, he caught a glimpse of a skywhal, drifting mouth-open on a trajectory that took it behind the moon. It was unusual to see one of the great beasts so close in to a planetary body, and Stom wondered excitedly whether it was going to beach itself. But, on closer examination, it was a small creature, its fronds little developed, and so was almost certainly still a youngster, still exploring, not yet settled into one of the great cometary orbits that mature skywhals preferred, away from the gravitational disturbances of planets.

Stom flew on.

He regretted, now, having finished off his whisky so quickly. He was sober again and a drink would have been very pleasant. He tried to concentrate on his book but kept nodding off. He dozed, half awake, half asleep.

Hours later the moon had grown until it filled most of the sky. Stom could make out features in its enormous face; lakes, canals, mountain ranges like trails of crushed nuts; broad patches of algal green, very sharply coloured in the eternal light of interplanetary spaces. There were narrower strips of cultivation, darker green. The desert areas, grey-silver, scattered a paler albedo across the great landscape. Three seas were evident, each of them, Stom knew from experience, no more than a few feet deep, though many tens of miles wide. His uncle Cleonicles lived on the shores of one of them, the Lake of Dreams, the *Lacus Somniorum*, as it was rather fancifully called. A sludgy pond stretched miles wide, too shallow and treacly with algae even to swim in. But Cleonicles' house was pleasant enough; not as large as so famous or senior a man deserved, Stom thought, and too much filled with machines and artefacts, but pleasant nonetheless. Four-legged birds, stork-boars, polopped their quiet way through the shallow waters, dotting the green sea out to the horizon; trees grew to spectacular height and slenderness in the lesser lunar gravity; vegetable worms crawled sullenly across the lawn. Some of Polystom's happiest days had been spent sitting in a comfortable chair on his uncle's lawn, overlooking the stagnant Lake of Dreams, chatting earnestly away whilst his uncle nodded and hummed. Cleonicles was a peaceful man, in this respect resembling his dead brother, Stom's father. He was not as silent a person as Stom's father had been, but neither was he the sort of person to monopolise the conversation. Stom had visited the moon many times since his father's death. He regarded it as something of a sanctuary.

Polystom's father had been dead four years, his co-father almost as long.

Polystom had married after his father's death, but the marriage had not prospered. The looked-for solace had not materialised. Stom had spent months in mourning for it. He lived alone now, often lonely and with a distant sense of something amiss in his life. To speak of the woe that is in marriage!

And so he came again to the moon. Picking out the horned shape of the Lacus Somniorum, away on the right-hand border of the moon, Polystom swung his plane's trajectory away from its dead-centre targeting. The gravity of the satellite was strong enough now to render the larger props redundant, and Stom spent several minutes changing them for the regular blades. Then he pulled into a shallower and still shallower approach as the moon swelled to encompass almost half the sky. Finally, as he had done many times before, he saw the curve of the Lunar Mount to his left, and set a course for a notch in the horizon that had opened up before him. The air grew warmer, and Stom turned off his flying suit, unbuttoned his jacket. His scarf sank slowly as it rediscovered weight, until it was draped in his lap. Soon enough the Lake of Dreams unfurled beneath him, glisteningly green and dotted with stork-boars. He passed over his uncle's house, circled round, and dropped easily down to land on the back lawn. The plane rolled, slowed, shuddered to a halt.

He had taken off his helmet and goggles and was clambering out of the cockpit before the engine had even started slowing; servants scurried towards him, and behind them he could make out the genial shape of his uncle waving his stick in greeting.

Cleonicles, Polystom's uncle, was at this time perhaps the most famous scientist in all the System. For long years he had worked on the celebrated Computational Device, the enormous valve-and-crystal machine that could undertake all manner of mathematical operations on a fantastic scale and with fantastic speed. He had been one of the party of three (this was many years ago, in his youth) responsible for initiating the project, his own, and later other patrons' money boosting construction of ground-based and later free-floating devices, vast scaffolds of electrical connection. The newsbooks called it the Greatest Work of Man, or sometimes the Summation of Human Knowledge.

Polystom, who knew his uncle as a genial old man with threads of white in his grey beard, had come late to knowledge of his uncle's celebrity. *Fame*, he realised belatedly, was something different from breeding, although of course his uncle was amongst the best bred in the System. This was something *else*, the young Polystom had realised with a jolt. His uncle, his pleasant-faced old uncle, was revered not just for what he *was*, but for *what he had done*. Understanding this marked, in an understated way, a revolution in the young fellow's thinking. He had been thirteen years old, and visiting Cleonicles on the moon in the company of his father. To stave off boredom on the flight, being too young to take the controls himself, he had read one of his father's discarded newsbooks, the *News Volume* for November. It was mostly given over to ecstatic reporting of the latest incarnation of the Computational Device, one larger than all the previous ones put together. The name Cleonicles appeared on every page, and towards the back of the book there was a lengthy word-portrait of him.

Latterly, Professor Cleonicles has withdrawn himself from the grander designs of the Computational Device committee; he lives now in 'splendid isolation', if we may be permitted to borrow a metaphorical phrase from the Political Military, on the moon of Enting, 'to be near my close family' he has announced. He devotes himself now to that arcane branch of scientific knowledge, star-research. 'I find the very notion of these superb, barren mountains of fire hanging in nothingness – literally nothingness! – to be poetic and engaging to the highest degree,' the Professor has said.

All through that visit, taking wine-lees tea on the lawn of his uncle's house, looking over the Lacus Somniorum, Polystom had been too excited to sit still. Had his co-father been there he would have been rebuked for fidgeting, but his father was too placid to care, and his uncle smiled his understanding smile.

'They called the Computational Device the great achievement of humanity!' young Polystom had said. 'And *you* invented it!'

'Hardly, my boy,' said Cleonicles. 'There were three of us in the initial team, and many more helped turn our rough-ready theories into the practice of the CDs themselves.'

'They're building the biggest Computational Device of all!' Polystom had gushed. 'It said so in the newsbook!'

'They've built it,' said Cleonicles, pouring his brother some more tea. 'Now they're just fine-tuning it. There are experiments, for which the machine was designed. Actually, they've run into a spot of trouble.'

Polystom's father, the elder Polystom, sighed and smiled as he lifted the cup to his mouth, as if to imply that trouble and error were inevitabilities in this System of theirs.

'Why did you leave that project, uncle?' Polystom asked earnestly. 'How could you leave something so exciting?'

One of the things that Stom loved about his uncle was that he never shirked or side-stepped a question. He always answered directly. 'Partly because the nuts-and-cogs of Computational Devicery aren't as exciting as they sound to young ears like yours. Partly because I had disagreements with the others on my team.'

'Distressing,' murmured Polystom senior, sipping his tea.

'Very,' said Cleonicles, with a sharp nod that made his beard waggle. 'But partly, my young bear-cub, I left because I found something *more* exciting.'

'Stars?' said young Polystom, unable (though he knew it was poor manners) to keep disdain out of his voice. At thirteen Polystom had never seen stars, and accordingly his imagination had no purchase on the idea of them.

'Certainly stars,' said his uncle, with pronounced though not unfriendly emphasis. 'After tea I can show you some photo-lithos that I've recently taken out near the upper-limit of the System.'

But Polystom was unconvinced. When tea was finished he trudged into the house after his uncle and duly gazed at some filmy pictures of what seemed to him very little indeed: black squares, each one an image, nine to a sheet; some pure black, like press-sheets at a printing house; most black but scattered with a dozen, or two dozen, white dots and smudges. What was so exciting about that? It looked spotty and miniature to Stom. Even his uncle's enthusiasm for *enormous globes of fire, burning in nothingness* failed to rouse his imagination. The whole business was just too fanciful.

So, now, seven years later, Polystom the adult, Polystom the seventh Steward of Enting, climbed out of his biplane and jogged over the lawn towards his uncle. Things had changed, of course. Old Cleonicles had been wearied and a little broken by the death of his brother, and his brother's partner. The war on the Mudworld had erupted into extraordinary violence. For long stretches of fighting as many as a hundred people, including two or three people from important Families, were dying every day. Cleonicles wrote dignified but furious letters to the newsbooks about the conflict, a war he viewed as a ghastly error of judgment by the Political Military. He had the grace not to force his views on his nephew, a discretion that greatly pleased the more warlike boy. But when a scientist of the stature of Cleonicles spoke, many people listened. *Blockade would be easier, less destructive and infinitely more humane than the senseless war being waged now. I urge all families of note to petition the Political Military, with a view to calling a panel to review strategy. Lives are being lost every day!*

'Helloë, uncle!' Polystom called.

'My dear boy,' returned Cleonicles, a little breathlessly. 'My dear boy!'

They embraced. 'A good crossing?' the old man asked, ushering Stom to a chair.

'Uneventful. Passed a balloon-boat; splendid thing. I saw a skywhal, too, in what looked like a close swing about this moon of yours.'

'I think I saw him myself, dear boy,' said Cleonicles, gesturing with his left hand at a five-foot-long telescopic tube erected on the patio. 'Very young one. Sometimes,' he added, as if unable to resist the urge to lecture, 'sometimes the things beach themselves on moons, you know, and I wondered if that was why he came in so close. But it's always mature fellows who beach themselves, and this one was clearly immature. Lost his way a little, I expect.'

A servant appeared, bringing a tray. On it was an exquisite blue glass samovar filled with coffee. Next to this was a bottle of black wine.

'Still *star*-gazing, uncle, eh?' said Polystom, throwing one leg over the arm of his chair, and tossing his flying helmet and gloves onto the grass beside him, in a rather self-conscious attempt to play-act *carelessness*. Maps and charts were spread on the table in front of the old man.

'Yes, dear boy,' said Cleonicles.

'I've been thinking about your passion for these *stars*,' Stom said brightly, putting just a hint of impertinent emphasis on the final word. 'Don't you think that they don't make sense? According to some of the

13

books I've been reading, there are theories that they don't exist at all. I'll tell you: I was talking to my Head Grass-Gardner, you know, about seeding a new lawn. And in amongst other things he told me that *he* doesn't believe in them, and he's an excellent fellow. At Grass-Gardening, anyhow.'

'If you can't see them they don't exist, eh?' chuckled Cleonicles. 'A veritably Grass-Gardneresque philosophy, that. If you can't run the seeds through your fingers, or feel the pressure of roller on lawn, then it's just a dream, eh? No, *coffee* for me, man. *Wine* for my nephew,' this last, in more severe tones, addressed to the servant who was about to pour a glass of wine for Cleonicles.

'But stars – you say that these things burn? In *vacuum*?'

'I am impressed,' said Cleonicles, smiling. 'You're keeping up with at least some of the latest science writing, if you know that word.'

'I'll admit,' said Polystom, grinning, 'that I dropped the word in for effect. But burning means eating air – don't it? How does a thing burn in a vacuum? It really makes no sense.'

'There's certainly vacuum at the limits of our system, you know,' said Cleonicles. 'That, at least, has been scientifically proven. Now, I agree with you, there are conflicting stories as to what the "stars" are – how far away they are, whether they are real phenomena or somehow fragmentary reflections of something else, whether they embody genuine fire or some pseudo-electrical phenomena. But you must concede me vacuum, at least.'

'What I read,' said Polystom, 'is that when scientists make up vacuum in a chamber in some laboratory, the effort is enormous; and that vacuum they make is the delicatest bloom of all the delicate blooms – the *least* thing destroys it. Now how can such a fragile and fundamentally *un*natural thing as this vacuum surround our system? Wouldn't mere contact with the ether collapse it?'

'This is a surprisingly good point, my boy,' said Cleonicles, sipping his coffee. 'I say *surprisingly* only because you've always devoted your energies to poetry and suchlike, so I'm surprised by the acuteness of your observation. But evidently you have the makings of a scientific mind too. It's a good point, and difficult to answer. Well, all we have are theories. Clearly you're right about the inherent instability of "vacuum" – all of nature detests a vacuum, you know. If we imagine a space the size of our system filled only with vacuum, you see, then it's clear – the maths confirms this – that any objects *at all* within this space would be vaporised and dissipated throughout the space, to produce – well, to produce what we see around us, the natural order of things, a more-or-less level pressure gradient, uniform ether. It is *in*conceivable that matter in gaseous, liquid or even solid state could survive the savage differences of pressure that "vacuum" physics implies.'

'And yet you say,' drawled Polystom, drinking his wine in great gulps, 'that outside the sphere of our system . . .'

'I know, I know. You sound like one of my scientific colleagues, dismissing my research! Well,' said Cleonicles. 'Well. One theory is that some from of force-field surrounds our System, to preserve the integrity of the vacuum beyond it. This is hypothetical, and goes beyond Science (if by science – I say, by *Science*, you mean experimental data and observation), but it has certain strengths, as a theory. And if "stars" are, as I think they are, bodies in the vacuum, burning and emitting light, then some similar force-field must exist to preserve their unity.'

But after his initial enthusiasm, Polystom was growing bored of discussing metaphysics with his uncle. 'Well,' he said. 'I'm sure you scientists will figure it out.' He stopped.

Now Cleonicles was silent, smiling slightly. Another thing that Polystom loved about his uncle was his sensitivity. His enormous tact. It was more than good breeding; it was a positive virtue in the old man. Cleonicles knew that Stom would not fly all the way from Enting to the moon merely to talk about physics. Something else must be bothering the young man. But the way to approach this was not to badger Stom, not to rain questions upon him, but rather to allow him the time to tell his own story, to unburden his heart.

'Do you know what?' said Polystom after a while, looking past his uncle at the mud-green stretches of the lake, and blushing slightly. 'I'll tell you; trouble sleeping. It's the oddest thing. Trouble sleeping.'

There was a pause. 'Go on, my boy,' prompted Cleonicles.

'That's all there is to it, really. That's all. Just that. I can drift off to sleep, in front of the fire, with a bottle at my elbow, very pleasant I'm sure. But I always wake up a couple of hours later, and then I can hardly ever get back to sleep after waking again.'

Cleonicles nodded; waited.

'Makes me muggy in the head. Tired all the time.' Polystom's blushing had taken on a deeper hue, now; but still he couldn't meet his uncle's eyes.

'Is there any particular reason for waking up?' Cleonicles suggested, gently.

'What do you mean?'

'I don't know.' Cleonicles spread his old hands on the table before him, the skin of them thin and sagged, marked with brown ecchymotic spots like a negative photo-litho of one of his own star-maps. 'There might be various things.'

'Do you mean,' said Polystom after a pause, still not looking at his uncle, 'things like . . . nightmares?'

'For instance,' his uncle agreed.

'Yes,' said Stom. He breathed in, but the breath caught in his throat and started throbbing out again in gasps. Alarmed, he realised that he was crying. Tears were leaking down his face.

'My dear boy,' said Cleonicles, with infinite compassion. 'My dear boy.'

He reached his hand over the table, and Polystom dropped his own hand on top of it. Just that human contact. The tears still came, languidly, wetting his cheeks and his lips. Polystom sobbed. Soon enough, the crying softened, and died away. Away in the lake behind him, the four-legged stork-boars took their gloopy steps through the shallow waters. Only that noise, and the rustle of the breeze.

'You miss her, I think,' said Cleonicles.

Polystom wiped his face on a napkin, and dropped it to the lawn with a snort. 'I'm ashamed of myself uncle.'

'Oh we shouldn't be ashamed of our feelings,' said Cleonicles. 'Not when we are amongst our loved ones. It's not as if we're entertaining guests!'

'Still, uncle, I hate to cry.'

'You miss her,' Cleonicles repeated, more matter-of-factly. 'There's nothing shameful in that fact, nothing hateable. Of course you miss her.'

'To think,' said Polystom, almost laughing at himself now. 'That she is still keeping me awake after all this time.' 'She' was his former wife, the only wife he had ever had. She had been called Beeswing, although her name had been Dianeira.

[second leaf]

They had married less than a year after the death of Polystom's two fathers. Too sudden a wedding, some people said. Stom's father had died of one of the illnesses that claim old men, and Stom's co-father had followed him into the ground within a month, despite seeming stronger and healthier than his partner. Polystom had grieved, but not alone. Naturally, at moments such as this, the family gathered round him. Two of his aunts, one of them his father's sister, and a dozen cousins ranging in age from eighty to twelve, came to the estate and stayed with him. Cleonicles himself, Polystom's favourite uncle, came down from the moon for a weekend; although he had important science to perform (he claimed) and didn't stay. All in all, Stom was glad of the company.

Aunt Elena, his father's sister, had been particularly wise in the ways of mourning, having lost her own love-husband several years before, and having watched a favourite cousin go down to the Mudworld to fight and not return. She had counselled Polystom not to attempt to restrain his grief for the first week, but thereafter to attempt a more manly self-control. Polystom had wept and wailed on his aunt's shoulder for the allotted seven days, and on the eighth had found it surprisingly easy to control himself. By the end of the month his co-father was dead as well, and Polystom wept again, although the fount of his tears was not as copious the second time. After that his family endeavoured to keep him occupied to the point where absorption in his grief did not stagnate into something unhealthy, but not so much that he was unable to work through the natural grieving process. They swam and fished despite the chill of the Middenstead in Winter Year; they played catch-hoop and netgame on the lawn. Polystom spent time with each of his cousins, getting to know them a little better.

After six months, Aunt Elena began talking of the need for

companionship. Firstly, she inquired, gingerly, after Polystom's pre-ferences. It was awkward, she admitted – given her nephew's relatively advanced years – that she needed elucidation upon this point: 'of course I ought to know, dear boy, but somehow I've remained in ignorance of the direction in which your passions flow.'

'Women,' said Polystom. 'As it happens, girls.' Then Aunt Elena began, delicately, discussing possibilities for companionship. Perhaps even marriage, eventually. With his father's death he had inherited a splendid estate. There was no denying it – it was a large estate, she said. Large, Polystom repeated gloomily, looking through the recep-tion-room window at the dusk-darkening forests, void now of his father's presence. Large and beautiful, of course, Aunt Elena had added diplomatically. A jewel in the crown of the System. But if Stommi (she used the childhood abbreviation) could find a heart's-ally, somebody with whom to share the burdens of stewardship . . . Polystom nodded. He had thought this himself, of course. Perhaps now he was ready for a wife. Perhaps that would mark his ascent into full manhood: inheriting the estate, carrying life onwards, becoming Steward, and marrying.

'Come to a party, then,' said Aunt Elena. 'I'll organise it, in my home. A fortnight today. You can fly over, and I'll introduce you to some interesting people.'

So Polystom had taken his favourite plane, the single-seater *Pterodactyl*, and flown over the Middenstead and down the spine of mountains to his aunt's elegant house, in the middle of beautiful olive-crop country. It was entirely right that the family be organising his bride for him. His sadness, still sharp, felt swathed about as with a bandage by the love of those close to him.

It became obvious that Aunt Elena had a particular girl in mind; a girl called Erina, who was the daughter of Eu Trachaea, the famous composer of modern operas. This Erina was a tall, slender woman, her skin the colour, said Aunt Elena, in a stage whisper, 'of coffee blended with the finest cream'. Aunt Elena introduced the two of them. 'You really must meet my beloved nephew,' she said, before drifting discreetly away. Polystom smiled, stood up a little taller in his bear-leather shoes. He bowed, kissed the front of Erina's wrist as was traditional, and offered his compliments. But he decided immediately that her skin colour, fashionable though it was, was false: there was a tannin-shaded uncertainty to the tone, as if nicotine had spread from her fingers (where she held her long brown cigarette like a pen) up her arm and across her torso.

'You don't smoke?' she asked.

'No,' he conceded. 'My chest is not strong enough for it. Childhood asthma, you know.'

'What a terrible shame,' she said, sipping at the end of her cigarette. The smoke tendrilled about her chin and neck. She pronounced the word *terri-ble* as two syllables. 'To miss such pleasure!'

They were at a garden party, a very select gathering, with no more than two dozen carefully chosen guests. Savoury-smelling cooked chittlings sizzled on hotplates, book-sized pieces of thin metal with flames burning intermittently blue or invisible underneath them. Servants carried wine between the knots of people dotted over the immaculate green sward.

'I have tried it of course,' said Polystom, clearing his throat in a half-cough at Erina's smoke. 'It didn't agree with me.'

'But my smoke is irritating you,' said Erina, smoothly. 'How awful of me.' She dropped the cigarette to the grass, where it stuck, glow-down, like a miniature javelin. 'Let's have coffee – I simply *must* have something to keep my fingers busy, and a coffee-thimble will do as well as anything. Over there.' She didn't point, but started languidly strolling towards a set of three outdoor sofas, laid out in a Π pattern around a low table, and currently unoccupied. Golden samovars of hot coffee on the table released threads of steam from their nozzles.

Erina slipped onto one of the sofas, curling her legs away beneath her, shedding as she did a pair of Hermés slippers. Her bare feet, whiter than the rest of her, flashed momently in the sunshine. One of the slippers tipped onto its side, showing its gaping mouth to Polystom in a toy imitation outrage.

'Do sit,' she said, tapping the seat beside her with her little finger. 'Sit down.'

He sat himself next to her, and poured her a coffee, passing the tiny cup to her by holding its rim so that she could take its ear-shaped handle between thumb and middle finger.

'Glorious weather,' he said, aware of a certain awkwardness between them, but not understanding why it should be there.

She looked up at the pure mauve sky, the sun's clear eye of light. 'Oh yes,' she said. 'Aunt Elena always manages to have her parties on the very best days, weather-wise. I don't know how she does it.'

'Is she your aunt as well?' Stom asked.

'As well?'

'As mine.'

'Why, yes. Are we related then?'

'I suppose it's no surprise,' said Stom, pouring his own coffee. 'Most of the great families are related to one another. If we traced it back far enough, I daresay we could prove everybody a cousin of everybody else.'

'Aunt Elena has been very dear to me, ever since I was a child,' said Erina.

'And to me.'

'Only lately,' Erina went on, tossing a sly look at her companion, 'she seems to have decided to matchmake. Ever since I reached twenty. Apparently' – she drew this word out enormously on its second syllable – 'I'm too old to be single.'

'She invited me over to this party with the same intention, I do believe,' said Stom, feeling a relaxation in the tension between them.

'Oh of course. I suppose she sees the two of us together.'

'I suppose she does. Do you think she's right?'

'About us?'

'Yes.'

Erina sipped slowly, drawing the moment out briefly, before saying 'I really don't think so. Do you?'

'Not at all,' said Stom, with genuine relief in his belly. 'I'm so glad we're of one mind on that.'

'Auntie doesn't care, I think, whether I pair off with a love-husband, or just get together to have some children. But she's said to me many times that an *official* pairing gives one's twenties some sort of solidity.'

'For me,' said Stom, 'I believe she has in mind a love-partnership. She thinks I need a companion.'

Erina looked coolly at him. 'Do you?'

'Well,' said Stom, a little flustered by the intimacy of the question, 'perhaps I do. My estate is rather large. And I have been by myself since my father's death.'

'Is your mother dead too?'

'Oh no, but I don't see much of her. She came for the funeral, of course, which was very nice of her, and left me with an open invitation to visit. She lives on Kaspian. I had a co-father, but I'm afraid he died as well, not long after my father.'

'Beastly,' said Erina. 'Were you close to them?'

'Yes,' said Stom, surprised again at the indelicacy of her questions.

'Beastly,' she repeated. 'Well I'm sorry I won't be able to be the balm for your solitude. But perhaps there's somebody else here?' She put her cup down, and pointed with a little finger across the bright green grass. 'There – Arassa.' She was pointing to a sleek white-skinned woman deep in conversation with two elderly men. This woman was wearing a white cotton dress and black knee-boots that looked shiny as liquorice. 'Dear Arassa,' Erina said. 'Perhaps she's the one for you. She's very . . .' and she searched for the word, as if retrieving it from some distant and quite alien language – 'very *loving*, I believe.'

'I don't think I've ever met her,' mumbled Polystom.

'No? She is charming. There was some story associated with her and her parents, I forget what exactly. Except that she lives with her grandmother now.'

'She's very – striking-looking,' said Stom.

Erina, catching his tone, looked quizzically at him. 'It *is* a woman you're thinking of?' she asked. 'Come, let's not stand on stupid ceremony. You can tell me. I know boys as well.'

'A woman is what I'm looking for,' said Stom, blushing. 'But that's not to say that I'm going to be equally attracted to every single woman I see.'

'Poor Arassa,' said Erina, without feeling. 'Too buxom? Her loss, I'm sure. Or there's Thekla,' pointing again. 'I was at school with Thekla.'

Stom squinted into the sun, and made out a thin body topped with massy scarlet hair wrapped about in gauze. Her face was freckled, her mouth open in the middle of telling some anecdote, her eyes wide. She was talking to an elderly woman, dressed in sober green trousers and jacket, who was in turn carefully shepherding another girl. Stom's eye went to this latter. Her hair was black, her face turned away, her slight frame swathed in pale blue silk that wriggled and moved in the breeze to cling about the contours of her arms, her hips.

21

'Who's that with her?' Polystom asked, blushing deeper.

'Beeswing? She's a tomboy. Oh, she's trouble. Don't you know her?'

'No,' said Stom, colouring deeper. 'What a strange name.'

'That's not her name, of course,' said Erina. 'It's a nickname, or something like that. I don't even know where it comes from. Her name's Dianeira. Are you interested in *her*?'

'I don't know her,' said Stom, the blush spreading from face to his neck and ears. The unknown girl turned, momentarily, and he caught sight of her face in profile; the delicate, almost faery features.

'How funny,' said Erina, and giggled in a low, languorous way. Stom flashed a look at her: that was really too rude, but she laid her hand on his sleeve. 'Oh I'm not laughing at you, my dear,' she said, adopting the tones of an old lady, 'really I'm not. Only I'm imagining poor Aunt Elena's face when she discovers that you've fallen for *Beeswing* of all people!'

It may have been the fact that Beeswing was not regarded generally as an appropriate choice that fixed Polystom's attention so forcefully upon her; or perhaps it was fate, karma, love, whichever of those sorts of hex-words you find most convincing. Certainly, in the early days of his infatuation, when he was most overwhelmed by the beauty of her face, the delicacy and grace of her body, and by the rumoured rebellious heat of her heart – in those days, Polystom most often thought in terms of *love*. He wrote poetry that expressed, in more flowery words than the occasion demanded, that the two of them were meant to be together.

Aunt Elena began by expressing disbelief, and continued by voicing an elegant sort of exasperation. 'But you don't know what she's like!' she told him. It was true, but it was also a large part of the appeal. Of course he didn't know what she was like. How, his soul cried (finely honed, he liked to think, with a genteel anguish) could any person truly *know* any other person? He had tried to put this sentiment into verse and had only distressed himself with the clichés that resulted. But that didn't stop it being true; and, he told himself, there *had* to be some connection between the two of them, some special speech in the air between Beeswing and him, or why else would he feel this way?

'Speak to her guardian,' Aunt Elena advised. 'If you really have got a crush on this girl, then at least you owe it to yourself to go into things with a full knowledge. Disabused.' He winced. *Got a crush.* So vulgar a phrase. His soul flinched from its crudity, or perhaps from the notion of transience it implied. To paint true love in such colours!

'Her guardian?' he asked, covering his embarrassment with a nonchalant smile. 'What's the story there?' The garden party was over now; some guests had departed, others were staying over in one of Elena's many, sumptuous guest rooms. Beeswing and her elderly companion were among the latter. Most of the guests had gone into the house; Stom and his aunt were walking together over the lawn.

Dusk had fallen. Moths dripped from the darkening trees in their thousands. Their colonies nested in the upper branches throughout Spring Year, and now they flew through the purpling sky in random flitters, a grainy and swirling cloud over the lawn. Servants were erecting ectoplasmic draperies before the open doors and open windows, gauze to prevent the insects getting indoors. Polystom parted one such delicate curtain to allow his aunt to step through the back door into the rear sitting-room.

'Her guardian,' Aunt Elena repeated. 'She had co-mothers, I think; her mother and her co-mother. Her father went off somewhere, got himself lost. On Kaspian, I think. Anyway, her co-mothers were strict – possibly a little over-strict. Shall I call for some liqueur?'

'If you like, Aunt. go on: over-strict?'

'Oh well,' she said, sitting down and beckoning a servant. '*Perhaps* over-strict. It's so difficult knowing how to handle the young. I'm sure the parents were only acting with her best interests in heart, merely insisting upon a certain discipline. Anyway, Beeswing didn't respond well to discipline. Yes, a half bottle.' This last to a servant, who hurried away.

Stom sat opposite his aunt. 'Really?' In his head he was imagining this fragile creature as a heart-strong rebel against heavy-handed parenting. A free spirit. A faery raised by cattle. He had already decided, with instant certainty, that the two of them were soulmates – decided this without having exchanging so much as a word with her. This particular romantic ideal, like something out of a poem, brought enormous solidity to his heart's yearning.

'She ran away. Several times. Talk to her guardian, and she'll tell you. Ungovernable, she's simply ungovernable. Oh Stommi,' added Aunt Elena with a gushing little rush of words, leaning forward to rest her hand on his knee, 'I can *see* you're smitten, it's *obvious* you're smitten, but *please* don't rush into anything. Will you at least promise me that?'

The next day he took breakfast at eleven, at a large round table set on the lawn, and made sure to sit next to Beeswing's guardian. This was a compactly stout little woman called Elena like his own aunt, and addressed by everybody as 'Elena Marina' to distinguish her. Beeswing herself was not at breakfast. 'In her room, reading,' said Elena Marina, a tinge of disapprobation to her words.

Stom almost didn't want to ask, for fear of being disappointed by a negative answer, but he had to know. 'Poetry?'

'She does read a lot of poetry,' Elena Marina conceded, as Stom's heartbeat sped with the thrill of confirmation. 'She reads a lot of everything. Too much, in my opinion. She doesn't spend enough time where she *is*; always running away, even to the point of running away from herself in her own head. Did your aunt tell you her story?'

'A little of it. She ran away from her co-mothers?'

'My cousins, both,' said Elena Marina. 'By different branches of the family, but both of them were my cousins. They worked hard with her, they tried, but she *won't* accept the need for discipline. That's why they were compelled to give up on her in the end.'

'They're still alive?'

'Oh yes, oh certainly. They do visit, from time to time. But mostly they spend their time on the moon of Berthing. They have a house up there, you know.'

'It was extraordinarily kind of you to take over as guardian,' said Stom. But the instant he said this Elena Marina blushed a bruise-purple colour from cheeks to neck, and he realised that he had touched a very tender spot. Despite her manner of easy gentility, Stom realised, she must have undertaken guardianship for a fee. It was her way of earning a living, which made her, in effect, a servant, although a servant of a slightly grander station than most: a governess or tutor, something of that rank. 'Aunt' was evidently a courtesy title, and when she had said that Beeswing's co-mothers were both her cousins (rather *over*stressing the fact, in retrospect), she must have meant on the sinistral side. Perhaps she was the offspring of a playful son's adventure with a servant, a daughter experimenting with a handsome field-hand, something along those lines. It was a common enough story. Stom smiled his most charming smile, and said something bland to cover her awkwardness, although inwardly he experienced a rush of lofty disdain for her miniature pride, her rather pathetic imitation of breeding. A servant! Passing herself off as the equal of the guests at the party! The very idea!

'How old is she?' he asked. It was rather a direct question, but the fact that Elena Marina was only a glorified servant rather relieved Stom of the need to be too polite.

'She's eighteen.'

'Old enough to do without a guardian.'

Another deep-coloured blush. Polystom understood that she had interpreted his observation as a criticism; *you cling to her for the money and status, instead of letting her go, although really she should be making her own way in the world*. He hadn't meant this, or didn't think he had, but didn't feel particularly awkward about her awkwardness. He couldn't help it if people misinterpreted what he said. And besides, there was no point in worrying about upsetting a servant.

'Her co-parents specifically requested,' she said, slightly flustered, 'that I look after her into her majority. In so many ways, you see, she's still a child.'

'Then it's *doubly* good of you,' said Stom, the hint of malice in his voice covered by his smile, 'to act as guardian. To steer a child to adulthood is chore enough; to continue the labour into adulthood requires particular devotion. May I ask an indelicate question?'

Even asking whether he could ask such a question was slightly indelicate, too forward, but Elena Marina was hardly in a position to refuse it. She nodded, lowering her eyes.

'Beeswing: is she spoken for? Does she have any – particular admirers?'

Elena Marina shook her head.

'And, if I may impose upon you,' Stom added. 'One further question.' This next question would make his intentions unambiguous, and was even more indelicate than the last. Properly he should have asked it of his aunt, or some other close family member, but he was enjoying the blushing discomfort of the old woman too much to let it go. 'Is she of good family?'

'Good family,' echoed Elena Marina, weakly. 'Yes, yes. Oh yes. Her co-mother is second-fourth-cousin to the Prince.'

'And her mother?' Because, when all was said and done, and despite the polite noises everybody made, blood was more important than marriage connections.

'Her mother's father owns the second largest estate on Kaspian. Very good blood. And her father – I know he was only a contract father, but nonetheless – her father is the son of Rhepidos. You know Rhepidos? The writer?'

Stom angled his head. Of course he knew Rhepidos.

Later that day, as Elena Marina doubtless scurried off to gossip about her momentous news with various people, starting with Stom's unsurprised Aunt Elena, Polystom contrived an hour alone with Beeswing. The pretext was a game of goal croquet; six players, as the rules required, in three teams. Polystom approached Beeswing directly and asked her if they might play together. She looked at him with so oddly distant an expression, as if he were hailing her from half a mile away and she couldn't recognise his voice. 'My name's Polystom,' he said. 'Of the Northern Estate. Actually, I'm Steward of Enting. My father was also called Polystom. You're Dianeira, aren't you?'

The faintest of nods.

'Do you mind – I don't mean to be forward, but . . .' said Stom, his self-confidence, his self-stature, slipping in the face of her cool beauty, 'but would you mind if I called you Beeswing? Some people call you it, I know. It's so strange a name, but somehow poetic. I adore poetry, you see. So, would . . . would that be alright?'

'Yes,' she said, softly.

Her first word to him: an affirmation. His head buzzed with the thrill of it. How he loved her!

The goal croquet began. They started off striking the ball, taking turns. He played the game extremely badly because his attention was entirely on her; her silky figure, as she leant forward a little to strike the ball. The way her arms appeared so slender and yet flickered with miniature musculature when she wielded the wooden bat. Her hair, slipping over her face, or bouncing back, a complex blending of dark brown and black. The butterfly blue of her eyes.

Their team lost the game comprehensively, but Stom didn't care. He had hoped to use the opportunity of the period of the first *jou* to ingratiate himself with her, to project himself as witty and man-of-the-world. But in fact he had been rendered silent by the strength of his feeling. Coming back down the course for the second *jou* he made more of an effort, but she met whatever he said with a dreamy indifference. Not rude, so much as removed. The effect on Stom was intoxicating. He could hardly describe her manner. It was oddly spiritual, yet strangely knowing.

Afterwards, as the servants started laying a trestle table with lunch foods, Polystom summoned his courage and asked Beeswing if she would come with him for a wander. 'Down to the copse over there, and back for lunch?' he suggested, almost stammering with nerves.

She didn't say anything, but she did accompany him, and she did allow him to take her arm in his. It was their first time alone together. Stom, obviously, should have made only small talk; should have arranged for a second meeting; should have established the common ground on which they could converse and find out about one another. He knew this, somewhere inside himself. But instead of doing this he found himself talking for long stretches, his own voice spooling itself out and out with details of his own family tree, of his status and his place near the upper echelons of the System, of his personal wealth and estate. It sounded like the preliminaries of a proposal of marriage. Stom was, on one level, appalled at himself, but at the same time he was strangely exhilarated. Beeswing gave none of the signals, as another woman might, of being uncomfortable with the precipitous nature of the conversation. It was as if she, somehow, understood.

They made their way down to a copse of seven goldenspine trees, grown into interwoven patterns and dressed with carefully manicured nettlemoss. The copse was for display, a sort of living artefact, and it was not possible to enter it or walk between its trees, so Stom and Beeswing walked beyond it, down and up the grassy hillock beyond it and into the Canal Garden, where dozens of little bridges humped over and over the lattice of miniature canals. There was nobody in this garden but an undergardener, trimming the scarlet show-weed from the banks of one of the canals, and of course they ignored his presence. Stom went on talking. They mounted one of the little bridges, and paused at the top of its hump, leaning on the handrail and admiring the view.

Polystom's family is one of the most respectably bred in the whole

System; one of perhaps only a dozen families to have the same provenance and familial longevity as the Prince of the System himself. His paternal great grandfather was Count Meli, the famous Count Meli, who (Count being a military title of course) formed the very first flying squadron of the Royal Military. His maternal great grandfather had supervised the creation of the canal network that brought ice down from the highlands of the moon of Bohemia. In a touch redolent of the time (this was nearly a hundred years ago, after all) this great man had ground the bones of those workers who died on the job and mixed them in to temper the cement of the canal beds and sides; slightly gruesome, we might say nowadays, but done with the noblest intentions. This way, you see (as the Count might have explained, were he alive to do so) they are forever memorialised by the great work on which they were engaged. Surely burial in a hole cut out of the earth is merely ignominious? Although they were only servants, their deaths are memorialised in stone almost as if they were people of Family. A cousin of Stom's grandmother's wrote a tragic operetta on the subject. Very moving. Plangent melodies, and lines beautifully crafted in Old Kaspian, the proper language of opera:

> *Paragei tina-a-a-ah kleoo-oona ton kaloumenon*
> *Paflagona ka-a-a-a-ah-ti bursopo-o-olen* . . .

But she will really have to excuse him. His singing voice is atrocious. He's very much ashamed of it, and if he hadn't got carried away in the moment – but poetry has always been important to him. Very important. His father had also loved poetry. But, really, his family; he mustn't get distracted. Well, on his father's side he was related to the early Princes of Enting. What else? His great-great-great-really-a-*great*-many-greats-grandfather had purchased the whole of the northern continent. He still has rights of authority over most of it; certain parts have been given away to friends and relatives, but his estate, the Northern Estate, is still the biggest on Enting. His grandfather, his father's father, had been a hot-headed type; called Polystom too, of course. He fought a duel, you know. There was a famous poet called Phanicles, you know. And the two of them had loved the same woman. So his grandfather called Phanicles out – shot him too, although thankfully for literature not fatally. This grand uncle was called Chruestom. He was an army commander; the General, he was called, although his rank was more properly Count and that outranks general, as of course you know. He received more decorations than any other military man. This was before the war on the Mudworld started, of course, so perhaps his record has been overtaken now. He put down several insurrections, you know, with bravery. Among his current living relatives, there are first cousins who act as Stewards of Bohemia and Berthing; the current Prince is a second cousin; and his mother's partner is the mother of the heir to the Princedom.

He tells her all this, in a tumble of lengthy sentences, and she stands next to him, saying nothing, taking it all in (he thinks) with fascinated absorption. Finally he reaches a pause. He has stunned her with the enormity of his breeding, knocked aside any but the most flibberti-gibbet reasons for objecting to marriage. This last word, though, the weightiest of words, has not tumbled from his mouth, however much he has thought it. That really would have been too forward. But it is implied in everything he has said. Surely she realises that!

After a silence, he starts again. 'Tell me about you,' he says, a little awkwardly.

'Me?' she says, softly. 'There's no me.'

Does this mean, Stom wonders, a little wrongfooted, that there's no life story worth relating? Or that there is no person behind the beautiful façade of Beeswing's face and body?

'You ran away from home when you were younger,' he says. She doesn't reply to this at first, so he prompts her. 'Why?'

'I felt buried alive,' she says, still in her dreamy voice, her eyes still focused on the distance.

'This was with your parents?'

'Yes. Their house.' She breathed out, a slow exhalation like a smoker enjoying a cigarette. 'It was a prison. Not *like* a prison, you know, but *actually* one.'

But she need say no more. His sympathy is entirely hers; his heart throbbing like it too was buried alive and is shouting for attention, 'bring me out into the air! Make me known to her now!'

And, although he says nothing more to her in the canal garden, this is what he does, in effect. He takes her arm and walks her back to the House, and they walk in silence the whole way because (he is so sure!)

they have established a real affinity. And the following day, when he arranges a meeting with his aunt and with Beeswing's guardian, and the three of them discuss marriage, the sense of the rightness of what he is doing hums in his very bones. And the day after that, when he makes his plans known to her – letting her know of her guardian's consent, that a message has been sent to both her mothers, that the ceremony would take place by the month's end – she didn't say yes, exactly, but she certainly didn't say no.

[third leaf]

After the wedding, Stom took the *Ornithos*, his two-seater biplane, and flew his new wife back to her new home. He made sure to circle through the air several times to give her the opportunity to see the estate in detail from above. But from his rear pilot's cockpit he could see that she wasn't looking down. Her head was cast slightly back, her eyes fixed on the blue-violet of the sky.

There was no point in calling to her during the flight. His words wouldn't carry. But on landing he stood up and leant forward, supporting himself on the rear rim of her cockpit: 'I was flying around,' he said breathlessly, 'to show you the estate. It's beautiful, you know.' He felt foolish saying this last thing. It shouldn't need pointing out.

'The sky is lovely,' she said as she took off her leather helmet. This wasn't a direct contradiction of his words of course, but in an obscure way it felt like it was. 'I'd like to be taught flying. I'd like to learn to fly a plane such as this.'

'We'll see,' said Stom, suddenly angry, as if thwarted.

They climbed out of the plane as servants steadied the wings. They walked over the turf together. Stom had told the Head Grass-Gardner to mow their two initials into the lawn before the house: P and D. It had been nicely done, the letters a slightly darker green against the brightness of the spring grass. 'Look!' he said, touching her elbow and again feeling foolish that he needed to point it out. She should, he felt somehow, have noticed it herself, gasped with delight, clung to him in happiness. Instead her eyes barely followed the line of his pointing arm, lingered less than a second and looked away.

Indoors, a sumptuous lunch had been laid in the Mahogany Room. The two of them ate, Polystom punctuating the silence with nervous comments about the food – these are grown locally, you know. This is balloon-boated in from Berthing, very expensive. She barely smiled.

31

Over coffee, as servants cleared everything away, Stom pulled his chair closer to her, suddenly intensely nervous. 'Look,' he said. 'We could wait until tonight, of course. But I thought, perhaps . . . you know? Consummation. Of the marriage, I mean. We could do it now, this afternoon.'

For once she didn't seem abstracted. Instead she seemed to be concentrating intently on his words, which was in a way even more alarming. Stom felt his hands trembling, as if the fingerbones were buzzing, like loose canvas on a plane in flight. She looked directly into his eyes. 'Whichever you would prefer,' she said.

'I wondered if . . . I think I'd prefer . . . well, once the food has gone down a little, of course, but I wondered if we shouldn't . . . wondered if we couldn't do it this afternoon?'

She nodded, as if she had deeply considered and was deeply agreeing; slow, careful nods. 'Get it out of the way,' she said.

Although this sentiment had been in implied in Polystom's words there was something about the way she said it out loud that was actually rather upsetting. Stom swallowed. In a way that *was* what he had meant. But did she have to say it right out like that? As if making love with him were, somehow, a chore to be disposed of as quickly and painlessly as possible. The quiet, singsong way she had said that, *get it out of the way*, sounded in Stom's ears as a rejection. An insult. Him! He was Steward of Enting, as if she didn't know. His estate was the largest on the world. The Prince was his second cousin.

'Well,' he said, nonplussed. 'If you don't mind.' And then, because that sounded feeble in his own ears, he amended it to, 'maybe that would be best. Yes, that would be the best thing to do.'

So he waited twenty minutes, fidgeting, attempting cul-de-sac conversations. Finally he stood up. 'Shall we go upstairs then?'

Servants had prepared a separate bedroom from the one he normally slept in. He'd pondered that point at some length, and decided it was a good idea not to be distracted by his familiar things during this, their consummation. Coming into the room behind Beeswing he regretted that decision. He felt surprisingly agitated at the prospect of having sex with his wife. He missed the comforts of being in his own space. It had never been like this before. Playing with the daughters of local servants and farmers, bringing them wide-eyed and palpitating into his own house, or coupling with them in fields and barns. In all the scores, hundreds, of such experiences he had always had the gut-solace of his own superior status. Now, and despite his better breeding, his greater wealth, despite his better education and everything else, he felt somehow lessened in the presence of his wife. She was a tiny human being, so fragile-looking you might fear to embrace her for the damage you'd do, and yet she walked with a straight stride into the bedroom, and it was Stom who shuffled behind her, tongue-tied and blushing. When she was inside she looked all about the room, pulling the drawers open, fluffing the curtains out to check behind them, before settling down cross-legged on the bed.

'Shall I?' Polystom began to say, but the words stuck in his throat and he coughed. 'Would you prefer it if I – wore a guard?' A reasonable question; one he had thought through in advance. They had not married, as many did, merely for legitimate offspring. It was a true co-coupling. Accordingly, whilst children would clearly be desirable at some stage, they – she – might not want to become pregnant too soon.

'Yes,' said Beeswing, with uncharacteristic firmness. 'I don't want to become pregnant.'

Stom coughed again, went to the bedside cabinet and pulled opened the little door. 'Eventually,' he said nervously, fetching out the prophylactic spray, 'you'll want children of course. Of course, we'll both want children eventually.'

'Pregnancy,' she replied, more dreamily, her attention apparently distracted by the lozenge-shaped patterns on the painted ceiling. 'It's not for me,' she said, distantly.

Stom thought of contesting the point, but was fearful of spoiling the mood. They would, he resolved silently, come back to that another time. So, holding the prophylactic spray in his left hand, he unbuttoned his shirt and eased his body out of it. Beeswing turned to look at him and her dreamy eyes rested on his belly, on his chest, and on his face in turn. Then she uncrossed her legs in a single graceful movement, slipping off the edge of the bed. She was wearing a double-skirt, gathered at a button knotted into her hair at the back of her neck. It looked like a complicated arrangement, the cloth bunched and buttoned, intertwined with the braids of hair, but it took only a single touch with her right hand to untangle it all and leave the dress sliding off her body to gather in folds on the floor. She stepped free and sat down again on the bed. Stom took in her nakedness with one look before blushingly turning away. Her tiny breasts seemed all nipple and aureole, bruise-coloured circles with tiny thorn-shaped tips; her belly curved inwards, her hips traced out the slightest of arcs; her buttocks were flat, her thighs so slender that an inch showed between them as she stood. Her bush marked out a precise triangle, black against the silver of her skin. Only her feet were out of proportion in this faery-frame, for they were surprisingly long and broad. Stom, looking away, not understanding why he felt so abashed, pulled off his trousers. He flipped the top off the prophylactic spray. Erotic tradition suggested that the woman apply the stuff, as one of the preliminaries of lovemaking, but Stom felt inhibited from asking Beeswing to do this. The awkwardness, the sensation of inward block, made him somehow, distantly, obscurely angry. His own member was hard as ivory, and he quickly sprayed the prophylactic around the end and up and down the length of it. It imparted its cold, plasticky sensation. He turned to face his wife again, and she was sitting, cross-legged, watching him. Again he felt an inward quailing, and he drowned it out by telling himself that she was his wife, that they were doing a proper thing, that he had a right to do this thing.

'Shall we?' he said, making himself meet her gaze.

She didn't reply, but she did unhook her legs and lie back on the mattress. His own urgency pushing him on, Stom clambered on top of her. She exhaled in discomfort as his elbow crushed into her ribs. 'Sorry,' he muttered, but he was already fumbling at her crotch with his right hand, inserting himself. There was a delicious sense of slipping inside. He could have cried with the pleasure of it. He started a rapid flexing motion with his whole body, going in, in, in, and arrived at his climax almost at once.

For the briefest time he was motionless, still inside her, his head clarified and free. Then there followed the sour falling away, the slippage back into flesh, the awkward sensation of post-coital belated-ness. He was aware that he had come much too rapidly, which in turn made him feel unmanned, lessened. She would have expected more. She wouldn't have enjoyed that very much. And, underneath that thought was a darker one: that it was somehow her fault that he had come so soon. If she had been more . . . accommodating. If she had played along, played with him a little; or allowed herself, somehow, to

34

take more pleasure, instead of simply flopping back and opening her legs. If she hadn't enjoyed it, then she had herself to blame. Sex was a two-way process surely. He pulled out, and rolled back, resentment curdling in his chest. She was doing it all wrong; this was not what he had the right to expect from a wife.

He pulled off the prophylactic. The gum adhered clammily to his now soggy flesh. A portion near the end had ballooned out into a little sphere, his seed, and he looked briefly at this little sachet of himself. He dropped the whole package over the side of the bed. Servants would clear it from the floor.

Beeswing was lying, breathing gently, still staring up at the patterns on the ceiling. Her placidity infuriated him. It seemed like a form of dumb mockery. Was she mentally judging him? Comparing him with better lovers? How could he break into the space of her mind, interpose himself between herself and her thoughts? He turned to her.

'Sorry,' he said, his words surprising him in their mildness. 'I was a little quick. I haven't had . . . it, since our betrothal.' He started to ask *have you?* but the words blocked in his throat. What if she said yes? She was no virgin, had clearly had lovers in her life. There was nothing shocking in that fact, of course, except that it opened the horrible vista of other men possessing her body. Better lovers. Better men. And Stom shrunken and unimportant beside them. Stom useless, ugly, clumsy.

'It's fine,' she said, in her distant voice.

At this, its suggestive indifference, anger fired up from Stom's heart again, and his member stirred with the rage's aphrodisiac. He reached out to grab her hips, to pull himself onto her again – this time without a prophylactic (because she wanted it with that protection, he would do it *without*), this time harder and longer – but he stopped, of course. His hand touched her skin, and it was cool and smooth. A piercing revelation went through him. He had made no mark upon her body. He had pushed himself upon her, had possessed her, and now that he had finished there was no indication that he had ever been there. The wind blows upon the green hill, moves through the blades of grass like a comb through hair, the wind knows the hill with absolute intimacy, and then it passes on, and there is nothing to say that it was ever there. A sadness at his own transience dissolved the rage to almost nothing. He flopped backwards onto the mattress.

They lay together for several minutes, in silence. Through the open window could be heard the faint rhythmic noises of the waves joining the beach.

Later he called for coffee, and servants brought it on a splendid platinum decorated tray. Dressed in wraps, he and his wife sat on the bed drinking, and she looked away from him the whole time, staring out through the open window across the lawn towards the boatshed, and beyond it to the glistening of the sea, visible as a shining banner between the strips of land and sky.

'This coffee,' he said, miserably, wishing she would say something, that she would make the conversation – that she would raise any topic, do anything at all – 'this coffee is from the Southern Continent. It's usually considered the finest in the whole System.' He despised his own inanities; but the silence was worse. It isn't supposed to be like this, he told himself inside. Why doesn't she act properly?

'This isn't my usual bedroom,' he said. 'It's called the Mahogany room.'

'Really,' she said, still not looking at him. She acted almost as if in a trance, as if some vital part of her spirit were missing.

'I'll sleep in my usual bedroom tonight though. Will you . . . join me there?' This sounded even more stupid in his own ears. His own wife! They weren't a contract coupling – they were really married. Of course they should sleep together! So why did he feel so nervous, so awkward asking? 'At night, I mean. You don't have to of course. There are plenty of bedrooms in the house.'

'I don't mind,' she said.

Don't mind. In a nutshell, he thought, that is the problem.

'You're not drinking your coffee,' he said, in a weak voice. 'I can order tea, if you prefer?'

Later, he set the coffee tray on the floor and rode one of his spikes of anger to a second sexual consummation. This second time he was not so premature in his climax; he pumped and pumped to the best of his ability, shooing away his own orgasm by deliberately taking his mind away from where he was, by separating out his bucking body from his thoughts. He thought of the *Pterodactyl*, his one-seater biplane. He mentally toyed with repainting her, imagining different colours. He thought of having all his vehicles, planes, boats, cars, redone in a new livery. Then he thought of taking a cruise, of having his boat brought out of the boatshed and dragged to the sea shore. He could motor over the Middenstead for a week or so. He could take Beeswing, just the two of them on the sea, in the sunshine. Doing it on the deck, her tiny body underneath his, him piercing her over and over with . . . and he was back, on the bed with her now, his orgasm unstoppable. He cried out in mixed pleasure and frustration.

He had worked up a sweat, and was panting a little. Beeswing was quiet. She did not look flushed. 'Did you climax?' he asked, ashamed that he hadn't noticed her reaction. But he knew the answer as he asked it. She didn't reply.

They spent the evening together, reading in the library, and for a while Stom believed that it was going to be alright between them. And that night they went to the same bed. He wasn't in the mood for more lovemaking, but he embraced her and she let him. He fell asleep more hopeful, but woke in the middle of the night. Sitting bolt upright, out of some agonising dream, and patting the flatness of the bed beside him. Alone.

He pulled on the dressing gown and wandered the corridors for a while, hoping to locate her, switching on the wall-lights as he went. He found her eventually, curled up under a silk blanket, on a couch in the library. She looked vaguely cross when he shook her awake, and there was even a small pleasure for him in that fact. 'Would you really want to sleep here?' he said. 'Really? There are many more comfortable beds in the house. Or come back with me. Come back to my bed.' His voice wheedled.

'I was reading,' she said, sulkily. 'I drifted off to sleep.' But there were no books about her, on the floor, on the arm of the couch, on the table, no books at all except the myriad volumes tucked away on their shelves.

She came back to bed with him, but when he woke up in the morning light he was alone again. It seemed that she had risen early. Stom, guided by Nestor, found her in the kitchen, huddled against the wood-cooker in the early morning chill. The servants looked embarrassed to have their mistress slouching in their space. Did she understand nothing? How could she embarrass herself in front of the servants like this?

She looked up when he came in and her face seemed almost pleased to see him. For a moment his heart bubbled with possibility; come to me, he thought, love me and I'll repay it! I swear I'll repay it sevenfold. 'What are you doing in here!' he said in tones of mock-rebuke, as one might with a child. 'Getting in the way of the servants!' He helped her to her feet and embraced her, to the further embarrassment of the cook. Then he led her gently away, up the steps, and into the breakfast room. But somewhere, on that short journey, his heart swelling with hope and the possibility of being loved – somewhere on that journey he lost her. Her face came over vacant, her steps absent. She slotted herself into her chair before Nestor had time to pull it away from the table. She was so slender that she could slip between the fat oak edge and the heavy arm-rest.

Polystom was tired from his interrupted night's sleep, but nevertheless he made a conscious decision to try to reach her. To find a piece of common interest. She kept staring out of the window, so she presumably liked nature. She could share his love for the forest.

'Do you like trees?' he blurted out, reaching for a bread-sweet, and breaking it with both hands. The hot sugared dough steamed.

There was a little silence.

'Trees?' she echoed in her small voice, as if from far away.

'I love trees. My father loved trees, and I have inherited that love. Most of my estate is woodland,' Stom said. 'Beautiful trees,' he continued, hoping to reach her with his enthusiasm. 'You'll love it.'

She looked up at his face, as if about to speak; paused. Polystom had the sudden rush of hope, that he had touched her. She drew a breath, let it out. 'I like open spaces,' she said in her sing-song voice. 'No walls.'

'There are no walls in my woodland,' said Stom, a little over-eagerly, still trying to reach her.

'Trees are like walls,' she said. The sentence was spoken with an enormous quietness that implied grave, sad wisdom. She waited a heartbeat, and said: 'trees are walls.' She looked away.

How wrong! For days Stom could think of nothing else than this little speech by his wife, rehearsing possible replies in his mind, circling round and round the little dialogue over and over until it had condensed into a sort of rage inside him. How could she be so blind? He thought he had been granted an insight into her; saw her

38

spirit fleeing for ever over endless plains, over grasslands, running and running. But this was an illusion, this sense of escape. Because what did it boil down to in the end? Beeswing's tiny body, her too-rapidly beating heart, her own being-in-the-world, it was that she yearned to escape. And there was no escape from selfhood, it was a responsibility, not a burden. Couldn't she see? And even though the two of them had not quarrelled *as such*, even though no voices had been raised or cross words spoken, nonetheless this little exchange had revealed to Stom the sheer unbending stubbornness at the heart of Beeswing's mind. The stubbornness of the child who has not yet learned (as Cleonicles would have put it) that the gap between wish and world must be accepted or it will shred us to pieces. That wishing is not a crime, but wish – like a metal – only becomes *useful* if alloyed, tempered, with a sense of *how the world is.* That was what growing up involved. Didn't she see that? That was what Stom's great poetry told him, what his reading revealed, what his late-night discussions with Cleonicles over a mulberry or ashberry whisky confirmed in him. This was his co-father's insistent refrain; and, more than all this, it was his father's very essence, every aspect of his silent passage through life. Acceptance, this was the key. The universe of things is all around us, it supports us, it sustains us. Why fight it? *I want to go diving today, papa!* Not today, Stommi. *Why not father, why* not *why not?* And in reply to this eight-year-old insistence his father would not even need words, just the slow turn of his head, his glistening placid eyes meeting his son's. At some level below speech the little Polystom felt the knowledge, the wisdom, slide into his soul. He was surrounded by the sustenance of things, and also, equally tightly, by his responsibilities. It was a *great* responsibility to be Steward, and this could not be avoided or shirked. It was better not even to try, but simply to accept. Why couldn't Beeswing see this? Surely his own wife . . . *surely* she should understand, if anybody should.

One of his favourite habits was walking in the forest by himself. On several occasions, early in the relationship, Stom urged Beeswing to come with him, but she declined, obliquely at first, and then more insistently. 'Why must you be so insistent! I'm no pet *dog*,' she said, one time, with a febrile edge to her voice, 'for you to take on walks.'

Stom had said nothing to this. He had turned completely about and walked away.

If she wouldn't come, then he would go without her. She was the one who lost out. She stayed behind in the house, doing whatever she was doing, and Stom felt himself buoyed up in the purity of his solitude. That was it, he told himself. He felt raised up, lifted by the purity of his solitude. Her loss. *Most of my estate is woodland* he had told her; so by hating trees she was spurning the bulk of his estate, rejecting him. He was not surprised. She was a child. Her child-like body harboured a child-like mind. He had been foolish to think otherwise.

The rage coalesced into something hard inside him. He would be doing her a favour by making her see, by *making* her leave childhood behind, taking on an adult's perspective. After five days this had settled deep, a subconscious sediment layering the base of his mind. He no longer needed even to think of it. Just as his responsibilities extended to educating the children of his workers and servants, so they extended to his wife. She was wilful, but once she had been broken she would be grateful. It was as universal a law as gravity, as omnipresent a fact of life as the air we all breathe. Afterwards she would thank him. She'd be happier too – healthier, live longer. All this fretful fighting against everything would wear her out otherwise. It was in her own best interests. He had not decided how to impose his will upon her just yet, but the need for it was certain.

For five days after their seemingly bland conversation the two of them spoke no words to one another. They slept in separate rooms, took their meals apart. They rarely passed one another in the enormous house. On the sixth day Stom's mind was made up; he mistook the burning inner solidity of his rage for certainty, mistook it for strength of will. It was nothing of the sort, of course.

[fourth leaf]

Most of my estate is woodland, Polystom had told his wife on the morning after their wedding. He had hoped to impress her, hoped perhaps to win her over to himself, to bridge the space between them. But there was no such connection; it had been impossible. It was still hard for him to understand how it was that the beauty of the trees had not reached her. The forest is a kind of prison, she had said. Was ever a more absurd thing said?

Most of my estate is woodland. He still felt the tingle in his abdomen – *my estate!* It had been three years since his father's death, and he still could not evade the sense that he was only playing at being Steward in the old man's absence. Here . . .

[*seven lines lost, including*:

> . . .

. . . by no means . . .
. . . ever since he was a child . . .
. . . something n[ever . . .
. . . y[es?] . . .

> . . .

> . . .]

. . . thoughts [of his] father. These thoughts were somehow – he knew not how – inseparable in his mind from thoughts of the woodlands that his father had loved so completely. The dark, shadow-sated forests, the elegant shafts of trees planted in the rich earth like javelins, and in the air the interlocking thick bushes of fir leaves. Seventy thousand hectares of new planting north-east of Moss Cove between the coast and the mountains, now seven years old, bristling sticky saplings covering the curve of the hills like stubble. Six hundred thousand hectares of ancestral forest, to which the Old Man had devoted all his energies and most of his love.

41

Polystom had wandered through those forests as a boy and as an adolescent; solitary, most especially the woodland between the Neon Mountains and the sea, to the west of the house. He still did, now that he was a man and Steward of the whole estate. The solitude there seemed cloistered by the trees themselves, an almost sanctified tranquillity. Their great black stems, around which Stom could just about throw his arms for his fingertips to meet. Their pure reach of height, fifteen or twenty metres before branches appeared. They were like sword-blade epitomes of the shadows they cast, like shadows themselves made material and tangible. Polystom could walk through the cool fragrance of the woods for hours, the brown fir-needles under his feet like springy gravel. He might catch himself, head back, staring up the length of a trunk to the starburst spread of branches and needles above him, with only shreds of blue-mauve sky visible in between, might catch himself staring upwards, and feel foolish. He wasn't a child! *This sort of mooncalfing around isn't dignified* (this was his co-father's voice in his imagination, this chiding). *It doesn't befit a Steward, a ruler.* But the shade of his father, in this shady place, didn't rebuke him. The spirit of his father would say to him that it was not displeased: drink the peace of the trees, this would be the Old Man's advice. Not words he had ever spoken to his son in life, of course, for Stom had never had the wisdom to solicit them when Old Polystom was alive. But his father had never considered it beneath *his* dignity as Steward to wander the trees. His arboriphilia hadn't diminished his gravitas as local ruler. Polystom tried to take consolation from this thought as he meandered amongst the tree trunks. He walked, and walked, until he emerged from the other side of the forest and strolled down to the shoreline of the Middenstead sea. Intensely thoughtful.

Polystom sat, that afternoon, for a long time, looking out at the unquiet Middenstead sea. Or not looking, really, but rather hearing the sound the wind made as it moved through mauve-dark sky. The sifting noise of wind brushing the trees behind him. The noise of the water touching and touching at the beach, and the sound of the sand itself, the sound of the sand lessening.

His father and co-father had died within weeks of one another. It was a sort of revelation to Polystom. He had only seen their relationship from the outside, and had taken the bickering and emotional turbulence for the entirety of their connection. So it is we mistake tics and superficial habits for a deeper truth. But Polystom's father sickened and died over six months, and by the seventh month co-father was gone too. It was as if his prop had been knocked away. Polystom realised, belatedly, that there were depths in his two fathers' relationship (and by extension, in any relationship) of which he had been unaware. For all their bickering, the two of them had been together without breaks for longer than Polystom had been alive. For all they had fought, their relationship had worked.

They seemed so incompatible, an ill-matched pair. His father so placid, a man who might go for a whole day without saying a single word. A tall man, skinny, but always a little hunched over as if in embarrassment at his height. Many mornings he would simply not attend to his hair, not even call a servant to smooth it down, so it flailed and spiked off the dome of his head. He would wear the previous day's clothes, stained as they might be with food. There had always been that quality in his father of elsewhereness. As a boy it had infuriated Polystom, because he had read it as a sort of withdrawal, a stepping away from Polystom himself, as if his son's demands were somehow irrelevant to the father. But perhaps there had been a greater peace in that elsewhere, wherever in his father's head it was located.

His co-father, on the other hand, had been a shorter, bulkier person, his body covered in hair. His beard had reached from just below his eyes right down to cover his face, chin and neck in sow-bristles. Even his back had been knitted with thick hair, as Polystom knew from swimming expeditions. And as if this bristliness were an index of sheer energy, as if the hairs were like iron filings standing up in the magnetic force of his personality, he had been enormously, bustlingly restless. Do! Do! Create! Create! What was needed was *action* – now above all! *Now* above all! The Mudworld was a threat to everybody, to the Stewardship of all the worlds! They must do something, organise, push *on*, sort something out.

'Why?' Young Polystom had once asked. 'How exactly is the Mudworld a threat?' The three of them had been picnicking on the eastern flanks of the Neon Mountains, father, co-father and Polystom, with servants and a car a respectful distance away. The afternoon had been hot and clammy, every crease of Polystom's young body stuck with sweat.

'Are you an idiot?' co-father had blustered. 'Don't you read the newsbooks? What's the matter with you? Your own cousin died fighting on that world!'

His father, slowly pulling free the cork of a bottle of black wine, had said nothing. Polystom, hot and young and feeling bad-tempered, had pointed out that he had hundreds of cousins, had lost count of his cousins, but co-father ground him down with the relentless force of his personality.

'Do you want me to recite the casualty lists? Don't you see how vital it is to contain them there, on that world, rather than have them come through interplanetary space and attack us here? The whole System of Worlds has never been so tested! Young men like yourself have never had such an opportunity for glory and honour, for good working towards the common wealth.' And so on, and so on.

'I still don't see why they're such a threat, on that world,' Polystom had grumbled; and co-father had gasped in exasperation, and father had silently poured three glasses of wine. Polystom had caught what he took to be a pained expression in his father's eyes, although whether in disappointment at his son's attitude, or distress that his partner and his son were fighting, was not clear.

And when not blustering at Polystom, co-father had blustered at father, sometimes with enough intensity to provoke a response even from that serene man. They would be arguing over nothing, some irrelevancy; and the servants would shuffle awkwardly in the background, uncertain whether to stay or go. Maybe co-father would goad Old Polystom with some perceived failing or other, going at him for a quarter-hour, half-hour, until finally father's colour would darken and he would reply. It wasn't so, he would say in his grumbling baritone. It wasn't like that. Then why, co-father would counter, is *such and such* the case? Eh? Why did *such and such* happen, if things are the way you say they are? I really don't know, father would say with quiet dignity, though his flushed face and hard-focused eyes gave away his anger. Perhaps because of *this*? Or *that*? How should I know? Of *course* you should know, co-father would shout.

Polystom had been witness to so many of these arguments that they ceased to alarm him. As he grew older he accepted it as simply the way his two fathers related to one another. On the rare occasion when he did think about it, he may have wondered why these two men, who

44

were supposed to be in love, gave one another so much distress; but it wasn't for him to say. They had made some secret pact with misery to spend their lives fighting, he assumed.

And yet they had lived together for many years, and it was only when they were both dead that Polystom realised they had been happy. That his quiet father had found a delight in the turmoil and passion of his partner; and that boisterous co-father had found strength in the calmness of his. As he presided over the funeral of his co-father, his second family funeral in four weeks, he finally understood, or thought he did, that the outward trappings of a relationship hold no more truth to internal health than the plainness of a person's face is an index to the beauty of their soul. At the funeral he read a poem from Phanicles, his father's favourite poet. His co-father had not relished poetry, but somehow Polystom felt that a poem was an appropriate gesture at a funeral. Poetry adorned the ceremony, he felt; and so he read something from Phanicles:

> the mountain silent after my lover's gone
> and ash like velvet on the hearthstone
> and the comet with its great wind-sock of light
> and ash like velvet, white
> and shamrock, violet, hidden in the hedgebank by the stream
> and the fire now slowly silting down.

Polystom chose that poem because of the delicious sense of sadness it brought to his mind. It wasn't specifically a funereal poem, although there seemed to Polystom to be something obliquely elegiac about the lines. But as he finished the final line he looked down from the funeral dais to see the bored, or even disgusted, faces of his co-father's relatives. This shocked him, and with a potent sense of inner revelation he realised that just as he had seen his co-father's blustery aggression as a flaw, a vulgarity, something to be disregarded before you could feel love for the man – just so, exactly, there were many people in the Stewardship who saw his own and his father's quiet love for poetry in exactly the same way. For them it was a weakness, a blot on character, a distraction from the life of doing and overcoming that properly defined a man. In the pulpit Polystom had a nebulous sense of understanding of what the world must look like to his co-father's kin; the way it must have appeared to his co-father when alive. Polystom and his boy, the two of them hidden away in this foppish nothingness, burying their minds in this nonsense, blind to the world around them. Unmanning themselves with this mental decay called *poetry*, not pushing themselves into manly assertion. There were things to do! Leadership meant stepping out in front of the crowd, not hiding amongst the trees. It was a sort of sickness, a self indulgence, the very opposite of a self-discipline. Polystom looked down on the curled lips of his co-father's brothers and cousins, and felt a needle of shame. Perhaps they were right. Perhaps it was a contemptible occupation for a man. Certainly it was inappropriate to read poetry at the funeral of his poetry-hating co-father. It was wrong because unmanly.

And with this realisation, Polystom felt a deeper awe at the strength of the bond that had tied his co-father to his father. That had kept the furious spirit of his co-father living in this house for nearly twenty years, cloistered away from the burly flurry of Stahlstadt where great men made great decisions, and shaped the destiny of the whole Stewardship of Worlds.

The two of them, father and co-father, had sometimes visited Stahlstadt of course, and on a few occasions young Polystom had accompanied them. The first time he had been overawed by the scale of the city, the luxuriance and heat of the planet of Bohemia on which it was located. The second time, he had swaggered more, being fourteen and of a swaggering age. The three of them stayed in the same hotel, his father and co-father in one room and Polystom in a room by himself. But he had not wanted the other people in the hotel to know how largely, still, the towers, high walkways and massy stone objects of the city intimidated him. He had pretended a world-weary confidence, strolling up and down the wide stone stairways, riding the sliding cars as if he had been doing it all his life. Everybody else seemed so much sleeker than he. Everybody else seemed to fit in. Once, foolishly, he slipped off a sliding car and grazed his knee on the track. He never saw anybody else do that. On another occasion he walked down a main esplanade so caught up in admiration of the trio of colossal towers that dominated the city centre that he put his foot in a grille and fell over. People were too well bred to laugh openly, of course, but he sensed their amusement. Back in the hotel, as the three of them were leaving, a hotel servant dropped one of Polystom's bags. There was nothing fragile in the bag, but Polystom beat the boy with a rage fuelled by relief that there were clumsier people on the planet than himself.

He had been glad to return home after the second visit, back to the estate where he knew every square metre of the wood around the house, where the servants respected him. He sank into his favourite poetry as a weary man sinks into a hot bath, for the comfort as well as the sensation of being cleaner afterwards. It was a month before his seventeenth birthday. He was reading Phanicles' 'Meadow Poems'.

> *Who is it, then, that imagines me out of my mountain lair*
> *and into the habit of hovering, here, at the doorstone,*
> *mornings, in the slant new sun, the cobwebs covering*
> *a whole field like a shroud of butter muslin*
> *woven, light and water, like a poem*
> *coming quietly into being?*

He had visited the arable land south and east of the Middenstead often enough, and it was pretty countryside of course, but Polystom's heart was in the woodlands. He wished fervently that Phanicles had written some 'Forest Poems', but there was a subject that had never inspired the great man. Polystom tried writing such poetry himself, tried to imagine himself becoming, after his father's death, the Poet-Steward, the ruler with poetry in his soul. But somehow the poems fell flat. No matter how excited he had been writing them, no matter how much of the thrill and energy of being in the forest he tried to pour into them, somehow they simply didn't work as poems.

> *I stand in the forest, still and straight*
> *as a tree, arms at my side*
> *and the mist wraps around my legs*
> *in the marvellous morning*
> *like a thought of the beauty of the trees all around me*
> *each tree like a beautiful thought itself*
> *here I can feel the cool quiet comfort*
> *of safety and satiety. The trees*
> *like arms, they protect me. The atmosphere*

of trees all
around me, like air upholding a wing, so here I am I.

  No, it was no good. He was ashamed to show his poetry to anybody in the family. He made his groomsman read it, but the fellow was a servant, and all he could do was nod and mutter appreciatively. One day, Polystom thought, one day I'll have a soul mate, somebody who'll understand my poetry and my love for poetry.

[fifth leaf]

He told her, one breakfast, 'we have not been together as man and wife for a week.' He meant *we have not made love*, but could not bring himself to speak so directly.

She looked at him, but didn't reply. She drank coffee for breakfast, ate no food. It was no wonder she was so slight in her frame. If she nibbled away a side of bread in a day it was a large meal for her. Eat! he shouted inwardly. Eat some damn food! Build up some small reservoir of strength, so that you can act as a woman and not as a ghost! But he didn't say any of this out loud, nor did his inward fury inform his speaking voice.

She was looking past him now, out of the breakfast room window. A brisk spring wind was blowing straight up the Middenstead. The glass was rattling gently in its frames.

'Nestor tells me,' Polystom said, after a while, 'that you have taken to sleeping in the Velvet Bedroom.'

She caught his eye briefly, with the most ghostly of smiles on her face. Was she mocking him?

'He *also* tells me,' Stom continued, gripping the handle of his butter spoon with unnecessary force, 'that you don't settle in any one bedroom for very long.' If only you took *one* bedroom, he wanted to say. If only you *settled yourself somewhere*. Then I would know where to find you. He spooned a lump of butter onto his plate.

'I found some sketches under the chaise-baissé in the Yellow Room,' she said, unexpectedly. This wrong-footed Polystom, who had become used to her unbroken silence at breakfast. She couldn't even be consistent in that!

'Sketches?' he snapped.

'Of dogs, I think.'

It took a moment for Stom to locate himself. 'My great grandfather

49

used to sketch. He assembled a bestiary of animal sketches. Perhaps those were discards. Or copies. The original are now in private collection – my mother's mother keeps them all.' He paused for a moment. 'Did you say dogs?'

She nodded.

'There aren't any dogs on Enting, you know,' he said. 'The climate doesn't agree with them. Lots of insects in the air here, aboriginal insects, and their bite kills off almost all breeds.'

There was a silence after this little lecture, broken only by the fluttery rattle of the window panes in their frames.

Shortly, Beeswing slipped out of her chair and through the door, vanished, as insubstantial an exit as befitted her.

All that day Stom cursed himself inwardly, marching vigorously through the forest to try and burn off his sense of indignation. His mood wavered between fury and self-pity. For a while he would be spitting with frustration that there had been the chance of connection, that her observation on the sketches had suggested itself as a bridge, that if he hadn't been so inwardly clotted with anger he might have responded kindly to her words, might have established a dialogue, and the two of them could have started the slow process of growing together. But this mood would flip about in moments and would be replaced by an anger as hard as knucklebones. What was the matter with her! Why couldn't she be a more conventional wife! It *wasn't* his fault, it really wasn't, he had tried over and over. It was *her*! She had abdicated the proper responsibilities of a wife and partner. Even if she *fought* him it would be preferable; even if she spat at him and flashed her nails at his face. Anything would be better than this grey passivity, as if she weren't entirely real, as if *he* weren't substantial and important – the Steward of Enting, after all! By this stage Polystom was kicking great patches of last year's pine needles into the air, like winnowing wheat, with swooping great swings of his legs.

By his return to the house in the evening this rage had shrunk, distilled itself into a pearl of rancour seemingly located in his gut. His wife did not appear for supper. Stom sent the underbutler to seek her out, but after twenty minutes the young man returned, red with embarrassment, to say that mistress wasn't hungry, chose not to dine with him. The rage flared in Polystom's breast again – to humiliate him *via a servant!* It was too much. He ate his food with a savage deliberation, and then asked the underbutler where his wife might be found. In the Print Room.

He thumped his way along the corridors and to the Print Room furious, determined to vent his anger at Beeswing. He decided he was going to tell her that it wouldn't do, that she was not acting in an appropriate manner, that she needed to pull herself together. But before he reached the door he was imagining both sides of the argument. *What have I done wrong?* he imagined her asking him. *In what ways, specifically, have I erred?* It wasn't *like* that, Stom told himself. It wasn't that he could say 'you have over-stepped the mark in this or that regard', or 'this offends me' or 'that is unacceptable.' It was more a question of her overall demeanour; her attitude, of her refusal to live the life demanded by the code that governed the whole of civilised life in the System. It was a sort of dumb insolence. And anyway (he was clenching his fists so hard that the muscles in his forearms were starting to ache) – and anyway! It wasn't his responsibility to explain all this to her! Even if he could, even if he *could* lower his mind to an actuarial listing of specific instances, it would be inappropriate for him to act that way. It would be beneath him, in a very tangible sense. Couldn't she see that? She was the maladjusted child of a lesser branch of blood. He was the Steward of Enting! His family line was one of the oldest, as well as the most distinguished, in the System. Presumably she had understood that, presumably that was why she had agreed to marry him in the first place. It was *her* job to accommodate him, and *not* the other way around. If he were to settle down beside her and start listing all the things she was doing wrong, it would be demeaning not only to himself but to everything he represented. He had given her a particular gift by marrying her! He didn't insist upon any sordid exchange-value propriety, of course, but surely she understood what it meant to be married to somebody so well bred? He *could* stoop, turn himself into an accountant of proper and improper behaviour; he *could* demean himself by turning into schoolteacher and take her step-and-step through the correct way of acting. But if he did that sort of stooping, he would make himself less worthy of her love in the first place!

Couldn't she see that?

He knocked on the door of the Print Room, but there was no answer. Opened the door to find Beeswing sitting at the window.

Somehow his resolve dripped away through him, like drainwater running down the pipe of his spine. She looked extraordinarily beautiful, her pale skin glazed with the windowlight, her eyes intensely focused on the outside, a weird and spiritual stillness in her posture. He joined her by the window, searching with his own eyes for whatever it is that has captured her spirit so completely. He couldn't see anything special in the view. The light was grey, although it was a bright grey, and clouds scattered through the sky like suds. He looked out over the familiar view, the lawn of the garden falling and rising like green sighs, the orchard and a glint from the roofs of the glasshouses. The forest gloomed over to the right, but Beeswing's eyes were on the sea, restless and full under the spring air, its surface further off (this was just visible) tickled by occasional showers.

'My dear,' he said, awkwardly. 'What are you looking at?'

'The sea,' she said.

'Ah,' he said. 'The sea.'

There was a pause, and then she said: 'I'll go there.'

'It wouldn't be a good idea for us to take the boat out in this weather,' said Stom. 'It looks bright, I know, but the spring winds are surprisingly vigorous, and sudden rain makes sailing treacherous, even for an experienced sailor like me.'

'I didn't mean,' she said, dreamily, as if not addressing him, 'with you.'

It took a moment for this to sink in. 'I don't understand,' he said.

But she didn't reply to this. He stood up. 'Now look here,' he said. 'This won't *do*, you know. It really won't. What do you mean by that, by saying you'll go away?'

'I don't belong here,' she said, in the same dreamy voice.

'Of course you belong here. You're my wife. I married you, and you belong here. You can't go. I don't give you permission.'

At this she turned her head and looked at him, her eyes moist but hard, bright as aluminium. There was the slightest question in her look; or, at least, he interpreted it as such. 'I won't be interrogated. I *won't* be questioned,' he blustered. 'You'll stay here. We need to do some work, you and I, at being husband and wife. It evidently won't come naturally, and we need to work at it.'

He marched out, then, because he had run out of things to say. Downstairs, through the main hall. His mind rifled through possibilities. Something was needed, some public affirmation of their marriage, something to encourage Beeswing to settle down. Sitting in an over-large padded seat, staring at the portraiture on the wall, he tried to be decisive. A newsbook, this week's, was sitting unread on the low table. He flicked through its pages, not taking in the words.

He shut his eyes.

Out of nothing, a decision came to him. A party. He would host a party, something the house hadn't seen since his father's and co-father's death. The actual wedding ceremony had not, he thought, functioned properly as the public endorsement of their union. No wedding can, he thought to himself, because at that stage the parties are relatively unknown to one another. But a party thrown by host and hostess, months into their lives together, would be altogether more effective at publicly acknowledging and therefore cementing their partnership.

He called Nestor, and explained his plan; and then hurried upstairs to tell Beeswing personally. She wasn't in the Print Room. It took a fifteen-minute search, in which more and more servants became caught up, before it could be confirmed that she wasn't anywhere in the house.

Polystom kept thinking of his Aunt Elena's words when she had first learnt that he had fallen in love with Beeswing. *She ran away. Several times. Ungovernable, she's simply ungovernable.* So now she had run away from her husband, as she had once done from her parents, and from her guardian. Stom thundered at his servants, for allowing it to happen, but inwardly he blamed himself. He should have foreseen this, should have taken steps to prevent it. It seemed ridiculous, but evidently his wife needed to be watched, perhaps even locked up, at least until they could work out a way of purging her of this ungovernable nature.

He sent out as many men as were to hand to search the grounds; but it quickly became apparent that she had taken one of the boats from the pier at the bottom of the garden. A servant, who had been cleaning the glasshouse windows, had seen her pass. 'My lady asked me to unhook the boat-rope,' this man said. He was old, his face creased and collapsed like a crumpled old pillow, and he was crying now, streaky tears falling as his master raged at him. 'I'm sorry sir, I'm

53

sorry. I didn't think any harm. She is the lady of the house, since your marriage, sir.'

This seemed to Stom a kind of hidden rebuke to him. 'You idiot!' he yelled, slapping the old man so hard that he fell to the ground. 'What reason would my wife have to go off in a boat by herself in this weather? You should have thought. You should have thought, and stopped her.'

The man sobbed further apologies from the ground, but Stom didn't wait. 'Take the twin-engine,' he told Nestor, 'and take a man with you. I'm going up in the plane. She will have gone east or west along the coast. I don't believe she has any experience of the sea, and she's surely not crazy enough to have gone out into open water.' He scanned the horizon. The clouds further out were grey and lowering. 'It's not good flying weather, but we need to catch up with her sooner, not later.'

'Yes sir.'

'The twin-engine is in the boathouse, I think.'

'It is, sir.'

'Get it on the water and start west. You'll see me flying soon enough. If I come back and then fly east again, you're to turn the boat and come back in that direction. Do you understand?'

'Yes sir.'

He sprinted to the front of the house, and across to the end of the runway. The planes had been stowed in the shed since the weather threatened spring storms, but servants were now hauling one of the craft out. In ten minutes Stom was airborne, spits of rain in the air blotting his goggles so that he had to wipe them repeatedly. The ground shrank beneath him, and he pulled over the sea.

She had only had a half-hour start on them, if that, and Stom set in a course following the coast. He passed over Nestor in the twin-engine boat, drawing a great traingular wash behind it, both engines clearly at full throttle. He flew on, and almost at once saw another, smaller boat. Flying low over this he could see one small figure at the wheel. It had to be her.

Climbing again, Stom now wished he had some way of communicating with his butler in the boat. He wanted to tell him to hurry, that she was easily catchable. He flew east, and circled the twin-engine, flying low over it and drawing it further on by flying away to the west again, this time so low that his propeller cut a shallow wave out of the water.

He wished he were in the boat. He could not catch her directly with his plane. There was nowhere to land west of the house; it was too wooded, and the coastline was too craggy.

Furious he cut inland, and flew over the treetops until he caught sight of his house again. He landed, and clambered out. 'The yacht,' he told servants. It had not been on the water since the previous Autumn Year, but it had three large engines. 'Make it ready. I need to get on the water.'

Men hurried to comply, and Stom dashed down towards the boathouse. But then he saw, with a spurt of rage in his breast, the twin-engine chugging into the cove. As soon as Nestor was close enough he yelled at him. 'What are you doing here?'

'Come east,' said the butler, waving his arms. 'You flew over us again. We turned back – to go east.'

'Idiots!' Stom yelled. 'Come here – come here – at least I can be on the water now. She's gone west, I saw her. I flew over you again to indicate that fact to you!'

He told one of the servants in the boat to go over and stop them putting the yacht on the water. Then he jumped from pierside into the twin-engine, and took the wheel, throttling as hard as he could, kicking up a standing wave and spray. The boat surged through the water and out on to open sea.

'I'm sorry, sir,' shouted Nestor, over the noise of engine and spray. 'I misunderstood.'

'Never mind now,' said Stom, the thrill of the chase upon him. 'We know which direction she's heading, and this boat is faster than hers.'

For half an hour things went well. They made excellent passage over a clear sea. But then the storm that had been threatening from the south broke upon them. The change in weather came with a ferocious suddenness. The rain was merely spitty, drops in the air like a swarm of icy insects, and then, abruptly, the climate changed completely. A violent wind started bashing huge dents out of the surface of the water. Rain filled the sky all around them, heavy as shot and thick as glue. Visibility disappeared. Everything instantly soaked to grey. Being so close to the rocks of the coast was very dangerous in this sort of weather, but Stom was worried less for himself – he was an experienced boatsman after all – and more for his impetuous wife.

There was nothing for it: he had to kill most of his speed. The boat was bucking underneath him like a child's swing. It was only a pleasure craft, not designed for these more violent conditions. Compelled by a great swell of water and wind they were thrown forward alarmingly. A black rock, fringed at its base with a doily of cold white froth, appeared suddenly out of the gloom before them. Stom fought the steering to the left, swerved through the bucking water, only just missing the obstacle. Then, throttling up, he jockeyed over a number of tumbling swells. Better to ride it out in the open sea than be dashed against the rocks, he knew, although the open sea might easily capsize his boat. He had just made the decision to take that risk when the squalls of rain lifted curtain-like to show a sloping black beach to his right. At once, Stom turned the wheel and gunned the engine, driving the boat hard up against the sand.

He didn't need to order the men. They hopped out as waves crashed against the back of the boat, and hauled it up the sand. Further up, the mealy beach gave way to tufts of grass, and then to turf. Black sentinels, trees, vaguely visible through the fierce weather, loomed on the edge of sight. The boat was far enough away from the waves now, and the men could take shelter. 'There's a boathouse somewhere along here,' yelled Nestor. But Stom had noticed an overhang, and the four of them clambered between the rocks to the east of the little beach, and round a bend to relative quiet.

They were all completely wet, their clothes and hair, through to their skin. They were all panting too, their breath coming out like steam. Above them the rain sounded appallingly fierce, and the angles of rock blew weird, inhuman whistles from the wind.

None of them said anything. All were thinking, Stom was sure, of Beeswing out on the water in this weather. But there was nothing to do but wait.

The rain died, drum-rolled up to a squall again, and then died once more, dropping away completely. Through it all Polystom was in a heightened imaginative state. He saw, in his mind's eye, his wife's boat ground to splinters between sea and storm, saw her body tugged down to the bottom, her face blank.

As soon as the rain had fallen to a drizzle he clambered along and out, and hurried over the sodden ground to the boat. 'Put your *shoulders* into it,' he shouted at his men – redundantly, as it turned out, because they were all there, frantically pushing the boat into the water. Through ridges of splash and spray, hopping into the craft and gunning the engine, and then they were away from the beach and pulling out to sea.

The air felt damp, ionised, but then, with the sort of breathtaking change of weather typical of the late Spring Year on Enting, everything was instantly transformed from grey to summer. A line of sharp sunshine rushed over the waves dragging behind it brightness and blue. As the storm clouds ran away through the sky it became so bright that Polystom had to shield his eyes with his hand. Now the swarming drops of spray thrown up by the nodding onward crash of the boat were diamonds, jewels, tiny mirrored pearls, and the tang of salt tasted clean and sunny. The scene cleared all around them, bright greens returning to the land, bright purples to the sky. The sea quieted, unbuckling, spreading its surface with sun-glitter.

'Keep your eyes open,' Stom shouted over the noise of the engine, the wind, the splashing. 'For wreckage.'

But there was nothing to be seen. They moved swiftly over now-calm waters, blue as Beeswing's eyes.

Eventually they came in view of a little fishing settlement, on the western coast of the Middenstead, perhaps forty miles from Polystom's house. Two dozen small stone houses, stacked up the slant of the coastline, arranged around a harbour made by a wooden pier-stockade in which a dozen tub-like fishing boats jostled one another. This was Yenia-port, one of the little communities of Stom's servants who lived off the water rather than the land. They fished, supplying the house with their best catches, eating for their needs and selling the surplus. Technically everything they fished belonged to Stom, as did they, but he continued his father's benign policy of granting them a degree of freedom. There was an overseer's house, on the highest ridge of the village, and the overseer's job was to keep an eye on comings and goings; he reported (Stom had no idea of his name; too lowly a figure) to the underbutler at the house, who in turn reported to Nestor, who could inform Stom if anything happened to be amiss.

Spring Year was the year for the biggest catches of fish, and normally Stom would have expected his fishermen to have been out on the waves, but the storm had corralled them in the harbour. Indeed, the harbour space was so packed with fishing boats that there wasn't room for Stom's twin-engine to squeeze in, and he guided it to the far, seaward side of the pier-stockade.

There was the other boat, the one Beeswing had taken.

One of his men tied the boat up, and Stom and Nestor clambered up and hurried along the wooden pier. Birdsong was audible; and the endless buzz of insects. From harsh winter storm, the weather had swung about almost to a summer scene.

The streets of Yenia were narrow and steeply inclined, ridged with logs inset into the compacted dirt to aid feet. They were slippy, after the rain, and Stom's white Stapiá closeweave trousers were spattered with brown at their ankle cuffs.

He had come to Yenia several times before, years ago, when his fathers were still alive and he had indulged an adolescent passion for boating. Then his wanderings had taken him up and down the coastline of his sea, and he had come here. The dark little houses, fish-smelling. The one tavern, where the ale was stored in barrels on the roof and fed through a flexible tube into glasses below, where even that yeasty brew had a fish-like flavour to it. The boat repair yard in the lower village. The sequence of low-ceilinged plaster rooms abutting the harbour where the catch was cleaned, filleted, and then refrigerated (if it was for the House), or packed in salt (if it was for home consumption). The stone of the houses was whitewashed, and shone like glass in the new sunshine.

The tavern had no name, but Stom knew where it was, and inside he found his wife, sitting laughing in the midst of a crowd of fishermen and fisherwives. She was laughing at something an old man, amazingly creased and wrinkled, was saying to her. Even with bright sunshine outside the tavern was so murky that it was lit with two oil lamps, and in this red-orange light Stom took in the whole scene. The old fisherman was telling some anecdote, perhaps an old fishing story, to Beeswing, and she was laughing. There was something wrong with the old man's face, more than just its wrinkles and great age; it was queerly distorted, as if it had been torn into half a dozen pieces by fate and reassembled indifferently. The right eye was a wide slit, pulling down into the cheek. The ear seemed to be missing; the nose was of unusual bulk and shaped like a piece of coral. Yet his wife, his beautiful wife, seemed to be enjoying herself more than Stom had ever seen her.

He ducked his head to step inside the tavern, and of course all eyes turned to him. The chattering faded to silence; Beeswing's smile slipped, settled into her more usual enigmatic expression.

'My dear,' he said, his voice unexpectedly booming in the enclosed space. 'We were worried about you. The storm . . .'

He trailed off. Silence.

The gnarled-faced old man shifted his seat back, away from the Lady. She stood up. She did not need to hunch over, despite the low ceilings. With graceful step, she came over to her husband, and took his hand.

'They were telling me,' she announced, as much, it seemed, for the benefit of the whole room as for Polystom, 'of the life they live; following the shoals through the Summer Year up and down the Middenstead. Of the amazing plenitude of fish in the Spring Year. It's all so captivating. Captivating!'

The crowd, uneasy in the presence of their master, shuffled, smiled, settled. 'Come along, dear,' said Stom, his relief at finding her alive sliding into anger that they must act out this scene in front of nobodies, servants.

'I'll become a fisherwoman,' she said. 'I like the oceans. They are free and wide and open.'

'And dangerous,' chipped in the gnarled-faced old man from the back of the room. *Day-jrus.*

'And in the danger,' Beeswing continued blithely, 'is the truest freedom. I told them that you'll surely build me a little house here, in this village, so I can follow this life.'

But this, to Stom, was too absurd even for joking. 'Come away,' he said, more pressingly, taking her arm and tugging it. 'Let's not do this thing here.'

He led her down the slippery alleyway, and out to the twin-engine. One of his men would bring the other boat back; Nestor piloted the twin-engine, and Stom sat in the back, his grip on his wife's arm so fierce that she told him to lessen it several times.

[sixth leaf]

After this Polystom made a decision. He called his chief butler to attend on him in his snug. His mind was made up. He informed Nestor that his wife must be restrained – 'you understand, Nestor? This *running around* of hers is simply unacceptable. Think of it,' Stom went on, leaning back in his chair expansively (although his palms were sticky with nervous sweat), 'think of it as a kind of disease, I would like you to think of it as a sort of disease. Fever-germs agitate the body, making it shake and jerk; she has some subtle fever-germ in the mind that makes her run away. Do you see this?'

'Yes sir,' said Nestor, with the faintest colour of doubting in his voice.

'We need to confine her,' said Stom. 'Confine her. Confinement is natural to womankind, you see?' (He had only a vague notion of what 'confinement' involved, except that it was a condition into which women sometimes entered.) 'We'll lock her in the Yellow Room – yes?'

'As you wish, sir,' said Nestor. Stom caught a momentary glimpse of something in his servant then, like a fish coming up through water almost to the surface and visible from the air, something of Nestor's own personality; his preciseness; of his minuscule discomfort at this stratagem, his distant coolness, of the impeccably structured and timetabled life he led. But then the fish sank away again into the indistinguishable grey depths, and Nestor was just a servant again.

Little insights like this, Stom often thought with regard to himself, were the hallmark of a poet.

When the day came, Polystom brought in one of the underbutlers – a tall, frothy-haired woman – to stand behind Nestor. This party of three came upon Beeswing in the Main Library. She was squatting behind a mauve settee, reading a book with the almost feral intensity of a child

61

devouring a sweetmeat. She looked up, almost startled, as the three shapes appeared over her. 'My love,' said Stom, his heart thumping hard, 'there's something I'd like to show you in the Yellow Room.'

'The Yellow Room?' she repeated in her limpid, little-girl's voice.

'The view,' he said, extemporising. 'I've fitted a fountain pump in the lake and you can see the effect best from the Yellow Room.'

She showed no suspicion at all at this unprecedented and rather implausible statement. She got to her feet and walked beside him, still carrying her book, out of the library, up the stairs, along the turf-soft carpeting of the upper corridor. She stepped blithely through into the Yellow Room. Polystom did not accompany her; he paused at the door as she stepped sleepily into the mustard-coloured space. Then, softly, almost like one trying not to disturb a light sleeper, he reached in, and tweaked the edge of the door so that it turned silently on its hinges towards him.

It closed with a click like a tongue popping against the roof of the mouth. Stom turned the key once and the bolt slid across with a deeper click, like a sombre echo of the former.

It was as simple as that.

For a moment he stood there, holding his breath. He didn't know whether he was waiting for her to cry out, to shout in outrage, to pummel the door with her fists. But there was only silence.

He wanted, urgently, suddenly, to be out of the house – out altogether. He was at the front door in seconds, pausing only to fit on his out-boots, and then he was marching briskly away. He walked over the lawn, towards the orchards. Trying to push out of his head the thought of what he'd done, perhaps.

Outside, fresh air. One step after the other, and he was at the blossomy rows of fruit trees before he knew it.

Focusing himself. It was the best for her, that was why he had acted. Best not dwell on it, not think of it. But it was the *best thing* for her. He'd keep her in there a few days, that was all. Have Nestor put food on a tray. And a commode. A few days, or maybe a week.

The orchard was possessed by a positive blizzard of butterflies, blue as shards of sapphire. They crowded the air between the plumapple trees, all the way down to the greenhouses on the seaward side. Walking through them, all Polystom's senses were taken up with their brief, seasonal joy – the dazzling sight of them, the sound of their papery burr as they flapped, even the feel of them bumping harmlessly against his face. On the edges of his vision he caught the ghostly bouncing shapes of nets, as servants harvested the swarm. But walking through the midst of it he was completely wrapped up in a vividly deep blue.

Best to put his mind somewhere else. Best not to think of his wife at all.

Soon enough he was out the far side. Skirting the greenhouses, their roofs neon-bright in the sunshine to his left, he wandered into the forest proper, the fir woodland. The butterflies did not come here. They craved plumapple blossom, perhaps were even repelled by the resinous perfume of the pines, so that only one or two stragglers moved, lost and meandering like torn-up pieces of evening sky, through the shadows.

He walked a long circle, as far as the western foothills, and slowly back. Beeswing, in his mind, was a sort of blank. He did think of her, he couldn't help himself, but he imagined her standing in the Yellow Room as motionless and empty as a stone statue. He thought of her looking out over the vista, through the window, mannequin-like. And vaguely, half-subconsciously, he imagined her mental processes, her brain ticking around its route like a clockwork device, until the trigger arm was finally reached and flipped and she *saw*, she *understood* how foolish she had been. Vaguely, Stom thought of her enormous remorse, her penitence, her humility and love for him gushing through her at that moment like an ecstasy, forcing out sighs and tears with the sheer pressure of the passage, consummating her revelation as a sort of sexual climax.

Back at the house, Nestor was waiting by the front door.

'My mistress,' he said, giving the phrase a vaguely faded tone as if he used it only because a more accurate was unavailable, 'has been, sir, calling out, and shouting.'

'Calling out?' repeated Stom, the unfocused mental image of his wife in an orgasmic intensity of remorse still swilling through the lower vesicles of his consciousness.

'Screaming, I should say, sir. And banging.'

'Banging?'

'Hitting the door. Kicking it I'd say, sir, to judge by the sound she's been making. It echoed through the whole house.'

Polystom kicked off his boots and went up the stairs, with Nestor behind him. 'I can't hear anything,' he said as he ascended.

'She stopped, perhaps half an hour ago. We weren't sure whether to open the door, sir, but decided to wait until you returned.'

Stom reached the door of the Yellow Room. The place seemed as silent as he had left it, but the quietness seemed an oddly accusatory one. Something wrong, some joint not right in its socket. Polystom's mouth was dry. Feeling the ridiculousness of his action, he knocked at the door. 'Beeswing?' he called out. 'My darling?'

Nothing.

Gingerly, he unlocked the door and opened it. The collapsed mess of an old dress on the floor, topped with a sprawl of glossy black silk, was Beeswing's supine body. Stom stepped over to her, and then stood, uncertain what to. Behind him, the door swung shut with a small groan, an uncanny and mournful noise. Its inside was spattered with blood. Polystom turned his wife's body over with his hand to see her hair clogged with her own plasticky half-dried blood, and pour-marks and spots of red over her face.

They moved her to another bedroom, and called for a doctor, who came flying over the Western Mountains that same afternoon.

'A terrible mix-up,' Stom explained. 'She got into some sort of fugue state in the Yellow Room. Couldn't open the door, and became hysterical – ran at the door head down.'

'Not once,' said the doctor, 'but several times. This sort of concussion is a serious business, of course, but probably not fatal. Have a servant watch her as she comes round; tell her not to move about too much. Bed-rest for her until the swelling around the temples goes down. A week at least, probably two.'

In the dark hallway outside, as Nestor sorted out the matter of fee, the doctor beckoned to Stom. 'My dear fellow,' he said. 'I wanted to tell you. There's a clinic, extremely well appointed, charming views over an ice-lake, on the moon of Rhum. Heated centrally throughout by means of hot-water piping,' he added, folding his payment into his pocketbook, as if this architectural detail were particularly important. 'I've referred a couple of hysterical wives and daughters there. I don't say send her straight off, you understand, but keep it in mind. Eh?'

'I will,' said Stom softly. He went through the ritual of bidding the doctor farewell at the front door like a drugged man. He felt as stunned as if it had been *he* who had banged his head against the door. Of course the clinic was out of the question; it would be an unacceptable blow to his status, to his pride, if he were compelled to take that course, and if it became widely known. And anyway, her episode had been a one-off. Surely it had been a one-off.

He left a woman in Beeswing's room, and went to his snug. It took several drinks before he began to feel more like himself. How could she do it? *Why* would she do such a thing? It passed beyond his comprehension. He tried to imagine himself, poet-like, into her body, but the effort was greater than his imagination could make. To put one's head down, as if bowing, as if in homage to something, and then sprint as fast as one could, to build up as much acceleration as was possible in the small space, *knowing* that one was about to thunder head-first into a solid wooden door? It was almost monstrous, the willpower required.

The impulse to leave the house was strong upon him again. Maybe it would be better for him to go. Fly away; visit his uncle. Cleonicles had not been able to attend the wedding, and Stom hadn't seen him since. Maybe a few days on the moon would be the best thing. Maybe he could return from such a little away-trip to a calmer, clearer sense of things between the two of them. The rightness of the idea seized him, with its deeper promise of removal from a source of pain, and he leapt up. He rushed through to his own bedroom, and started packing a satchel to carry with him. Uncle Cleonicles would have some advice for him, some guidance on how to resolve this sorry situation.

A serving girl was at his doorway. 'Mistress is awake, sir,' she said in a small voice.

'Oh,' said Stom, still thinking he could dash out. But it would be better to see her first. Better to let her know that he was going away, going partly to give her time to think through her own foolishness.

He traipsed through to the little bedroom where his wife lay, her head grown huge with bandages, inflated. She lay perfectly still, her arms straight at her sides, her eyes looking directly ahead.

Stom moved into her line of sight. 'Hello,' he said, forcing a goofy smile. 'How you feeling, my dear?'

She breathed in, and released the air in one short sentence: 'you locked me in.'

A hissy voice, snake-like. Stom almost stepped back, alarmed at the malicious power this tiny woman appeared to possess, almost scared by his own wife. Why should *he* feel bad? She was the one who'd surrendered herself to insanity.

'You went a little crazy, I think,' he said, forcing the smile again. 'Why would you do such a thing, my darling? We were just on the other side of the door.'

Another indrawn breath. 'Don't lock me up.'

'It was a simple misunderstanding,' said Stom. 'You didn't need to act the way you did! That wasn't normal.'

Beeswing's expression was enough, without words, to convey her contempt.

'Don't look at me that way!' Stom barked. 'You're the mad thing. Bashing your head half in – it's crazy.'

The serving girl was looking extremely uncomfortable, blushing. She couldn't leave because Stom hadn't dismissed her. He stood up, ready to go himself. 'I'm going away for a few days,' he said, pulling down the front of his waistcoat with dignity. 'Think about what you did,' he said to her, as to a child. The words sounded hollow and bizarre in his voice, but they were the right sort of thing to say, surely. That *was* the point, wasn't it? He almost added *and I hope you're sorry for everything*, but decided against it.

He paused. Beeswing was looking straight ahead, looking now at the level of his midriff. She didn't say anything else.

He flew to the moon, arriving at Cleonicles' in time for supper, and greeted his uncle heartily. It felt so good to feel the wind over his face, to cruise the enormity of space, to be able to reach his arm out of the cockpit and feel the interplanetary ether slipping through his fingers. For an hour or so this mood buoyed him up, and he joined his uncle for wine and metaphysical discussion. Then he found himself crying. It was the sort of thing that, had anybody else seen his weakness, would have been unbearable; but his uncle had seen him cry before, and wasn't fazed by it. He didn't rush to offer pointless condolence, but sat and allowed his nephew to cry out the worst of it. Once the initial pressure was voided, and Stom could speak, only then did Cleonicles offer tactful questions, as another man might offer a handkerchief. Under this loving application of wine and sympathy,

Polystom unspooled the whole story. Beeswing's flight, her recapture, his decision to lock her up until she saw sense. Her running headlong at the closed door, not once but several times, until she had all but brained herself.

'What shall I do, Uncle?' Stom asked. 'I don't know what to do.'

Cleonicles didn't hurry his advice. He sat and swilled the last mouthful of wine around the bottom of his wineglass. The sky outside was purple-black now, stained by the blue and green earthlight; the night calls of the stork-boars making mournful glupping whistles in the darkness.

'You are Steward,' he said eventually. 'There's no point in disputing the fact, it's a feature of the natural world, as solid as a mountain. If an underling disputes it we think that disgraceful. But just because a person is married to a Steward – that doesn't give them the right to dispute that fact either. All are bound by the great structure, high and low. Or else,' he said, with an almost tripping gloominess in his voice, 'or else everything crumbles.' He downed his wine. 'Being of a proper family, being close to the power, makes insurrection worse, not more creditable. At least some pitiable servant may excuse himself on the grounds of ignorance. A Steward's wife has no such defence.'

Stom had never seen his uncle like this before. 'Insurrection, uncle?' he said. 'That's a strong word.'

'Oh I dare say, I dare say. Yes, it overstates it a little to call it insurrection. But, then again, what *else* can you call a struggle against proper authority?'

He refilled his glass.

'You're at a crucial point, my boy,' he said, his lips glistening in the lamplight as he took a long draught. 'She's struggling against author-ity, which is as stupid as banging her head against a wall, if you see what I mean. She'll either learn this, and her life will settle into a better course; or else she'll deny herself the chance to grow up.'

Stom nodded. 'You're saying,' he said, 'that I should stand firm with her.'

'Yes,' said Cleonicles. 'Yes! You *must* stand firm. This womanly trick of knocking her head against a wooden panel and falling down, this is calculated to prey on a man's sense of pity and wife-protection. But don't be taken in! She's trying to manipulate you, and you – a Steward – must not be manipulated! If I were you, boy, I'd fly home

67

tomorrow. Not that I'm trying to get rid of you; it's delightful to see you, as ever. But it's more important that you establish the proper authority at home.'

His uncle's words sounded very wise to Polystom. They struck a chord of rightness inside him. He flew back the next day, his head muggy with old booze and his headache worse than it might otherwise have been.

He arrived late in the afternoon, with the shadows of the mountains starting to lay great wedges of dark over the forest. As the engine cooled, and he unbuckled his helmet, a servant appeared with a wooden ladder to help him from the cockpit. 'How is she?' Polystom asked the man, who blushed and stuttered, lowering his eyes and muttering that he believed the Lady to be taking some supper.

Stom walked round to the conservatory at the back of the south wing, and saw a table laid out in the lawn, just past the shadow cast by the house. There, Beeswing, her head still bandaged, was sitting, attended by a servant. He made his way over, trying consciously to put command and authority into his stride.

'Hello my dear,' he said, or announced rather, sitting himself and reaching for one of the little roast zulu-birds. 'I'm back from Uncle's. How are you feeling?'

There was no answer to this question, and there seemed to be a certain hardness in her eyes as she looked at him. But at least she was feeding herself, at least she was eating something. The servant hovered uneasily behind.

'You look better,' he offered.

'My head hurts,' she said, in a quiet voice, with that infuriating way she had of suggesting a metaphorical as well as a literal freight for her words – your hurt, Stom wanted to say, is the result of your own ridiculous attitudes. Your problems inside your head are the result of your own wilfulness. But he held his tongue.

Instead he stood up. 'I'd like a chat,' he said. 'I want the two of us to talk. Later. In the Library if you like. You do like the Library, don't you?' He left a pause, in case she wanted to drop in a meek 'yes', but she said nothing. 'After you've finished eating, of course.' He was still holding the little spitted zulu-bird, and he took a bite out of its flank, before dropping the remains to the lawn and going inside.

He had a bath, and took some food. He had a fire made up in the library; although it was late in the Spring Year, with Summer Year only months away, nevertheless the nights were surprisingly chilly. He had a bottle of black wine carried in to him, and then he gave instructions that Beeswing's nurse was to bring her into the Library. He expected her to be wheeled through in a bath-chair, but when she did come she was walking, supported by an arm from her servant. Stom stood up until Beeswing had been settled into one of the mauve chairs.

Stom waved away the nurse-servant. There were several minutes of silence, during which Polystom put his head a little to one side and listened to the snapping noises of the contorting flames in the grate. Like limbs being broken and ligaments twisted out of hard joints, he thought to himself; the crackling and popping of a young fire.

'You could have done yourself a serious injury,' he said, without preliminary. 'How could you be so foolish?'

'You locked me into that room,' she replied.

The boldness of her direct statement shocked him, a little. 'Whether I did or not has nothing to do with it!' he said. 'You shouldn't have . . . hurt yourself, and . . .'

'You hurt *me*,' she said, interrupting him with her deceptively soft voice. 'By locking me away.'

He stopped. Flustered. 'You're missing the point,' he said. He tried to remember what his uncle had said, what his exact words had been. 'It's about growing up, you know,' he said. 'It's about necessity. It's for your own good. You need to learn, you see. Necessity and authority. The point is,' he said, warming up a little, 'that you don't seem to understand what a wife should be. How a *wife* should act. You are a wife, you know. You don't seem to have the . . . proper attitude, the appropriate attitude. You see.'

There was another silence, with the only noises the hum of the flames and the intermittent gunshot bangs of sticks splitting as they burnt in the fire. Then Beeswing did something she had never done before in all the time that Polystom had known her: she asked a question.

She said, 'What have I done wrong, as a wife?'

The fire bickered at its log.

Polystom leaned back. He was tempted to snap at her, *what did you say?* but he knew that she would not retract the question, not even repeat it, and would merely look at him with her infuriating eyes. Perhaps it was a breakthrough, the first step on the road to true sorrowfulness and associated repentance. He refilled his glass and sipped at the dark wine once, twice, three times, trying to compose an answer that would make it plain to her that he had seen through her, that her subtle routines of insurrection were obvious to him, that the game was up. But now that he came to think of it, it was very difficult to put into words exactly what the issue was. It was in the slippery nature of her transgression that words failed to encapsulate the nature of her wrongness. And even if he could express precisely how *this* and precisely *that* needed to change, he would somehow be serving her lack of respect, he would somehow be lowering himself in front of her.

'I think,' he said, slowly, sipping again at the wine, 'that you know very well what the problem is. I think you know just as well as I, what the problem between us is.'

He expected a denial, but instead of saying *no I don't know what the problem is* she said nothing. Her attention appeared to have wandered.

'I don't deny,' he said, filling the uneasy silence, 'that it may have been difficult for you, adjusting. Adjusting to your new life, you know. But the sooner you make that adjustment!' He beamed at her, his false smile ghastly in the flickering light. 'Do you see what I'm saying? The sooner you do adjust, the better for you – never mind the better for me, although that is also true. But the better for you!'

She was on her feet now, a little unsteadily, and with her left hand touching the side of her bandaged head as if supporting it. He stood up too.

'Tired,' she said. 'I'm going to bed.' And she turned round, and half glided, half staggered out of the library. She disappeared so quickly that Stom did not have time to say anything.

In the morning, he sought her out after breakfast. It was past eleven, and after the chills of the night the sun was hot and bright. Beeswing had eaten outdoors again, and was being helped inside, into the shade, now that the sunlight was too hot. Stom waited until she had been settled into a settee, and then waved away her servant.

'I wasn't satisfied,' he told her, having prepared this opening sentence, 'with last night's conversation.' He sat down opposite her, and folded his arms. He expected her to respond, but there was nothing there. Her expression was as distant and vacant as if her whole mind were a space of interplanetary ether.

'Look,' he said, meaning to say something decisive. But he couldn't think of a suitably decisive statement. 'This won't do,' he said, eventually. 'This is mad. Insane! We can't go on like this. Look – let me ask you a question.' He felt a bubbling excitement inside him as if the two of them were about to breakthrough, and everything was going to be all right. 'Let me ask you a question.' Leaning forward, fixing her languid eyes and her perfect, faery face. 'Are you happy? Answer that question. Are you happy?'

She looked at him with one long unbroken stare, as if trying to answer the question with her eyes alone. Then she moved her head, slowly, sweeping her glance away from him, moving across the far wall like a searchlight, and finally to the window. The grass gleamed bright green in the sunshine. The funnels of a petrol-delivery ship poked above the curve of the hill, outlined against the grey-blue of the Middenstead behind. They slid, disembodied pillars, across the garden landscape and went behind the trees.

A minute stretched to two. Two stretched to five. This was absurd. Was she going to answer him? He stirred uneasily. Clearly she was not happy. That was evident! Does a happy person dash themselves head-first against a heavy wooden door? She didn't *need* to answer him – all he had to do, to reach her, was make her see that the thing standing between her and her own happiness was herself. Once she grasped that idea, things would start to go well between them.

'I want,' he said, gruffly, and cleared his throat. 'I want,' he continued more smoothly, 'you to be happy. I want us *both* to be happy. This insurrection of yours,' he said, finding his uncle's word on his tongue, 'only adds to the sum of unhappiness. Believe me; people have married and settled for a thousand generations. There's a profound truth in it, you see.' He knew a poem about it, a trio of lines that expressed the inherent rightness of what he was trying to say, but maddeningly he couldn't recall them. *Come*, no, *You forget so easily, come*, no that wasn't it. Never mind. It wouldn't be quite right to borrow the eloquence of a poet; he had to make her see for himself. 'Ownership and being owned,' he said. 'It can only make us happy – we can only be happy – if we allow ourselves to be. These structures, they surround us, they surround us completely, supporting us, lifting us and not letting us to fall.' He wasn't capturing his mind's gleam in words. He reached out and touched her knee. 'Do you see?'

She shifted a little, her gaze still through the window on the range of the shifting sea. 'Man,' she said. He word hung, peculiarly, in the air. Stom didn't take the sense of why she used the word. Was she addressing him? 'You own a world, and the people who live in it,' she said softly. 'But you'll not own me.'

It took a moment for this rebuke to sink in. Stom's hand was still on her knee, but when the sting of her words pricked home his body stiffened. He pulled away, sat back, and then almost at once he got to his feet.

'You don't wish to be *owned* by me,' he said, fiercely. 'Very well. But you are my wife. We are married. I am a Steward of this System, and it is not possible for us to unknit our bond. It would be untenable, for me. You understand this?'

She was looking at him. It was only a look, but it fired up his rage again. He could hardly bear to be in the same room as his wife now. 'Say yes,' he barked at her. 'Say that you understand what I've just said to you.'

Her eyes were almost placid.

Stom crashed out of the room and went upstairs, to the Lesser Library. It was maddening, impossible. He marched the length of his room, spun like a jaguar in a cage, and marched back again. How to reach her? To compel her – to *make* her understand the idiocy she pursued?

[seventh leaf]

With whatever thready knits of commonsense still holding his sanity together, he knew that he could not confront her in his present mood. He needed to be calm with her, and rational. He understood that she would rebuff any too aggressive insistence on his part with an automatic stubbornness of personality over which – perhaps – she had little control. It was infuriating, but he would have to cool himself down, and try and reach her with a more rational discourse. She could hardly fail to see how her present behaviour contributed to her own as well as his unhappiness, provided only that she thought through her actions intellectually.

Stom called for Nestor, and had him bring up some lunch, a bottle of blue-wine, and a gramophone. He would, he decided, sit and collect himself, listening to some music. 'Bring up the disks for *Nephelai*,' he told Nestor. 'I want to listen to the final arias.'

And so he sat, drinking, whilst Nestor busied himself plugging in the gramophone machine and pulling out the final one of the seven disks from the box marked *Nephelai*. He set the machine playing, and slid away. Polystom wriggled himself deeper into the cushioning of his settee and let the music wash through him. Erodeo had composed few operas, but those few were all masterpieces. The tenor was Hippocles, and the soprano Meleta, and their voices intertwined and arched into the ether of pure song. She – Nephela – had been betrayed by her lover, and was consoled by her childhood friend Touto, but he hesitated to declare his own passion, believing himself unworthy of her. The delicious, agonising, uncertainty of the middle act of the opera was precisely captured in Erodeos's extraordinary, stichometric music, which managed somehow to be simultaneously brittle and yearning. Then, as that act closed, Touto had resolved to declare his love, regardless of its impossibility.

But Nephela, never suspecting that her friend carried adoration for her in his heart, has learned that her first love, a warrior called Stasimon, is returning from his distant campaign. She plans a spectacular suicide, eating a certain poison that will (with the strange logic that is found in operas) cause her flesh to dissolve and disappear into the air over a period of hours. She vows to attend Stasimon's homecoming rally with this poison in her system, and to sing her final song of love rejected to him and his followers as she passes away. Touto discovers the empty phial of poison too late, and the tragic conclusion is inevitable. This was the scene to which Polystom was now listening: Nephela sings her great aria, declaring that she will soon die, but that a fading-away death is inevitable for those spurned in love. There is consternation amongst the followers of Stasimon; but before the soldier can himself reply, Touto rushes onstage declaring that love can be spurned by fate as well as by individuals, and singing a matching aria that bewails circumstance and the poison, now rooted in her flesh and unretrievable. Stasimon himself now intervenes, with a song to a martial melody but in a minor key, where he reveals that he has loved Nephela all along, and had returned specifically to claim her as his bride. But the poison is now taking effect, and Nephela is fading away, dissipating into the cosmos, something Erodeos captures in music with a long drawn-out diminuendo, very difficult for a singer to sustain. In this final aria she sings of the beauty of the air into which her constituent elements will soon dissolve; of the clouds moving slowly like lovers' limbs and the birds fluttering like lovers' hearts, of the warmth of the sun and the cool of the night like an indrawn and outward breath, repeated through eternity. Then, softer and softer, she sings that her love for Stasimon had been a kind of illusion, fostered by his magnificent reputation and his splendid armour; but that she has come to realise that her true love was for Touto. As both men weep, she passes away on an upward-drifting melody line of such sweetness that Polystom, listening to it, cannot prevent tears from coming out. The softness of the music is so exquisite that it brings the hairs at the back of his neck ticklishly to life.

Aenaoi Nephelai—
Arthomen fanerai droseran fusin eu ageton

74

Aenaoi, Aenaoi—
Patros ap' Okeanou baruacheos . . .

She dies into silence, and silence is maintained upon the stage for fully four minutes, a bold move for a composer of operas (whose job, after all, is to fill his listener's ears with music). Then Touto and Stasimon conclude the piece with a mournful coda-duet, in which they declare their intentions to act as brothers to one another, and return to the wars to seek an honourable death.

For some reason, Stom's tears, and the blue-wine he had drunk, had exhausted him, and he found he couldn't keep his eyes open. He slept. He awoke with a jolt, the turntable of the gramophone still rotating, and sat up with his mouth dry and his head strained almost to the point of headache.

He switched off the machine, and poured a glass of water from the jug Nestor had left for him.

He descended the stairs with Erodeos's melody still in his head, humming it as he stepped down, *Patros ap' Okeanou baruacheos*. But there was confusion downstairs, people hurrying back and forth across the hallway and spilling out through the front door. Stom, his tranquil mood dissipating, dissolving into air like Nephela's dying body, found Nestor waiting just outside the front door.

Beeswing had disappeared again.

'How can she be gone?' Polystom blustered at Nestor. The butler had fortified himself with company before breaking the news to his master, gathering round him half a dozen anguish-faced underbutlers.

'Sir,' said Nestor, 'she just slipped away.'

'A nurse was with her!'

'Chrysorosa,' confirmed the butler. 'Yes, sir. A pantry and laundry girl, normally. The Lady seemed to get on with her. She liked few enough of the servants, to be truthful, sir, but she tolerated Chrysorosa.'

'Collusion?' shouted Polystom, his anger now feeding on itself. 'Between mistress and maid?'

'Almost certainly not, sir,' said Nestor, involuntarily stepping back half a pace, his normally slow eyes darting back and forth. 'Almost certainly not. They were in the garden. The Lady sent her in to fetch a shawl. When she came back out the Lady had gone.'

'Why didn't you wake me immediately?'

'This was only ten minutes since, sir. Perhaps twenty. I thought to . . . recover the Lady, and . . .'

'You searched the woods,' interrupted Stom, his rage riding him. 'The orchard? The greenhouse? What about the boathouse?'

'I've had men in all these places. Immediately, sir, I sent men out to look for her – as soon as—'

Strom hit him, a cross between a backhand slap and a rabbit punch, on his cheek. Not hard, but it froze the scene completely.

Everything hung, for an awkward moment.

'I,' said Stom, feeling as if he ought to explain himself, and yet feeling even more furious that he felt that need (to a *servant*!) 'I left her in your trust! I trusted you!'

'Sir, I'm sorry,' said Nestor, quietly but a little hoarsely. A red patch like a blush rouged his cheek. Stom saw, uncomfortably, Nestor's wearied age – he'd never really noticed before how old the butler was looking. There were dark areas of tiredness below his eyes, like drooping petals. His skin looked thin, its wrinkles more like cracks in a potter's glaze than creases.

'She can't be far away,' said Stom. His innards were tumbling with impotent anger, leavened with fear, and a kind of self-disgust that was an unfamiliar and unpleasant sensation. 'She's ill! She's still wearing the bandages on her head, isn't she – the doctor said she should stay in bed – this might *kill* her,' he added with a nauseous glee compounded of anxiety and hope. 'She might *die*, if we don't get to her soon. Send the men out again – we'll search again.'

'The men are still out, sir,' said Nestor.

'Then, more. Send out everybody. Where would she go? Where would *you* go?'

But this was an impossible thing for Nestor to imagine (a servant? Running away?).

'Did she take a boat again?'

'No, sir, all the boats are accounted for. And cars.'

Polystom had the weeping nurse-servant brought to him, but she had no idea where her mistress could have gone, and could barely speak through her enormous, epileptic sobs and the copiousness of her tears.

Stom hurried out of the house, agitated by emotions greater than he could articulate. He took two young underbutlers whom he sent off left and right on little running excursions. For some reason he got it into his head that she was hiding in the glasshouses; and so he had both exits manned and went inside. Nestor assured him that the place had been thoroughly checked, but he looked through each of the glass rooms anyway, finding only the hot plants waving their fronds and leaves at him in the draught he caused, in what he took to be languid mockery of him; and one broken pane of glass whose punched-out hole formed a jagged heart-shape.

Made even more furious by this wasted time, Stom hurried to the waterfront. The tide was out, and the beach dotted with servants checking the great haystack heaps of seaweed. The stone pier lay over the beach like a great serpent. Prompted by something, he didn't know what, Stom ran all the way along to the end of this, to where the water still sucked at the base of stone. He tried to fight the sense of certainty, rising inside him like bile, that Beeswing had simply come down to the water and drowned herself. Perhaps she had flown along the spine of this very pier, on her delicate feet, to drop herself off the end into the water. He wanted to order servants to drag the water below him, but the words stuck in his throat. It couldn't be. Was she there, below him now, mocking him again in death? Should he leap into the water and dive down to try and find her?

Stupid thoughts. 'A net,' he yelled. 'Somebody bring a net down here!'

As figures scurried in response to his words, Stom looked out again at the shuffling surface of the Middenstead. It stretched away to the horizon; and beyond that, he knew, it reached as far again, before sweeping eastward in a great arc and filling a large depression that reached as far as the southern hemisphere. Its immensity, like the immensity of the sky above him, had always given Stom a sense of security, of being surrounded by a greatness that supported and sustained him. He thought of the fishing trips he had taken with his father and co-father; of swimming expeditions from boats or from this very pier. Had Beeswing polluted even that childhood memory with the ultimate transgression? Had she filled his sea, his childhood bathing ground, with death?

Nestor was at his side now. 'The tide turned only quarter of an hour ago, sir, if that,' he said breathlessly. 'If she went in the water it won't be far from here.'

But even as men arrived with the weighted net, and others came dragging a boat over the sand, Polystom felt the urgency go out of his body. He turned, waving Nestor on, and started walking back along the pier. There was an utter certainty in him, as deep as his bones, that his wife was dead, and sodden in the water behind him. The awfulness of it settled over the surface of his thoughts like snow; but deeper down was a curious feeling of vacancy.

He reached the grass, when he was overtaken by shouting. Men were running down from the west. 'The woods! The woods!'

Stom's heart leapt up again. 'Is it her?' he called, breaking into a jog. 'The woods?'

'Sir!' called his servants. 'Sir!'

Nestor, despite being twice his master's age, was at his side in moments. They ran together up the sloping grass, past the orchard to their left and towards the gesticulating men at the borders of the forest.

'Did you deal with the fishers?—' Stom gasped.

'Yes sir!' bolted Nestor.

'—with the fishermen?—'

'Yes sir!'

'Was she heading in their direction again?' Stom asked. 'Is she going that way?'

They ran for two minutes, three, before a growl behind them announced one of Stom's automobiles, creeping over the grass on its narrow wheels, driven by a jerky-faced undermechanic. Stom spun about and pulled the door open, heaved the driver out, clambered in. The engine grumbled, and caught, and he drove up the slope and between the wide gatepillars of the trees, leaving a wake of two lines behind him, tyre marks deeply scored into the turf.

He drove as far as he could, Nestor running in front of him and the hallooing of other servants audible through the open widow, until the trees were too narrow to pass between. Then he tumbled out of the car and sprinted the last hundred yards to a knot of people. Pushing them aside, he saw, with déjà vu, the crumpled heap of clothes on the forest floor, a flimsy silk gown, a pair of house slippers, and the turbaned mass of bandages.

'How is she?' he asked.

'Breathing,' said somebody.

Stom gripped her tiny shoulder, and pulled her body over. Her eyes were open; her expression looked, indeed, rather comical, mouth pursed and eye-shaped. She met his eyes.

'Did you trip over a tree root?' he asked her.

'Yes,' she said, in a voice small but not diminished. And then, miraculously, a smile flicked over her mouth. It only lasted a moment, but it completely changed the mood of the moment.

Stom sat down on the pine needles beside his wife. 'Where did you think you were going?' he asked, not unkindly. The entire encounter, its emotional swellings and anticlimaxes, had now taken on the flavour of a ridiculous comedy.

She was staring straight up, now, at the canopy of fir branches. 'Away,' she said.

'Away – through the forest? In house slippers?' He chuckled. 'How ridiculous you are.'

'Away,' she said.

'You,' said Stom, gesturing messily at one of the servants standing nearby. 'Pick her up and take her to the car.'

The boy stooped, and stood again with Beeswing in his arms. She seemed dreamily removed from events happening around her. 'No,' she said softly, without struggling. 'Let me go.' Stom sat until his breath was back, and then got to his feet, walking the hundred yards back to his car. The afternoon sun was intermittent through the tops of the trees, making scribbling patterns of light on the forest floor.

At the car Beeswing was sitting on the running-board, her hands on her knees. '*In* the car,' said Stom, coming over to her. 'I can't drive you back on the running-board.'

'My head feels funny,' she said.

'The doctor told you bed-rest,' said Stom, helping her to her feet and opening the door behind her. 'He didn't say flee through the woods. No wonder your head feels funny.' He was impressed again, as he helped her to a standing position, by the sheer lightness of her, as if her bones were hollow as a bird's, as if her flesh were not filled with blood in the hot-water bottle fashion of Stom's own body but was instead suffused with ichor, with air itself. And there was even a little elation in himself. The quicksilver shifts in mood, in the air around his wife, bubbled a hopefulness up in his own mind. Perhaps this ridiculous little adventure was going to mark the turning-point in their mutual relationship. They could learn to laugh together at the absurdity of her escape attempts, and by laughing they would bond. He wanted to be alone with his wife in this fragile moment of bonding. 'You men,' he called to his servants. 'Back to the house with you.'

The servants, half unwillingly, left, stepping between the trees. They too had been wound up tight by the trauma of Beeswing's vanishing. They shared, in their reduced way, his sense of anticlimax. 'In the car, my love,' said Stom, a smile on his lips, turning to face her.

She wasn't there; and he turned his face again, smile-less, to see the back of her bouncing away deeper into the wood. He started after her, immediately, caught between laughing at this child's game of chase-and-kiss-me, and scowling at her continued intransigence. It was possible to take a game too far. And underneath was the suspicion, hardened by his earlier anger into grimness, that Beeswing was playing a different game to him. Chase-and-kiss-me meant I expect to be caught, I relish being caught. Beeswing's running was the reflex action of the instinctual runaway. She continued betraying him, abandoning him.

Stom's longer legs covered the ground between him and his wife swiftly, and as he reached out to apprehend her he decided that he would root out this insurrectionary streak in her make-up once and for all. He would lock her up, and keep her locked up until her spirit broke a little – or if not *broke* exactly, then at least softened to the point where it could bear the imprint of reality. Tie her to a bed, perhaps, so she couldn't hurt herself. He could not play this game for ever. Marriage was a more serious business than this. And thinking so, he reached forward and grabbed with both hands at Beeswing's moving hips, one hand on each side, gripping and pulling her down. His greater weight and momentum carried him over her and forced her down on the ground.

He stumbled, his foot caught against her legs and he almost fell; but he recovered himself, staggered on several steps and brought himself up against a treetrunk. She was lying face down again, as she had done before. 'To me!' he called, angry now, wanting his servants to come quickly, to pick her up and make sure she was deposited inside the car. 'Over here!' He turned his wife's body over with his foot, looking down at her with a certain disdain, as if to say *I'm not amused by this childishness, you know*. The irritant was that, even in something as tender as the bond of joint amusement, she did not understand where the boundaries lay. Had she got straight back in the car, the fragile mood of happiness might have been maintained on the drive back to the house. Then this first point of connection could have been firmed up. But this second running off had spoiled that. And playing dead, as she was now doing, only made matters worse. The games were over. No point in lying there white-eyed and pretending motionlessness.

He bent over her, to look more closely at her fogged eyes. She had rolled them back in their sockets. Her mouth hung slack. The first of his servants had reached him before he realised that she wasn't breathing, and that her pulse – never a strong thrum – was entirely absent.

The doctor, that evening, could offer little precision of diagnosis. A blood vessel had exploded in her head, he said. This was probably a weak area from her former injury, some vein torn by her banging her head against the door that had only partially healed, and had been knocked loose again. He couldn't say whether it had been Polystom's tackle that had done this, or whether she had done it herself simply with the action of running, 'this latter,' he said, 'as distinct a possibility as the former. With this sort of injury, bed-rest is absolutely required, you see. Sudden movement can easily be fatal. It's also possible,' he said, 'that she hit her head in the forest going down, and caused a wholly new injury. I could open her head with the knife,' he explained, smiling at Stom's wince, 'and wouldn't be able with certainty to determine which of these scenarios was the proximate cause of death.'

'Thank you,' said Polystom.

Nestor, his cheek still red, although the ruddiness had not darkened into a bruise, saw the doctor out. Stom stood in the ante-room into which Beeswing's body had been brought. The bandages had been removed to reveal two smile-shaped cuts, half-healed and rusty with dried blood, just above her hairline. Otherwise, there was nothing about the body to indicate that it had died prematurely. He touched the forehead, expecting instinctively to feel warmth and instead found it dry and cold, an unusual combination. The sweatless fever-free chill of polished stone.

Nestor, tentatively, looked round the door. 'Sir?' he asked.

But Stom felt cool himself, infected by her coldness. He was conscious of the absence of the violent emotions he had felt at the deaths of his father and co-father. He felt no desire to cry; and no capability of tears even had he wanted them. 'Her manner,' he said, 'in the woods, when we found her. She was fey, then. Do you think the aneurysm had already happened, and her head was filling with blood as we spoke to her?'

'I don't know, sir.'

'That would mean,' he went on, 'that she was dead when we found her. Dead but still playful. I'd like a bottle of wheat whisky, Nestor. There should be half a dozen bottles from the case Aunt Elena gave me for my birthday. Bring a bottle to my snug.'

The chill unreality of this death continued through the next few days, as Stom organised a funeral. Few came; although Aunt Elena and Uncle Cleonicles both appeared – which was surprising, given that neither of them had come to his co-father's funeral the year before. Beeswing's guardian came, but neither of her parents appeared. Polystom wrote up the record of her life the day before the ceremony. It had taken him nearly a week to write up records for his father and co-father, but he managed hers in a day. There seemed so little to say about Beeswing: the bare facts of her life, fleshed out with a few observations on her character from her husband. It was as though she would leave as light an imprint upon the biographical record as her delicate body had left upon the material word. 'There was something elfin about her,' Polystom told the few assembled. 'My feelings were touched,' he said, having decided against using the phrase *I fell in love*, 'my feelings were touched by her lightness, her delicate but fiery spirit, by her faery beauty. She was a creature of the air, a spirit of the air, like the sprite Aethra from the opera *Tettixes*. She has left this material world now, and I'm certain she finds a purer existence amongst the clouds.'

He could see Aunt Elena nodding, gently; but there were no tears.

Afterwards there was a brief funeral meal, and then the guests went their various ways. Only Cleonicles loitered. 'Are you bearing up, my boy?' he said. 'This is a bad business, I know, but are you bearing up?'

'Could I prevail upon you, Uncle,' he said, with the brittle precision of the bereaved, 'to stay tonight?'

'Of course, of course,' said the old man. 'As long as you like.'

That evening, over drinks on the patio (for the night was a warm one) they talked for many hours. Or, rather, Polystom talked, talked on, dry-eyed but urgent, and Cleonicles listened. The talk was, to begin with, of Beeswing, but of course it elided easily into talk of Polystom himself. She had never understood him; she had ignored the gift he had given her. It was an appropriate way to die, really, he said. There had been something wrong in her head all along. Why should it be that healthy individuals are drawn, as some undoubtedly are, to the marks of sickness in others? Where is the sexuality in pathology? Health should be drawn to health, surely. But there was a sort of sickness in me, too, he said. He had craved a soulmate, a partner, and this craving was a sort of weakness. A weakness. And the talk wound down into drowsy wine-fuelled pleasantries. And after this into silence, a comfortable silence between the two men.

After a while, Cleonicles said: 'you don't blame yourself, dear boy?'

And this was a thought that had literally not occurred to Polystom. 'Blame myself?' he repeated. 'For what?'

'Quite,' said Cleonicles. 'Quite.' And he looked into the fire, as if his science-refined spirit could foresee the future, the innumerable visits that his nephew would go on to make to his house, the innumerable tears he would shed, the pitiable talk of *missing her* and *bitterness of life* that Cleonicles would have to listen over the coming year. It may have been that he did not suspect such a future. Or perhaps he had some inkling of the way his nephew's spirit would run.

'There's no reason why you can't marry again,' he said, offering the remark with a forceful voice, knowing it to be one of the uncomfortable sorts of truth that a recently bereaved husband doesn't like to hear, howsoever truthful it may be. 'Not just yet, of course, but in time. And marry somebody more settled, perhaps.'

Polystom stared gloomily into the fire. 'I know you're right, Uncle.'

'May I take the record of her life with me?' Cleonicles said. 'When I go back to the moon, I mean?'

Stom looked up, startled at this request. 'If you like, Uncle,' he said. 'But why on earth would you want it?'

'I have my reasons,' he replied. 'Scientific reasons, perhaps.'

'Does – she – come within the remit of science, then?'

'We all do,' said Cleonicles. 'All of us. An eccentric, as she was, is more useful to – certain scientific investigative procedures than a run-of-the-mill type. My boy,' and he leant forward. 'You mustn't be ashamed.' Polystom started to protest, feebly, but Cleonicles quieted him with his heavy hand. 'No, you mustn't be ashamed to have fallen in love with such a creature. It's one of those passing things, and had you not followed it through you would have regretted it. Regret nothing! Never apologise, never explain. And always remember that love comes in a variety of species. There are healthier forms of it waiting for you!'

They chatted on, for an hour or so, before the older man drifted into a sleep in his chair, and Polystom looked thoughtfully upon the heap of glowing ash that filled the fireplace.

It was not until a week had passed that Nestor told him that one of the servants had almost died the same day as Beeswing, death hovering twice over the house. 'She didn't die, though, sir.'

Polystom stared at the fire. Nestor was giving his weekly report. 'Did this happen this week?' he asked.

'Yes, sir.'

The fire crackled into the silence between them. 'Well?' prompted Polystom. 'What happened?'

'I wasn't sure if you wanted all the depressing details, sir. The point is that she's better now, with the loss of one hand, and she's recovering her health.'

'Tell me the depressing details,' said Polystom, his voice freighted with a curiously self-satisfied gloominess.

'Oh, sir,' said Nestor, a little flustered. He was wearing all black, in honour of his master's mourning. The new black velvet of his coat crinkled and flexed as he shuffled uneasily in his seat, grins and smirks appearing and disappearing in the cloth as if it were making wicked faces at its master. 'It was only a lower servant girl, a garden worker. She pushed her hand through some glass in the glasshouse. We don't know why. But she's fine now, recovering.'

This tale was not morbid enough to satisfy Polystom's soul; he waved his butler on with his report.

[eighth leaf]

[*this leaf is very fragmented at start and close, and its order is uncertain. It is impossible, from internal evidence, to know whether the event it relates comes from before or after Polystom's marriage to Beeswing, or how the original author intended it to relate to the other events in the narrative. It is placed here at the end of the sequence only tentatively.*]

[. . . looking into]
[. . . (*masculine word ending*)]
[. . .]
[. . . and f(rom?) above]
[. . . variegated]
. . . that [there were?] bears in his woods. Some estate-owners had their aboriginal bear-populations culled, 'clearing their woods' as the phrase went. Polystom had read about the Steward of the main Estate on Rhum having all his bears killed, stuffed, to be animated stiffly with rods and cogs and little electrical motors, before placing them back in between the trees. Such artifice was not for Polystom. He hired hunters (on leave from the army, and glad of the pay) to shoot two hundred of the beasts in his own woodland, but impressed upon them that they must kill no more. He liked the idea of a score or so bears roaming his lands. He went so far as to ship a whole herd of cows to pasture south of the Middenstead to save the valuable creatures from ursine depredation. [There were?] enough boars, rabbits and fish living wild in the forest and streams to keep a limited population of bears fed.

And once, magically, dangerously, Polystom had come face to face with one of his bears. It happened towards the end of a Winter Year, just as it was turning to a Spring Year. He had been wandering further than usual; the sun was slipping away. It was late in the afternoon, dusk permeating the gloom of the forest with sepia, and the fragrance of pine-needles and resin sharp in the cold air. Polystom had been walking for many hours. He had heard the moans of bearsong several times through the day, but had ignored them – they sounded distant, and his mind had been elsewhere. He had wandered on. The moon was low in the sky, its green-silver circle of light bitten into by the silhouettes of trees, and more trees, and then the up-line of a mountain. Soon the sunlight drained away entirely and green moon-light on dark-green trees gave the woods a spectral, unreal aspect. Sighing with the beauty of it, the melancholy loveliness of his lands, Polystom stopped where he was. He slipped his backpack from his shoulders and rummaged through it to bring out his torch. It would be time to go soon; not to walk home – that was too far – but to cut down through the trees to the nearest inlet or cove of the Midden-stead, and then along the coast until he found one of his boat huts. Inside would be a kettle, a larder of dried food, bottles of pineberry wine – and a telephone, from which he could call his main estate and have a servant come collect him in a boat. He switched his torch on, not wanting to stumble and twist an ankle as he picked his way through the shadow at his feet. The light, a bright and syrupy yellow, sprang all about him, enamelling the tree trunks in their own sharp shadows, turning indistinctness into the upright painted flats of layered stage scenery.

And there was the bear, directly in front of him.

It hallooed, rather sorrowfully, at the suddenness of the light, more groan than roar. Polystom froze. The bear was twice his height (probably less in fact, but surprise and fear exaggerated the pro-portions). It looked, in fact, surprisingly unlike a bear, or unlike Polystom's memories of bears – more like an enormous shaggy brown lion standing on its rear legs. Its fur was seaweedy and matted, hanging in strands from its huge body. Perhaps the creature was not in perfect health. But its teeth, stained yellow by the lamplight but presumably white, jutted proudly out; and its eyes, so glossy they looked like globes of black oil, caught starbursts from the torch and glistened. Its front paws dangled in the air before its chest, like a man leaning on an invisible rail. Each paw sprouted long thorn-shaped claws.

The bear moaned again.

Polystom's first reaction, when he had unfrozen enough to act, was to pull his thumb back over the switch of the torch. The yellow light vanished, his retinas' recoil leaving everything utterly black for a moment until the softer silver-green moonlight faded up the world into half-vision. The outline of the bear was still there, one kind of dark massed against the variegated darkness of the background. For a time the scene stayed as it was, until Polystom saw, or thought he saw, the shape melt, droop, dissolve, and vanish. When he finally summoned the courage to move he backed slowly until his hand, reaching behind him, touched a tree trunk. This he slowly slid behind. Could bears see in the dark? He couldn't remember, wasn't sure if he'd ever known. His own breathing seemed appallingly loud.

When, after an age, he decided to risk the torchlight again, the sudden brightness showed only trees. The bear had gone. Pricking his courage, he forced himself towards the water. He had the superstitious sense that the lamp had somehow summoned the bear to him, or even called it into being, so he moved through the dark with the light off, tripping often over bumps and roots and twice falling completely. But he made it down to the glittering expanse of moonlit water, and then after a short trot into one of his boat huts. Inside, with the door bolted, he was trembling so hard he couldn't stand up.

Later, with a boat on the way, and most of a bottle of wine inside him, he felt more self-congratulatory – his encounter took on resonances which fear had, at the time, blocked out. He *had* stood his ground. It had been the bear that departed. And, the more he thought about it (jotting with drunken-messy handwriting in his little note-book) the more the encounter took on a magical or mythic quality. The bear, rearing up from nowhere in the middle of the moonlit forest; Polystom standing so close (not true, this part, but in his lubricated imagination it became true) that he could smell the odour of bear-pelt, the hot exhalations of old, eaten meat on the beast's breath. It had appeared to him in a burst of light. Then it had vanished into darkness again. It came to seem to Polystom almost a blessing from the land, from his estate. It came to seem to him, obscurely, almost a materialisation of truth itself.

The moon like a perfect circle of green-and-silver stained glass, brimful of light. [*this last sentence is of dubious provenance, and may not belong at this point in the narrative.*]

TWO
Cleonicles

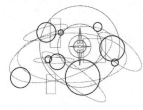

A Murder Story

[first leaf]

Cleonicles' last day alive began exactly like any other day, with the routine he had inhabited now for fifty years. He woke early, sunlight filtering beautifully through his bedroom curtains, and got himself out of bed. His morning servant, who slept on a pallet-bed outside the bedroom door, came in as soon as he heard his master stirring, and took him through to the annex. In this little cubicle Cleonicles sat on the lavatoire and moved his bowels whilst his servant lathered his face and shaved him. Decades of the procedure had made the old servant adept at guiding the razor smoothly over the knuckles and ridges of Cleonicles' face. By the time the residuum of foam was being wiped away with a large damp cloth, Cleonicles had emptied his bowels. He came back through to the bedroom, with his servant behind him, and servant helped master into his underjohns, into his Daverné trousers, his undershirt and overshirt. Dressed, his feet slipped into his favourite houseshoes, with the lambs-wool linings, Cleonicles made his own way downstairs leaving his servant behind to make the bed, tidy the room and clean up the lavatoire. Breakfast was cooking; Cleonicles could smell it.

Naturally, he did not realise that this was his last day alive. He had every reason to expect, throughout this day and for many others, to continue his science. In fact, so established was his comfortable daily routine that he didn't even look forward with any conscious shaping of his thoughts. If he had done so, he would have imagined working this day and the next on stellar observation and theory, with other work – covert work, for which he was still employed by the Prince – taking up a proportion of his time. Had he bothered to articulate this to himself he would have thought of spending the next month in this. But he did not need to look forward: habit and contentment had positioned him in an eternal present where nothing in the future, and nothing in the past, could disturb his happiness.

His nephew Polystom had stayed three nights, but had left the previous day for his estate on the world above – the green-blue sphere of Enting, huge in the sky. He loved his nephew, of course, and enjoyed his visits, but there was also a certain relief in having the house to himself again. A troubled soul, his nephew. Something not quite in harmony within him. And on the occasions that he stayed some of his unsettled spirit percolated through into the general atmosphere.

After his breakfast, Cleonicles strolled on his front lawn and smoked a cheroot. The air was clear today, the booming chuckling of the stork-boars clearly audible over the sounding-board of the waters. They were gathering in a flock at the near shore, and Cleonicles wandered down to look at them. They were peculiar beasts. He had published a paper on them soon after moving to this house – decades ago, now. The shallowness of the Lacus Somniorum (which was generally two feet deep, sometimes three, across almost all of its enormous breadth and length) meant that there was virtually no tidal action, despite the colossal gravitational pull of Enting in the sky. But the birds seemed to flock in a tidal fashion, as if they were being pulled west and east by the gravitational tug. Cleonicles had dissected many of the creatures and was certain that he had found a small metallic node deep in their brains. It was nothing more than a piece of metal grit, but Cleonicles' theory was that it in some way enabled them to orient themselves in the gravitational and magnetic fluxes. It was a difficult theory to prove.

Looking up, Cleonicles saw a rice grain-sized speck in the sky.

A plane?

No, the wrong shape.

It could have been a balloon-boat, a long way off, or then again a skywhal close by.

He trotted an old-man-trot up the lawn to the patio where his smaller telescope was set up. Angling it and settling his eyes against the eye-pieces took only a moment. It *was* a skywhal! Another one, flying close to the world. Once again it was a young one, its fronds underdeveloped. Extraordinary! This was the third he had seen in as many months. In his previous three decades on the moon he had never seen one of the shy beasts come so close up. They were sensitive to the gravity dip of any large body and preferred to stay away from them. Young ones could be curious, and had been known to stray close to worlds – although never this close, and never thrice in three months! More mature beasts kept themselves on languorous cometary orbits around the sun, sweeping endlessly through the interplanetary sky, feeding, growing, mating, eventually dying. Very rarely an elderly and perhaps sick skywhal would beach itself on a world, crashing to the ground to be dashed to pieces. This had not happened in Cleonicles' lifetime, but it was well documented – happening once a century, perhaps, it could be expected. But why would this young creature return three times to the dangerous gravity of the moon? Assuming it was the same beast.

Cleonicles hurried indoors and returned with one of his sketch pads. Most scientists had cameras fitted to their telescopes, of course; and Cleonicles himself used a camera, attached to his major telescope, for his stellar work. But he still loved the older discipline of making sketches. He shifted the telescope minutely, tracking the great sky creature as it swam, and sketching its lenticular body, its mouth like an enormous leather catch-all bag left wide open, its stubby fronds. There was no doubt, as he compared his sketches, that this was the same beast he had seen before.

Why was it visiting him?

It wasn't visiting *him*, of course, it was merely drawn for some reason to the moon, or perhaps only tracing out a peculiar trajectory through the sky for its own reasons. But Cleonicles had always found it hard to separate himself from his science. Part of the thrill he had tended to experience as a scientist came from his own soul, his own sense of engagement in the cosmos. He couldn't quite shake the sense, somehow, that the beast was seeking him out, nosing through space to come to him. Foolish. The fondness of an old man.

Cleonicles stretched himself at the telescope. He *was* an old man, after all. And, yet, wasn't there some special connection between the skywhals and himself? Between those great dumb sky-cows floating between worlds, and Cleonicles, most famous scientist in the cosmos? It was Cleonicles who had first thought of charting skywhal movement to index the concentrations of scilia in the sky. The beasts flew in arcs where they could be sure of scooping up the maximum amount of the microscopic creatures. Scilia were present all throughout the inter-planetary sky, of course, and received wisdom had been that this distribution was uniform. It had been Cleonicles who had been able to show that in reality the scilia grew much more prolifically in certain areas than others; and that the skywhals organised their trajectories to sweep through these places. His early research had been mostly on scilia; this was how he had made his reputation in the scientific community as a young man. The miniature unicellular creatures that lived throughout the interplanetary atmosphere, billions upon billions of them, he had often observed through microscopes.

He had known from an early age that the excitement to be felt at observing such things outweighed any excitements generated by human contact. It wasn't that he was a misanthrope, exactly. He liked people well enough. He valued the time he spent with his family. In his younger days he had taken lovers. But the tang of that pleasure had always come abruptly upon him in the act, and had faded rapidly afterwards. The pleasure science gave him, however, was of an altogether deeper sort. It grew within him, a warmth in his viscera, at the prospect of study. It swelled to a sort of subdued thrill that permeated his whole body as his scientific endeavour – whatever it might be – occupied him. It lasted longer and gave more satisfying excitement.

He had come to understand this early in his life, probably, in fact, from his very first microscopic observations of scilia. That very first microscope, pronged and angular like a petrified branch. He had settled himself over the device, rested his eyes on the brim of the eye-piece, fiddled with the nipple that adjusted focus until the two bleary circles of light coalesced into a single bright disk. And there they were! Sluggish under gravity (for their normal environment was weightless), but vivid and beautiful, each one as though carved with infinite attention to detail out of a microscopic speck of glass. Each scilion was a sausage-shaped nodule, with a transparent cell wall and strands, almost eyelash-like, in a ridge along its 'back'. At the centre-line of this tiny transparent lozenge were the tiny particles of cyanophyl with which the things converted sunlight into energy. The specks looked almost colourless under the microscope, with only the very faintest suggestion of mauve about them. It was these that provided a reaction surface where the carboniferous gases of interplanetary space were oxygenated, locking the carbon into their bodies. Cleonicles hypothe-sised it was the countless billions of these creatures, and their tiny

94

specks of cyanophyl, that gave the interplanetary sky its colour. This theory, published in *Proceedings of the Chemical and Royal* as one of Cleonicles' earliest papers was not uncontested – the prevailing view was that atmospheric colour was a gaseous phenomenon. Cleonicles argued that the gradations in the intensity of colour were the result of greater or lesser concentrations of scilia. Others denied this, explaining these nebulous patches with reference to various, purely chemical, reactions. But that dispute, conducted with a gentlemanly and gentlewomanly restraint, had never especially engaged Cleonicles' heart. His heart belonged not to the society of scientists, and their antique rituals, but to science itself – to his true bride, science itself. He had lost his heart to her as soon as the two blurry circles revealed by his microscope had swum together into the sharp one, and the secrets of the miniature world had been opened to him. It was *seeing*. It was being privy to details fundamental to the cosmos that were nonetheless overlooked by almost the whole population of the System. It was the awful beauty of these glass-coloured specks, the incredible precision with which they were fashioned.

Some of the scientists with whom the young Cleonicles mixed – some of these venerable men and woman saw Divinity in the precision. They saw God in the staggering profusion of miniature perfection. But not Cleonicles. For him, science had been a liberation from the foggy doctrines of 'God', not an endorsement of them. It had struck him sometimes, as he worked carefully at his early scientific projects, that this elimination of faith in his heart had not been accompanied by any depression of spirits, any pangs of angst. Probably there was a deeper faith than religion in Cleonicles' heart: one planted by his childhood sense of the closeness and permanence of his family – the careful attention and more carefully delineated boundaries of proper behaviour laid down by his parents; leavened into something less military, something more human, by the love he shared as a small boy with his brother. His parents had been distant figures, perhaps, but he had never doubted the bond between himself and his brother. It was love, a deep love.

Growing older, he realised that this elegant structure, rigid yet yielding, was more than family. It was society as a whole, the whole marvellous intricacy of humanity itself. And science first drew Cleonicles for the same reason. It gave him an insight into the deep structures that underlay everything, and the sense that the apparent randomness and diversity of the visible System was governed, underneath, by certain simple, immutable laws. The fact that the principles of order and structure were fundamental chimed with his own sense of things. The beauty of science lay precisely in this feeling of *rightness*. It was not 'God' – any more than a crystal, a painting, a population of mice, a nest of orbits around the sun, any more than *any* pattern was 'God'. But it was *ordered*, and that was enough.

Order was important to him.

At this early stage in his life (he lost all pretensions to religion in his late teens) science was a pastime; he was just one more gentleman amateur, dabbling in the prettier disciplines. His life ran, still, in conventional channels. He drank. He intrigued. He enjoyed love affairs. He even played sport, although his lanky, unmuscular frame was ill suited to it. And his whole life might easily have worked it way along those lines, with science as no more than a hobby, except for one thing: a flaw in the symmetry of structure he observed that snagged his attention.

It grew out of his observation of scilia, the very same microscopic free-floating creatures that played so important a role in interplanetary space. Cleonicles watched them through his microscope. He sketched them, marvelled at their jewel-like beauty. Then he read a study of the skywhals – the enormous, floating beasts that basked through interplanetary sky with mouths agape, gill-grilles filtering out hundreds of pounds of scilia a day. The scilia fed, in a manner of speaking, on the sun; the skywhals fed on the scilia. Like a planet-bound natural chain of being, Cleonicles saw structure and harmony here just as it existed in human life. But there was an absence in the pattern, and it was this absence that attracted Cleonicles' attention.

He knew the generally accepted theory, called by some 'evolution' and by others 'progressive alteration'. He had read the classic studies by Anhydrocles, Pelias and others, of the slow accretion of biosphere on each of the System's worlds. First, microscopic life, then progressive alteration and growth to multi-cellular creatures; then larger and more complex patterns feeding on the simpler, until complex life evolved, honed either to defeat predation by numbers or agility, or else to predate more effectively. Cleonicles saw in the microbes, plants, insects, birds and ornithophages of, say, his home world Enting a beautifully balanced structure, as glittering and precise as crystal. But comparing the situation, he couldn't see why a similarly complex chain-of-being had not progressively grown into interplanetary space. Out there were microbes (the scilia) and large-scale grazers (the skywhals), but there was nothing else.

This perceived imbalance led him to look more closely at the habitat provided by interplanetary atmosphere, and these enquiries, casual at first, then more committed, pulled him with inexorable and delicious force into science as a whole. By twenty-three he was history's youngest-ever member of the Prince's Scientific Society, with seven published papers to his credit, including groundbreaking research on skywhals and on interplanetary sky. By twenty-five he had published a book-length study, part observation and part hypothesis, on the interplanetary habitat – arguing that freak mutation had given certain high-gliding birds float-bladders that had lifted them higher still, and the pure emptiness of interplanetary sky had meant that no rivals prevented these birds from colonising the new realm. It was still the most widely accepted theory for skywhal 'evolution'. And from there he had worked on the very first Computation Device; and then, opening up whole new worlds of science, into other arenas. He had pioneered stellar research as a scientific discipline. He had financed the first experiments out of his own pocket. And, now, an old man, he could look back on his life with satisfaction. He could have done so, except that such a degree of introspection was alien to his nature. As he had always done, he absorbed himself wholly in what he was doing, in the now. His memories were hazy and rarely consulted (except for strictly scientific recollections), and his sense of the future as unformed as a baby's. Nonetheless, or perhaps because of this, he was as contented a man as lived in the whole System. Of course he did not know, as he continued to track the skywhal with his telescope, that this was to be his last day alive.

Eventually the skywhal swung round the globe and out of sight of his telescope. This was, Cleonicles calculated, the beast's closest approach to the moon yet. His mind worked through possibilities. Was it deranged in some way? Was this bizarre flight-path merely the skywhal equivalent of youthful high spirits? Was the beast suicidal, to tempt the fatal tug of the gravity of this world?

Cleonicles went back inside and took a glass of coffee and some marinated and freshly grilled chitterlings, before writing up his observations properly. Something very interesting going on, he was certain of that.

He took an interest in everything, as was (he thought) proper for a scientist. But he had given over the majority of his energy, in these last years, to the mysteries of the cosmos beyond the System. Stars! Vacuum! A scale that some experts calculated at thousands of miles, some at *billions* – difficult to judge which was more likely. For the man hungry for mystery this arena was the most mysterious of all. It was this impossible place, outside the cosmos, that chiefly animated him now. If he had one regret at devoting his life to science, at choosing his researches over partner and family, it was simply that he now had no son with whom to enthuse over each day's new startling discovery. He tried, sometimes, to engage Polystom; but much as he loved his nephew he had to concede the boy's mind was weak and vacillating, infected by what the great physicist Cinesias called 'the virus of subjectivity'. For a time he had come close to irritation (without, luckily, actually succumbing to the vulgar impulse) at his nephew's presence. It was that period of six or seven months after his wife's death when he seemed forever visiting, forever sleeping in a guest room, forever wearying Cleonicles' ear with his sorrow and his self-pity. Throughout those months he had distracted Cleonicles from research at a particularly exciting juncture, and it had crossed the old man's mind simply to ask him to go. He was glad, in retrospect, that he had never given way to so base an instinct. It wasn't Polystom's fault that he had fallen for a madwoman, and when all was said and done, he was family, after all.

The mail had arrived.

An official-looking letter, the envelope crested with the Bear of Enting, had come from some officious civil service officer. It related to the execution of a servant that had taken place two days earlier on Cleonicles' estate. Cleonicles glanced at it: an endorsement, nothing more. A waste of paper. But this other one looked more interesting – a long pale-orange envelope, evidently a communication from his onetime rival and now occasional collaborator, Scholides. Cleonicles pulled the corner off the envelope and slid his finger in to rip away the top. What was the old boy saying?

98

... my preference, as you know, refuses to apprehend 'vacuum' as any but an extreme, laboratory-induced phenomenon. And, dear friend, although I know you mistrust numerical sciences, I have brought 'mathematics' to bear on the issue. Following on from my recent paper, the one you kindly endorsed, I worked with a notional 'planet' with a notional atmosphere existing in the sort of 'vacuum-space' you postulate as existing beyond the borders of the cosmos. I have now utilised a force algorithm to examine the effect of the pressure gradient from one bar to zero bar over a length of seventy kilometres. Now you will say that this final measurement is arbitrary, and so it is; but I would counter that it needs must be arbitrary, believing as I do that no such situation could ever actually obtain in the universe! And given the need for this arbitrary number, I have taken seventy thousand metres from your own models! With these initial data, and the equation $F = G[(m_1)/x - (m_1 m_2)/x^2]$, such that x is the figure of seventy thousand which we have mentioned and the ms 1 and 2 the respective atmospheric pressures, we arrive at a force of one seventh of a Kratos – a small force, but one capable of accelerating a particle as tiny as an oxygen or nitrogen particle up to fifty thousand kilometres an hour! Accelera-tion of such force, occasioned by the effective decompression of going from one bar to zero in so short a space of time, would, as I have demonstrated, suck any atmosphere clean away from any planet. Any liquid would also be boiled away into space, and some mineral matter, although minerals such as granite or compression-formed marbles may possess tensile strength enough to resist the force (a related question is whether rocks as we understand them could form in the extreme conditions you posit). You will note that assuming a vacuum of zero bar effectively eliminates the second part of the equation, but even if we assume a vacuum of very low bar – say one one-thousandth – it does not materially affect the equations. The gravitational G in the equation might be thought to have the power to rein in some small proportion of the particles, but only if G approached infinite levels could an atmosphere be maintained – atmosphere being at the molecular level, as we both know, billions of individual missiles travelling ballistically at velocities great enough to escape the gravitational attraction of any world. Clearly, then, no worlds as we understand them could exist in the conditions of a

vacuum cosmos: and if my own world of Rhum were translated
there by magic the 'vacuum' would boil its atmosphere and seas
away in moments, rip away its biomass and whirlwind away much
of its soil and rock.

Only two postulates can possibly follow from this state of affairs.
One . . .

From the flowery language it looked as though Scholides was planning
to publish this letter; the 'My Dear Cleonicles . . .' at the top would be
enough to find it a home in half a dozen respectable journals, and it
was a quicker way of publishing than working through the tortuous
rituals of refereed *Proceedings* and *Journals*. Well, let him publish. It
was dull stuff, and not particularly original. Worse, there was a degree
of dishonesty about it: for Scholides knew perfectly well (though
he didn't say so) that Cleonicles had never suggested this bizarre
model . . . planets existing out in vacuum, beyond the cosmos, with
atmospheres that simply *sat*, like pools in an indent. That was patently
ridiculous. Clearly any such atmosphere would be boiled away into
space, either immediately or else through a process of depletion over
time. He folded the letter to throw it away, and then thought better of
it. Perhaps it was worth checking the 'two postulates' that the old
rogue mentioned. Maybe he had something new to say.

Only two postulates can possibly follow from this state of affairs.
One is that the 'stars' and 'atmosphere-bearing planets' of what we
may be pleased (in your honour) to term Cleonicles' vacuum cosmos
– that these stars and planets preserve themselves against the
tendency of universal vacuum to dissipate their constituents by
means of some force-field or barrier. So incredible this barrier would
have to be, of such surpassing might and power, draining such
quantities of power, that it has properly been called not a function of
Physics at all, but rather a manifestation of God. For the renowned
atheist Cleonicles to be endorsing a Religious reading of the universe
is ironic indeed! The second postulate, on the other hand, is to my
mind the inevitable one – that there is no 'vacuum' beyond our
cosmos, and that no planets and no stars exist in the mighty
imaginary emptiness of 'Cleonicles' Space'. That the objects observed
at the boundary of the cosmos have some other, more rational

explanation. Is there any way, my old friend, in which I can convince you of the folly of denying . . .

Cleonicles dropped the letter to the floor. A servant would clear it away. A less placid man might have been annoyed by the impertinent tone of Scholides' communication, but Cleonicles had been through so many petty disputes with so many petty scientists he no longer cared. The introduction of religion was a clever twist of the argument, though; he had to concede that.

Polystom – for some reason, this day, his mind kept wandering back to his nephew – Polystom had once advanced the 'religion' argument. It was a fundamentally unscientific manoeuvre, which was why Scholides had inserted it into his letter, hoping to discredit Cleonicles' theories by association. Of course, to simply brush everything a man could not immediately understand into the satchel marked 'God' was nothing more than intellectual laziness. So people had once called the planets 'gods', shining through the sky, before the age of flight; the same planets that the descendants of those same people now inhabited. 'But uncle,' Polystom had said, his face flushed. 'What holds the System together?'

'Gravity,' said Cleonicles.

'Isn't this *gravity* just another name for God?' he had said, wide-eyed. But Cleonicles had no desire to be unfair to his nephew, even in his own mind. When he had said that he had been fourteen years or so. It was of course a characteristically adolescent way of seeing things. The boy had grown up a little since then, if only a little.

It was mid-morning. Cleonicles was in his study, with charts in front of him. He had, the previous year, calculated the relative luminosities of the various stars to be observed from the margins of the cosmos, and using a candle-scale of his own devising he had calculated and plotted their distances. The scale had much educated guesswork about it, of course, and it assumed that all stars were the same size and luminosity as the sun. Latterly, Cleonicles had begun to doubt this postulate. The sun, after all, burned air, as all such fires did. The electrical combustion of 'stars' must needs follow some different, anaerobic physics, and this in turn implied a different refractive index. But until he understood exactly how the 'stars' shone, he could not properly map them out.

He went through his charts. According to these earlier calculations, the nearest star was less than four thousand miles beyond the outer limit of the System. But a recent paper in the Proceedings of the Organisation of Constitutive Sciences argued for distances of millions or even billions of miles – an impossible gap to bridge. Cleonicles still nurtured the dream of one day reaching out into the emptiness at the edge of the System. Of course, conventional flying devices had no purchase upon vacuum, for their wings and propellers needed atmosphere in which to operate. But a projectile fired from near the edge of the cosmos might hurtle to a nearby star. He had drawn up plans, once, long ago: a sealed projectile, fired by an enormous tube; a second projectile fired afterwards and carrying enough explosives for the voyagers in the first projectile to be able to blast themselves back into the cosmos when their journey was complete. There were difficulties, most particularly, the difficulty of not killing the crew with the severity of the acceleration at firing. But if they could be overcome! Scientists could travel to these stars, to other worlds, and all this tedious debate would be superseded!

So much depended upon accuracy of observation. A journey of a few thousand miles would be nothing, but millions of miles? Billions? It would take up the whole lifetime of the crew; and of their children, and their children's children. There had to be a way to determine what the distances were to the stars. But it was hard! Many scientists, like Scholides, refused to accept that 'stars' existed. They argued that Cleonicles' observations were amenable to some other explanation. For many years now, Cleonicles had tried to find a definite proof for his speculations. Alas, the fundamental *relativity* of observation thwarted him. Was he looking at great objects far away, massive globes of fire in a vacuum? Or small objects very close by? Had the photographic lenses fitted to his balloon-probes captured miniature sparks, atmospheric effect? Was it some sort of fogging of the film? Were they flecks of the stuff that marked the border of all things?

Cleonicles tried, for the tenth time that day perhaps, to focus his mind on the physics of this, but his mind slipped from the problem, and once again he found himself thinking of his nephew. It was puzzling. For some reason the ghost of Polystom lingered still about the house he left only days before. It had been a good visit, better than most. The boy had not whinged endlessly about his nightmares, his loneliness, his – worst of all! – sense of purposelessness. He had attended the execution of the servant with Cleonicles, which was good for morale all round, although he had (it was true) gone unwillingly, and grumbled about it. But still! The two of them had chatted, uncle and nephew, about stars again, which Polystom had insisted interpreting in a 'poetic' rather than a 'scientific' manner . . . a common fault of his. They had taken a stroll down by the lakeside, and had talked about the management of the estate on Enting. Cleonicles had suggested, as gently as he could, that it would soon be time for the boy to visit Stahlstadt, to take up some of the larger responsibilities of Stewardship. The System didn't run itself, he chided gently. Order was a fragile blossom, a delicate crystal, and needed constant attention. Polystom had nodded, sucked at his lower lip, plunged his hands into the very bottom of his pockets, and said nothing.

What a pitiable, and yet lovable, figure his nephew cut sometimes! The mannerisms of a teenager in an adult man. His belief, evident in all his actions and all his statements, that he had suffered appalling and soul-forging tragedy . . . and why? Because some ridiculous girl had put her hands down his pants and then gone off to die. This wasn't tragedy! This was an interlude, symptomatic of an inability to see the larger scale of things; as if – and thinking about the boy seemed to trip Cleonicles' mind unconsciously towards poetry – as if the lad perceived all his own emotions through a microscope, magnified, and everything else out of view. And yet, despite this immaturity, Cleonicles couldn't help loving the boy. His earnestness! The vertical crease running up his brow, already distinctly marked despite Polystom's youthfulness – all that fretting and worrying. There was something oddly refreshing about it, Cleonicles supposed, or he'd have long found it tiresome. It was the *positive contrast* he made with the languid good manners of most of polite society. Cleonicles could see Stom now: his jerky long limbs, arms dangling at his sides and bouncing like a girl's two long pigtails, like a rag-doll puppet's arms. His legs, all angular knees and jutting feet, linked by long-boned thighs and shins like the handles of hitball bats. His eyes always wide, his mouth always drooping open. His brown-blonde hair cut short, starting to thin a little even at his young age, the fine strands stirring in any breeze to show flashes of scalp. He was his father's boy in a great many ways. It was his father in him, if Cleonicles was honest with himself; this was probably the root of his affection for the lad. Cleonicles had loved his brother so deeply. Old Polystom had been the one person to whom he had felt bonded when he was younger. But now Old Polystom was dead, sucked into the vacuum of death (to turn poetic again), and young Polystom his only relic.

Death, not something Cleonicles would usually spend time thinking about, had been the topic of many of the conversations he had had with his nephew, ever since the death of the girl, the death of whatever-her-name-was. Young Polystom's grieving for his dead wife, it seemed to Cleonicles, had passed through the stages of absence, sorrow and regret into something much less healthy, into something obsessive. The lad had forgotten, or chose not to remember, how unhappy he had actually *been* when she was alive. Or so it seemed to Cleonicles. One evening, the two of them drinking together, he had suddenly said: 'Uncle, what is the name you scientists have for this groove in the upper lip?' He ran his hand from the underside of his nose to the centre of his top lip. 'This little downward guttering, here, this little crease?'

'I'm not sure, my boy, I'm not sure of the technical term,' Cleonicles had replied. 'I could check in Validicles' textbook of anatomy – shall I have a servant fetch it?'

But Polystom hadn't really been interested in the name. 'Isn't it strange?' he had said. 'The way it divides the upper lip into two, like two fleshy epaulettes. It's like the contour made by roof-tiles meeting. Don't you think?'

'How fanciful your imagination is,' Cleonicles had said, with a hint of severity. Being fanciful was, after all, in itself no virtue.

'I dreamt about it the other night,' Polystom said, with the gloomy little shrug that tended to accompany his pathetic indiscretions concerning his own emotional turmoil. Cleonicles didn't say anything. 'I dreamt I was looking at Beeswing's face, and in particular that I was looking at that ridge. That beautiful little mark. I told her that I . . . I loved her because of that line, because of the way it pointed me towards her lips. And because of the unbrushed, pale, ghostly little hairs lined up upon it.' Wasn't that just the way? A scientific question – a scientific answer – and then off into these windy irrelevances. Epaulettes? Hardly!

After a suitable pause, Cleonicles had said: 'you need a new wife, I think, my dear boy. It's time to put your first marriage behind you, your unhappy first marriage.' He repeated this last phrase, to draw his nephew's attentions back to the facts of the case. 'Your *unhappy* marriage.'

But the boy's young mind had drifted away, into whatever melancholic poetic inner wildernesses it visited. Cleonicles, clucking his disapproval, had given up.

The very next day, Cleonicles had gone off to preside over the hanging of one of his servants, and he had invited the boy to accompany him. It was one of the estate servants, a man who had been caught stealing several times, and who had tried finally to abscond by making his way through the Speckled Mountains. He had been caught, of course, and now he was facing the consequences. It was rare for Cleonicles to have to execute a servant – he was pleased to say, because it was not something in which he took any pleasure. But on the occasions when it was necessary he preferred hanging as more humane, in its way, than flogging. Flogging was more common on the sunward worlds. Hanging was regarded as a better method on the outward planets. And so Cleonicles had set the time, and decided that the best place was one of the courtyards in the western stables, a forum large enough for all the servants from that part of the estate to assemble. Their watching the event was more important than the execution of the individual, in fact, which was why (in Cleonicles' opinion) hanging was more effective than flogging. Watching a man flogged roused levels of passionate excitement in the breasts of servants, he thought, that counteracted the deterrent effect. Hanging was a cooler business, more rational, and more likely to promote serious thought. It was also good, of course, that several representatives of the governing class be present, to give weight to the proceedings. And so Cleonicles asked Polystom to attend.

'Come along to it, my boy,' he had said. 'Ten-minute drive, the whole thing won't take half an hour, and we can be back for tea.'

'I'd rather not, uncle,' Polystom had said.

'Rather not? Have you something better to do?'

The boy had mumbled something about doing some reading.

'Reading? Nonsense! Come to the hanging. It'll do you good. It is a bracing experience, you know. And it'll do the servants good to see some true blood there.'

'Really,' Polystom had said, colouring, 'I'd prefer not to.' And as soon as Cleonicles saw the blush he realised, with a little shock, that his nephew was actually *squeamish* about watching a man hang. The very idea! 'I won't hear of it!' Cleonicles had said. 'You're Steward now. You'll have to preside over your own justice system. You'll have to discipline your own estate. I *won't* hear it!'

So he had bundled the shy fellow into the car, and talked to him all the way there about the necessity of enforcing discipline, about how hanging was *far more humane* than flogging a man to death, about the stupid servant's multiple crimes and about his eventual dash for freedom into the Speckled Mountains – 'what else can I do with him? He's tied my hands, my dear boy.' And Polystom had said, 'yes Uncle, I know Uncle, of course Uncle.' But at the vital moment, when three servants had leaned into the rope and pulled with all their strength, and the hoist had gone up with the curiously slack figure of the condemned man hanging from it – during that time Polystom had blushed again, and looked away. Looked away! Imagine it! 'You're missing it,' Cleonicles had hissed. The hanging man's feet were tied together, naturally, as were his hands, but instead of bucking and twisting as some executees did, he simply dangled. The three men had not pulled with enough force to break his neck (a sign, Cleonicles knew, that the fellow was not well liked amongst the servants), and so was alive for a while, his face puffing up and darkening and his tongue coming out like a mass of blown bubble-gum. But still he didn't struggle. Eventually he was just a limp quantity of dead flesh, rotating with meticulous slowness to the left, stopping, rotating back to the right, stopping, and going through the same motion again.

In the car back to the house Polystom had stared out the window at the passing scenery, and had responded to his uncle's conversation only with grunts. Foolish boy.

The charts curled unregarded on the table in front of the old man now; he was pressed back against his chair, his eyes shut. Memories were seeping through his mind like alcohol. He was not used to wallowing in his memories in this fashion. They made him sleepy. His eyelids came down with that fuzzy droopy blur-darkness. Not the clean-cut image of a shutter descending that he had once thought, as a boy, ought to be the way the retinas observe, from the inside, the closing of eyes. How certain he had been! How worried that there was some pathological degeneration in his eyes. Sitting in a corner shutting and opening and shutting his eyes, wondering *does everybody else see this as a hard focused line coming down? Is there something wrong with my eyes? Am I going blind?* The anxieties of being a boy. But the old man's eyes were shut now, and a darkness as dark as vacuum itself smoothed the old man into sleep.

Cleonicles snoozed. He often napped during the day. Unless particularly gripped by some scientific endeavour, he would sleep two or three times. This was something over which he felt no shame: it was important to rest his brain, after all, if he expected it to function at full efficiency. And as he slept a dream swirled into being in his head. It was the sort of sleep, propped upright in a chair, the windows bright, where the sleeper half knows that he is sleeping, and yet is sleeping still. He is so far into the subterranean location of sleep that he cannot move his arms, but he knows that he has arms, and that they are draped in his own lap. He is half conscious of life going on around him, and yet the fragments of subconsciousness that constitute dream-state came swirling up around him, blizzard-like.

This dream was one he had had before. He seemed to become a world himself; to swell and circumbobulate into the weighty, iron-souled globe of a planet. And he was spinning, whirling through the sky, tethered by an invisible rope to the sun. And as he orbited, he became aware, as if this notional tether were an actual umbilicus, of the warmth and life that flowed out from the sun every moment. Each separate atom of light was nourishment to him. And as he fell in his great orbit, circling and circling, he became aware of all the other items caught in that great swirl of orbiting dance: the other worlds and their moons, the wallowing skywhals, even the microscopic-gritty trillions of atoms of air and other gases, each one a globe in miniature and each one swimming in its own great arc round the sun – more likely, perhaps, to be deflected by collision or other turbulence than larger bodies, but still in motion. The whole gorgeous mess of it all. A comet plunged through the more orderly ring of orbits like a bather diving into a body of water; and the ripples of its passage caressed the side of the Cleonicles-planet with delicious intimacy.

'Sir! Sir!'

With an almost electric jolt Cleonicles woke up, bucked out of sleep by the voices of excited servants. They were calling to him from outside the house; running up the grass towards the back door, yelling out. 'Sir! Sir! Come quickly, sir!'

He sat forward, his mouth gummy, and wiped his eyes free from the bristly flakes of sleep. What was going on? His butler was knocking at the door, a discreet tapping that might have been going on for some time, since it was of itself too low a noise to have penetrated Cleonicles' doze. 'What is it?' he said, hoarsely.

The butler slipped the door open and stepped inside. 'Sir,' he said, 'something has happened. A skywhal, we think, sir. It's beached itself on your estate.'

This woke him up. He was out of his chair immediately, stomping out of the study and down the corridor, firing questions at his butler, who, being only a servant, was no use *at all* with the answers. A mature skywhal? Or the immature one observed before? How long were its fringes – the prongs, along the sides of its body? 'You're useless man! You have no powers of observation! Where did it land?'

At least the fellow knew the answer to this one: 'In the lake, sir.'

'The lake? It must have made an enormous noise!'

'On the far side, sir. The splash *was* audible from the house, sir.'

Outside, Cleonicles stomped along the pier. He climbed into one of the flat-bottomed air propeller-driven lake boats and tapped the driver on his shoulder with his stick. Away! They buzzed over the water, scattering stork-boars before them. In minutes the carcass of the skywhal was visible, a hump of grey and black on the horizon. Minutes more, and the whole silhouette of the thing, tragic and magnificent, was there before them lying in the shallow water. It was the same youngster that Cleonicles observed earlier in the day, it must be – it must have beached on its very next orbit! Extraordinary, and unprecedented. But why had it happened?

The boat hummed to a halt alongside the carcass, so close that Cleonicles could reach out and touch the rubbery, scale-dotted skin. Imagine it – beaching in his own lake, on his own moon. It was almost as if the creatures were intelligent enough to know that he, Cleonicles, was the single human who had studied them most thoroughly. As if this young beast had come specifically to see him.

He was not wearing his waders, but in his excitement he hardly cared, and he hopped cheerily out of the boat, sinking into the lake up to his knees and ruining his Lassé Pedi shoes in the process. But to be able to touch the carcass of a skywhal! He sloshed along its length, tapping at the left-side vertebrae with his stick, counting them. Seven, eight, nine, ten: skywhals' spines bifurcated just below the brainstem, running in twin lines down the left and right flank, joining up again at the sacrum from which the tail began. There were conflicting theories as to why this was, but Cleonicles himself believed that it speeded nervous reaction that would otherwise be too sluggish for so enormous a beast. Fronds sprouted from every third spine-node. Now, in the unfamiliar gravity, they drooped like strands of seaweed, but in flight they fanned out left and right, helped the beast steer and sense its surroundings.

Other servants came wading over to him. *Sir! Sir!* Voices like birdsong. *It's amazing, sir! Amazing!*

Cleonicles put his walking stick underneath the drooping length of one of the left-spine fronds, and tried to lift it. The fronds looked like filigree through a telescope, but the thing was in fact so heavy he could barely move it. Why had the creature fallen? Was it diseased – or dead, in flight? Or was it a healthy young animal that had, somehow, conceived the desire to die?

'Sir,' gasped one servant. 'I watched it come down!'

'It came from the sky there, yes?' said Cleonicles, pointing back in the direction of the house.

'Yes, sir,' said the servant, unsurprised at his master's knowledge. The master knew all sorts of things. 'I watched it fall. I saw two of them break off and float to the east.'

'Break off?' said Cleonicles sharply. 'What do you mean, break off? Two of them? Fronds?'

'Yes, sir,' said the servant. 'I took them to be.'

'Well,' said the old man, thinking. 'We can recover them later if they did fall free.' But what a strange thing! He had never heard of a frond disengaging from the main corpus of the skywhal. Was it some sort of unusual wasting sickness? Was that why the beast had crashed to earth?

Then, splashing through the sour waters, gleefully counting vertebrae and fronds, Cleonicles went right round the great body before realising that all the fronds were present. 'No frond came off this corpse,' he told his servant. 'So what was it you saw?'

But servants make poor scientists. Their powers of observation are simply too limited. The man stuttered and grew blotchy-red in his embarrassment, and Cleonicles dismissed him. His butler was approaching on a second boat whose engine noise grew from hum to buzz to grainy roar. It swung to, coming to rest alongside the carcass just behind Cleonicles' own boat, and its wake slopped water further up his *blair-trou* clad legs.

Cleonicles was looking into the creature's enormous mouth now: as large as an open barn, with the deeply ridged and liverish mucus membrane of the inner mouth folded into two channels that led air through to the gill-grilles. The interference-pattern shading of these grilles was just visible to the light of Cleonicles' electric torch.

'Sir!' said the butler, excitedly, coming over. 'It's astonishing, sir!'

'Isn't it, though?' agreed Cleonicles.

'It's so *big*!'

'Small for its kind, though. A young one. Mature skywhals are three, four, even *six* times as big as this.'

'It's rare, sir, isn't it? For one of these beasts to come down to the ground?'

'Very rare. Rare even amongst elderly skywhals. I believe it absolutely unprecedented among ones this young.'

'So why did it happen?'

'You are asking a good question. There are signs of predation on the far side – wounds above the right-spine fronds, some half-healed. They're fairly extensive.' Cleonicles sloshed round the mini-island of dead flesh, his butler in tow. 'There,' said Cleonicles, pointing with his stick. 'You see?' Six great gashes were visible, reaching up over the back of the great carcass from above the saddle of its fronds; two of these showed the grey scaly growth that indicated healing but four were still raw, the violet-red blood glistening within. Each gash was the size of a door, and the flesh inside two of the cuts had been scooped out.

'It is like the marks left by the swoop of a giant claw, sir,' said the butler. 'What could cause such great injury?'

'Not the monster you seem to be imagining,' said Cleonicles, chuckling a little. 'There are no such beasts as that, not in inter-planetary sky nor anywhere else. Indeed, these skywhals have no predators – except for us men, of course. No, no,' he added, poking the end of his stick into the wound, 'these strange gashes are extremely unusual. Unusual indeed. Male skywhals sometimes fight,' he said, more to himself than to his companion, 'when the mating fever is on them. But that fever comes once in seven years only. And, besides, this fellow is far too young to be a mating buck. Could he have been struck by some debris, up in the sky? A comet, perhaps? But no, no, that makes no sense either – to leave six such stripes in his skin? So regularly spaced? It's a puzzle, certainly.'

He returned to his boat, and gave orders for the thing to be dragged over to the shore and there, he said, grandly, embalmed. Although, as he gave the order, he found himself wondering how this enormous feat was to be achieved. He would return to his house and work on the problem; it would take his men a day or more to pull the body over to the shore and then cover it with oilcloth. In that time, he told himself, he would be able to work out some impromptu method of preserving the creature's flesh. He clambered back into the boat, and tapped the driver again with his cane, forgetting for a moment that it was still gory from the skywhal's carcass, and leaving therefore a splatch of purple on the man's uniform jacket. As the boat roared away over the water, and the wind rushed to embrace his body and face like a lover, pulling back his hair and making him crease up his eyes, Cleonicles thought through the alternatives. He could use a large copper pot that was lying empty in an outhouse to brew up some preservative fluid; but the difficulty would be in putting enough of it through the blood-lymph system of the creature. Skywhals lived in a weightless environment; unlike planet-bound fauna they did not have the disadvantage of gravity to impede their circulation. If a man's heart did not pump his blood throughout his body it would pool, under this gravitational influence, in his legs and feet. But skywhals do not exist under such constraints. Accordingly, their hearts were small to the point of vestigiality, blood moving through their bodies chiefly by means of inertia. This in turn meant that their vascular system was much less clearly defined than many creatures', and it would therefore be hard to ensure that any preservative permeated the entire system. But, Cleonicles thought to himself, smiling into the wind, he would find a solution to this particular problem. The beauty of science lay in finding solutions to problems.

[second leaf]

And so the hours of Cleonicles' last day used themselves up. He took an elongated lunch hour, chewing bread dipped in brine wine, with strips of chargrilled fish and whole roasted pot-tomatoes, accompanied by a tart little radish wine, all the while reading the latest newsbooks. He was particularly interested in events on the Mudworld, because he had been so closely involved in the circumstances that had led, indirectly, to that world's situation. Every now and again he would shake his head at the folly of mankind, at the great loss of life.

After lunch he started a letter to his nephew. *My dear Polystom. It was wonderful to see you again, naturally. I hope your nightmares ease themselves. I repeat what I told you; from the vantage point of science nightmares are a natural phenomenon, a way in which the brain purges itself of negative energy. In time they will subside. And I urge you, my dear boy, to consider remarrying. The time has come for it, I sincerely believe.*

Writing to him brought a sharp memory of the boy into Cleonicles' memory, like a pungent whiff of some odour. His goofy smile, creasing the chin beneath it into a visual echo of the wide split mouth. For some reason (the points of connection in the brain relating to memory, Cleonicles had often thought, have a random quotient to them, so one memory will often trigger a completely unrelated one) – for some reason he remembered now travelling to Stahlstadt with the boy and his father, Cleonicles' own brother. The three had flown to Kaspian. It had been their second visit, or conceivably their third. He remembered them all standing on a wide esplanade, paved with a complicated tessellation of Kaspian eagles and Enting bears, with a splendid view over the spires of the city. He remembered the weight of sunshine and heat, the sheer pressure of sunshine against his skin in the Stahlstadt summer, the world of

Kaspian being that much closer to the sun. And he remembered looking down to see young Polystom sprawled, face down, like a diver interrupted by the ground. His satchel was beside him, its mouth open as if it had been sick on the pavement: a red notebook, a small drinks flask, a pamphletty book of poetry waving its comb of pages in the air, a clutter of pens, a virgin chequebook, a squashy bar of chocolate. Polystom had tripped over his own feet, in the way that tall and gawky adolescents sometimes do. No permanent harm done. His servant had dropped to the floor, pushed the various ejecta back into the mouth of the satchel, and the boy had picked himself up, red-faced with embarrassment and rage. Cleonicles remembered that sunny afternoon so vividly. How Polystom had beaten the servant boy! His falling over had been no fault of the servant's, but that wasn't the point, of course. And to think that this same Polystom was now, fully grown, too squeamish to watch a delinquent servant being hanged by the neck! How curious a thing was human nature. People invented 'compassion' to fill all those parts of their lives that weren't reserved for their own rage, embarrassment, and pride.

The memory flickered briefly to the body of the dead servant, two days ago, hanging from the spar. The way it had rotated slowly left, right, like a great slow shake of the head.

The most amazing thing has happened, Cleonicles wrote. *A skywhal had beached itself in the Lacus, not three miles from my house. As I'm sure you know such an event is almost unprecedented in the natural history of our System. Occasionally, but very occasionally, a senescent adult will beach itself; but this beast was immature, no more than thirty-five yards long, barely twenty years old by my estimate. More mysteriously, there were several parallel wounds on its anterior right-spine side, each six feet or more in length and of some depth. The surface fascia had been separated so far that healing was only intermittent; and from what I could see there were associated deep internal cavities as well. I'm having the carcass carried ashore where we will – somehow! – improvise an embalming strategy. Then I'll be able to study it at my leisure. You must come again, my dear boy, and examine it for yourself! Perhaps it will kindle your interest in natural history, and thereby your entry into science! I can see your sceptical expression in my mind's eye as I write, dear boy; but would ask you to allow an old man his dreams, howsoever implausible. You have my love, dear boy. C.*

He sealed up the letter and took it down to one of the footmen, who hurried away with it. Forty miles east was Rompez, where the balloon-boats docked on their regular trading jaunts; a mail-boat would pick it up today, or the next day, and carry it over to Enting.

As the footman bicycled away with the letter, Cleonicles stood in the doorway thinking. Something felt sluggish inside him, something weighing him down and preventing him from concentrating his energies on science. He didn't understand his own recalcitrance. There was, after all, a pressing problem, which was how to administer embalming fluid adequately to a carcass the size of the dead skywhal. But instead of going through to his study, or out to one of his laboratory sheds, he stood musing on the front door. What was wrong? Why had he been unable to settle to anything solid, con-structive, this day?

It was unsatisfying. Frustrating But sometimes days were like this.

Memories kept popping unbidden into his mind. It was curious. Usually Cleonicles thought little of the past, except to draw on his enormous body of scientific knowledge. Something inside him kept triggering the memories. He thought again of his nephew, the flush on his face at the hanging two days earlier. Something nagged him about the servant's execution, but it was not immediately clear what this might be. The whole thing had gone very smoothly. It hadn't been pleasant: the face gargoyling like a child making himself ugly on purpose; the latrine smell wafting over the yard as the dying man had soiled himself; the front of the tongue, a solid convex, coming steadily further and further out of the mouth. But these things weren't supposed to be pleasant. They were supposed to be educational.

'Parleon?' he called from the door. 'Parleon?'

The butler emerged from a side door, hurrying across the grass towards his master.

'Parleon,' said Cleonicles. 'Drive over to the west stables, and have the body of that servant taken down.'

The slightest hesitation. 'Yes sir.'

'You think I should leave it longer?' Cleonicles asked.

'A week is traditional, sir.'

'I know. But I think two days is enough. He was a solitary criminal, stealing by and for himself. It wasn't a more general insurrection, you know. It must be horrible for the estate servants to go about their business under that—' *bulging black eye,* he was going to say, but thought better of it. 'Under that presence,' he said. 'And the weather is warm. It's probably smelling by now.'

'Yes sir.' The butler departed.

But still Cleonicles wavered at his own front door. What was the matter with him? Something felt clogged inside; in a metaphorical sense, but also in practical terms. He had emptied his bowels that morning, but there was a distinct pressure down there now. Perhaps he needed to go again. Ah well.

Cleonicles crossed the hall, went through to the lower master bathroom. He tugged the light on; it was a silk cord weighted with a plug of amber. There was a tiny asterisk, a dead fly, in the heart of the amber. The stone's soul perhaps. The cord yielded with a click and flooded the room with white brilliance, where the fittings in the room sparkled with their usual opulence. Two great marble baths, shaped like cupped hands, lying empty to the right and the left. Two polished granite commodes were positioned like thrones at the far end of the room, and to either side of them two sinks carved each from single pieces of green marble. The whole of the far wall was mirrored. As he settled himself onto one of the two toilets, Cleonicles found his eye drawn by the lazy meandering oscillation of the amber ball at the end of its length of cord, pendant from the switch in the ceiling. It moved through the air as a fly might on a summer day, sweeping a small figure of eight, the motion that his pulling hand had imparted to it. Would it be possible, he thought to himself, to create a mathematical equation that would describe both the sinusoidal trajectory of that body, that cord-dangling sphere of amber, and also to describe the rate at which the circles lessened and therefore the amount of time the whole system would take to reach equilibrium?

He could do it, probably; but he was too tired to do it now. Maybe at some later stage. And his bowels were refractory, refusing to play along. He had definitely felt the inward yawn of something, some lower food-canal bolus of digested food ready to emerge. But now that he was here, sitting on the toilet, it seemed that nothing wanted to emerge. Tiresome. A waste of time.

He stood and pulled his trousers up again. Out of habit he washed his hands anyway, and then left the bathroom, turning the light off behind him and imparting who knows what erratic new orbit to the amber-weighted string.

Outside he went back to his study, but he was not comfortable in his bowels, he could definitely feel the turd still inside there, skywhal-shaped and pressing against the walls of his lower intestine. He paused on the stairs, and debated with himself whether to return to the bathroom. It was possible that, were he simply to be patient, he could just sit on the toilet and wait until his sphincter decided to release itself. But he had no time for that. He had work to do! And he closed the door of his study behind him with an air of decision.

But in his study he could not settle to work. Instead his mind went back six years; danced over that intermediate bar of time like a hurdler. As he leaned back in his chair he was six years younger. He was back in the middle of his last prolonged sexual experience, a year-long dalliance with an estate servant. He had not come from the stable estate to the west, but from the hop fields of the east.

Melesias, he had been called. A fine young man.

Why had his wandering mind lighted on sex? What had triggered these memories? The cause-and-effect was too tenuous. And why should he be reminded of this particular dalliance, out of all his life's sexual encounters? Something somewhere in his brain wasn't right. Perhaps it was a sign of incipient senility, of a degeneration of the mental will. Had the bulging body of the man he had hanged two days earlier linked a chain of memory in his mind? From one servant to another. Even as he indulged his remembrance, the more scientific part of his brain was cogitating on ways of experimentally testing the functioning of memory. Had there been any serious research pub-lished on the topic? Not that he knew about. The corpse hanging loose, limp, a general image of detumescence despite the fact that the individual features of the hanging body strained and bulged.

The way it swung, gently, almost lullaby-like.

As a young man, Cleonicles had been close to his younger brother. Had loved him more deeply than any other human being. Had spent most of his time with him. Indeed, he had admired him on occasion to the point of hero-worship. There was a solidity about Old Polystom's character, a stillness of spirit, that touched Cleonicles deeply. With it went a sort of automatic certainty about things. Polystom simply knew, for instance, from an early age that he preferred boys to girls, and he went through no inner anguish or uncertainty over the fact. Following in his wake (though he was the older brother) Cleonicles too experimented with male sexual partners to begin with. But his sexual drive was not as powerful as Polystom's; the real urgency with him was intellectual. He sometimes chose partners, or picked out attractive servants, and played the active role in a same-sex coupling. He even tried the passive role, in the spirit of experiment (he *was* a budding scientist after all, or so he told himself), but he enjoyed it less. Something about being dominated in this fashion excited his body, but the sheer discomfort of it, and the indignity of it, was just not compatible with his mind, his sense of self. After he moved to his own house, he ceased playing with boys, and on the rare occasions he did indulge it was with women. As science took a larger and larger role in his life, so sex waned. He stopped having proper relationships, with real people, altogether; and only occasionally availed himself of the servants.

But, in the latest decade of his life, he had found his taste changing. He was not entirely sure why. Sexuality was not a topic he thought worthy of properly scientific exploration – it was surely too unpredictable, too capricious, as well as being too *low* – and so he did not attempt to analyse himself with any precision. Nonetheless, for some reason he found himself fantasising, on the rare occasions when sex did enter his mind, of males rather than females. In his last decade, he returned to men for his rare outings into sexual activity. He didn't understand it, and didn't especially want to understand it. Over a period of three years, he had a number of fairly long-lasting 'relationships' with several of the servants, the last of them with Melesias, the young, strong hop-hand from the east of his estate.

He had spotted that one on a tour of the hops one harvest time, and had called him up to the house to work on the hothouse flowers. Observing his fine touch with plants, the way he could seemingly draw life up through their stems so that even sickly growths grew well and strong, Cleonicles had remitted him to one of his experimental greenhouses, growing plants not native to Enting. Growing mutated forms of algae that helped the old scientist approach some of the mysteries of the scilia. Now, sitting in his chair on his last day of life, Cleonicles' memory was strong with the image of this man, this

Melesias. He had had a feminine skin, smooth, with only wispy hairs growing on the underside of his jaw, and a curved womanly chin like a billiard ball. But he had had strong masculine eyes, and a good jutting skull at the back of his head that Cleonicles associated with intelligence. His body was slender and dense with muscle. It had been a month or more before he had summoned him to bed, and then for a further month all he had been able to do was wrestle impotently with him under the sheets. Cleonicles was, indeed, getting old; and although his member perked up at odd moments, it refused to perform on demand. There was one occasion when he managed to get it up and in before it softened, but this achievement alone gave him little pleasure. The placid, work-horse manner of Melesias did not help him gain erotic arousal, he decided, and over the weeks that followed he ordered the servant to be more dominant. There was something paradoxical in ordering such a thing (dominance should assume control automatically, surely, it shouldn't have to be *told* to do so), but it seemed to answer some deep need in Cleonicles. Melesias pinned his frail arms behind his body, used his superior strength to move him about the bed, pressed him face down into the mattress. It was a novel, humiliating and deeply exciting experience: the sort of excitement that grew from the belly to thrill through all his limbs like a slow explosion outwards. 'Order me about,' he ordered, the fizzing sexual excitement dissolving the illogic of the statement. Clumsily, warily, Melesias had played along. Come here, the servant had said. Lie on your front. Like this, not like that. *Now*, Cleonicles insisted, *put it in! Do it, do it!* The first time the servant had tried, he had pulled out quickly at Cleonicles' wince and grunt of pain, and the old man had shouted at him, beaten him with his feeble arms, for his tenderness. *Again! Again!* And this time it had not been so hurtful; maybe the little ring of muscle had sagged with age, or maybe his excitement covered the pain. *Don't move it! Just leave it in there!* And Cleonicles, panting under the weight of the man on his back, had fumbled around underneath himself and brought himself off easily.

But afterwards he had been deeply bothered by the encounter. The thought of it nibbled away at his well-being. It was hardly dignified; to allow a servant such dominance, even in play. Three days later he had called Melesias back and had tried to reverse the roles, smacking the young man's broad back with his stick hard enough to bring up weals, like brushstrokes of red oil paint. But scream and beat as he could, his own member refused to do anything but hang dead from the scaffold of his torso, flopping from side to side.

Sexuality was not something, Cleonicles realised, that could be gainsaid or argued down. As immutable in its own way as gravity. There was no point in fighting it.

Months had passed, most of a year, and each time Cleonicles indulged himself he felt less comfortable in his mind. But each time he did it, the bodily thrill increased. He had the servant ride him, pump him, and it had been extremely uncomfortable, so much so that for an hour or more afterwards he had been unable to hold his stool in, and had sat on the toilet glum and sore. But at the time, whilst it was happening, it had fuzzed his mind with a sort of animal bliss. It would not be quite right to say that he was disgusted with himself, since he was too well-bred to allow that sort of vulgar slackening of character. But he was unsettled, and his unease went deep.

Eventually, the balance between pleasure and unease tipped away from sex. Cleonicles reached a mental place where the sight of the servant revolted him. He sent him away: first of all to the furthest reach of his estate, and then, when the irritant of knowing that the man was on the same world as him grew too great, further away than that. He gathered together two dozen fit men, Melesias among them, as an Enting platoon of foot, and sent them off to his friend Amynseis as a sort of gift. *Thoughtful and patriotic,* the old general had replied by letter. *Unlooked for, my dear old friend, given your current public position on the war; but I can see that your common sense runs deep. Be assured they will be put to good use on the Mudworld!* Cleonicles replied that he would prefer it if his platoon were not mentioned in any public despatch as being his – say, rather, 'a volunteer unit from Enting' – and that he specifically *did not want* casualty reports sent to him. And that was the last he had heard of Melesias. Five years since. General Amynseis was dead now, of course. He had died of an apoplectic seizure whilst commanding troops in combat (the fit so fierce, apparently, that his aide-de-camp had thought he had been shot) and a new general had taken charge of the offensive. If any men remained out of Cleonicles' little platoon, they had surely been reassigned to different battalions.

In that intervening time Cleonicles had been pleased to observe, of himself, that he no longer craved the sexual encounter. He had indulged himself, once or twice, after Melesias, but latterly had simply not thought of that subject at all. Blessed release, he told himself.

[third leaf]

[*this leaf does not appear tattered or degraded, and yet it is unusually short, which may indicate a hiatus. It is given here whole; emendation in this case would self-evidently be spurious and hypothetical.*]

And the time still ticked away, as Cleonicles mooned in his study, thinking of the past. The hours bore down upon him, passed through him and swept away, the last ones that Cleonicles would ever know. Eventually, the hold of memory released him a little, and he wandered downstairs and out onto the lawn to smoke a second cheroot in the afternoon light.

His butler drove up the long lakeside driveway, and parked the automobile outside the main garages. He clambered out and puffed over the lawn to where his master was sitting. No longer a svelte man, Parleon: his waist bulging out like an onion, oedematous wrists, his eyes sinking into the flesh of his face, his forehead reaching now almost to the top of his skull. 'Sir! Sir!' he panted.

'Did you do it, Parleon?'

'They cut the body down, sir. Buried it out behind the hillock, at the back of the furthest stable.'

'Away from the regular servant graveyard, I hope?'

'Yes sir.'

'Unmarked grave?'

'Yes sir. But sir, there's something else.'

'Really? Something else?'

'Yes sir. Several of the estate servants out there reported seeing strangers.'

The word was like electricity in Cleonicles' body. He sat straight up in his chair. 'Strangers?'

'Interlopers, sir. Nobody they recognised. Dirty-looking men; three

123

of them. One woman I spoke to said they had a disreputable look about them.'

'Really?' said Cleonicles, sitting forward. 'Strangers, eh!'

So the end began.

Cleonicles was on his feet, reaching for his stick, which he had propped against the back of his recliner. 'We'd better go in and phone the militia captain,' he said. 'The last time we had interlopers they turned out to be deserters from a military balloon-boat – do you remember?'

Parleon nodded. Naturally he remembered. They had been scrawny fools from Rhum who had jumped ship when it docked at Rompez. The two of them were both thinned by their three-day run-about, both blackened with dirt. They had been hung upside down by their feet over a wall, four hundred yards from the main house. Parleon had handled it personally; tying the sobbing men's feet together and looping the rope round; draping it over the wall and having two underbutlers haul the rope on the far side so that the bodies were drawn up the face of the brickwork. As they hung that way, arms free to flop and wave, their matted hair hanging in strands, the militia had lined up and shot them. Two volleys of bullets, and afterwards the sound of somebody pissing noisily on the far side of the wall: except that it wasn't piss, as Parleon discovered coming round to the front, but blood, tumbling in a strong stream from a wound in one man's neck. They were young men, very young. Boys probably. They had been fools. Their photographs had been taken, dead and upside down, for publication in one of the military newsbooks. Deterrence an important part of the function of news-reporting in the media.

'Have any balloon-boats docked today?' Cleonicles asked.

'No sir. There's a regular postal boat coming in this evening. But no boats today.'

'Admetus would have called if any of *his* servants had absconded,' Cleonicles said, thoughtfully. Admetus owned the estate on the far side of the Speckled Mountains. 'This is a puzzle. Still, let's get some militia over here, and then we can investigate. If it's deserters, we'll *have* them.'

'Yes, sir.'

Cleonicles eyes were gleaming now; there was a smile on his face.

The two of them hurried back towards the house together, the old man marking the grass at regular two-stride intervals with his stick.

And now events were moving swiftly to their inevitable conclusion. This was Cleonicles' very last hour alive, his last hour of breathing and seeing the sunlight. He left the butler at the front door, and made his own way in to the downstairs study. Something to do! Calling through on the telephone immediately, connected to the militia base at Rompez in moments. Cleonicles, here, Captain. Dangerous men, disreputable types, hanging about. That's right, Captain. If my people say 'disreputable', then you can be sure there won't be an innocent explanation for their being here. That's excellent, Captain; I'll expect your men within the hour.

Cleonicles came out of the study, strangely energised. A chase! A search! *That* would take a shapeless, unsatisfactory sort of day and give it purpose! He would drive out with the militia and track the vermin down. Excellent!

The hall was brighter than it had been before, and it took him a moment to work out why. Both leaves of the front door had been opened wide. Usually only one of the two large doors was opened. Why were they both open?

The sun printed a clean-cut rectangle of brightness on the marble, and Cleonicles stepped into this bright space. A lumpy draught excluder was lain neatly against the bottom of the left-hand door. Odd, in this hot weather, to lay out a draught excluder. And stepping closer, Cleonicles could see that it wasn't a draught excluder, but rather a stretched-out body, its arms up over its face as if shy, the fingers tangled together. He barely had time to register this.

It was his butler, dead and dragged halfway through the doorway.

'Parleon?' Cleonicles barked, in a cross voice.

Steps behind him.

He turned, although not rapidly – he was an old man, after all. He did not spin sharply about. He pulled himself round with his stick, using its leverage against the marble floor to give him torque, *ploc* and turn, *ploc* and turn, and there were the two strangers coming across the hallway towards him. They were, he saw, dressed in raggedy-fringed coats marked brown and black by dirt. Their feet were naked, and so blackened with grime that they looked as though they had been painted. The thought started to form in his head that they would, surely, be leaving ugly footmarks on his beautifully polished marble; but that thought was chased away by a more adrenalised realisation. These two tramps, these two nobodies, were looking him straight in the eye! One had a sort of hat on his head, as close-fitting as an acorn's cap on an acorn; the other was bareheaded, his hair cut very short, a crescent scar on his forehead. This man, the closer of the two, raised his arm, straight out, elbow locked, like a shy person ill-trained in social graces offering to shake hands. There was a beautiful silver ornament in his hand, something polished and gleaming, the last sort of thing you would expect two such down-at-heels to own. Had they stolen it? Something valuable from Cleonicles' front room – and now, caught, guilty, was this man offering it back to him with his outstretched arm? No, he wasn't offering anything. It was not an ornament. The last thing Cleonicles deduced with his conscious science mind was that this object was a gun, a polished slot-revolver, army-issue. He looked from the gun to the face of the man just in time to see him screw his eyes shut. Like (the thought popping into his head with lunatic irrelevance) a man opening a bottle of champagne, worried that the cork might fly off into his face.

There was a fanburst of smoke and a loud smashing noise. Cleonicles' chest clenched with pain, as if a sword had been instantly sheathed between his ribs. All his breath went out of him. He felt as if he had been punched in the torso, very hard, and the world wobbled and swung around him. A heart attack would have felt like this, perhaps; the explosive agonising pressure of it right in the middle of his chest. And silence. The detonation had numbed his hearing, possibly, or else the fall was a kind of swoon, because the world was rushing away from him now, down a long tunnel, the edges of his sight grey and out-of-focus, and even the sensation of pain from his damaged chest was oddly muffled, detuned, so that the bang on the back of his head as it collided with the marble floor was nothing more than a tap; and through the wrong end of his eye's telescope Cleonicles saw the face of his assassin, peering down at him with an expression it was possible to read as concern. The pain was still there, somewhere, disassociated from his chest now, flowing up and down his bones. And worse than that was the swelling sense of breathlessness, the need, like the urgent need to piss on a very full bladder, the need to draw in a breath of air. Yet he didn't draw any air into his lungs. He might as well have been breathing the vacuum which he had spent so much of his life studying. And the throbbing of the pain was removing itself now, slipping away, draining out of him, with something (the assassin's foot, although there was no way Cleonicles could have known it) levering him over onto his side, and then onto his front, face splashing into a puddle of something wet spread on the marble. But even those sensations, of warm wetness, of cold hardness, were becoming indistinct, and the last cotton-woolly patches of Cleonicles' consciousness dissolved into nothingness, moments before the second bullet impacted with and penetrated the back of his head.

[fourth leaf]

The six planets and three moons of the System had been inhabited for over four hundred years. The community of mankind had advanced a great way in those years. All the various families and peoples of the system derived from the one world of Kaspian, the originary world: *ka* means 'earth' in one early idiolect. The *-spia* termination is variously interpreted; the school of the linguist and historian Hierocles argue that it means 'of the Goddess', and relates it to an early religious cult. On the other hand, the Comparative Languages Scholar Trygaea links it to other words from early vocabularies including *sca* and *spoh*, both of which mean 'roundness'. Trygaea, therefore, dates the suffix from the earliest realisation that the world was not flat as common sense dictated, but actually a globe.

The older monarchy on Kaspian, under the progressive rule of King Morza, circumnavigated this globe, ships of trade and conquest fanning out over the whole bellied expanse of it. His grandson, also called Morza, presided over an empire consisting of most of the world, and *his* child Queen Abeth sponsored the first Bird Flight Prize, for any scientist-inventor in all her realms who could create a machine to mimic birds and fly through the air. Such a leap! From crawling through the crumpled, horizon-hugging seas in servant-powered paddle-propeller boats to flight in less than a century! Once the Asimov brothers had theorised the fixed wing, everything else follow-ed. The propellers that pushed ships over the sea, turned by sweat-shiny servants, could be adapted to haul craft through the air. The coal-dust engine was reworked, made more efficient, more powerful, smaller, and then fitted to 'air propellers' (petrol engines were another hundred years away). Rigid wings fixed crossways gave lift when pushed through the air with enough velocity. Suddenly man was up, flying. Queen Abeth conceded the prize to the brothers Asimov, although one died of a tumour between this announcement and the prize being received, and the remaining brother refused to take the half of the amount he was offered, insisting that the whole sum be his. In the end he got nothing and died bitter. But this is a footnote to history. The important thing is that men now owned the skies.

Perhaps it is surprising that it took nearly fifty years before an adventurous soul flew high enough to realise that Kaspian's moon was a relatively easy flight away. But then again, perhaps not: the peoples of the System have always been conservative. They trust to the time-endowed structures that guarantee the smooth running of things. Even so profound a change to culture as the Colonisation Revolution (history books call it by this slightly fanciful name) – even this had surprisingly little impact on the polished surface of genteel life. Soon enough explorers charted first the moon, and then the nearby worlds of Berthing (sunward) and Enting (in the opposite direction); but still life went through its well-oiled motions at home as if the travellers' tales reported in newsbooks were fiction rather than fact. Families intercommunicated; there were parties, balls, hunting and fishing; there were reading groups, scientific discussion senates, giving and taking in marriage. By the time the explorers had reached out more adventurously to the comparative heat of fern-covered Aelop (not yet known as the Mudworld), or out to the relative chill of Rhum and Bohemia (where the frost that coated each blade of glass was as fine as etched glass and silky to the touch) – by the time explorers had mapped and flagged the remaining worlds and pushed to the edge of the envelope of air encompassing all the System – only by this time were the first actual settlers moving to Enting and Berthing. Planes were joined in the sky by the ample profiles of balloon-boats, larger and larger as time went on, to ferry people and their servants, livestock, possessions. Traffic between the worlds became something of a craze, albeit one that still existed only on the margins of polite society. Society was slow to accept technological novelty, but once the technology became familiar to well-bred people, once its use was established, it was developed and spread widely with alacrity.

Four thousand two hundred miles to the moon; fourteen thousand miles from Kaspian to Enting; three hundred and seventy thousand miles from Aelop to chilly Bohemia – a year's grand tour could take you to every world. And each world was a sight to see, with its own fauna and flora. Scientists postulated that airborne bacteria and microbes, and even some hardy insect-eggs and other forms of life, had disseminated themselves throughout the System. But each planet's ecology had developed along unique lines. The great forests of Enting, for instance, had evolved many thousands of varieties of insects, but relatively few higher animals: some wood-rats, birds, fish, tree-pigs and, of course, bears. But on Bohemia it was the other way around. Few breeds of insects could flourish in the chill there, but a great many breeds of mammals were indigenous.

The transition from one-world to six-world Realm happened with an extraordinary smoothness. Indeed, the sixty years or so that elapsed between the first settlers arriving on the Kaspian moon and the ratification of the Protocols of Principality as governing fully six inhabited and commissioned worlds with three attendant inhabited moons saw only two events that could in any manner be described as 'disruptions'. The first of these was the unpleasantness that occurred on the Southern Continent of Bohemia, when a population of masterless and vagrant servants attempted to set up a secessionist stateling, and it proved necessary to apply military force. But in actuality the whole of this campaign lasted no more than three months, with another year or so for mopping up stragglers and resistance in the mountainous territory around the frozen high-altitude lake of Gauldas. Moreover, the greater proportion of casualties was on the side of the secessionists. Reputable historians deal with the whole sorry affair in a few sentences, and pass on to more important subjects.

The second, and far more significant 'event' marking the transition from one world to six was not, in fact, an event at all, but rather a smooth and largely painless transition from one manner of constitution to another. One of the things that made it painless was the fact that the ruling Dynasty had ruled the world of Kaspian for less than a century before humanity moved up into the sky. So, without bloodshed or war, the six worlds evolved six separate characters, distinct cultures, and their own local centres of authority – necessarily so, of course. The notion that they were all centrally ruled from Kaspian was little more than a polite fiction, although a fiction all parties piously followed. Fact, however, presented itself as five Princes, not necessarily of the Royal Blood Direct (although, of course, all of good breeding), declaring nominal affiliation to the monarch on Kaspian but actually ruling their various worlds after their own pleasure. From this it was a short step to the monarchy of the original world itself coming to refer to itself as a 'kingdom' and adopting the title 'Prince' (or, as it might rarely be, 'Princess') of Kaspian. So for a while six Princes governed as one, and the paraphernalia of joint rule – royal council, a senate, stewards beneath them to undertake the less ceremonial aspects of rule – came into being, almost of its own accord. Three hundred years of peaceful, slow growth testified to the stability of this System, and time's slow mutations continued until we arrive at the constitutional situation now prevailing. Of the six Princes only one remains, and the Stewards (who had been de facto rulers for some time) are responsible directly to him. And the source of the greatest pride for Polystom, as he grew up and was educated in the glorious history of his System, was that 'rule' involved so little actuality. The machine ran so smoothly, he was taught, so evenly, so perfectly har-monious was the social sculpture that 'governance' could be enacted with the lightest and most occasional hands upon the tiller.

The single focus of social disturbance, in these latter days, was the Mudworld. The war there had begun before Polystom's birth. The fern-covered hills and blue-green marshy lowlands of Aelop were almost entirely gone by the time he reached maturity.

There was a mysterious aspect to the war. Polystom had realised, growing up, that it was one of the things polite conversation abhorred. The newsbooks, weekly or monthly, were full of reports from the fighting, of course: so much so that the names of the geographical features of the place (the Western Mire, bordered by the Lesser and Greater Broken Headlands, the Dash, Slops) acquired the familiarity of famous writers or operatic singers. People mentioned it, but nobody *discussed* it, nobody really *talked* about it. Questions from the boyish Polystom would be blocked with a polite 'and what an inquisitive little thing he is!' His father would look pained if pressed on this issue; his co-father would be more direct and straight out rebuke him for asking something so indelicate. Even his uncle Cleonicles was strangely reticent – strangely for him, because more usually he delighted in explanations and discussion. Polystom, not one to persevere at anything too disagreeable, soon gave up the issue. There were many things it was not possible to discuss.

Once the little planet had been called Aelop: a steamy, marshy little world whose aboriginal life had been ferns and grasses, a large family of fat, semiaquatic cow-like beasts and innumerable insects. It had been settled; the cows had been farmed; peat had been dug out for its rich deposits and as fuel; estates had been established. Dwellers in the outer planets, where the air was cool in summer and frosty in winter, took to holidaying on Aelop, for the novelty of it. Pleasure palaces had been built overlooking the small seas of the place. That was the past. *Now* the whole geography of the place had been transformed by war. At some stage, clearly, things had changed. Polystom assumed, without really thinking about it, that the servants had behaved badly in some way. The proper population of Aelop had presumably been small; few people of breeding could possibly enjoy such heat all year round. But a large population of servants must have been required, tending the swamp cows, digging, as well as serving their masters. Maybe this imbalance had been dangerous. But Polystom didn't pursue the line. If it had been an 'insurrection', it was beyond deduction why it had gone on so long. Any insurrection would be put down in months as a matter of course. Perhaps it was something else, although what else eluded him. All he knew was that many men flew to that world to fight there; that many glorious reputations for bravery and strength were made there; and that some died.

Polystom's first reaction upon hearing of Cleonicles' death was a calm one. 'Dead,' he had repeated, and then turned his whole body through ninety degrees, facing himself deliberately away from the servant who had brought him the news. 'Dead.' As if saying the word would act as the open-sesame for his emotions.

Nothing. There was a space where his reaction should have been, almost as if marked out in his mind, like a chalk sketch on a wall made by an artist before he filled in the design with colour and shading. But nothing more.

'Murdered,' said the servant. 'Assassinated. It was three men, they say. Shot him with a firearm.'

'Dead,' said Polystom a third time, still trying the word on for size.

'They killed his butler too. But they didn't kill anybody else on the estate. The militia is all over the moon, now, of course. Extra troops have been sent from Kaspian, they say.'

Polystom looked at the servant. He had come directly from the moon. He was one of Cleonicles' own servants, travelling with the postal balloon-boat. He was carrying a letter: Stom assumed it was an official account of the death, written perhaps by one of his uncle's estate managers, but Stom didn't take the letter. 'Assassinated,' he said, and then again with an upward intonation. 'Assassinated? By whom?'

'Three men,' said the messenger again. 'They were seen loitering about on the estate earlier that day.'

'Who were they? I mean, where were they from?'

'Not from the moon, sir. All the estates have counted heads, and nobody is out of place. They must have come from offworld, sir.'

'Offworld?'

'Yes sir.'

'What do you mean, offworld?'

'Nobody knows, sir. Only they weren't servants from the moon, sir.'

'Were they servants at all?'

'Masterless men, sir,' said the messenger, gabbling the words in the horror of them. 'Vagrants, is what people are saying. They looked dirty and disreputable.'

The whole thing had an unreal timbre. Perhaps that was why, Stom thought to himself, he couldn't register the sorrow of his uncle's death. He couldn't quite believe that the old man wasn't breathing any more. 'This doesn't make sense,' he said. 'Vagrants? How could vagrants have come to the moon from another world? Vagrants don't buy tickets to travel by balloon-boat.'

'They weren't off any balloon-boat, sir,' said the messenger. 'Nor any plane. That's all been checked . . . the first thing that was checked.'

'So how did they come from offworld?'

'A skywhal beached itself in your uncle's estate that same day, sir. We all saw it. And they say that three figures leapt off it when it was still in the sky, and floated to the ground by parachute. That's what they say, sir, though I never saw it with my own eyes.'

It was clearly all a joke. In poor taste, but it was surely too ridiculous to be serious. 'And you say,' Stom repeated, 'that my uncle is dead?'

'Yes, sir. Dead, sir.'

The messenger had a coldsore on his lower lip, towards the left: the scab of dried blood was perfectly oval, flat, like a ruby planed and buffed and fitted into the skin. It was fascinating. Polystom couldn't stop looking at it. It was simultaneously revolting and oddly ornamental.

He felt like laughing. The hilarity bubbled up out of him like champagne bubbles in a flute-glass. But a gentleman did not laugh. It was an ill-bred things to do. He turned another ninety degrees, so that his back was now to the messenger.

'Thank you,' he said, keeping his voice steady with some effort. 'That's all. If you go down to the kitchens, they'll find some food for you.'

'I've a letter for you too, sir,' said the messenger in a wretched voice.

'Leave it on the side there,' said Stom. 'I'll see to that later.' He didn't feel like laughing any more.

His nails needed paring. Usually he had one of his servants attend to them whilst he listened to music. But he felt like doing them himself. He went upstairs to his own bedroom, and through to his annexe bathroom. There he sat down on the edge of the bath, and brought out the nail scissors from their ledge. The left hand was easily trimmed; little finger first, curving the scissors in a tight arc as he cut, cutting away a crescent moon. The ring finger, releasing another splinter of cut nail like a discarded shirt collar in miniature. The middle finger, cutting off a lopsided shred, and then cutting again to balance out the shape of it. The pointing finger, cutting the nail away, and then using the blunt side of the scissor blade to push back the encroaching skin from the bed of the nail, tidying it up, like pushing down the earth around a newly-bedded plant. Finally the thumb, a different shape altogether, a flatter curve, that Stom cut straight across and then cut the corners off of. Transferring the scissors to the left hand and starting to cut the nails of the right-hand fingers was trickier. The coordination did not come naturally. The little finger. The ring finger, where the pink nail displayed a curious little splash of darker pink within, like a fly squashed and trapped in amber. The middle finger, where the nail, uniquely, sported miniature corrugations from left to right. Pointing finger. Thumb. He was finished. The floor was scattered with the splinters of his cut nails, like broken frosted glass.

Polystom got to his feet. His uncle was dead. Surely he should be upset? No more trips to visit him on the moon. No more conversations with him about science. Why didn't he feel anything?

He contemplated the situation. In four years he had lost his father, his co-father, his wife and now his uncle. This was surely a great loss, a kind of tragedy. Wasn't it? This accumulation of grief.

But there was nothing. He took some food, and felt the savour of the food and the intoxication of the wine, but nothing more. He received reports from subsequent messengers, and later in the day a great-aunt came to stay for a week. The two of them discussed how terrible it was, but Stom's concerned face and woodpecker tut-tutting were acts, carefully performed to catch the appropriate degree of grief. The days went by, and the weeks, and there was no grief in his heart for his dead uncle. The sadness refused to grow.

He watched his great-aunt weeping, discreetly, into a gold-embroidered Kaspian-silk Sagé handkerchief. Her tears were like little hiccoughs. But he couldn't imitate the crying.

He discovered, by accident, ten days later, the letter that the first messenger had been bringing, where it had been tidied with other mail. Most of this pile consisted of condolences, families striving discreetly to out-do one another with the opulence of their crested paper, some sheets as thick as cotton. In amongst them Polystom discovered his uncle's handwriting, and he held the slender envelope up with a sudden, fierce joy. Some part of him thought that this sheet would be the tocsin to bring out tears. He thought: Cleonicles must have written this letter shortly before he died. Reading it will be like hearing him speak again, from beyond the grave, for one last time. Surely it will move me, and make me cry? There was something grisly about the eagerness with which he ripped the envelope:

My dear Polystom. Wonderful to see you again, naturally. I hope your nightmares ease themselves. I repeat what I told you; from the vantage point of science nightmares are a natural phenomenon, a way in which the brain purges itself of negative energy. In time they will subside. And I urge you, my dear boy, to consider remarrying. The time has come for it, I sincerely believe.

Nothing. No emotional response at all, except for a faint, and under the circumstances wholly irrelevant, flutter of irritation that the old

boy was still meddling in his personal life. He read on: Cleonicles'
personal version of the dead skywhal, the beast that had been freighted
with his own death.

> *I'm having the carcass carried ashore where we will – somehow! –*
> *improvise an embalming strategy. Then I'll be able to study it at my*
> *leisure. You must come again, my dear boy, and examine it for*
> *yourself!*

Nothing at all. The mind of Polystom noted the small ironies in the
words, and even the spookiness in receiving an invitation from a dead
man. He was able to read the letter as a reader of poetry might, the
hulking carcass as a metaphor for the old man's own death – a mighty
creature fallen from high, his flesh raked, turned into so much meat to
be manufactured into remembrance. But none of this moved him.
Other things did: Phanicles' *Rhum Elegies* still tickled his eyeballs with
tears. Listening to beautiful music did it too. He still had the capacity
for feeling. It simply didn't assert itself over his uncle's death.

Eventually Stom reached a state of mind in which he was indeed
distressed. Upset not by the death of his uncle, for on that topic he still
felt nothing, but upset rather by precisely the fact that he felt nothing.
He *ought* to have felt devastated, he ought to have grieved. The fact
that he did not experience that emotion troubled him, to a certain
extent. If he searched himself, he came to the conclusion that he did
not and could not find the death of his uncle distressing. It was not
'tragic' or 'appalling' or any of the things the newsbooks called it,
except in a purely intellectual sense. The word that occurred to Stom
was *preposterous*. It was, simply, preposterous that Cleonicles could be
dead, and doubly preposterous that he had died the way he had. It was
absurd. If Stom had invested any feelings in the fact – he did not think
this consciously, but we can assume that this was the subconscious
factor behind his emotional numbness – if he *cared* at all, then it
would endorse this preposterousness, and in turn this would render
the whole of the cosmos chaotic and absurd. All this wonderful order!
This filigree network of relations and forces, orbits and growth – all of
it would become nonsense the moment he allowed this ridiculous
event to take root in his heart. For the universe to bring a con-

sciousness into existence, to allow it to grow and develop and mix with others and gain understanding, to achieve so many things only, in the end, to achieve nothing – to die at the hands of servants. Not even of servants, but vagrants. It was intolerable. A life needed a pattern, just as society did. Some psychological muscle in Polystom's subconscious mind refused to relax enough to allow this notion through: his uncle had died an absurd death.

Lacking the self-knowledge to understand this, Stom was merely baffled by his absence of grief. He felt as if he were unable to do the proper thing, in a culture where doing the proper thing was all-important. The more he searched himself, hoping for tears and gloom and not finding them, the more upset he became at his strange behaviour. He began, in a half-focused manner, to wonder if there were something withered and monstrous in his soul. Hadn't he *loved* his uncle? Well yes, he thought he had, Didn't he *miss* his occasional visits to the moon? Well, yes, in a distant sort of way, he did. So why didn't he cry? Not a single tear?

Not a single tear.

The sense of distance from the event was compounded by the funeral. He began busying himself to prepare it, his fourth death ceremony in as many years, when he received notification that the event had been taken over by General Demus, one of the leading figures in the current war effort, subordinate only to Counts Meton and Euelpides, and the Prince himself. This funeral, Stom was told, was a matter of military honour and the patriotic pride of the whole of the System. The General trusted, his aide-de-camp told Stom in person during one visit, that Steward Polystom was not inconvenienced by this move, and hoped indeed that it would be of assistance to him in this time of great grief to have the responsibility for organising so complex an affair taken out of his hands.

Polystom, thrown, not wanting to betray that fact that he felt no grief at all, had assented too quickly. Very kind of the general. Please carry my compliments to him.

The two of them had been sitting outside Polystom's house, the Autumn Year well underway. A friend, or a family member, might have asked how Stom was bearing up under his terrible blow; but the aide-de-camp, though a fellow of good breeding, was no friend and no relative. He said nothing.

'Will it,' Polystom asked eventually, 'be held on the moon?'

'The General plans it so,' replied the aide.

'And quite a large do?'

The very faintest of quizzical looks crossed the aide's face. 'Naturally. Cleonicles – your uncle – is a great hero of the System.'

'Really?'

A slight, embarrassed pause. Polystom had not meant to be so abrupt; his single word had sounded like a contradiction. 'Of course,' said the aide.

'It's only,' said Stom, 'that I've always thought of him as just my uncle. You know? Although naturally I see what you mean. His science was terribly important, I know. Terribly important.'

'As a scientist, yes,' said the aide. 'But more than that. A great patriotic hero. A key figure in the war, on the Mudworld you know. Count Meton himself will be attending.'

'He will? I didn't realise they were friends.'

'Oh yes. The Count himself said, yesterday, that Cleonicles was one of the most significant figures for the military campaign on the Mudworld.'

This was entirely new to Polystom. 'You'll pardon me,' he said, 'but I had believed my uncle opposed to the war.'

'You'll pardon *me*,' said the aide, with an ingratiating smile, 'and of course you know your own uncle better than I, but his engagement with the campaign goes right back to the beginning. I know he had disagreements with some aspects of the *prosecution* of the war, but not with the war itself, never of that.'

'Fascinating,' said Stom, weakly.

'The Prince – this is confidential, you understand,' said the aide, leaning forward conspiratorially (although there was nobody in the garden but them), '—but the Prince is bestowing on him the Order of the Sun, and of the Eagle. Posthumously. It will be announced at the service.'

'An honour indeed,' Stom mumbled.

'And, to be confidential again – I hope you don't mind –'

'Not at all.'

'—I don't know if you're aware that your uncle raised a platoon for the war from his own estate. It was entirely characteristic of the man, I think, that he insisted on his own anonymity; that he took no public credit for this most patriotic act.'

Polystom hadn't known this either. Clearly the war had meant more to Cleonicles than the nephew had realised. And, a week later, at the service itself, the rank upon rank of gaudy, embossed uniforms amazed him further. The entire affair was so martial it gave the impression that Cleonicles had been a general or a count himself; instead of being a scientist given to writing sharp-phrased letters to the newsbooks about the poor management of affairs on Mudworld. It all added to Stom's sense of removal from the old man's death.

A great tent, more like a canvas barn, had been erected on the flat land south of his uncle's house, with tiered scaffolding for the seating and a wide entrance through which the cortege could pass. It took all morning for the place to fill, the brilliant colours of three dozen varieties of uniforms, the cream silks and pale wormskin dresses of the women, servants in white with bands of white cloth drawn about their mouths (an ancient symbol of mourning, once common amongst actual mourners, now worn symbolically by the servants) moved up and down between the seats with drinks. At the apex of all this attention was a raised dais on which the coffin was placed precisely on the chime of noon. Polystom sat behind the wooden box, with Count Meton and General Demus on either side of him. Once the servants had deposited the coffin and stepped away, the silence in the tent was complete, intense, like a concentration of the heat of this sunny autumn day, oppressively all about him.

He spoke first, standing, leaning over the coffin as tradition demanded, and addressing those gathered: talking waveringly of the role his uncle had played in his life, of how he had been aware of the greatness of the man only distantly, and had always treasured the closeness of his family relationship instead. It was a weak performance; the audience, military uniforms splashing a disconcerting quantity of colour about the usually bleached experience of a funeral, sat absolutely still.

Finally Stom fished a poem out of his back pocket. He had debated with himself about this, remembering only too well the stony response he had got at his co-father's funeral. But in the end he had decided to read it anyway, as a personal communication between himself and the memory of his uncle, and also – perhaps – to offer his own social embarrassment on the altar of his guilt at his continuing grieflessness.

He read aloud, one of Phanicles' Rhum elegies, adapting the final line to the circumstances:

> *I was alone at the well.*
> *I was doused in shadow and in deed.*
> *My yoke lay on the ground, waiting.*
> *I cannot say what I mean.*
> *I was come upon.*
> *Death has carried away my loved man, my family man.*

The crowd of dignitaries, luminaries, military men and women did not react with any obvious discomfort at this reading of poetry. Neither were they visibly moved or touched by it. Their blank faces held a mirror up to the blankness in Polystom's. He sat again, feeling only a weird, mystic disconnection from everything.

Then General Demus stood up, and delivered a rousing piece of military oratory. Cleonicles the hero! Little sung as a hero true, by temperament disinclined to seek public recognition for his work, and in some respects out of line with current military philosophy – nonetheless, he had done more than any man in the cosmos to help make the war on the Mudworld winnable, and winnable in as brief a time as possible. His innovations in Computational Devices alone marked him down as the greatest scientist and inventor the cosmos had ever seen; which was to say nothing of his work in the fields of natural history and cosmology. He had personally raised a platoon of men from his own estate, and sent them to General Amynseis – General Demus's esteemed predecessor as Ground Forces Commander, now resting in the realms of glory – and had done so without the usual fanfare and nonsense that so many people expected as their due for such recruitment. 'He did it purely as an act of patriotism. His example stands before us! He was a great man! We shall not allow the weasly nobodies who struck him down to deflect us from our path!'

Had it been proper for a crowd to applaud at a funeral, this crowd would surely have applauded. It was a rousing performance indeed.

Count Meton spoke perhaps twenty words, wishing his friend glory in the next life, though he had, alive, always disavowed belief in such a place. But he deserved his place amongst the honoured dead. Then, the Count sat down again, red in the face – with emotion? With the effort of standing and speaking? A piercing musical note, vocal and metallic at once, wavered through the tent. The horn player was standing behind the raised tiers of seats. He played the melody line of the death-march from Erodeos's *Diepus*, then he paused, and played it again. Servants appeared, lifted the coffin, and processed out.

Afterwards, at the wake, both the General and the Count consoled Polystom in person, and assured him of the greatness of his departed uncle. The theatre of the whole experience moved Stom even further away from grief. All these implausible creatures, in their stagy, bizarre colours, moving to and fro. Everybody eating fine food. The warmth of the Autumn-Year sunshine. Stom thought to himself that the servants had carried his uncle's body to the cold store in which meat was kept during the summer months. The refrigerating grumble of the store's motor would lullaby the corpse for two months, until the marble mausoleum was finally constructed on the east bank of the Lacus Somniorum, and Cleonicles could finally be put to rest. It wasn't that the funeral seemed premature to Polystom. It had certainly happened at the proper time. It was that it all seemed to relate to a different person than his uncle.

[fifth leaf]

After the funeral, Polystom stayed at his uncle's house for less than a week. There was a great deal to be sorted out; an executor had arrived, and was working through the instructions of Cleonicles' will. The executor was a young military officer, First Flying Squadron – another surprise, for Polystom had expected a civilian executor. But he was efficient, and deferential. 'You're chief heir, of course, sir,' he had said. The *sir* was a little problematic: as an officer, the executor was of approximate social standing to Stom. Polystom had no military ranking, and so it wasn't a military courtesy. To call Stom *sir* because he was the seventh Steward of Enting was technically correct, but a little stuffy and unfashionable. But Polystom couldn't correct the usage without embarrassing the man. He coughed, put his hands deep into his pockets, and ignored the fellow's use of the honorific.

'But your uncle suggested,' the executor continued, 'that a cousin of yours – Pithycles, I believe is the name – should take up residence in the house and rights over the estate here, on the moon. Is this agreeable to you, sir?'

'Of course,' said Stom. Running this estate as well as his responsibilities on Enting would be far too much bother.

'There are various other tabled items in the will,' said the executor. 'Perhaps too many to detail at any length with you, here? If it's alright with you, sir, I'll deal with them myself.'

'Whatever you think best.'

'Your uncle's main butler was killed with your uncle, of course. The underbutler in line is a young man, name of Agor. It would be appropriate, I think sir, for you to interview him, to ascertain whether he's ready to take on the responsibilities of acting as butler to the new master.'

'Very well.'

So Polystom interviewed the nervous young servant, asking him a few desultory questions. He seemed shaken – by the two deaths, he said. He'd never seen anything like it, he said. His father and grandfather, both still alive (this was said with an apologetic duck of the head) said *they* had never seen anything like it. It was terrible. It was awful. What was the cosmos coming to?

'Never mind that, now,' said Stom. 'It's terrible, yes. But the purpose of this interview is to determine whether you're ready to take over the responsibilities of being chief butler.'

'I think so, sir,' said Agor, miserably.

'Did the previous butler . . .' (Polystom had met him a hundred times on his visits to the moon, but now couldn't recall his name) '. . . did he show you the ropes, as it were? Do you know what your duties are?'

'He was very good at bringing me on, sir,' said Agor. 'I'll try my best, sir.'

'Then that seems fine. That's the proper order of things. Of course you'll want to speak to the executor, when he gets back from the Eastern Estate. And of course you'll want to decide on which under-butler should follow on from you.'

'Yes sir.'

'That's all.'

'I should take up running the estate straight away, sir?'

'Of course,' said Polystom crossly. 'The estate won't run itself, now, will it.'

'There's just one thing, sir. It's a slightly out-of-the-ordinary thing, sir, and I'm sorry to bother you with it. But I'm not sure what to do about it.'

'Well? What?'

'It's just that a skywhal beached itself a couple weeks back, and the master told us to store it until he could embalm it. For study, he told us, sir. So we pulled it out of the water and put it in a barn west of the lake. Only I don't know what to do with it now, sir. The master told us to keep it. Should we keep it? If it's to be embalmed, then there's nobody on the estate who knows how, except Old Epops, who used to help the master with some of his experiments, and he says he doesn't know how to deal with such a large carcass. Or if we're supposed . . .'

'Yes,' said Polystom, bored with this speech, interrupting the servant's gabble. 'The skywhal. I heard about that. It's a very unusual thing, I suppose.'

'It is, sir.'

'Well, I suppose Uncle wanted to keep it for science. But Pithycles has no interest in science. There won't be any of that going on when he's master in this house. I suppose we should do something about the skywhal – I tell you what,' said Polystom, his interest pricked for the first time since he had come to the moon. 'I tell you what. I'll come and see for myself.'

'Very well, sir.'

So he had taken that afternoon to drive out along the slurpy shallow coastline of the lake, with the new butler Agor at the wheel, fifteen minutes to a large, dark, wooden barn perhaps two hundred yards from the water's edge. All the way out there Stom was wondering what the actual sight of this extraordinary thing would be like. It was, he had decided, inherently poetic. It was a symbol somehow connected with his uncle's death. He had been toying with the idea of writing a poem. Or perhaps, if he could find somebody to write the music, an opera. the subject would be his uncle's death, and the extraordinary events of his last day alive. The skywhal and his uncle would be the main characters, the one singing the eerie music of the skies, the other singing verses to do with down-to-earth subjects like science. In his mind Polystom thought of the fallen skywhal and his uncle as symbols of one another; or perhaps of the skywhal as a symbol of himself, poetically floating Polystom. Whichever, it was clearly important for him, if he wanted to write poetry, to see the beast for himself.

The car had stopped, and Stom hopped out.

There was a bad smell, a miasma, in the air around the barn, and when Agor pulled the door open it washed out over him like a breaking wave, a ghastly stench of putrid flesh and ground-down faecal liquefaction. A mass of flies ducked under the eave and poured out into the light, the cloud of them flexing and spiralling outwards like pollen billowing off a tree-top in spring. Agor pulled wide the second leaf of barn-door, and the barn again spewed out a massive bolus of flies. There were countless more insects inside, their buzzing so drowsily intense it sounded as if a petrol motor had been left running in there. But the stink was so fierce, so overwhelmingly horrible, it had swept past the borders of the single sense to which it should properly have restricted itself – it was more than just a smell, it was a tangible pressure upon the body, it was a horrible, groaning noise of flies; it was the sight of a mountain of slimy decaying flesh; it was heat.

Polystom buried his nose in the crook of his arm, but the wide-weave cloth of his Parca jacket was no filter. He stepped back, and back again, as if the smell had physically pushed him. Lifting his arm as he lifted his head, he squinted into the barn. The skywhal was just a dark mass; its mouth, open, had half-collapsed, and any features that might have made it recognisable as a skywhal – fronds, eyes, markings – had dissolved in putrescence. Rusty streaks of grey, mould perhaps, lay over the thing's back; a piss-coloured treacly pool of something unspeakable had filled the floor of the barn, and was now creeping out through the open door.

'Horrible!' gasped Stom into the crook of his own arm. 'You didn't tell me it was like this.'

The servant couldn't hear him over the crescendo of insects, so Stom motioned to him to shut the doors again. Doggedly Agor pushed first one, then the other, great door shut. The buzzing dropped in volume, and Polystom trotted down to the water's edge to breathe again.

When Agor was at his side, he said: 'How foul that was!'

'Yes sir.'

'Burn it. Burn the barn with it. No,' he added, looking out at the placid stork-boars, who were stepping stealthily through the water, occasionally dipping their beaks into it for food, 'no, on second thoughts. I wouldn't want to burn a barn. Pithycles might need it. But you must bury that monster – take some men, remove the beast and bury it deep, away in the hills behind. Then wash the barn out properly.'

'Yes sir,' said Agor, somewhat glumly.

'Drive me back now,' said Stom.

Polystom stayed in his uncle's empty house for four more days. One day he took a tour through the whole estate, driven again by Agor. They drove completely around the lake, calling in at the stables and arable lands west, the dairy to the north, the orchards and hop-farms to the east. Everywhere Polystom noticed a subdued misery in the servants' faces that seemed to him to go beyond bereavement for the death of the master. Their mood jarred with the clear purple-blue sky and bright sunshine.

At their second stop, amongst farm buildings west of the lake, Polystom said conversationally to Agor: 'I was here a couple of weeks ago. In this very yard.'

'Sir?'

'Saw a man hanged here.'

'I know sir. I was there. Met, he was called.'

There was a pause. An autumnal bluefly drifted through the air in lazy curlicues, dragging its fizzing noise along with it.

'That fellow,' Polystom said, his mind running on the execution now, 'he ran away, didn't he?'

'Sir.'

'You say you knew him? The man who was hanged?'

'Yes sir.'

'A bad sort, I suppose?'

'Worse than some. Not so bad as others, perhaps, sir.'

Polystom was looking around the yard. A young girl appeared from between two buildings, carrying a laden pole across the back of her neck. It was an apple-stick for the horse; the apples as fat as footballs, gathered in bunches that dangled almost to the ground. She passed, her face carved in motionless unhappiness. 'What do you mean when you say that?' Stom asked Agor, as the girl went into one of the stables.

'Sir?'

'When you say this fellow wasn't as bad as others?'

'I'm not sure it's my place to talk about it, sir.'

'Not when,' Stom said with sudden fierceness, 'I asked you a *direct* question?'

There was an awkward pause. 'He wasn't much liked by the stable-staff, sir,' said Agor. 'He started out working the cows to the north, and was moved because the underbutler up there wanted him out of the way. Something about a woman, I believe, a woman they both wanted. So the underbutler moved him down to the stables, and several people here took against him. He was a difficult character to get along with. I'd play dice-dominos with him sometimes. People didn't much get along with him. Often he would be left out at mealtimes.'

147

'What do you mean, left out?' Stom's attention was only half on the story. The girl had come back out of the stable; a pretty girl, but her face looked palsied by misery. Couldn't she manage a smile?

'When slops – which is how they're named, sir, I should say mealtimes – when slops are called, it's down to the underbutler who sits where. If a fellow's excluded from the table he goes hungry.'

'What?' asked Stom. He hadn't been listening. The girl disappeared again, between the buildings, and Stom turned back to the servant. Agor repeated his last sentence.

'Is that why he stole?' said Stom. 'Because he was hungry?'

'It was partly that, I think, and partly just his cussedness. He had a wish for self-destruction about him, I think. He welcomed being caught. He was almost glad at the hanging, it seemed to me.'

Stom remembered the hanging. How *unaesthetic* that had been. 'That girl who just passed us. Do you know her?'

'Yes sir.'

'She looked extraordinarily glum. I mean, I'd expect her to be glum at the death of her master, but that was something else. Why's that?'

Agor looked extremely uneasy. 'Sir?'

'Come on man!' chivvied Polystom. 'Do you know, or don't you?'

'Yes sir.'

'Well?'

'Her brother was knocked over last week sir.'

'Knocked over?'

'By the militia. They came through the whole estate like a dose of salts. Looking for the assassins, of course, and looking for them pretty vigorously, sir.'

'They knocked him down?'

'Yes, sir.'

'Why?'

'I'm not sure there was any particular reason why, sir. They were bustling, in a hurry, rifles out and shouting and running around. They weren't particular, I think, sir.'

'Is he going to be alright? That girl's brother?'

'No sir, dead, sir. He broke his back, took a high fever, and died in days.'

'Broke his back?'

'Sir.'

'Did he fall off a roof or something? What an unfortunate accident.'

'No sir, just fell to the ground. I think it was the rifle butt in the small of his back that did the damage.'

'What an unfortunate accident,' Stom said again, a little vaguely. 'Anyway. Anyway. Back to the car.'

They drove on, up the western edge of the lake, past the barn with the decomposing carcass of the skywhal in it. The stench was noticeable even from the moving car. Figures were shuffling with doll-stiff awkwardness, scarves around their faces, carrying buckets in and out of the barn. The car carried Polystom on, and the air cleared.

They called in at outhouses, straggly collections of servant cottages, and then drove past the broad arable fields that constituted the bulk of Cleonicles' farmland. The lunar gravity, less than two-thirds that of Enting, enabled super-plants to grow, great towering cob-corns and a special breed of wheat that resisted insect depredation by exuding a waxy resin from a nodule at the top of each plant. Seeing the monster wheat, twice or three times his own height, reminded Stom that he was indeed on the moon. He had visited so often that he hardly noticed the difference in gravity now. He perceived it a little on landing, but after half an hour one tended to forget about it, and to be aware only subliminally of a sprightlier step and a lightness in one's bones.

They called in at an enormous barn, less a barn, more a great wall-less roof on six pillars, in which the autumnal harvests were stored. Servants were sheaving and piling the hay, and tipping drums of wheat into specialist winnowing machines. Stom stood, bored. There was hardly any arable growth on his own thickly forested lands. The thing that struck him most forcefully was the mournful looks on the faces of these servants, their sluggish, depressed manners. Back in the car he asked Agor whether this was also the result of the militia. 'Well, sir,' said Agor, raising his voice to be heard above the roars of engine and wind, 'perhaps the way to put it is this: servants don't like change. We like to know where we stand, sir. This whole terrible business with your uncle, sir, and then the militia shaking everything up and rushing around, it's a terrible disruption.'

'And that's why people seem so depressed?' Stom asked.

'That's it, largely, sir, yes.'

They drove on. Round the northern shore of the lake, back down the eastern shore, stopping off when the whim took Polystom. They took a look at the dairy herds, animals half as big again as Enting cows, but creatures whose milk was hopelessly watery and which had to be skimmed and skimmed to produce something drinkable. They drove through orchards of huge trees, on which grew cherries the size of apples, apples the size of melons, pears like gourds, sourberries in clusters like strings of black onions.

They drove through the hop farms, stopping at one of the breweries, for Stom to take a look at beer-brewing and at hop-wine and hop-whisky distilling. Stom wandered dreamily around this place, sniffing up the rich, sweaty aroma of stewing hops, tapping the fat metal bellies of the great copper stills. In another shed he climbed the ladder and peered over the lip of a beer tub, bigger than a swimming pool, where the sweet-salty smell and the foaming bubbling surface of the great lake of brewing beer seemed almost to hypnotise him. He stayed up there for many minutes. 'Like looking into the crater of an active volcano,' he said to the underbutler in charge of the distillery as he came down. 'A beer volcano. Think of that!'

'Yes sir,' said the underbutler blandly.

But they had used up most of the day by now, and Stom, bored, told Agor to drive him home. He leant back in his seat, and watched the scenery whip past: hops growing in their chesslike grids on the left, the placid waters of the lake on his right. He was asleep when Agor pulled in at Cleonicles' house. He woke to Agor's tapping him on his shoulder with a start, stumbled into the house half-awake, and fell asleep again on a chaise-riche downstairs.

There were a great many military people coming and going. General Demus himself came back to the Moon from Kaspian. 'What a pleasure, General,' said Polystom. 'An unexpected pleasure.'

'I need, personally, to supervise a search through your uncle's papers. I'm sure you understand, my dear Polystom,' said the General, as his batman, crouched at his side, tidied up the gold-braid stitching on the rim of his jacket with a short needle. 'There are a number of things we hope to uncover. Your uncle was involved in a number of confidential military projects. Intelligence for this, new weaponry for that, and always, naturally, the Computational Device.'

'I must say I didn't know anything about this,' said Polystom. This little conversation was happening in the early afternoon, and Stom had drunk a fair amount at lunch. 'Uncle never mentioned anything to me about it.'

'Oh, he wouldn't,' said the General, slapping away the batman with the back of his hand. 'He wouldn't. He respected confidentiality. A trustworthy man, your uncle.'

'Join me, General,' said Polystom, indicating a free seat at the table. The table had been laid for six, in the garden, in the rich autumnal afternoon light, although Polystom was actually lunching alone. 'Some apple wine? It's most refreshing.'

'Thank you,' said the General, seating himself. 'No wine for me. I have to work, this afternoon, you know. Coffee.' This last word, spoken more severely, was addressed to the hovering house servant.

'I was meaning to ask you, General,' said Polystom, emboldened by slight inebriation.

'Ask away, my dear boy,' said the General.

'I was reading some of my uncle's letters to the newsbooks. Their tone is quite anti-war, I'd say.'

'Yes?'

'Well, I'm not sure in my own mind whether my uncle was pro-war or anti. At the funeral the orations all stressed his belief in the war.'

'Oh, Cleonicles believed in the war. He thought our tactics were skewed, that's all. He thought he had a better way of winning.'

'*Are* your tactics skewed?' Polystom asked, with a slightly louche forwardness. The General smiled at him, as if to say, *I know you're a little tipsy* and *we understand that you've been a little knocked off the rails by the shock of your uncle's death.* But he didn't say anything.

'General,' said Polystom. 'Have you caught the assassins yet?'

'Ah,' said the General. 'The coffee. Not yet, I'm afraid. We suspect that they are being harboured somewhere on the moon.'

'What a frightening thought,' said Polystom, languidly.

'Isn't it?' said the General, lifting his glass of coffee to his lips. 'One wants to trust one's servants, but there are bad apples every-where. Even on the best-run estates. Do you trust *your* servants, my dear boy?'

'Let us say,' said Polystom, feeling quite grown-up and sly, 'I know which ones to trust. Who can say better?'

The General only smiled.

'I'm foolish, I know,' Stom went on. 'But I still can't understand what anybody could hope to gain by murdering my uncle. I've been trying to think it through, and I can't see how it benefits anybody.'

'Terrorists,' said the General. 'Extremely dangerous, dedicated men.'

'Is it true they came all the way from Mudworld?'

'Very likely.'

'By hitching a ride on a skywhal?'

'Stranger things,' said the General, 'have happened. My dear boy, we're looking for certain papers of your uncle's, a particular sheaf. They were stacked neatly in a green canvas box, with a C on the front. You wouldn't happen to know where they might be?'

'Sorry, General, I don't recall ever having seen them.'

The General's face was as unreadable as ever.

'Are they important?' Polystom asked with faux-innocence.

'If you do see them,' said the General, getting to his feet. 'Let one of my aides know. Good day to you, my *dear* boy.'

'Good day.'

Perhaps it was the presence of so many military people about the house. Or perhaps it was, as Polystom later told himself it was, a longer-standing yearning of his. The fact of the ongoing war on the Mudworld began to intrude itself into Polystom's consciousness. He had always been aware of it, of course, but now it loomed large. Every time he saw one of the brightly uniformed staff officers coming or going about the house, or the estate, he thought to himself *you've been to the Mudworld, you've seen things and done things about which I have only imagined.* He realised, one morning, that he had never actually made up his mind about the war. He had never fashioned for himself strong feelings, pro or anti. The most he had done was soak up the prevailing atmosphere at whatever gathering he had been attending. Visiting his uncle, for example, he had assumed what he took to be his uncle's position – which is to say, a generally conceived though nonetheless patriotic opposition to the campaign. Now he discovered that Cleonicles had been considered a hero of the war! That the old man had actually levied a platoon from amongst his own servants! And, in the bustling, elegantly purposeful atmosphere of the house as it now was, with each of the handsome officers strutting up the stairs or across the lawn, Polystom started, osmotically as it were, to soak up a different perspective on events. He fished out copies of

Phanicles' *War Hymns* and Oenophanes' *War's Glory* and read them. *Life's but a sword's length, at best*, said Phanicles. The great Phanicles, who had fought on Bohemia; wielded rifle and bayonet amongst the snow. A terrible thing, of course, but marvellous as well. He took both books out with him, and sat by the lake in the whisky light of a late autumn day. He read a sonnet by Oenophanes about men marching in step, their marching pounding the ground, their hearts marching in step as well, their rhythmic pulses connected, their sensations heightened by the presence of glory. They marched over a bridge and shattered it to timbers with the sheer force of their coordinated marching. *A phenomenon*, the author observed in a tiny-print footnote at the bottom of the page, *which has often been observed by military leaders, and to prevent which men are trained to march out of step when crossing a bridge.* Polystom wasn't so sure about that one. All the men in that poem ended up in the water. What was so glorious about that? But, turning the page, he found something more stirring:

> *This is the eternal Might and Right*
> *By which all life is sifted, slain and shed!*
> *Lord make me hard like thee, that day and night*
> *I may approve thy ways however dread!*

A little stuffy, Oenophanes, but stirring stuff. Rather old-fashioned now, and nothing compared to the fragile beauties of Phanicles' verse, but it made the pulse hurry a little. *Life's but a sword's length, at best!* That was true, surely. How could a man *be* a man unless he had tested himself in the crucible of battle?

The following day, Polystom came across one of General Demus' two aides. 'Have you found the sheaf of papers you were looking for?' he asked.

A slightly suspicious flutter passed over the man's face, but then he smiled again. 'We've found a great deal that will be of use to the war effort, sir,' he said. 'I wonder if it would be convenient for you to lunch with the general today?'

'I'd be delighted,' said Polystom.

The two of them walked inside together. There was a chill in the air, more characteristically autumnal than the weather had been in the previous few weeks, and lunch was being taken indoors. As they walked together, Stom asked the aide, 'tell me, have you been in action yourself? On the Mudworld, I mean?'

'Yes, I have.'

'Really!'

'It's hard fighting down there, sir,' said the aide, although his smile seemed to undermine his words rather. 'Hard fighting.'

'But – you know,' said Stom. 'Glorious?'

'Of course.'

The general was already at table, his other aide beside him. Polystom settled into a chair beside him, and filled his own glass with apple wine, whilst a servant portioned apple-and-salmon pate onto a plate.

'My dear Polystom,' said the General. 'How are you?'

'Bearing up, General,' said Polystom. 'I have something to ask you. It's more, I suppose, that I'm asking your advice. Or your blessing.'

'And I have something to ask *you*. But you go first, dear boy.'

Polystom, smiling, looked straight into the general's eyes. His face was broad, friendly-looking, almost babyish, with ink-blue eyes and pale bristly hair. Well-formed, except for the wormy bruise-red ridge of an old scar, running down the right side of his face, wriggling like a live thing when the general smiled. 'You told me about my uncle raising a platoon from his own estate.'

'I did, my boy.'

'I'd like to do the same. From my estate, on Enting. Would that be of use to the war?'

'Indeed it would. What an excellent notion.'

'My estate is rather larger than my uncle's. I don't see why I couldn't manage say – fifty men.'

'Tremendous.'

'You'll pardon my ignorance . . . I don't know how these things work. These would be servants, of course. Officers would . . . ?'

'Would come from one of the academies on Kaspian or Berthing. I could introduce you to the lieutenants personally – over dinner. That might be pleasant.'

'Let's say,' said Stom, feeling increasingly nervy and gauche, holding his wine glass by its stem like a flower and angling the cup to watch the light reflecting from its surface. 'Let us say that I were interested in leading my own men. Would that be . . . ?' He fizzled out.

'That would be an act,' said the general, beaming at him, his scar curling, 'of patriotism and bravery. Splendid! Splendid! I can see the same blood runs in your veins as ran in your uncle's.'

'Is that – a done thing?'

'It is indeed. Some people prefer not to become personally involved. Your uncle, for instance, went so far as to insist upon anonymity. And there is, as you know, a degree of danger involved. But that's the glory of it.'

'How would it work? Practically, I mean?'

'Well,' said the general, raising his own glass. 'First, a toast.' The two glasses kissed, with an icy little *tink*, and Polystom took a long draught of wine. He felt more nervous now than he had done before. 'Well,' the general said again. 'The practicalities are that it's usually best to leave the nitty-gritty of command to your lieutenants. They'll order the men directly, enforce discipline, that sort of thing. It's better that way, my dear boy: they're specifically trained for battlefield command.'

'I quite see that,' said Stom. His heart was pumping. Was it too late to back out? Or would a change of mind at this stage effectively brand him a coward?

'But your presence would be an enormous benefit. For one thing, your men know and love you. That makes for a very healthy command dynamic. The men can hate the lieutenants, for punishing them, for ordering them into lethal situations. But because they love you, they don't hate command as such. It works very well. Respect for authority is the key to military success, you see.'

'Would I have to be trained myself? Military training, I mean?'

The general pursed his lips and shook his head genially. 'If you like, dear boy, but it's not essential. Not essential at all. You know how to fire a gun? Of course you do. There's not much else to it. This is an *excellent* decision you've made.'

'It is?'

'Certainly it is.'

Stom smiled, goofily. 'I'm glad you're pleased, General.'

'I am. Fifty men, did you say? That's a marvellous contribution to the war effort. It really is. And you'll be getting *in* before it's over,' the general added with enormous gusto. 'Think of the honour! Think how jealous other people will be when the war's finished, when you have a distinguished record and they don't!'

This was an altogether more appealing perspective on things. Stom took another slug of wine. His belly was warming. 'I'll fly back tomorrow, and gather my men together.'

'Good idea. My aide here will have you sign the commission papers before you go. He can also take you through the hoops, as it were, so you know what to do.'

'Thank you, General.'

'Don't mention it, my dear boy. Thank *you*! Now, there was just *one* thing I wanted to ask you.' He poked at his as yet uneaten lunch with the back of his fork. 'Come to think of it, it may involve you staying on the moon, here, for a few days more.'

'Ask away, General.' There was a slightly manic elation inside Stom now. He had taken the step. He was, essentially, a soldier now. He was on a level, now, with his eminent lunch partner. A petty pride swelled in his breast. He would prove himself worthy! He would open himself to new experiences. He would gather glory to himself. The general was looking more serious now.

'It's to do,' he said, 'with your father's assassins.'

'My uncle's,' Stom corrected, automatically, but the mood had instantly shifted, chilled.

'Yes, yes, I do beg your pardon. Your uncle's assassins.'

'Have you caught them?'

The General's smile had a slightly forced look about it, as if Stom had said something indelicate. 'Not yet. We'll find them, to be sure. They must be hiding with somebody, somewhere on the moon. We'll deal with them soon, don't worry. But it's important for morale, for authority you know, that we make an exhibition. That justice is seen to be done, and quickly. You do understand?'

'Of course,' said Stom, not understanding at all.

'I think it best in a case like this to use the skin-frame.'

'The skin-frame,' Stom repeated, the words cooling his heart.

'A bit gruesome, I know, but it's imperative we send out a signal that the whole System can hear. Now, we've – this is hush-hush, naturally – but we've pulled over a couple of prisoners from the Mudworld. Dangerous men, criminals of the worst sort. We've flown them over in secret, and now they're in a cellar under the house.'

'From the Mudworld?'

'Yes. The general population of the moon, the servants you know, don't know what the assassins actually looked like. Only that there were three of them.'

'I've heard some servants say there were four of them.'

'Two, three, four. If the stories continued circulating, dear boy, there would be a hundred of them by month's end. We'll say there were three. We'll disseminate the news that we caught all three of them on the Speckled Mountains, hiding in a cave. Then we'll say that one of them was shot resisting his arrest, and that the other two were captured. Then we'll bring out our two Mudworlders, execute them by skin-frame . . . oh, shall we say, the day after tomorrow?'

The aides, on either side, nodded.

'Yes. That will give people time to assemble. Ideally, we want a very large crowd. And photographers, newsbook-men, the whole caboodle. Now, the reason I mention this to you is that the best thing, clearly, would be for you to be there. As your uncle's closest surviving relative, you know.'

'I see,' said Polystom. He had no desire to watch men executed by skin-frame; it was the most unappealing way to die he could imagine. But, he told himself, he was a soldier now. He had to harden his sensibilities. Perhaps, he said to himself, putting the wine-glass to his face and sucking down another mouthful of wine, perhaps he could use this as an opportunity to train himself into familiarity with blood. 'Of course I'll do it.'

He sent a letter to Nestor, his butler, telling him that he'd be staying on the moon for another three days at least, but that he'd be home as soon as he could get away; and also instructing him to draw up a list of the fifty likeliest soldiers on the estate. *I intend forming a platoon, for the war, with myself as captain,* he wrote. *I'll leave you in charge of the estate in my absence, of course, but I need good men under me.*

The night before the execution he had trouble sleeping, and in the morning he lay in bed, trying to determine whether it was indeed a sort of squeamishness, a boyish cowardliness, that made him disinclined to watch men put to death. If so, then he needed to purge that weakness.

The squeamishness, if that was what it was, hadn't dented his appetite however; and he ate heartily at breakfast. Agor, attending him, talked about the crowd. 'I've never seen anything like it, sir. There must be thousands of people. Most of them slept on the hillsides west of the estate sir; but they've all come to see the assassins get their desserts.'

'It's an important thing,' Stom said. 'An important lesson to be taught. For the whole System.'

'Yes sir.'

After breakfast, Polystom went with one of the general's aides to the cellar to visit the condemned men. 'Do they know they're facing the skin-frame?' Stom asked.

'I'm sure it's all they expect,' replied the aide. 'And if they don't know, they'll know it sure enough when the executioner comes to prepare them.'

'Prepare them?' Stom asked, half wanting to hear the details, and yet with a fluttery heart.

'They'll be basted, as it's called. A tannin cream rubbed into the skin, which toughens it a little. It's no good if the skin rips or tears, you'll understand. And they'll have been starved, to loosen the subcutaneous fat a little. It's an old procedure, sir. The executioner knows what he's doing.'

Stom said nothing. The cellar door was opened by a uniformed guard, and behind it was a small grey room, the stone floor and walls empty and clean except for its occupants. Two men, grimy and sullen, sat in the coign of wall and floor. Their arms were over their heads, chained to a hook halfway up the wall. Their was a blank, animal ferocity in their eyes. Stom leaned forward a little, fascinated by what he saw. There were little cuts and marks over their bare legs, up their bare arms, over their faces. They were so dirty it was impossible to tell which blotches were bruises and which were grime. Their hair had been shaved, revealing half-a-dozen or more circular marks of red, like tiny fairy rings, over their stubbly crowns. One of them was opening and closing his mouth, like a man chewing air, and Stom could see that he had no teeth, and was mashing his gums together, although he couldn't tell why.

'These men,' he said, in a hushed voice.

'Sir?' returned the aide.

'How were they . . . I mean, what were they . . .' But the question wouldn't frame itself.

'They're bad men,' said the aide. 'I wouldn't worry about that. These are no ordinary prisoners of war. Those, naturally, we execute quickly and cleanly. These have done *much* worse than average.'

Bad enough to merit the skin-frame? Stom wanted to ask. But he didn't say anything. He drank in, again, the unthinking venomous hostility of their eyes, and then turned away.

The skin-frame was an antique execution device, rarely used these days, or so Polystom had always thought. Perhaps it was still usual in military justice. A wooden frame, fifteen feet tall, with two hand-rails at the top, spaced so that a man could support himself by holding them. Two bars, like a piece of gymnastic equipment, but with the difference was that three feet below these, fixed to the side, was a metal cradle. The condemned man was suspended in the middle of the frame, his hands tied to the bars and his arms bent a little at the elbows. The skin around his ankles was cut clear about and peeled a little way up his shins, this bloody end of flayed flesh being fixed with many little hooks via springs to the cradle. Then the condemned man was left to hang. As long as he could support himself on his bent arms, he could limit the area of his skin that was pulled from his flesh to two circlets of agony around his ankles. But as his grip weakened, and as he sank, his own body-weight flayed him: the weight of his body pulling him down and peeling off his own skin as he went. It was an unusually horrible way to die.

'Have you ever seen a skin-frame used before?' Stom asked the aide, as they climbed back up to the house.

'I have,' replied the aide, benignly. 'A few times.'

'It's a military punishment, then?'

The aide nodded.

'I'm just wondering,' said Stom, trying to keep the quaver from his voice. 'What to expect, you know.'

'Depends. It depends, for instance,' the aide said, 'on the strength of the man. You'll find that they hold out for a while. Then they drop a little, and the pain of that gives them the strength to pull themselves up again. This could go on for a while, dropping, pulling free more skin from their legs, the agony inspiring their tired muscles with a little more energy, struggling up, drooping again, crying out, struggling up again.'

159

Stom nodded. He felt sick in his stomach now. He wished the aide were not being so graphic. But perhaps it was better he know in advance. And, anyway, wasn't he a soldier now? A soldier couldn't afford squeamishness.

'Their hands are tied to the rails, of course,' the aide continued. 'They can't just drop completely off the device. That would end it too quickly. Though, actually, I doubt if any man would have the strength of character to just drop off – the pain would be unbearable, all at once. So, they drop lower and lower, and the skin is flayed off up to the middle of the thighs. Eventually they reach a stage where they can't support themselves, no matter now hard they struggle. Then they do flop down. The executioner makes a slit, running up the skin of the inside of each leg and across the skin of the perineum before the execution, you know, so that at that stage the whole skin should come away quite easily. They're left hanging, nude, as it were, except for their faces and their arms – still tied above them, you know. The top part of the hanging body is, well, sheathed as it were, so you can't see the face unless you look down from above.'

'And they're dead by then?'

'It doesn't take long for them to die then, if they're not already. I'm only telling you this,' the aide added, 'so you know what to expect, sir.'

'Yes,' said Stom. 'Thank you.'

The aide clapped him on the shoulder and laughed abruptly. 'How pale you look sir! Don't worry about it, really. They deserve it, these criminals; keep that in mind. They're just insects. They're lower than animals. They're not anybody.'

'I'll try and keep that in mind.'

They wandered out onto the flat ground east of the house, where the frames were being assembled. The two main skin-frames were fully built; and now the long beams of the two lifting scaffolds were being hauled up. 'One thing occurs to me,' said Stom.

'Yes?'

'What if they shout out that they're innocent, that they've been brought in from the Mudworld. I daresay that people wouldn't believe them, of course, but it might spoil the effect a little.'

'Don't worry about that, sir,' said the aide, pulling a cigarette white as a bleached finger-bone from a silver packet and slipping it between his lips. 'Their tongues were pulled out yesterday.'

And, later in the day, in the cool sunlight of another autumnal afternoon, with an enormous, murmuring crowd of onlookers gathered in the open ground east of the house, Stom tried to focus himself. To act like a soldier. The two condemned men were being led out, their bodies naked but unwashed. Stom sat next to the general and his two aides on a platform, raised opposite the execution frame. It was, the aide explained, important they be seen by the crowds. That was a large part of the point of the exercise. And so the four of them sat virtually enthroned, as the condemned men were brought out by the executioner and his uniformed assistants. They were lifted up, dangled in the air from the rear scaffold, the rope under their armpits forcing their arms forward into a gorilla's pose (that mythical beast), as the executioner positioned them; flashing his large knife around their ankles to cut the skin, fitting their feet into the network of sprung hooks of the cradle, tying their hands to the rails. One last touch involved him running the point of his knife up the inside of one leg and down the inside of the other, doing this for both men, like a tailor measuring fittings. Blood oozed out, red sap, and dribbled from their pinioned feet to drip to the ground. Then the scaffolds were removed, the executioner untying the supporting ropes, and leaving the men there. The crowd, which had buzzed and shuffled as the elaborate preliminaries were undergone, had fallen absolutely silent. Polystom, too, was rapt, staring at the condemned man nearest him. *I doubt if any man would have the strength of character to just drop off*, the aide had told him. *The pain would be unbearable, all at once.* But, Stom wondered, how could you *not*? How could you do anything other than try and end it quickly? What would it be like to hang there, knowing what inevitable agonies awaited you? The two scrawny bodies hung, displayed, ribs standing proud of the skin like thick scars, faces crumpled in pain, the surprisingly large genitalia of the nearer man dangling like sausages in a butcher's window, the other man's shrunken and snail-like, the circlets of bright red around both sets of ankles surprisingly decorative, like red cloth tied there to brighten the picture. They hung there on their own muscles' strength, arms crooked out at the sides like lizards, as if frozen in the middle of press-ups. They strained. There was something in them, Stom realised, that refused to give up to the experience. They clung on, quite literally, for their lives.

Turning to the aide immediately on his left, and lowering his voice, he hissed into his ear: 'these were servants, on the Mudworld, originally, I suppose?'

'Years ago,' the aide whispered back, without turning his head. 'On Aelop, yes. The insurrection is so old now that they've long since forgotten servantly ways.'

And yet there was something almost noble, in a grotesque sort of way, about the effort they were putting in. Work was a servant's only currency, a servant's only freedom, and these two were working at their last few minutes of existence with a worthy intensity. Stom tried to think himself into their position; mouth ragged and sore, starved, agony gripping around your ankles, the prospect of worse agony to come, and yet hanging on, hanging there though your muscles were popping and screaming with the effort of it. Everything in the cosmos focused down, reduced to that effort, to the pain and that effort. To pain and will power. Stom shut his eyes. But the general was saying something to him, leaning across his aide to talk to Stom. 'This is,' he was saying, sotto voce, 'a much better – I mean, by that, much worse – version of the execution than I'm used to. The – lesser gravity of the moon means that they can hold themselves longer, and it also means that the process is that much more drawn out. I wonder,' the general mused, sitting upright again, 'if we shouldn't schedule all such executions for a lower gravity world, rather than a higher?' 'A good idea, sir,' said the aide. 'A good idea.'

THREE

The Mudworld

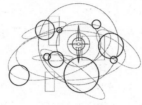

A Ghost Story

[first leaf]

The two lieutenants, younger sons of good family, flew down in the same plane. They were called Sophanes and Stetrus, and they were two young men formed from a similar mould: tall, svelte, their uniforms the dark brown with gold trimmings of the Ground Corps. Long-featured faces, long slender noses, wide mouths rimmed with thin lips, lenticular eyes, eyebrows as long as a finger reaching out from the middle of their brows on each side almost to their ears. Handsome, but severe. To Polystom they looked like killers, trained killers. They could have been brothers, although in fact they were only second cousins. They called one another '*Sof*' and '*Stet*', without inviting the same intimacy from Polystom, although he was their superior officer now.

They called him 'sir'.

They came to train the platoon, the fifty men that Polystom had chosen – or had Nestor choose for him. As the Autumn Year moved towards its close Stom had a barracks built on land east of his house. He hired three tailors from the southern hemisphere, and housed them in his own house. He ordered so much brown bolt-cloth, so much leather and cotton, that a special delivery was made by balloon-boat, landing on the lawn, unloading their bales and departing. The three tailors took a dozen servants under their temporary command, and set about making seventy Ground Corps uniforms; fifty for the men, twenty as spares. The number of spares had been Stom's own ideas. 'Sof' and 'Stet', when they arrived into the middle of all this busy-ness, were unimpressed. 'If the men think there are spare uniforms just sitting around,' drawled one of them (Stom found it hard, initially, to tell them apart), 'then they'll not treat their clothes with the proper respect. A better way is to have none spare, sir, and punish the men for any raggedness in their own uniforms. That encourages them to keep themselves neat.'

Polystom, still unsure of himself, feeling almost completely unlike a captain, had acquiesced. He didn't like the lieutenants' insouciant tone, felt it almost as an affront, but he fretted about it in private rather than challenging them directly. They knew more about war than he did, he told himself. Told the tailors that only fifty uniforms would be needed. Or, rather, fifty-three; because he, as captain, needed three uniforms: one for battle, one for travel, one for dress occasions. A tailor attended Stom in the Velvet Room, measuring every point on his anatomy. When the travel uniform, the first of the three, was completed five days later, Polystom strutted around before a mirror for hours, admiring himself. He did the same with the battle uniform: a more severely styled garment, but still elegant, gold braid covering the stitching between body and arms, gold hemming the rich brown at bottom and top. Stom sent all the servants away and danced around his bedroom with an empty rifle, hiding behind the bed and pretending to shoot at himself in the mirror.

His two lieutenants, on the other hand, had embarked on a two-month training process with the men. This began with long runs, through the forests and to the mountains, then back: the lieutenants shouting all the time, the men carrying sacks of stones in each hand. Each evening Sof and Stet dined with Polystom in the main house, where of course they were staying. They laughed a great deal at one another's stories, laughter in which Polystom tried, slightly awkwardly, to join. Some of it frankly passed him by, and many of his own conversational sallies fell flat. 'Do you two read at all?' he asked once, to be met by blank expressions. Evidently they did not read. 'Poetry?' Polystom pressed. 'There have been some superb martial poets, poems about war. Phanicles himself fought on Bohemia, you know.' 'Phanicles,' said Sof. 'No, never heard of him.'

'Knew a major called Palicles,' offered Stet.

At dinner they might vaguely ask his permission for some aspect of training or other. 'We'll need to dig up a field, put some trenches in it, lay some logs. For the training you know. That alright?' Yes, said Polystom. Of course. But their easy, almost insolent manner grated on him. Perhaps they were more experienced in war, but he was still Steward of Enting – they ought to be more respectful. He wanted to express this feeling, but couldn't think of the form of words.

Obviously he didn't want to rebuke them outright. He didn't want to alienate them. But, after all – he was the Steward.

The next day's training saw the men out digging, turning the daisied turf beyond the airfield into a plain of mud. The day after that, the two lieutenants sent all the men to the far side of it, and ordered them to advance from trench to trench whilst Stet and Sof stood firing shots at them. Polystom came out to watch this exercise. His men were scrambling desperately out of each trench, running low and zigzagging, dropping to their knees and crawling through the mud, hauling themselves prone over the logs laid in their way, and dropping into another trench. All the while, the two offers were firing live ammunition at them. It looked to Stom, and presumably felt to the men, as if they were shooting to hit. They took aim, fired, swivelled the gun, took aim, fired again. One man was shot in the thigh, and without a cry fell back into the trench from which he was emerging. After the exercise, Sof stood over the man whilst another soldier, a man appointed corporal medic despite his lack of medical knowledge, bandaged the wound. 'He can have five days rest,' Sof said, loftily. 'Then I want him training again. And he'd better patch the hole in his uniform. He'd better patch it, or his friends had better. Or he'll be on punishment detail. Wound or no wound.'

'Sir!' barked the medic. 'Sir,' groaned the wounded man.

Despite the injury to one of their own, or perhaps because of it, the men were in high spirits that evening. Polystom, in his own house, stood in the Yellow Room looking over the lawn to where they massed by the sea's edge, rinsing their mud-clogged uniforms in the water. Some were naked, some in longjohns, but they laughed and joked, splashing one another and larking about in the paling light. Stom returned to the dinner table. 'I must say,' he said to his two lieutenants. 'It looked like you were having a jolly go at shooting them this afternoon. I mean, *actually* trying to shoot them.'

'Trying to shoot *near* them,' said Stet. 'So they know what a bullet sounds like cracking past their heads. But it's good practice to shoot one of them, in an exercise like that. Toughens them all up. Keeps them all on their toes.'

'I see,' said Polystom. He felt an obscure unhappiness pressing inside his solar plexus.

'They'll face worse on the Mudworld,' Sof observed, pushing his silver knife through his fillet of trout with chicken and sourberry stuffing.

'Have you seen action there?' Stom asked.

'Certainly have,' said Sof. 'Both of us. I say, Stet, do you remember the Pencil Ridge? That was no picnic, *if* you like. The enemy had dug themselves into the ridge, actually into the ridge.'

'How they do it's a mystery,' put in Stet. 'Why they don't drown in mud and earth. But they don't.'

'So they had a troop on the top of the ridge, and we were ordered to take it. So we pushed forward with two hundred men, and got cut in half, fighting uphill you know and so on. But we took the ridge. And just as we were settling ourselves, weapons unready, ciggies out, didn't they just pop up from the ground?'

'They?' asked Polystom.

'Sir?' said Stet. The two of them managed, continually, to give the impression that they weren't really paying any attention to him.

'You said they just popped up. Who? Who do you mean?'

'The enemy, sir,' said Stet, as if explaining to a child. 'Coming out of the ground, where they'd dug themselves in. Up they came, and cut us in half again. Only a dozen or them, but wild, and with that element of surprise.'

'That element of surprise is a killer, sir,' said Sof.

Sometimes, Polystom felt he ought to attend more closely to their conversation, and especially to their military anecdotes, as a way of preparing himself for war. But the impression of war he got from the two of them was that it was a giant playground, where kicks and knocks were of the same order as amputation and death. He didn't much care for that version of war. He wanted to believe it something altogether more enormous, great glory, intense tragedy. Something poetic and beautiful in the terror and pain; something meaningful in the carnage.

The training continued: sometimes brutal ('toughening them up', Stet called it), sometimes merely gruelling. Polystom occasionally toyed with the idea of joining in, but his lieutenants dissuaded him. Best not diminish yourself in the eyes of the men, they said. You need the manner of command, they said, that's the important thing. And you have that already, of course, sir, they said, possibly smirking a little as they spoke; it was hard for Polystom to tell. As Steward, you automatically have that.

'Is there nothing I can do?' Polystom had asked, a little plaintively.

'Well,' said Stet, tapping a cigarette against the back of his hand prior to smoking it, 'you could practise your shooting. An officer can always stand improving his accuracy with the gun, you know.'

'Rifle,' said Sof, 'and pistol both.'

'Oh yes. Pistol especially.'

Accordingly, whilst his two lieutenants were making the men clamber up and down the trees, under fire, to retrieve parcels from inaccessible branches, Polystom made his way to a different part of the forest. He carried an elmwood box, like an attaché case, which he opened to display two perfectly crafted silver slot-pistols. He had had them made by a specialist gunsmith who lived on Rhum. Polystom levered them both out of their velvet surrounds, and then unhitched a layer of stiffened cloth from the lid of the box to reveal a layer of polished metal bullets, like fish-eggs crammed in together. It reminded him of a chocolate box. He fitted five bullets into each slot, and then turned the pistols over and over in front of his face, examining them carefully, their symmetry, their craft, their weight. The handles were inlaid with flat panels of teak, scored and criss-crossed with lines like wood engraved for printing. The barrels were straight and hollow like birds' bones. The slot fed into the trigger casing. There was something delightful about the intricacy of the clock-like machinery. Standing with his feet apart, Polystom held both pistols away from him straightening his arm and aiming each at the trunk of a tree a hundred yards distant. A mutual clench in each trigger finger and the things exploded, a colossal synchronised bang, like reality itself splitting and cracking.

All around, birds flew upwards with an amplified shuffling sound of wings and rustling leaves.

Polystom had wrenched his left wrist with the recoil and, muttering curses to himself, he replaced the guns in their box and sat on the floor, nursing the jarred joint. For five minutes he wondered, bitterly, if he had broken it, but he seemed to be able to flex it slightly, and he probably (he told himself) would not have been able to move it all if he had snapped any bone. But it was hugely sore. Sprained. The stupidity! He'd tried to brace his joints, he really had. But now he knew he was facing the ridicule, howsoever elegantly expressed, of his two lieutenants. How did your pistol practice go sir? Hurt your wrist sir? What a shame, sir.

With his good hand he packed away the guns and shut the case. Only as he was leaving did it occur to him to check whether he'd hit his target. Holding the case in his good hand, and clutching his sore arm against his chest, he made his way over to the tree. A portion of the bark on the extreme right edge had been splintered by the passage of a bullet.

He had Nestor bandage up the wrist with a splint of cured leather that allowed a degree of movement. 'Try and make sure the bandages are underneath the sleeves,' he told his servant, unable to keep the peevishness out of his voice. 'Sir,' said the butler. 'I think it needs to come up over the base of your hand, sir, if it's to do you any good.'

Supersensitive at supper, Polystom thought he detected sly smiles being exchanged between his lieutenants, but neither of them spoke directly about his sprain. They started on a lengthy military anecdote, swapping the narrative voice between themselves, their hilarity spiralling higher and higher as they proceeded.

'. . . so the order comes down to dig out the old river bed . . .'

'. . . although the mud is practically fluid, but nonetheless . . .'

'. . . *digging* for hours and hours, but every spadeful slops back . . .'

'. . . and then . . . and then the colonel himself comes down . . .'

'. . . to see what's taking the platoon so long . . .'

'. . . and he doesn't recognise *any* of us because we're so muddy . . .'

'. . . and he's shouting and waving his pistol around, when . . .'

'. . . plop!'

'. . . plop!' (They made this sound by flicking their tongues inside their cheeks.)

'. . . he *loses* his grip on it and it goes flying *into* . . .'

'. . . *into* the mud . . . disappears *completely* . . .'

'. . . and how he raged! "Dig over here, now!"' (A gruff, doggy voice for the colonel.)

'. . . "you lot! Stop digging there and dig here!"'

'. . . "I want my gun back! That was my grandfather's pistol!"'

'. . . "Where are your officers? I want them to report to me now!"'

'. . . "Been in the family a hundred years!" . . .'

Until they couldn't continue because they were laughing so hard. Polystom smiled, leaning towards them, trying to get caught up in their manic hilarity, but he felt excluded from the game.

That night, in his bed, his wrist throbbing and keeping him awake, he told himself that things would be different after a tour of active service. That was the thing, he said to himself, that separated him from the younger officers. They had seen battle, and he hadn't. Once he had been there, once he had purified himself in the heat of battle, then he would be one with all other soldiers. Then he would feel *real*.

That night, Polystom's men were sleeping naked under the stars. The Autumn Year was practically at an end, and the nights were very chilly. The point of this exercise, the lieutenants had said, is to toughen you physically. You must be ready for every hardship. You will sleep tonight naked, on the lawn, under the chill night sky. We'll be keeping an eye on you from the house! And as Stet and Sof slept the heavy sleep of the wine-sozzled, under their blankets, the mass of their men, acting without conscious decision, contracted and contracted, bodies pulling closer to bodies for the shared heat, until the whole platoon was a connected mass of bodies.

Polystom found it hard to sleep. He had nightmares. Most nights he woke, sobbing, from horrible nightmares.

In a week Polystom's wrist recovered, and he spent long days alone by himself in the forest, honing his pistol shooting. He held one gun in his right hand, braced his right wrist with his left hand, squinnied along the length of the barrel and fired. Powdery clumps of tree-stuff spread and flew. The sensation of action at a distance was a very agreeable one. Once expected, the loud crash of the firing action did not startle, but rather exhilarated. He varied his practising from day to day. One occasion he would shoot trees, aiming for the dead centre of the trunk. Another day he would wait until a bird settled on a distant branch and then he would take aim at that.

His lieutenants had constructed a massive grid of felled logs which they floated out past the pier. Days of training now involved, it seemed to Polystom, the genuine attempt to drown the men. He occasionally came down to watch, but the antics depressed him. He felt a sick kind of sadness in his gut at it all. Playing at war. He was impatient now for the real thing. He wanted the charade-death to vanish, and real-death to come onto the stage. Was he really eager for death? He couldn't decide. Partly it was a desire to remove himself from this home environment in which Sof and Stet could be so carelessly insolent to him. Surely things would be better on the battlefield. Then he would have actual command, instead of this courtesy title – a courtesy title that invited so much discourtesy from his lieutenants. Or, if not precisely discourtesy, then at least an unquantifiable lack of deference, a something not-right in their manner.

Their twin faces, grinning, as if sharing their secret joke. As if Polystom was the butt of their joke.

The last day of the year arrived, and Polystom held a Year's-End banquet for all his men. On the *ting-ting* of midnight, as the clock marked the transition into Winter Year, everybody cheered. Polystom gave a lengthy speech, not especially coherent, but his men cheered his every sentence. Before dessert was served Polystom was so drunk he couldn't coordinate his spoon, bowl and mouth. Nestor, as discreetly as was possible with a figure sitting at the top table, crept in and helped him away. Carried him like a baby back to his own bed, put him into his pyjamas and left him sleeping. Polystom woke several hours later, into the chilly small hours of a new Winter Year, and vomited copiously, liquidly, all over his bed. The choking, gushing noises brought Nestor through, and servant helped master to the bath-annexe, washed him, dressed him in clean pyjamas and helped him, groaning and limping, to a new bedroom. The following morning he was too ill to leave his bed. Nestor brought him honey-broth at eleven, and he could barely keep that down. But through the open window, the chill fresh air touching his hot face, he heard Stetrus and Sophanes drilling the men in a jog round and round the house. Left *hep* left *hep* left *hep* jump! Left *hep* left *hep* left *hep* jump!

They trained for a further three weeks. Polystom wrote to General Demus requesting embarkation orders, informing the general that the platoon was now ready to report for action. He informed the general that it had not been possible to hire a private balloon-boat, but said that they would be travelling charter to Berthing, and would take military transport from there. The general's aide wrote back, detailing the code of an appropriate transport, the destination on Aelop (the military brass, Polystom realised, tended to use the world's less familiar name in official communication), and the name of a colonel who would meet them on their arrival. Polystom replied with his gratitude, and in a PS asked after the folder, marked with a C, for which they had been searching in his uncle's estate? Had they found it, in the end?

Polystom received no reply to this communication.

'We'll be needing some rifles for the men,' drawled Stet over dinner one evening.

'The army doesn't' said Polystom, meaning to go on *provide the rifles itself?* But that was ridiculous, of course it was. 'Have any particularly favoured models?' he concluded lamely.

'They need to be able to fire bullets,' said Sof. A slight pause, and both men chortled in unison.

Polystom ordered fifty rifles from the supplier of his pistols. There was no point in skimping on such a thing. With an order so large, the gunsmith sent a partner down by company plane. Polystom, his two lieutenants and the gunsmith took lunch together, looking through a calf-bound catalogue book. The lieutenants, both smoking and gesturing vaguely, systematically chose the most expensive of everything; the most expensive barrels; the most expensive bayonets; the priciest stock. 'We'll need several thousand rounds of ammunition for each of them,' said Sof. Polystom, a wealthy man, raised to regard the particulars of money as vulgarity, blenched a little. Each rifle was worth, in money terms, ten men. The price of each weapon could feed a servant for a year or more. And this expense was merely laid over the top of all the other expenses, all the enormous expenses accumulated during the months of this military experiment.

Later, drunker, laughing genuinely at a joke told by Stet, he felt less bitter about the transaction. Best that the men be properly armed. No point in going to all this bother and then giving the men inferior weaponry. Stet, standing on a chair in the garden, was doing the characters in his joke in different voices. Sof had wet his face with tears by laughing so hard. The gunsmith's agent was nodding and beaming. *And then the ghost is there*, said Stet, barely able to get the words out between his own volleys and detonations of laughter, *and he's holding a sock! A sock! And the ghost says*, slipping up an octave to do the ghost-voice, *what's this for? And the butler replies*, dropping deep and gravely, *you put that over your foot. Your foot? says the ghost. What's a foot?* And so on.

And so on.

The guns arrived within the fortnight. So did the first heavy snowfall of the Winter Year. The two lieutenants, as inseparable as twins, forced the men out, uniformed but bootless, marching and hopping through the snow. Left *hep* left *hep* left *hep* jump! Left *hep* left *hep* left *hep* jump!

At lunch, Polystom decided to call in at the barracks, to show his face amongst his men. He did so occasionally; showing his face. But this day he paused at the door, where he could see that inside the men were all treating themselves after their march: buckets of waters heating on the central wood-oven, towels soaked and wrapped around their red-blue feet. He decided not to go in. They would have had to stand to attention, and that would have been extremely uncomfortable for them.

The snow fell, stopped, fell, stopped, making the daylight grey and filling the landscape. Polystom, in uniform, overcoat, scarf, gloves, hat, three pairs of silk socks beneath his boots, wandered the woods. His woods.

His entire estate looked austere in the snow: beautiful.

Colours had been wiped away, until only black, blue and white remained. The trunks of the trees have darkened in contrast to the white brilliance of the snowfall. Polystom walked with a slow, careful, snow-walker's tread; cracking the surface of the frost-drifts like opening a new pot of coffee, and then sinking in up to his calf. His figure vanished into the space between the trees, leaving a crocodile of oval shadows lined behind him over to the white lawn, like two columns of dark tortoises imperfectly synchronised.

He had been suffering from nightmares for weeks now.

Out in the forest, where the air was cold enough to scrape his lungs, where frost had furred the pine-needles with a white imitation mould, he felt himself escaping the horror of the nightmares. He had been too ashamed to tell anybody. Of his many anxieties, one of the more acute was the fear that his saggy-eyed exhaustion would give away the fact that he had not slept properly for such a long time. But his two lieutenants seemed oblivious to his haggardness. 'Of course,' they confided, over beef shreds in wine and glazed root mash, after another day's unrelenting training in the icy weather. 'They'll find no snow on the Mudworld. No, it's a deal hotter than that. But it's always worth toughening them up.'

Toughening them up.

His nightmares concerned the flayed men. The curious thing, he thought to himself, was that they had taken such a long time to manifest themselves. The experience itself, watching the execution in the grounds of his dead uncle's estate, had been unpleasant. Of course it was unpleasant. But he had sat through it, believing his duty required as much. And afterwards he had told himself that it hadn't been so bad, drinking with the general and his aides back at the house, laughing at the experience. We got *under their skin*, laughed the general. Justice is more than *skin-deep*, he said. All of them laughing a little over-loud, drinking a little more than they otherwise would. Polystom's dreams that night had been unfocused, menacing but not specific. The following day he had flown himself back home, and that night in his own bed he had slept deeply. For weeks, he succeeding in blotting the spectacle of two flayed men out of his head. Sophanes and Stetrus had arrived, and the various other distractions of assembling his platoon had crowded other thoughts away. There had been a single night when he had woken moist with sweat from a dream of being pursued. In the dream he had not looked behind himself at his pursuers, but with the logic of dreams he had not needed to because he had known that it was the flayed men who were after him. He woke, gasping, his bedding in a ruckled heap where his flailing arms and legs had messed it up. It had taken him three tall glasses of wheat whisky to settle his nerves. He had settled to sleep again nervously, tentatively, like a man who has been shocked by a bare wire reaching out to touch it again to see whether he had indeed switched the thing off now. But this second sleep had been blissful, blank, and Polystom had woken late in the morning. The following night was alright, and the night after that too. He had congratulated himself that he was past the experience.

Then, for no reason apparent to him, the nightmares had come flocking down to him. In the first week of the Winter Year, training almost completed, the prospect – exciting – of embarkation, and out of the mauve (or out of the purple-black of the night sky) came the phantoms of the flayed men to disturb his sleep. The dreams were more or less the same, with subtle variations that deepened the horror. He was on a flat, treeless plain. The two men, flayed red and purple, rose out of the ground and came towards him. Their legs and torso were as Polystom remembered them from the execution, glistening wetly with scarlet, pulsing, marshy, livid and vivid, the inner skin turned out to the world. But in his dream the flaying had extended further, each face ripped clear of skin, each halfway to skull, the pouched and streaming redness running up to eyelidless eyes that stared and stared and swivelled and stared. The arms were flayed too, blood oozing up on the grainy muscles, like red sweat. They held their arms towards him, and he shrieked and ran, ran as fast as he could except that he could not take his eyes off the grisly pursuers, he was running with his head over his own shoulder. And they came after him effortlessly, red gleaming legs covering the ground in great scything motions. Their white teeth. And he was running, sometimes over a flat surface, sometimes over cobbles like a million bubbles turned to stone. One of them, grinning all the time, reached his flayed arm towards him, and the arms seemed to be stretching like red elastic, until the bony fingers clasp around Polystom's ankle and he felt himself falling.

Waking up.

Sometimes, this was the moment Polystom woke. Sometimes, however, the dream would extend, and both flayed men would lay hold of his legs, two hands to each ankle, and yank his legs in disparate directions. These dreams were the worst, because no matter how Polystom kicked and writhed he had the unshakeable sense that he was about to be split in two like a green twig.

One time he woke to discover he had pissed himself as he slept, and his sheets were cold and oily with it. Another time he woke so wet with sweat that he thought he had pissed himself again, until he realised there was no smell of urine. Often he was screaming as he slept, and bucking about, which would summon Nestor, and Polystom would wake to see his butler over him, concern in his face, holding his shoulders down against the mattress.

The afterimage, when awake, lacked the immediacy of terror that he felt in the dreams, but had its own horrors. The *idea* of it, of being flayed alive, was more insidiously awful than the reality. The reality was just a painful death, that was all; but the *idea* was the bearing of everything that was inside to the outside world. The idea was replacing the skin of ordinary sensation, of caresses and sex, with a membrane dedicated only to pain. Everything that a person hid away inside themselves flipped out, displayed; for everybody to see. It made his guts clench to think of it.

The nightmares settled into a pattern. He had them two nights running, and then slept fitfully though nightmare-free for a third. Then another two nights of nightmare. He called his doctor, who attended, but who could offer him nothing more than a sleeping tablet. Polystom took the tablet, and slept eleven hours, waking feeling sluggish and sticky with sweat. He had no memory of a nightmare, but his sheets were cast off his bed in a heap, and there was a pungent smell of piss. He took no more tablets.

His sleep had been disturbed before. After Beeswing's death, for instance, he had woken throughout the night for weeks. But there had been no nightmares as such. These bad dreams he was experiencing now – they were so severe they bled into his exhausted waking hours. He watched Stet and Sof parade the men back and forth, and the image kept flashing on his eyes of one of them stripped of skin. Stripped doubly naked.

He was drinking far more than even he had been used to do.

[second leaf]

He had arranged with the Multi Planet Line to have a charter balloon-boat come down to collect himself, his two officers, and his platoon of men. Three first-class berths, fifty in steerage. It had taken some doing. To begin with the agency officer had insisted that the whole party travel to Apolis, on the southern shore of the Middenstead. This would have involved hiring a large boat. 'It's the time delay,' Stom told the agency officer, although a more pressing worry in his mind was the added expense. He was a wealthy man, but there was a limit even to his wealth, and a boat large enough to carry fifty-three plus crew would be expensive. 'We would not be at Apolis in time to catch the next balloon-boat, and would have to wait until the one after that.' 'Docking at a private house,' said the agency officer. 'Even so splendid a house as yours, Steward. It's most irregular. There are insurance complications, should anything go wrong.' Polystom was tired, and reached easily for his anger. 'I'm not prepared to argue this point with you, man,' he snapped, his voice rising almost to a screech. And then, a moment later when he'd controlled himself a little. 'I'm Steward of this world. I order you. I have that power, I feel sure. I'm sure I do. I order it! I am taking a platoon of soldiers, my own, to fight on the Mudworld. Where is your patriotism? Where is your company's patriotism?'

'It's not a question of lack of patriotism,' whined the official, on the other end of the phone. 'We have certain restrictions, pertaining to our insurance premiums . . .'

'I undertake to cover you for any loss incurred in collecting us,' said Polystom grandly, hoping devoutly that no such expense would be necessary. 'I expect the boat to land on the flat ground behind my house the day after tomorrow.'

They held a passing out parade two days later: a grand business, all uniforms clean and all buttons polished, the troop presenting arms and marching round and round the house. There was nobody to see it but a gaggle of ooh-ing and aah-ing servants, but Polystom felt a certain pride swell in his chest nonetheless. He had the lieutenants assemble the men behind the house, standing to attention, whilst they waited for the balloon-boat to come down. The [? (so)?] . . . [eleven characters missing] . . . from the clear sky. Snow lay in uneven stripes over the lawn, where . . . [six characters missing] . . . in the fragile patterning of its decay. When . . .

. . . [never]

. . . [surely, with]

. . . [eyes upwards

. . .

[Even]tually the balloon-boat was visible in the sky. It swelled, slowly, as it sank through the atmosphere. It was a passenger liner, not one of the super-carriers that ferried cargo along with the people, and . . . [eleven characters missing] . . . [B]ut despite this, it was a huge thing. It lowered itself down until the curve of its green-cloth belly blotted out the moon and filled the sky over the back of the house. Its whirring props growled enormously; their turrets angled down, sucking the buoyant body down through the air. It came down steadily, swelling, growing, the house-sized compartment underneath the balloon coming close enough for people to be visible at the portholes, the whole mass of the craft sinking sinking slowly, slowly, until the props were level with the assembled people throwing their hair back in the force of wind they threw off, pushing their clothes back against their bodies so that the contours of their legs, torsos, arms were sculpted. Then the bottom of the great ship kissed the turf, wobbled, and settled; and the propellers died away.

The enormous balloon roofed the garden. Everybody was in shade.

Traps opened and crewmen leapt out with tether ropes. But there was no ceremony, no carpet laid out. Instead a crewman hurried over to the assembled soldiers, stopped at Sof, was directed onwards, and came at last to Polystom. 'Sir?' he called. 'Can we get everybody aboard as quickly as possible. Our captain is eager to get on.'

'Certainly,' said Polystom.

He walked, a little stiffly, over to the opened hatch and clambered inside. One of the men, once a fisherman called Hath, followed with his luggage. Then came the men themselves, stepping smartly through and in, with Sof and Stet following behind, shouting at them to hurry themselves along. The crewman showed Polystom his quarters. 'I want a view of the take-off,' Stom said. 'This way, colonel,' said the crewman. Stom didn't bother correcting him.

He came through little metal corridors to a more spacious bar at the front of the capsule; one hundred and eighty degrees of window, glazed in a chevron bulge, gave panoramic views. A carpeted expanse of floor, dotted with tables and settees, lead back to a broad bar. A dozen or so passengers, all in mufti, were lounging, drinking, chatting. Two or three were standing at the rail by the window, looking out at Stom's house. There were rails on the ceiling too.

The lower array of propellers could be seen, idle, on either side of this viewport, but the great green-canvas ceiling that bellied out above hid the upper array. It was these props, angled upward, that now ticked and roared to life, their blades whirring to grey dials, the pitch of the engine noise rising to a scream, then a whistle. With a barely perceptible wobble the balloon-boat left the ground.

Polystom collected a drink, a large blackberry whisky, and went over to the rail at the fore of the bar. Already his house was toy-like below him. The ruffled cloth of the Middenstead. The individual strands of trees still visible in the carpet of the forest. One swig of the burning drink, and the woodland shrank to a smooth uninter-rupted green, and the Middenstead contracted, as if a speeded-up drought were pulling the shoreline in and in like a tightening noose of cord.

'Sir,' said Stetrus, appearing at his right hand as if from nowhere. The lieutenant was holding a glass of wine.

'Stetrus,' said Polystom. 'The men settled in?'

Sophanes was at the bar, fussing over his drink. His voice, boomingly insistent. 'I specifically said I didn't *want* ice. Pour it again.'

'We dished out the battle ranks yesterday, sir,' Stet was saying. 'Your man, the Orchard-Gardner, Crius. He's going to be sergeant. He's a good sort. Reliable. And Droy, he'll be corporal. Your batman you already know; Sof and I chose our batmen weeks ago. That's everybody, I think.'

'Medic?' asked Polystom, only half his mind on the conversation, his eye snagged by the diminishing scene below him. The curve of the horizon was visible now, and the purple-blue sky beyond.

'That's not a ranking position,' said Stet. When Polystom looked at him, he smiled. 'Faba's picked up a few tricks during training. He can stay as platoon medic.'

Sof joined them. 'Here's to your lovely planet, Captain,' he said, raising his glass. 'And to your hospitality, putting us up for all those weeks.'

'Not at all,' murmured Polystom.

It took a little time to get acclimatised to the microgravity of interplanetary flight. The balloon-boat interior was designed with handholds on all surfaces, and food and drink was served in containers to prevent unnecessary mess. If left alone, objects tended to drift in the direction of Enting, the direction they were leaving behind; but it took almost no effort to leap and sail through the air. At exactly the neutral point on the way to Berthing, they were told, the planetary microgravity would cancel itself out; but there was always the slight tug of the sun, which meant that genuine weightlessness would be experienced sooner than that. The experience of most travellers was that they adapted extremely quickly to the weightlessness. 'After all,' said the captain, in the middle of a conversation halfway into the flight, 'we were all mostly weightless once – in our maternal wombs!'

Polystom smiled, nodded. He did not feel comfortable.

The captain introduced himself the second day of travel, a smooth-mannered man with an oily, shiny face. 'Delighted and honoured,' he said. 'Captain, lieutenant, lieutenant. Dine with me? Later this evening? Excellent, excellent.' He bowed, slightly. 'I must say it's a proud voyage. Multi Planet Line is honoured to be doing our bit for the war. A small bit, I know.'

'And one,' said Sof, who was quite drunk, 'for which you're being well paid.'

The captain smiled, ignored the comment. 'I was in the Flying Corps, myself,' he said. 'Before taking up this civilian posting.' He laughed, as if he had said something funny.

The two lieutenants' manner towards him changed at once. 'Really?' said Stet, leaning forward. 'Flying Corps?'

They were all of them in the bar, seat-belted round a low table.

Polystom had been trying to reread a volume of Phanicles until his lieutenants had joined him. Now the captain lowered himself gingerly onto the settee, making the party four. A barman appeared almost at once, with a sealed-lid glass of white wine. Evidently his crew knew what their captain liked to drink without having to be told.

'Second biplane command,' murmured the captain.

'The second,' said Sof, and whistled. 'You were at the Sink?'

'I was,' said the captain.

There was a short silence. Polystom cursed himself silently that he didn't know which campaign, of the many there had been on the Mudworld, the Sink related to. He couldn't think of a way of asking.

'I crashed there, actually. *That* was one time,' and the captain laughed his strange, forced-jollity laugh again, 'one time when I was grateful for the mud. Cushioned the blow, though I did break both my shins.'

'Ouch!' sang Sof, raising his glass. 'Ouch ouch!'

'Indeed,' said the captain.

The three men fell to reminiscing about the Sink, about the tactics, about the casualty rate, about the knack the insurgents had of burying themselves into the mud to emerge at inconvenient moments. They laughed. They clicked glasses together as smartly as an officer might click heels.

Polystom smiled, and nodded, and interjected comments once or twice, but as always he felt almost entirely excluded. After ten minutes or so he excused himself, and went to the lavartoire, even though he felt no physical need to go. He belted himself onto the commode, pressing his forehead against the wall where the thrum and vibration passed into his skull, into the depths of his brain. It was soothing. It was like the sound on the other side of silence.

Eventually he returned to the bar, but instead of joining the guffawing, shoulder-slapping party of three around their table he ordered another drink from the bar and pulled himself along by hand-holds to the rail by the observation window. They didn't seem to miss him. Outside it was the eternal day of interplanetary space. The violet shade of the all-encompassing sky. Away to his left and right the lower array of props carved out their moon-like silver circles. Steep-jacks had fitted high-sky propellers, and now they hauled the boat sunward. Polystom's homeworld seemed to have rushed away behind them, visible now only from the extreme left of the observation rail as a distinct half-circle. Before the boat was only sky, and the sun glowing white, like a beacon. They were not aimed directly at the sun, and in fact their passage was taking them almost forty degrees away from it, so that it gleamed well over to the right of the panoramic window. They were to dock at Kaspian, and then to fly on to Berthing, where Polystom would disembark his men and liase with military transport. Only the military flew to the Mudworld now. Or flew from it. Although, of course, the assassins somehow made their way from it as well. Polystom still marvelled that two men had been able to make their way off that world and through space to his uncle's moon. Human ingenuity was a wonderful thing.

The balloon-boat captain insisted on giving the party of three officers the grand tour. They trailed through the metal corridors, and rode up in a rectangular elevator for an awkward two minutes, as the four men stood inches from one another, in silence. Then the lift settled, and the doors opened. 'Here is the main cabin,' said the captain, holding his arm straight out before him.

'Marvellous,' murmured Stet, lighting a cigarette.

The cabin was as large as the bar, and with more extensive windows. In the middle of the space were several consoles, metal sheets pimpled with bolts, levers and dials, a blue-uniformed crewman belted to each, monitoring it intently. A phonebox-sized case stood, unattended, in the dead centre of the room. But the captain was more interested in the view, leading his guests over to the front.

The cabin was in the middle of the top tiers, perched above the enormous belly of green. Like the billowing skirt of a giantess green cloth stretched away in all directions below them, and to their left and right the banks of huge propellers were clearly visible. Where . . .

[. . . violet-mauve, and]

[. . . nevertheless (?dialogue?)]

[. . . if]

[. . .]

[. . . (')that coin-sized object there?' The captain was pointing. That's Kaspian. That's our next destination.'

'Extraordinary accuracy, really,' said Sof. 'Is it all your own judgment?'

'No, no,' said the Captain, turning and indicating the six-foot tall metal box in the middle of the control space. 'We rely quite heavily on our Computational Device. This is its terminal.'

'You carry a Computational Device aboard this balloon-boat?' said Polystom. 'How marvellous.'

'All the larger boats carry one now. It's amazing the difference it makes. And amazing how far these machines have come in the – what is it – fifty years, since they were first developed? The main body of our own CD is in a ballast section of the balloon itself, but it feeds through to this relay, and we can work out any amount of complex mathematical and other material upon it.'

Polystom had half a mind to say *my uncle invented this device you know*, but that would have been mere bragging, and he resisted the urge.

Talk of Computational Devices preoccupied the dinnertime conversation as well. The captain, over a plate of vinegarised eel-heads accompanied by split-roasted parsnips, expanded royally on the enormous benefits the devices had made to interplanetary transport. 'Revol*u*tionised it,' he said, lifting his goblet of sour wine. 'Simply revolutionised it. We can now calculate orbits, free-forms, trajectories, optimum fuel-use, everything – we can calculate it all in moments – literally moments. The sheer speed of computation is extraordinary.'

'Jumped-up counting box,' said Stet, who had eaten perhaps a quarter of his meal and was now smoking, despite Polystom's polite coughs of annoyance. Stet had to keep the cigarette in constant motion, or the smoke accumulated around the top and extinguished it. This meant that he dispersed the smoke in a wide swathe around him.

'Oh no, *much* more than that – much more,' said the captain, earnestly. 'In the early days, perhaps that's all these devices could do. But now! Why, some of them are as smart as a human! As smart as a servant, certainly.'

'This,' said Sof, whose appetite was healthier than his lieutenant-comrade's, and who was helping himself to a second portion of the eel, 'this is what I don't understand. These machines are clever as a servant, yes?'

'At least.'

'So why not just buy a servant? As I understand it, the Computational Devices are terribly expensive, and really quite large.'

'Enormous,' said Stet, smoke dribbling from his mouth like the ghost of vomit.

'So they're enormously expensive, and enormously large – which means, I daresay, unwieldy. So where's the advantage? A servant is cheaper. Buy a very clever servant.'

Polystom smiled weakly.

'Oho,' said the captain, jovially. 'You're being deliberately obtuse, I think! The things these Devices can do – no servant could achieve it! The speed and intricacy of calculation! More, they can be *written* to do all sorts of wonders.'

'I'm sorry?' said Stet, a little over-loudly. 'What?'

'Written – it's a technical term, lieutenant,' said the captain, with fatuous patronage. 'One of the things a modern balloon-boat captain must know about! Think of these Computational Devices as sheets of paper. This is how I explain it to my children . . . if you'll excuse the impertinence of comparing you to children.'

'Not at all,' drawled Stet.

'Rather accurate,' agreed Sof.

'Then we might think of the Computational Device as a sort of magic paper. In its raw state, each Device is simply valves and crystals, arranged in such as way as to be able to compute very rapidly. But when the Device is *written*, it becomes capable of coherent operation. What operation depends upon the form the writing takes: you've heard of the Master Machine, of course?'

'Can't say I have,' said Sof.

'Loafer,' grumbled Stet.

'Really? It's been in the news a great deal. The biggest Computational Device ever assembled. Cleonicles . . .'

'My uncle,' said Polystom.

The conversation stopped. Everybody looked at Polystom.

'Cleonicles,' he said. 'He was my uncle.'

'In that case,' said the captain, earnestly, 'I'm doubly honoured to have met you! You are the nephew to the great Cleonicles? Extraordinary!'

'Had no idea,' said Stet, dipping his head in a languid salute.

'Go on with what you were saying,' said Stom.

The Captain chuckled, nodded, raised one hand. 'It was nothing – I feel embarrassed to talk about it in front of the inventor's own nephew!'

'I know almost nothing about Computational Devices,' said Stom.

'Well – well – I was only going to mention the Super Device.'

'It was in the newsbooks,' said Stom.

'Exactly so! Ex*actly* so. But the general newsbooks haven't covered the detail. The things this machine is capable of! The incredible *penetration* of its computation.'

'Large, is it?' said Sof.

'Very,' said Stet. 'Huge. Out in space somewhere, because it's so big.'

'No, no, gentlemen,' said the captain. 'I'm sorry to correct you.'

'I could have sworn,' said Stet, absently, examining the glowing tip of his cigarette.

'The original plans were for a weightless construction,' said the captain. 'It would have been suspended in the sky, of course. But the problems were with power source. So the machine was built on Aelop.'

Both lieutenants sat forward.

'Really?'

'On the Mudworld?'

'Didn't you know?' said the captain, looking flustered for the first time. 'I do hope I'm not being indiscreet – I thought it was well known. The decision to locate it there was well enough reported in the technical press at the time of construction – this would be, what? Fifteen years ago now?' He looked to Polystom, appealing for confirmation, but Stom had no more idea than anybody else.

'Well,' said Stet.

'So,' said Sof.

'Perhaps it has become more secret,' said the captain, his face flushing in a dappled pattern of red. 'It's true that it *isn't* really reported nowadays. But it was in the technical press at the time. It was the closeness of the sun which helped power the thing – the machine's very large and takes a deal of power. And then there were certain crystal lattices, underneath the surface of the world, that were useful for confirmation in the establishing of the Devices.'

'This was before the place turned into the Mudworld?' asked Sof.

'Before the war?' said the captain. 'Yes, yes. Although the one followed closely on the other, I believe.'

'The servants didn't like having the machine there, I suppose.'

'But what a machine!' said the captain. 'A Computational Device, large as a mountain – buried under the ground. Written by experts – including, sir, your esteemed uncle. By the most brilliant men in the System! Who knows what marvellous things it has achieved.'

'Is it still there?' asked Polystom.

'There?'

'Working, I mean? Not damaged by the war?'

'No, I don't think so. I mean, yes, it's still there. It may be,' said the captain, nodding slowly at his own surmise, 'that the secrecy is part of the war effort. Perhaps the machine has a role in the war.'

'First I've heard of it,' snorted Stet.

But the dessert had arrived; blackberries stuffed with sweet-olives, and drizzled over with wine-cream. The conversation moved elsewhere.

Sof and Stet settled easily into the routines of the ship, making friends with the civilian passengers. Polystom did not have that knack. He spent long hours in the bar by himself, reading and gazing into space, whilst one or both of his lieutenants chortled and heehawed with wealthy wives and mousy husbands.

'A skywhal!' cooed somebody one afternoon, and the occupants of the bar all made their way to the windows, drinks in hand. All save Polystom, who stayed back, and poured himself more drink. He thought of the stinking carcass of the skywhal on his uncle's estate. That thought, by an inevitable process of association, brought to mind the flayed man. The figure still haunted his dreams, monstrous ghost.

A week of further travel, with Polystom feeling increasingly alienated from his fellow passengers, whilst his two lieutenants formed a widening circle of friends, and the boat slipped into orbit around Kaspian.

'We stop here,' the captain announced, 'for two days. Please be sure to be back aboard within that time, if you require passage to Berthing.'

They circled Kaspian for hours; beneath them lay its frayed continents and cloud-speckled seas. Finally the balloon-boat began its descent, the rotors tugging against its anti-weight, against its buoyant desire not to sink into the thicker air at the bottom of the gravity well. Cloud swirled around the observation window, veiling it completely for several minutes, and then clearing suddenly to reveal the landscape around Stahlstadt: a few scraps of green parkland, the squares and squares of suburban houses and their gardens, but directly below them the splendour of the city itself – the largest conurbation in the System. Silver threads, rail-lines, stretched taut south, east, north-east, north-west, and the city clustered along those lines in each direction, like a giant splashmark. As they came lower more detail was revealed. The passengers crowding round the observation rail clapped and cooed with happiness. There were the famous triple-towers, throwing long shadows over the complex of esplanades. It was even possible to make out the miniature bristles on these broad stone areas: people! There was the Prince's Palace! There – there – the bisected dome of the Library, the tiered shell-shaped erection of the new opera house. The balloon-boat swung lower, and Polystom found himself lost in his own thoughts, distanced from the excitement of his fellow passengers. To him the city looked oddly naked. It looked like the insides of some electrical device, with valves and juts and spars in some complex arrangement, the roads linking them gleaming grey in the light like solder. Everything displayed, as if some machine had had its cover ripped away. It looked, somehow, vulnerable.

They stopped two days and one night at Stahlstadt. For many of the passengers it was the highlight of the trip; the opportunity to sightsee in the System capital. Even the two lieutenants wandered out, and for the single evening of their stay Stom, on their advice, allowed the men a furlough. But he himself stayed on board ship the whole time. He had seen Stahlstadt before, several times, he said. In fact, the shock of having a full gravity's weight again, after a week of microgravity, depressed him. He spent the first day in bed, where even turning over made him feel exhausted. By the second day he felt as if he had a little more strength, but he was relieved when the balloon-boat lifted off and he returned to microgravity.

The journey to Berthing was five days more, and there the balloon-boat voyage ended. Stom was met at the broad stone-slab airport by a military subaltern. It was hot. The sun looked bloated with fire and light, larger than it should be. The hills around Berthing Main Airport were grass-covered, but on an enormous scale, the green enormity of them sweeping up and up. Polystom found that oppressive too. He was, in truth, hungover, and content to stay in the shade of one of the balloon-boat hangars whilst his lieutenants unloaded the men and signed-in the company. Berthing's gravity was actually a little less than Enting's, but after weeks of microgravity it felt abominably heavy to Polystom. He had his batman bring him a chair, and then he sat in the sunshine, underneath the unpleasantly huge architecture of the hangar, gazing up at the seemingly neverending green sweep of the hills.

'We'll put you on a military transport tomorrow, Captain,' said the subaltern. 'I'm not giving anything away when I say that there's a push coming, and your men will be very useful.'

'Splendid,' said Polystom, sourly.

He slept badly, kept awake first by the weight of his own chest, and then – when exhaustion sank him into sleep in the small hours – he woke again with another nightmare of the flayed man. He was grateful when he was hurried onto a sleek-lined military transport that buzzed and lifted away from the world. Microgravity returned him to a good mood, like an addict getting a hit of his necessary substance.

They flew sunwards, the observation portals of the military craft occupied by stronger and stronger light hourly, or so it seemed. Stet and Sof, sensing their captain's grumpiness, had gotten into the habit of giving him a deal of space. But without civilian passengers to chat to and impress, they too became grumpy. They took out their bad tempers on the men, shouting at them and making them clean their kit over and over until it gleamed with a weary brilliance.

The journey took three and a half days. Finally the Mudworld itself came into view: a dull-coloured blob, then a whole sphere. The landscape was divided between caps of blue-green at north and south (seas, said the pilot officer, the polar seas), and a broad band of brown at the equator. The whole was so covered with cloud that the surface only showed through in the torn-cloth gaps of the white cover. As they passed the nightside flickers of what Stom took to be lightning gleamed, like a torch flicked on-off under a bedsheet. They swung round, twenty minutes later, and the sunlight dazzled from the whiteness.

'Hot down there,' was what the pilot said.

[third leaf]

It was very hot. Polystom and his troop unloaded at a military balloon-boat facility, and spent three days acclimatising to the new gravity. The Mudworld was a only little larger than the moon of Enting, so its gravity was not so oppressive as either Kaspian or Berthing. After a day Polystom was walking around, feeling fairly comfortable.

The embarkation camp was not architecturally very attractive. Pathways of stone slabs had been laid over the ground in a zigzag pattern, but the mud was visible beneath. If sunshine occupied the sky for any length of time this mud dried to a stony hardness, but rain fell frequently and hard upon the little world and this turned the mud into brown sludge very quickly. The buildings were stacked blocks of stone, bolted together: boxy hangars, inside which partitions were fixed into the floor. Men marched and drilled up and down the central esplanade, stomping along in time to the shouting of a sergeant or a lieutenant.

His first evening on the new world, his shirt dark and smelly with his own sweat, Polystom had dinner with a fellow captain: a wide-faced man ten years older than Stom was himself. 'Captain Parocles,' he said, introducing himself. 'My boys have been waiting for your boys. I think Command have something special in mind for the two of us.'

'Really?' said Polystom. He had spent the day groaning under his new weight, and had given no thought to the thought of battle. But, he told himself hopefully, that's why they had come all this way. That was why he was here, when all was said and done.

'Oh yes. There's a big assault underway. Colonel Thakos will be popping down here tomorrow morning to fill us in. But I think we'll see some action soon enough.'

'You've been here a while?'

'Best part,' said Parocles, beaming, 'of a year.'

'Hard fighting?'

'Oh, very.'

Polystom fell asleep that night drunk; when he bolted awake, sitting up sweat-washed, with the flayed man still vivid in his thoughts from the nightmare he had been having, it was almost dawn. He congratulated himself on getting most of a night of sleep.

He washed in cold water, and went outside. The sun was only just up, but already it was warm. Polystom wandered to the outskirts of the embarkation camp, and climbed a low thin-grassed hill. From the top he could look east to the rising sun, north, west where the shadows were long. The landscape was bleak: brown, rising and swelling but pitted with meteoritic craters that Polystom realised, his heart hurrying with excitement, must have been caused by shellfire.

At breakfast, which he took with Captain Parocles, they were joined by a colonel from Command. 'Good to meet you, captain,' he said, shaking Polystom's hand. 'Have your boys been here long?'

'This is our second day.'

'Acclimatised to the gravity?'

'Pretty much, I think.'

'And the heat? It's hot, though, ain't it?'

The two captains agreed, smiling, that it was hot. The colonel leant in towards Polystom and said to him, in a low pleasant voice, 'you ought to call me "sir" you know. Not that it bothers me overmuch.' He stood up straight. 'Breakfast!'

As their food was served to them, the colonel gave them their orders. 'Day after tomorrow,' he said. 'There's a mountain fifty miles south of here: a very important strategic site. Now, a number of ridges run out from this mountain, and they're pretty strategically important too. There's been some fierce fighting down there, I can tell you. The enemy has pushed in a deal of its force, and we're aiming to break them there.'

Polystom, his mouth full of apricot bread, nodded. *Break them there.* It was exciting to have the force, the focus of military expedition, stated so nakedly.

'You two, my dear captains: we'll run you down there, and day after tomorrow we'd like you to get stuck in. Alright?'

'Alright,' the two men said, together.

In fact it was three days before the transports arrived: enormous canalboat-shaped vans, running on vast swollen rubber wheels that were taller than the van itself. 'To enable it,' said Stet, informing Polystom, 'to run over the mud, you see.' Three of these great buses were required to ship all of Polystom's men and all of Parocles'.

The fifty-mile journey took over four hours. Polystom, his spirits unusually elevated, chatted with Stet and Sof. 'It's smooth enough, this mode of travel,' he said.

'Ought to be,' said Sof. 'The wheels are soggy enough.'

Pressing his face to the window, he could see the mud churning into the air behind him. Clouds darkened the sky, and rain started spotting against the glass. In moments it was lashing down, covering the window in writhing strands of water. 'Weather seems changeable here.'

'It most certainly is that,' said Stet.

'So,' Polystom said to his lieutenants. 'The company's first engagement. How do you think we'll do?'

'It's a *little* harsh of Command,' said Sof, pursing his lips. 'To put us into combat alongside a battle-hardened troop. I think so, anyway. Parocles' men have a head start on us, so to speak. But I daresay we'll acquit ourselves acceptably. I daresay we will.'

'I'm certain of it,' said Stet. 'Besides,' he added, as the rainclouds cleared away and sunlight sparkled against the glass, 'It's a heavy-armament advance. We'll pound them and pound them with big guns, until they're smashed to strands and threads. Then we'll just walk up and take the site.'

That didn't sound terribly glorious to Polystom. Privately, he hoped for something with a little more glory.

They arrived at the base in the afternoon, and the men were easily and quickly billeted. Polystom himself had his baggage taken into a dugout, timber-pillared and with a rough plaster on the walls, but still evidently a hole under the clay. It wasn't handsome; and when his batman hung a mirror on a hook on the wall he saw that his face was scowling. He rebuked himself for this. It was idiotic to expect hotel accommodation. He was at a battlefront!

He spent an hour walking about. There was a network of trenches, from which doorways led to various dugouts. Men stood to attention as he strolled past. Standing on toes, to look over the lip of the trench, he could see the long ridge they were ordered to capture; the hogsback. 'Isn't it exciting?' he said, addressing an ordinary soldier, and gesturing at the salient, their military objective. 'Tomorrow we'll be up there!'

'Yes sir,' replied the soldier, a slightly wild look in his eyes.

That night Polystom had the jolliest meal with his two lieutenants in all their time together. When enough drink had passed into them all, he became almost confessional. 'You boys know,' he said, 'that I've never been in battle before.'

'You'll do fine sir,' said Stet.

'Absolutely fine.'

Polystom waved their words away. 'Just let me know what to expect.'

'Ask us,' said Stet, 'when there's a *real* battle in prospect. The bombs'll fall over the ridge tomorrow, and pound the enemy into the mud. Anything alive will be . . . well, won't be alive after that.'

'Hurrah!' chimed Sof.

They clinked glasses.

'It'll be a walk,' said Stet,

'A walk through the mud,' said Sof.

That night Polystom slept soundly, with no nightmares about flayed men to wake him up. He was shaken into consciousness after dawn by his batman, and he got out of bed with the thrill in his belly of a child expecting to receive presents on the morning of his birthday.

The attack took place late in the morning. For twenty minutes aircraft droned overhead, and the sounds of muffled explosions drifted on the air, one after another, on and on. 'That looks like quite a severe pounding,' Polystom muttered to his sergeant.

'Yes sir,' said Crius, fervently.

'Not just smoke and noise,' said Polystom, wanting to convince himself as much as anything. 'Real bombing.'

Finally the bombing stopped, and everything fell quiet. Polystom took his revolver from its pouch, and timed off five minutes on his watch. His stomach was tense, burning a little on the inside with the excitement. But there was a faint sensation of sourness at the back of his mind. This would be too easy a first experience of battle. All the defenders on the hogsback would be dead, smashed to scrags of flesh, and all he would be doing would be leading his men on a jog-trot through the mud. Perhaps, he told himself, he would see a more glorious battle some other day.

There was a shout, orders being issued, followed closely by another further down the line. To his right and left, men pulled themselves over the lip of their trenches, Stet and Sof taking their men up there.

Everything was quiet. Polystom sent four men up, and then clambered up after them. The mud was soggy, clutching and sucking at his boots. All clear: he waved up the remaining men from his trench, and hefted the weight of his pistol.

He stood for a moment, looking around. The plain was a dark expanse scored out with thousands of tiny craters, like a turbulent sea frozen in brown. His men, and, further off, the men of Captain Parocles, were drifting forward in a great line. The sky was an untouched pale purple from horizon to horizon. The sun looked swollen, ripe with heat. It stung his eyes. His skin was prickling with sweat. Before him the ground was more or less flat for half a mile, rising sharply to the ridge, the hogsback itself. The indistinct promontory looked as shapeless as a mass of modelling clay pummelled and pummelled by children's hands. Nothing was alive up there, clearly.

It was going to be a hot walk.

'Come along then,' he said to his men. With a sharp sense of insight he realised that he was actually there – he was in the middle of a battle. He had arrived. In the future, he thought, I'll be able to say *I was at the battle of the hogsback*, and fellow military men would nod, and non-military types would look on with awe. He had done it. Pride bubbled in his chest.

It was not easy walking: each step had to be dragged out of the clingy mud, and carefully placed to provide a solid enough pivot for the next step. Polystom marched on for ten minutes, perhaps fifteen, struggling a little to keep pace with the main body of men.

There was a whistling sound, away to the left. One of the men was warbling some song or other. Polystom looked in that direction, annoyed; Sof, or Stet, would, he decided, isolate the fellow after the attack and punish him. On his orders. Just because the march was going well, under a sunny sky, was no reason to ignore discipline. Whoever the whistling man was, he certainly wasn't taking this assault seriously enough.

The whistling stopped with a faint *thud*, as if the whistler had been punched in the stomach. Serve him right. Then somebody to the right started whistling, and there was another thud, and Polystom's eye was distracted by the sight of somebody tumbling backwards out of the line. He had been punched too hard, perhaps. The whistling was reprehensible, but there was no need for excessive violence. The delinquents could be disciplined later, when the assault was over.

Another man started whistling, but had barely started when the thud came and he tripped forward. Two whistles, one on either side, two thuds like knocking on a padded door, *knock, knock*, and two men fell. Sweat was dribbling from Polystom's forehead, where the brim of his hat pressed against the skin. It was dripping a little into his eyes. This place was altogether too hot. Uncomfortable. The men were moving more rapidly now. The whistling seemed everywhere, and more men were falling down. The sun was too bright. Polystom couldn't see properly. And then somebody was screaming, but screaming impossibly, up in the sky, a weird howling that changed in pitch, changed again and then broadened violently into a crashing drumroll.

Away to the right a tall, brown-branched willow appeared from nowhere, hung in the air, and fell away in shreds of dirt.

Everybody was running, sluggishly but earnestly.

Polystom tried to pick up his feet. There was another crashing sound of detonation, and another enormous tuft of mud sprouted and wilted away to the right.

Then, much closer, there was an explosive double compression, *boum-boum*, and Polystom was flattened, flicked over by the force of it. Face to the mud. He couldn't hear properly. His head wobbled, his thoughts scribbling like sunlight on choppy water. Trying to get to his feet, the clay clutching at his legs. He rose up, overbalanced backwards and fell again, the pale mauve of the sky above him. The whole battle had gone eerily silent. There was nothing except a high-pitched sound of birdsong. Bird? No, it was tinnitus, singing inside his head. Trying again to get to his feet. Up, unsteadily. One of his men was in front of him. He could feel the man's grip on his shoulders, see his anxious face right in front of him. He was yelling something, his mouth working vigorously, but Polystom's ears weren't functioning. The man was waving his arms. Waving, and then pushing, pushing him back towards the trenches, go back now, and Polystom, stunned, turned unsteadily and started heaving his steps through the mud. Back in the direction he had come. It was all silent. Epileptic flashes of light blinked in the corner of his eye. A series of ragged lumps of smoke barrelled past. The singing noise in his head rose a tone, a tone and a half, and then popped into muffled sounds.

'. . . on the hogsback,' a voice was yelling behind him. 'They must have heavy guns up there. Get the captain under cover.' Other figures, bent forward, were on the edge of Polystom's vision.

'Get him back to the dugout!' Behind the words was a grumbling sub-bass, the deepest of organ notes, punctuated by crackles and thuds. And it was so hot. Too hot. Sweat was dribbling into his eyes, soaking down his neck, as his legs laboured and laboured through the mud. Polystom saw the wooden pegs that marked the outer edge of the trench, and turned to see who it was had guided him back. He saw the man's face for only a moment.

There was an enormous clatter. The air all around buckled and twisted like a great sheet of steel being crunched up. Sight dissolved to smoke. Polystom felt a smack, a punch, in his gut, and almost at once he was in the air, flying backwards, the world caught in an impossible perspective of vertical horizon and bleaching sunlight, and then with a soggy crunch his shoulder bashed into the back wall of the trench, the rest of his body colliding into the mud a moment later. The next thing Polystom knew he was on the floor of the trench, on his side, winded, panting, the sweat still dribbling into his eyes and over his face. There was a fierce pain in his gut. He had been shot. Shrapnel had penetrated his abdomen. He was going to die.

With a steady sort of panic, a sort of panic that he had never experienced before, cold and intense and terrifying, Polystom pulled himself into a sitting position and started unbuttoning his jacket. He had to see the wound for himself. Men were on either side – 'you alright, sir?' 'Caught one, sir?' – but he had no time for them now. He had to be alone with his wound, alone with his own death. He hauled the jacket off his back, pulled away the tie, and started scrabbling at his shirt buttons, imagining the gaping hole that must be there, the blood-rimmed emptiness, and finally the shirt was off.

He looked down at himself, panting. The skin of his stomach was whole, entire, white, unmarked except for the snail-trail lines of his own sweat. There was a slight redness to one side.

He breathed, breathed. The stomach pulsed in, out.

He looked up at the men who had gathered around him. 'What are you looking at?' he shrieked. 'Man the trench! Are they counter-attacking? The enemy, are they coming?' He pulled his shirt shut over his torso as they scattered.

It was five minutes, fully five minutes, before the panic relaxed sufficiently to allow himself to dress himself again. His jacket, thoroughly muddied, was stiffly recalcitrant as he tried to button it. Finally he tried to stand, like a newborn deer, wobbled, slipped back down, and tried again. His pistol was not in his hand. He must have dropped it out on the battlefield. He needed a pistol. His other one was in his digs. He needed his batman to retrieve it for him. Where was the man? Twisting his head left, right, looking up and down the trench.

Men were tumbling back into the dugout now in ones and twos, and the crashing explosive sounds were still beating out a dull, sodden rhythm in the air.

Twenty minutes later the barrage had ceased. A man helped him, wobbly, along the trench to his hole.

Everything was still, as if there had never been anything but silence and sunshine on this world. Polystom was sitting, his hands trembling slightly, holding a metal, book-shaped whisky flask. He had drained it, but the shivers in his hands hadn't stopped. He was sitting in the door to his digs, watching men come and go along the trench.

A shadow spilled up and embraced him. Sof was standing over him. Or was it Stet? No, it was Sof. 'You alright sir?' he drawled.

Polystom thought of saying something, thought again. Took a deep breath. 'Did you find my batman?' he asked.

'He caught one, sir, I'm sorry to say.'

'Caught one? Dead, you mean?'

'Come inside, sir,' said Sof, helping him to his feet and leading him into the muggy darkness of the room inside. He settled Stom into his chair, and sprawled himself nonchalantly over the edge of the table.

Stom watched him as he fished a cigarette packet from his upper pocket, pulled a white stick from inside, popped it into his mouth and replaced the packet, all with one hand. It was remarkably dextrous. The same hand located the lighter, and placed a glowing dot of red at the end of the cigarette. His eyes had their usual lazy, dreamy look, although there was a red cut, thin as an insect's leg, running up the middle of his forehead, and small marks and bruises on his nose and chin.

'Quite a party, eh, sir?' he said, finally.

'Party,' said Polystom, numbly.

'I'm sure you're just about to ask, sir, so I'll tell you. We lost nineteen, sir, with another seven wounded too badly to fight tomorrow.'

Polystom tried to think of something to say to this, but couldn't. Sof seemed to be in no hurry. He sucked in the smoke, and it poured out of his face, white dribbles from his mouth, his nostrils.

'Is Stet dead?' Polystom asked, his face in his hands.

'Sorry, sir? Didn't catch that?'

'Lieutenant Stetrus,' said Polystom, sitting up properly.

'Stet's fine,' said Sof, sucking in a great lungful of smoke. 'He's sorting out non-commissioned rankings. We lost both sergeant and corporal. Unlucky that.' He exhaled, and the smoke drained out of him. Polystom noticed that it was coming out of the middle of the man's cheek as well as his mouth and nose. A spike of smoke, thrusting out from the exact middle of his cheek, like steam coming out of a boiling kettle.

'What's wrong with your cheek?' he asked.

Sof opened his eyes marginally, his dumb-show for surprise, and put his free hand to his left cheek. Polystom shook his head, and Sof touched his right cheek, fingering the hole there. 'Well well,' he said, getting to his feet and wandering over to the mirror. 'I must have got a bit of scrap metal through there. It's a hole as big as my big finger.' He leaned into the mirror, slipping a finger inside his mouth and poking it out again through the hole in his cheek. There was something obscene about the gesture. 'Will you look at that,' he said, with his mouth full of fingers. He withdrew the hand, and laughed: short, donkey brays. 'That'll spoil the face a little. I'd better have it sewn,' he said, squashing the cigarette under his heel. 'Back in a moment.'

He wandered out.

Polystom's hands were still shaking.

He unbuttoned his jacket and took it off, holding it in front of him. It was completely crusted with heavy, dark-brown mud. It looked as though it had been dipped it in a tub of boiling brown wax and left to dry.

A messenger arrived an hour later, looking for Polystom. 'With your permission, sir,' he said, handing over a black cloth-sealed envelope. Polystom opened it, read the order slip inside, nodded to the messenger, and sat down again. *Assault to recommence. Bombing run in thirty minutes.*

The last thing, the very last thing, he wanted to do in the remnants of the afternoon was to step out again onto the battlefield. He felt sick at the very thought. He felt tired, a sweeping tiredness that came down on his head like a hammer blow. He would curl up in his bunk and sleep; he would sleep all the way through to the next day, and then everything would be finished – the hogsback would be taken, and he could take the next balloon-boat away from the world. He would go home.

He leaned back in his chair.

'Helloë,' said Stet, from the door. 'Was that a command orderly I saw coming and going? Have we orders?'

Polystom stared at him. He wanted to deny that he had received any orders. He knew, in the honeycombed centre of his bones, that he could never fight again. He just couldn't.

'And these,' said Stet, stepping inside the digs, with what struck Polystom as a near-obscene jauntiness, 'must be they. Shouldn't leave them lying around on the table, sir.' He fished up the sheet of paper and read it.

Look, Polystom wanted to say. *Can't we just forget we received this? But his mouth felt gummed up. It's clearly a mistake. Look, I'll send to Command for clarification. Can't we wait? Can't I . . . can't I go home now?*

'Right ho,' said Stet, beaming. 'Ho ha hum. I'll get the men organised.'

I won't be going with you this time, Lieutenant.

'The men,' said Polystom.

'Sir?'

'Casualties were . . . ?'

'Nineteen dead, sir. Five injured. Another half dozen minor injuries, but they'll be alright to fight again.'

'Lieutenant,' said Stom, slowly. His brain didn't seem able to process the words properly. 'Lieutenant . . .'

'Sir?'

'Lieutenant Sof was . . . injured, I think.'

'Oh I *know* sir,' said Stet, with a broad smile. 'I saw him trotting up-trench to get it fixed. Quite a hole, that. Quite a beauty spot, it'll make. There,' he said, angling his head. 'There they go.' Polystom could hear the drone of planes overhead. He found himself on his feet without quite instructing his muscles to stand up. *That's not half an hour! That can't have been half an hour!*

'I'll whip the men up,' said Stet, and slipped easily through the doorway.

Polystom was planning his excuses as he stepped into the trench outside. He felt dazed. There were flickers of light passing in front of his eyes, perfectly transparent globular blotches, like a magnified image of unicellular life, drifting across his line of sight. Like clouds. He had injured his head. He had been blown up, and needed medical attention.

He had changed into his regular jacket and trousers. They were mud-free.

The noise of the bombing died away, as it had done earlier that day, and lieutenants up and down the line shouted the order to advance. Once again, soldiers scrambled over the lips of the trenches and out of the dugouts, and started across the broken ground. Polystom stood motionless in the bottom of the trench, until a passing soldier – one of his own, or another platoon, he didn't know – slapped his shoulder. 'Need a hand up, sir?' And then, like a triggered clockwork toy, he sleepwalked up the steps and out into the exposed territory.

What are you doing? Go back! But there seemed some disconnection between brain and muscles, because he was trudging forward through the mud as before, the sweat was oozing into his eyes as before, and at any moment he expected the explosions to begin, the men to start falling all around him, the concussion to strike him, the metal scraps to come hurtling towards him. He plodded on.

Stupidly, he realised that he hadn't brought his revolver with him. He had had one before, he knew, but he'd dropped it somewhere in the mud. Perhaps it was around here somewhere? Without breaking his stride he started scanning the ground about him. Dead men were inserted into the mud like static swimmers in the static sea: arms propping out, faces, backs, legs at queer angles. A clay-smeared man caught in the middle of some balletic pose, body twisted like the letter M. A leg lay, severed, by itself. Here was a face, a framed oval in the mud with nothing else around it to indicate head or body: like a discarded mask. There was a hand reaching out of the ground, its fingers curled into a miniature model of a winter tree.

You ought to, said his inner voice. You ought to have a weapon, you know.

Who could he send back for his pistol?

But looking around, everybody was so intent on marching onwards. The land was more uphill now, and the going tougher. He didn't feel he could interrupt anybody's procession. Perhaps it didn't matter.

Perhaps nothing mattered. Every second was the last second of his life. He marched on and on, and he knew with every step that he pulled out of the mud that he would never plant that foot. Never lean into it, drawing the other foot out with a squelch. Never swing that forward, and plant it in its turn. And then, the slightest pressure on his shoulder, and it was Stetrus, beaming at him.

'How focused you look sir!' he said. 'Well, you can stop now, sir. We're here.'

Polystom assumed the bombing had been more effective than the first time, and that all the defenders had been eliminated. Stet was of the opinion that the enemy had simply pulled back. 'Their heavy ordnance has vanished,' he pointed out. 'I think they've scarpered.' Either way, the elation at obtaining their objective lifted Polystom's spirits. He felt absurdly, ridiculously happy. He danced, as well as he could, in the mud, lifting each clay-weighted boot with ponderous grace and dancing about.

'Best not let the men see you do that,' said Stet, from behind him. 'Shall we dig in, sir?'

'What?'

'Dig our position in, sir? I'll tell the men to get going on the digging straight away. Until we receive further orders, you know.'

Polystom stood, grinning, dazed.

'Best get to it, I'd say, sir,' Stet went on. 'The sun's hot. Ordnance has softened this mud up some, but it'll dry out hard as stone quick enough. Assuming there's no rain.' He went off.

Polystom looked up at the beautiful blue-mauve sky, at the glorious hot sun. Life! The men were standing around, their rifles across their shoulders, running up into the sky like horns. The lieutenants were going amongst them, barking at them. Shovels were being unpacked, men were leaning into their work, heaving dirt aside.

Polystom sat himself down on the lip of a larger crater, and reached into his breast for his whisky flask. Only when he'd twisted off the cap and lifted it to his mouth did he remember that it was empty.

There was a dead body, half buried in the mud, inches from his hip.

Polystom carefully rescrewed the cap and put the flask away. Then he leant forward a little. The dead body might have been naked, might have been in full dress uniform, it was so caked in mud it was hard to tell. Only its left hand was clear of dirt; that, and its cheek. The top of its head was missing. Its legs were buried in the earth, its torso lying along the contour of the crater, one arm lying forward alongside its face. It looked like it was sleeping, except that its head ended in a shear-line of red. The insides of the cavity were filled with mud also. What most caught Polystom's eye was the quality of the dead flesh, like soft cheese.

In an hour the lieutenants had overseen the construction of a trench along the line of the ridge. The men had been able to dig in a small room at the end of it, bracing the ceiling with some pieces of wood hauled up from the camp at the root of the ridge. 'Captain's dugout, sir,' said Sof.

'What about Captain Parocles?' Polystom asked.

For a fraction of a second, the expression in Sof's eyes was that of a tired parent dealing with an awkward child. Then he smiled, ducked his head forward. 'The captain caught one in the first attack, sir. Weren't you told?'

'No,' said Polystom. 'So I'm in sole command?'

'That's right sir,' said Sof, complaisantly. The stitched wound in his cheek looked like a tiny mouth caught in the act of gobbling a fly. Polystom didn't like the look of it.

Clouds spooled and curled in the sky, and in half an hour all the pale mauve was swallowed up by a greasy, low-slung ceiling of raincloud. A shower splashed abruptly down upon them, lasting five minutes and then passing by.

There were three more brief, intense showers in the next half hour. Polystom sat in his dugout, looking down the line of the newly constructed trench. The men were working on, digging side-lines and excavating quarters for the lieutenants at the end of the thing. According to Stet, nineteen men survived from Parocles' company. Nineteen men and no officers. 'What should I do?' Polystom asked. His euphoria had dissipated entirely, and now he felt disoriented and powerless.

'Absorb them into your platoon, sir,' said Stet, as if it were the most obvious thing in the world.

'Right,' said Polystom.

The men were working energetically, the rain bouncing off their bent backs. A puddle had formed at the foot of the trench, a few feet wide but many yards long. In the rainstorm, splashes made a hundred transient little nipples out of the surface of the water.

Parties of men hurried up and down the ridge, bringing chairs and tables, Polystom's possessions, moveable things from the lower dug-out.

The thought that kept dribbling through Polystom's mind was: Captain Parocles is dead. If one captain is dead, why not the other one? Why not me?

A colonel flew down to them, in a one-man mono-wing miniplane. Its engine could be heard clearly in the damp air. It swooped over the ridge, and circled round, the single wing gawkily long, the pilot's cradle slung underneath in front of a chugging motor. None too skilfully the colonel brought it down to land stickily in the wet mud alongside the new trench.

Polystom received him in his digs.

'I've just come direct from Command,' said the colonel, without so much as introducing himself. 'We want to say, firstly, well done, captain. Taking this ridge is very important. Now we want you to hold it.'

'Hold it,' said Polystom. His own voice sounded funny to him; tinny, somehow. Unreal.

The colonel looked at him. 'I know what you'll ask me,' he said.

'You know,' repeated Polystom.

There was a pause.

'You'll ask,' said the colonel, a little less gung-ho, 'for reinforcements. I can't give you any. There's been a most enormous push by the enemy, west of here.' The colonel stood, and pulled a square of paper from his jacket. It was spattered with dried droplets of mud. Polystom was struck by how much they looked like blood. The square unfolded and unfolded, and the colonel spread out a map covering the whole table. 'You can see,' he said, 'these ridges fan out from this central peak.' Geographical features were marked on the map with numerous straight marks, like laughter lines. 'Four ridges. We hold them all, now that you've taken this. That was why we put such an effort into isolating and then retaking this ridge. You see?'

'Yes,' said Polystom, although he didn't.

'The enemy were trying to defend this ridge,' said the colonel. 'Your ridge. When they realised that was hopeless, they pulled all their forces into an attack on this one here – it's a bigger feature, and it runs directly to the peak. Your ridge is not such a good path to the mountain, because we've mined and wired the further reaches of it. So they're pushing hard to take Camel Ridge, here, do you see?'

'Yes,' said Polystom, again.

'There's no doubt,' said the colonel, folding the map up, 'that the enemy is going all-out to take the peak. All out. They've realised how important it is. How important,' he repeated, fixing Polystom's eyes, 'it is.'

'Yes' Polystom asked, although he had no idea what the significance of the peak was.

'Now, Captain,' said the colonel. 'I'm about to tell you something top secret, *top* secret. Your specific orders, you understand, are to tell nobody. Not even your lieutenants.'

'Alright,' said Polystom.

'You may know of the existence of a Computational Device of enormous size and power on this planet.'

'I'd heard.'

'The peak I'm talking about is the central section. It's part of a naturally occurring crystalline-rock prominence. When the device was being constructed it utilised the natural crystal in its circuitry. This was augmented with valves, of course, and with a series of separate power sources. But the crucial thing is this: the Computational Device is of the *utmost* importance to the war effort, and to the System as a whole. Do you understand? The *utmost* importance. It *cannot be allowed*,' said the Colonel, becoming quite fierce in his emphasis, 'to fall into enemy hands. I *cannot* stress this too greatly. Your orders are to hold this ridge. It may be that the enemy attempt to retake it when their attack on the Camel falters – or maybe they'll try a diversionary attack. But they must not be allowed back up here.'

Polystom, a little wide eyed from the urgency of the colonel, nodded.

'So, Captain,' said the colonel, standing up. 'I'm sorry I can't let you have any reinforcements. I can, however, let you have two guns; your men can pull them up this evening. How many men have you got left, by the way?'

Polystom had no idea. 'Sixty,' he said, randomly.

The colonel's eyes widened. 'I must say,' he said, 'that you and Captain Parocles both deserve especial commendation – you two retook this feature with less than fifty per cent casualties. Superb commanding, sir! S*uperb*. Both of you will be mentioned in the Command Account, sir. One last thing.'

'Yes?'

'I'll need your men to lift my monoplane out of the mud, and help me aloft a little. Just running along, helping me catch the air. The lift of these single wings isn't too good, and in the mud I can't manage enough speed to get airborne.'

'Of course,' said Polystom.

The colonel was outside now. A light drizzle was falling. Pinheads of water started accumulating in myriads upon the colonel's jacket and cap. Polystom relayed the colonel's needs to Stet, and a dozen men were detailed to haul the airplane onto their shoulders and stagger through the mud with it. The last thing the colonel said, from his cockpit, was: 'I feel more confident than I can say, leaving two such distinguished captains in command here.' Then he was off, jerkily transported along the ridge and finally hurled into the sky, where his engine caught and swung him away. It occurred to Polystom that the colonel did not realise that Captain Parocles was dead.

'How many men do I have?' he asked Stet.

'Forty-five, sir,' he said. 'Forty-five and two officers.'

The clouds were breaking up into sudsy patches. Within an hour the sky cleared to reveal evening purple. Two large guns were sledded up the bank of the ridge by teams of straining soldiers, and established (Sof's positioning) at either end of the new trench. The air was thickening with dusk, the sun burning as red as the tip of one of the lieutenant's cigarettes, the atmospheric purples becoming denser and denser. Rations were served, and Polystom ate in his dugout with Stet and Sof.

'What did the colonel fellow say, then, sir?' Stet asked. 'Orders?'

'We're to hold this place. Hold this ridge.'

By the time they had finished eating it was dark outside. Polystom accepted a cigarette from Sof even though he didn't smoke. He lit it, sucked it, pulling on it like a teat, but only swilled the smoke around his mouth. It wasn't very pleasant. But it helped keep the night midges at bay.

Conversation limped along. Inconsequential observations and long silences.

Polystom was in the middle of telling his lieutenants that they needed to find him a new batman, when the air growled with the distant sounds of multiple detonation. Stepping out of the dugout and clambering up the side of the trench, the three of them looked west. The land leading towards the horizon was black, but the sky behind gleamed with red and orange blurs and patches.

'That's west,' said Stet. 'North west.'

Knots of the men were standing about, all eyes in the same direction. *Boum-boum*, and the splashes of vivid colour in the night sky. There was something clothy, to Polystom's ears, about the sounds of the explosions. So muffled by distance as to be almost mellow. But the fire-coloured billows looked fierce enough.

'That's some party going on over there,' observed Sof.

'Are those our bombs?' Polystom asked, his head muggy with smoke. 'Or theirs?'

The two lieutenants looked at him, and then at one another. 'No way to tell, sir,' said Stet.

The distant bombardment continued for several hours. Polystom lay down on his bed, in his dugout, clutching his one remaining pistol to his belly. He had brought up some blackberry brandy, and sipped at it, sipped at it. He couldn't sleep.

The thump, thump, sounded through the walls like the mud's own pulse.

Beeswing was in the room with him. His dead wife, here with him on this terrible planet. She was looking in at the door. Her hand, pale as life, was on the wooden doorjamb, and her beautiful, fragile face was peering round it at him. There was a question in her eyes. The vision was so vivid that Polystom's heartbeat deepened and sped. He pulled himself upright, his pistol in his left hand.

He yelped with surprise.

The ghost did not back away, or vanish into nothingness. The roseate light from Polystom's lamp caught and reflected from the planes of her face, twinkled orange in her eyes. Her lips looked plump, filled with blood. There was the aura of presence about her. He swung his legs round and stood up, dizziness whirring in his head. 'Bees-wing!' he called out.

She looked up, looked into his eyes. The faintest of smiles animated her lips.

'Hello,' she said.

And then a powerful clatter shook the air, and the blackness behind Beeswing's form flashed yellow. There was a crack, a rolling boom, and several coughing hacks of rifle fire. This was much closer than the distant bombardment. Beeswing turned her head, looked over her own shoulder, and then withdrew. She didn't disappear in a puff of ghost-stuff: she slid backwards through the door into the night.

For a moment Polystom stood, motionless, a disconcerting sensation of intensity in his chest. Was this what it was like to encounter the dead? Was it a hallucination? The fact of her having been there hung, somehow, in the air, like perfume.

Then there was a second thunderous explosion, and he lurched forward, through the door and into the night.

Outside a cool drizzle was in the air, and the shadowy forms of men were hurrying up and down the trench. Another explosion threw orange light over the night-sky, blocking out a wedge-shaped shadow in the trench. Stom grabbed the nearest man to him.

'What's going on?'

'Attack, sir.'

'Where are the lieutenants?'

'At the guns, sir.'

Polystom lumbered up the slippery steps and out of the trench. The two big cannons had been hauled up, and were now in position. The nearer of the guns was being rotated by a group of men, shadows in the darkness heaving the great weight round. The air was crackling with the sound of small-arms fire. 'Stet?' yelled Polystom. 'Sof?'

'Sir,' Sof called back.

Polystom was at his side in moments. 'Are we under attack?'

'From the west, sir, we think. Flare!' He shouted the word over his shoulder. 'Now!'

A man raised his arm, and a flare exploded from the end of it. It burnt pale blue phosphorescence into the air, and the landscape around them swept into visibility. Polystom could see Sof's face, glass-pimpled with droplets of rain. The gun's metal arm pointing at the horizon. The gaggle of men hauling at its base. He turned, as the flare sank, and saw the mud at the base of the ridge heaving and squirming with horrible motion. There was a powerful explosion, very close, away on the other side of the ridge, and yellow-orange mixed garishly with the blue. Sof and Polystom flinched simultaneously, drawing their shoulders up in a hunch.

'Where are they firing from?'

'Shoulder cannon, from down below, sir,' grunted Sof, leaning forward. 'You men in the trench,' he bellowed. 'Return fire. Now!'

From the trench below them came the snapping of rifle fire. 'You'd better get back inside your dugout, sir,' Sof gasped, turning back to the cannon. 'Take cover, please sir.'

The blue light was fading, the darkness intensifying around the flare, and with a sputter it was gone. Sight vanished. Polystom was too stunned by the suddenness of the attack, and a little too drunk, to think clearly. He stood, uncertainly, turning left, turning right. As his eyes accustomed themselves to the renewed darkness he could see the darker gash of black against the ground that was the trench, needle-pricked by stuttering light as rifles were discharged. He could make out the massy shape of the gun. The shuffling figures at the base. He wanted to do something, to say something. Was there any point in the men firing into the darkness like that? Surely they couldn't see to hit anything.

He thought of himself seeing his dead wife's face in his dug-out moments earlier. Had he been dreaming? Was he dreaming now?

'Flare!' ordered Sof.

Another fizzing beacon soared pale-blue, and again the seething landscape was laid before him. The blue light gave it a spectral quality. He could make out the individual humps of enemy soldiers making their way up the side of the ridge. He could see, further down, the crouching shapes of combatants peering out of the lower trenches and aiming shoulder-cannon. Then the flare started to fade, the light shrinking back to its source and disappearing.

A moment ago the ghost of his dead wife had said *hello* to him.

With a horrifying jolt immediately behind him, his own cannon fired. It startled Polystom so much he almost fell over. The barrel thrust out a spike of white fire, and everything went dark again. Over the chatter of rifles Polystom could hear the whistle of the shell, and then the distant crash it made. Below them was a splash of white orange light, and the rolling *boum* of impact.

Polystom put his hand to his forehead. His heart was racing. Startled into action by the gun going off unexpectedly. He could hear the muttering of the men at the gun, and then Sof's voice softly, almost coaxingly, 'fire.'

The gun spoke again; and again Polystom flinched. The gun crew scrabbled, the barrel sank a few inches, and there was a wash of heat as the chamber opened.

The gun spoke again, and spoke again. Polystom turned, and turned again, dizzy with the unreality of it. Then the gun at the far end of the trench clattered out a shot, and the nearer gun spoke once more in appalling harmony. Down below them, patches of white fire flurried and died away.

The rain was still ticking gently into Polystom's face.

'Here they come!' shouted somebody.

The big gun spoke again, and by the subliminal illumination of its flame Polystom saw a figure rear up from the mud right in front of him, almost as if it were made of mud itself. The enemy was here. The enemy was upon him. Its head and torso gleamed, brown-shiny, and it was holding a rod or pole of some sort. The light faded quickly and again it was dark. Polystom stood stupefied. Away to his left the flicker of rifle-fire pocked the darkness with little jagged spots of light. Without thinking consciously of what he was doing, Polystom saw that he had raised his own left hand. But that was absurd, because he wasn't left-handed. Except, there it was, his left hand out in front of him, and with a jarring pressure up his arm that hurt his wrist the pistol in his hand discharged, discharged again, and then again. With each shot, the figure before him was strobed standing, lurching back, tumbling away.

The rain was falling with infinite softness.

The clatter of gunfire increased in intensity as the rain died away, making a mechanical echo of the rain-patter. A third flare flew upwards, and once again the landscape was coated with the eerie blue light. Polystom saw figures all around him now, some raising weapons, some shouldering fatter tubes, the enemy was upon them. His men, in the trench and around it, were standing taller, firing as rapidly as they could. Polystom's own left wrist was sore. He swapped the gun into his right hand, raised it, checked that the slot was primed with bullets, and fired. He fired, turned, fired, fired again. The flare-light was dying. The enemy was upon them.

It was inky dark again. Polystom shot bullets into the darkness.

Something whistled past him in the dark, away to the left, briefly making the sort of pure harmonic that shatters wine-glasses. 'Sir!' gasped somebody, at his side. One of the men. 'Sir! Take cover, sir!'

The great guns bellowed. Rifle bullets flew. A pressure on Polystom's elbow drew him to the left. He reached out with his right hand, where the gun weighed against his forearm and wrist, firing once, twice, into the night. 'This way sir!' And then his feet were on the steps going down into the trench. The rain had stopped falling.

At the bottom of the steps he was shuffled through into his dugout. The light made his eyes wince. He sat himself down in his chair. Only then, as his eyes accustomed themselves to the brightness of light, did he realise that he was panting. Excitement? Terror? The soldier who had brought him in was streaked with watery dirt; blood was coming sluggishly out of a wound on the side of his head. His ear seemed clipped, halved, and blood oozed out in visible pulses to run down his cheek and over his shoulder. 'You're shot,' he said.

But the man was already turning away, going out of the door, returning to the battle.

[fourth leaf]

Outside, the sounds of battle sounded clatteringly though the night air. Polystom sat in his chair, his gun in his lap. The barrel was hot, but soon became cold. There was an enormous inertia in his body now; not a tiredness, for he felt he could not sleep under any circumstances. But something that rooted him to the chair.

The staccato of battle slowed, the booming of the guns became more infrequent. It stopped. A silence more strange than the noise settled in the air. Still Polystom sat. Nothing was real, evidently. This silence was more tangible than the gunfire and cannonfire. Nothing was real.

Somebody was at the door.

'Beeswing?' he said.

But it was Stet. He came inside, exhausted-looking, and lit a cigarette. 'We beat them off, sir,' he said. 'But it was a major attack. We might expect another one before dawn.'

'It really happened, then?' Polystom asked.

'Oh yes, sir. Seven dead, and seven wounded. I'd get some sleep, sir. You should be able to manage a few hours.'

He left. Polystom looked at his bed, and hauled himself out of the chair. It took an enormous effort to reach the bed, and to sag onto it. But it wasn't tiredness that weighed his limbs down. Something was wrong.

Perhaps he was stupefied by the unreality of things.

The light was still on. He hadn't the strength to get up again and turn it off.

He lay on the bunk.

Night midges buzzed through the silence. Polystom could not sleep. He turned on his bed to face the wall. Mud. The silence was so intense it seemed to make a high-pitched hum in his ears. He turned again.

It had seemed so vivid, his vision of Beeswing. It had really been as if she were materially present in the room. Some sort of hallucination, possibly. Brought on by the pressure, by the stress of it all. Standing at the threshold. She had said *hello*. Had she been about to come in? Had that been it?

She had been about to come in, to greet him, to embrace him, to tell him something, some message from the other side of death. But the sound of the assault outside had scared her away. It was ridiculous, of course, he told himself, to think in these terms. Clearly, the stress of the situation had overburdened his mind. And yet, he thought, and yet even if she were nothing more than a figment of his heated imagination, it would be good to hear what that figment had to say. What might it have been? *I'm sorry.*

He turned in his bed again, facing the wall.

I'm sorry.

He turned again.

There was a massive explosion, outside in the night air. His heart thumping, Polystom leapt from the bed and rushed to the door. At the threshold there was another violent noise, and heat washed over him. Fires were burning, red and yellow, on the ground at the top of the trench, throwing a sinuous light over everything. Polystom stumbled over a supine body, and tripped, falling onto his knees. As he was getting up he heard the sound of his own big guns returning fire, bashing the night air, crash crash, crash, and then only the voices of his men calling out in the dark.

He took the stairs one step at a time, emerging cautiously from the trench. The fires were still burning, illuminating the scene garishly. 'What's happening?' he called out, querulously. 'You.' A soldier, flat on his belly, was aiming his rifle down the side of the ridge. Polystom, feeling vulnerable in the light, bending over, hurried to him. 'Tell me what's happening.' But he had mistaken a corpse for a live man, mistaken the hunch of its shoulders for the missing head.

He picked up his pace, and ran to the nearer of the two guns. Sof was there, looking through binoculars.

'What's going on?'

'Sir,' said Sof, not removing the binoculars from his face. 'You should be back in the dugout, you know.'

'I want to know what's happening.'

'Petroleum bombs. They explode and throw burning petroleum sludge over everything. There!' he called out, pointing. 'That's the little pig! Down, seventeen, eighteen at the most.'

The gun crew hauled the gun through five degrees, and lowered the barrel an inch. There was a breathy sound high in the air, like a sigh, and then the sound slid down the scale and collided with the mud in a fireworks splatter twenty yards from the gun. Red brightness. Everybody flinched. When Polystom looked up, the ground between him and the detonation was sown with fire, and gobbets of a snot-like burning substance adhered to the metal guard at the front of the gun.

'Take the pig!' shouted Sof. 'Now!'

The gunner hauled on something, and the gun uttered its enormous shout. Polystom put his hands to his ears and shut his eyes, curling up like a child. He felt the heat of the opened chamber as a new shell was inserted, and heard the dialogue between Sof and the gun crew. He had no place here. He should be back in his dugout, safe. 'I think I'll go down again,' he said, but only the first two syllables sounded, the rest of the sentence battered into nothingness by the second eruption of the gun. He turned his back on it all and started scurrying back to the edge of the trench. Back to the safety of his dugout.

There was a great force of heat and pressure behind him, accompanied by the sound of the air and the land being chewed and crunched up. Polystom was on his knees. He had been pushed down. The back of his head stung, as if bitten by an insect. He got unsteadily to his feet, and turned to see the gun covered in fire, snakelike wriggles of flame leaping off every surface. A person-shaped shadow, also wreathed about with fire, danced and kicked in the midst of it all. This burning shadow-figure danced away from the gun, and dived, describing a perfect arc through the air and into the mud. There he wriggled and wriggled, turning over and over, until all the flames were done.

Another sighing sound in the air, over Polystom's head, and away behind him, halfway down the far side of the ridge, there was another great bang. Polystom's own shadow leapt away from him, spotlit by fire light, and wriggling over the ground.

Stom made his way over to the burnt man. By the time he got there the figure wasn't moving. People were shouting. 'The gun!' 'Watch for them from below.' 'Sir! Sir!' Polystom leant over the figure on the ground. He couldn't tell, in the uncertain firelight, whether he was breathing or not.

A soldier was at his side, and then another. 'Where's the medic?' Stom demanded. 'Who's acting doctor?'

'He caught one yesterday, sir,' said, one of the soldiers.

'Are you mine? Or the other fellow's?'

'I'm sorry, sir?'

'Are you *Polystom's* company or *Parocles*?'

'I'm yours, sir. I'm Lamba, sir. I worked in your orchards.'

'Our medic is dead?'

'Yes sir.'

'And what about the medic in Parocles' troop?'

'I don't know, sir. I think he died yesterday too, sir.'

'Is there nobody in this body of men with medical knowledge?'

Another petroleum bomb exploded on the far side of the wrecked gun. Red and white light blossomed. 'Get this man,' Polystom shouted, 'into the trench. Do that now.'

He didn't wait to see his orders followed. Instead he lurched towards the steps, and slid ungainly down them, back into the safety of the trench. 'You,' he said, grabbing the first soldier he could see. 'Fetch me Stet.'

'Sir?' Startled, wide-eyed, in the red light.

'Lieutenant Stetrus – go get him, bring him to me.'

The man scurried off. The burnt body was being brought down the steps. At the base of the trench they laid him in the mud. 'Is he alright?' Polystom demanded.

'Alright, sir?'

'Is he *alive*?'

'Think so, sir.'

Polystom bent over the figure. It was impossible to tell if he was alive or dead. The soldier he had sent off came panting back.

'The lieutenant sends his apologies, sir,' he said. 'But his time is currently—'

His words were broken off by the sound of the one remaining cannon firing. Second later came the sound of its shell detonating, and after that the distant watery sound of men cheering.

Polystom pushed his way along the trench, and up the steps at the far side. 'Stet?' he called, as he made his way over to the gun.

'Sir?' replied Stet. 'We got them sir. *That* was a direct hit.'

'Really?' Polystom said. 'Well done, Stet, well done. Only – Sof, you know . . . dead . . .'

'Here they come again!' bellowed somebody.

At once the popcorn snaps of rifle-fire started up. Stet was very near, his face close up, his hand on Polystom's shoulder. 'You really ought to be in your dugout sir. We wouldn't want you to take any unnecessary risks.'

Polystom made his way back to the trench and down the steps, but instead of going along it he took up a position beside a couple of his men. They were leaning over the lip of the thing, firing their rifles. He peered over. The firelight was still burning from the debris of the petroleum bombs, giving intermittent glimpses of the approaching enemy soldiers. One fact cut through Polystom's dreamy dull-headedness: if those figures got all the way up here, they would kill him.

Kill him.

There were three more attacks that night, and each time Polystom's men beat back the advances. The enemy were attacking up both flanks of the ridge now, Stom's men swapping sides to fire down through the dark. Eventually the burning petroleum sludge died away, but as it did so the dawn lit the eastern horizon, and the indistinct figures of mud-coloured enemy soldiers started to acquire solidity. The big gun could only be swung around with great effort and difficulty, so Stet decided to keep it aimed at the complex of trenches and dugouts at the foot of the feature – the same trenches and dig-outs that Polystom's own men had excavated days before, now occupied by the enemy.

As the night wore on, Polystom became more and more tired. For the first few attacks he leaned over the lip of the trench with the rest of his men, firing his pistol. Later he slipped away, and lay down in his dugout. He fell into and flipped out of sleep intermittently: drowsing until some loud shot or explosion woke him, drifting away again. Finally the attacks died down, and he was able to sleep more deeply.

He dreamed of the flayed man: dancing out of flame, with all his skin burnt away, but the same horrid knots of naked muscles, the same moist-eyed grin. As with his earlier nightmares, the figure stretched his arm out and out and laid hold of Polystom's ankle. Usually he awoke at this point, but for once – fatigued as he was – he didn't. He looked down at the gristle-glistening hand that gripped his ankle, and then looked up at the face of the creature who held him. It had skin again. It had Beeswing's face.

'Hello,' she said.

He awoke, lurching to the left, toppling from the narrow bunk onto the floor. His breath stuttered. He was lying on the floor.

Light was pouring in through the door of his dugout.

He got to his feet, and adjusted his dress as well as he could in his mirror. Then he stepped out, rubbing his eyes in the light.

Bodies lay neatly along the side at the bottom of the trench where they had been placed. Stom stopped to examine one sooty corpse. Was this the one he had carried from the burning gun in the phantasmagoric night? The uniform was charred and blackened, revealing various layers like the pages of an unequally burnt book. The braiding at his left shoulder was still intact, marking him as a common soldier. But here the jacket had peeled away to reveal smoke-blackened shirt, and here peeled further to reveal vest, to reveal skin, to reveal bone turned charcoal.

Polystom stood again. 'Stet?' he called.

Several of the men stirred, leaning over the lip of the trench.

'You men,' he called. 'Where's the lieutenant?'

'He caught one about an hour ago, sir,' somebody replied.

Polystom's stomach chilled. 'Dead?' he asked.

A man took him along the trench to the lieutenant's dugout. The air inside smelt foul; a burnt, foetid, spicy odour. Inside Polystom saw another charred corpse, laid on the floor on its front. No, on its back; the face burnt smooth, the hands and feet unrecognisable. It might have been on its front or its back, it was impossible to tell – except, there was the line of white mosaic tiles that were its teeth. Was this Sof?

On the bed was Stet. He was sitting up, still alive, but looking terrible.

'What happened?' said Polystom, pulling the chair over to sit beside him. It was a foolish question, he realised, as he asked it: foolish because the answer was obvious, and foolish because Stet could certainly not say anything by way of answer.

Stet waved vaguely with his hand, gestured towards his throat. A bullet, shot from below, had passed up through his throat and come out through his cheekbone. Two wattles of blood and torn skin hung from the mess of his adam's apple, like exterior tonsils. The right side of his face was as smashed as if somebody had stamped on it with a heavy boot. Tiny rice-grain splinters of bone poked out, edging the wet red cut. The whole of that side of his head was blackened with bruising, and his eye had vanished in the pleats of puffiness. A cravat of bandage hung loose around his neck, where Stet's finger twitched restlessly at it.

'Do you need anything?'

A half-shake of the head.

'A drink? I have some brandy in my dugout.'

A half-shake of the head.

Silence. Polystom sat as the implications of this thing started to sink in. It meant he was in sole command. This was no good. This would not do. He couldn't command the men by himself. He would have to get in touch with Command, have them send out some more lieutenants – or at least, a sergeant, or somebody. Or better still, relieve them altogether. Send in some new troops. Or at least let *him* go. Send in another commanding officer to take over and let him go home.

Stet's forefinger twitched and tugged at his neckerchief of bandage.

Polystom cleared his throat. 'You heard about Sof?'

Stet could barely manage a nod.

'Terrible,' said Polystom. 'Terrible.'

He sat with the injured man for several minutes, before excusing himself and going outside again into the sunlight. He made his way up to the gun, and found the gun crew dozing. 'You men!' he called. As one they leapt to life. 'Men! Attention!'

'Sir,' they replied.

'Do I have a sergeant? A corporal?'

Nothing but sullen, exhausted faces.

Polystom, feeling more and more despairing, less and less in control, made his way along the trench. 'How many men are left?'

'Not sure, sir,' from one figure.

'A dozen, perhaps, sir,' from another.

'Shouldn't stand upright, like that, sir,' said a third. 'Make a nice target, I'd say.'

Polystom looked nervously over his shoulder, and dropped into the trench again.

Flies, fat as raisins, droned through the fresh sunlight, drawn to the bodies at the bottom of the trench. Polystom waved them away from his own face. At the far end of the trench he crept up the steps, and hurried as fast as he could over exposed ground to the ruined gun. Its barrel looked serviceable, sticking straight up into the sky, smoke conjured from its end by the heat of the new day. Like an enormous metal cigarette. But the loading mechanism was melted, the tangle of levers bent and waxy, and several blackened corpses appeared to be actually stuck to the metal. It was a mess.

Polystom turned back. Squinting, he counted the figures lining each side of the trench. Add three for the far gun. Best not count Stet: he was in no position to fight. Thirteen men.

Not many.

His head was starting to buzz with the preliminaries to panic. What should he do? Was there any way they could make their way off this ridge and to safety? They needed to contact Command. They needed somebody from Command to come to them, give them new orders. He scanned the lower ground, trying to spy out enemy soldiers, placements, but he could see nothing. Perhaps they had pulled out. If so, he could lead his dozen men down off the peak and away. Where to? He wasn't sure. He didn't know which direction was the safe direction.

Back at the trench, he tapped the nearest man. 'You.'

'Sir?' He pulled his rifle in at his side, stood straight.

'Name?'

'My name, sir?'

'Yes, yes.'

'Mero, sir.'

'Are you one of mine? Or were you Parocles'?'

'Captain Parocles,' said the man. 'But the captain's dead, sir, so now I'm yours.'

'You're my sergeant,' said Polystom.

'Sir,' said the man.

'I want a corporal too. Who shall we have as corporal?'

The new sergeant looked left and right with unease. 'Don't know sir.'

'Come on, man. Give me the name of one of your friends.'

'They're dead, sir.'

'All of them?'

'Sir.'

'Anybody – you!' Polystom tapped the next man along.

'Me sir?'

'You're corporal.'

'*Me*, sir?'

'Yes. Battlefield promotion. What's your name?'

'Rai, sir.'

'Were you one of Parocles' as well?'

'No, sir. I was a fisherman on your estate, sir.'

'Oh, you were a fisherman, were you? Now you're a corporal. You and the sergeant here – you, what did you say your name was again?'

'Mero, sir.'

'Yes, you and Sergeant Mero.'

They both looked at him.

'We have to work out what to do, you see,' said Polystom.

'Yes sir.'

'Yes sir.'

There was a silence. Polystom became aware of an emptiness in his belly. He had not eaten since the night before, and it would soon be time for breakfast. Maybe he should retrieve some rations from his dugout.

From the other end of the trench, somebody's voice rang out. 'Here they come again! West flank!'

Everybody still capable of movement hurried to the west side of the trench. Polystom had left his pistol in his dugout. He ran through to the door, skidding on the threshold and tumbling through. He located the pistol, loaded the slot with bullets, and turned back to the door. The first snapping sounds of gunfire were sounding in the air outside.

[fifth leaf]

The attack was beaten off easily enough. The enemy deployed no heavy ordnance, and no more than a dozen individual enemy soldiers made a rush up the west flank. They retreated under fire.

After the attack, Polystom told the men to break out their breakfast rations, having no idea what those rations might be or even whether the men possessed them. Then he told his new sergeant and corporal to come into his dugout.

'Now,' he said to them, attempting to act with a proper authority. 'You know that Lieutenant Stetrus is too injured to be able to command properly. This means that the burden of command falls to us. You – sergeant – I'm afraid I've forgotten your name again.'

'Mero, sir.'

'And you?'

'Rai, sir.'

'Good. We need a plan. Our numbers are dwindling. Now, we were ordered by Command to hold this ridge, but I suppose that there . . . eh . . . you know. That there's a level of manpower, you know, below which it's not practicable to follow such an order.'

The two men looked blankly at him. With a swallowing sensation in the base of his stomach, Polystom realised that neither of these men had the vaguest clue about the principles of command.

'Now,' he said. 'I want your opinion. Does the enemy . . .' He paused, thinking how best to frame the question so that it didn't appear he was advocating ignominious retreat. 'Does the enemy control *both* the west *and* east flanks of the ridge? Is there any way we could slip away from here?'

'In the night,' said the sergeant, 'they attacked from both sides. I think they're all around us.'

Polystom considered his options.

'We could withdraw up this ridge,' he said. 'The ridge leads to a mountain, I think.'

The two men were looking at him.

'I'm certain there's a concentration of our troops on this mountain,' said Polystom, trying to make his voice sound as if he were certain. 'If we can make our way along to them. The Computational Device . . .' He stopped, unsure if he had said too much. 'Have you heard of the Computational Device, either of you?'

'No, sir.'

'No, sir.'

'You know what a Computational Device is, though, yes?'

Blank looks.

'We fight where we are placed, sir,' said the sergeant. Polystom had forgotten his name again, but didn't want to admit the fact by asking him once more. 'That's all we do.'

'Well, a Computational Device,' said Polystom, uncertainly, 'is a sort of machine. In this case, an enormous machine. Do you understand? In the mountain. In fact, I think it *is* the mountain. Now this machine is very important to us.'

'Why?'

'Well,' said Polystom. 'Well. It can do extraordinary things. It can calculate at a fantastic rate. And if it is written . . .' He screwed up his eyes, trying to remember what he had been told. 'If an expert writes into it, in some way, it can think like a person. It can perform any tasks you set it. It is one of the hubs of the war. If we can make our way along to it,' said Polystom, 'then things will be much better. We'll join larger units, and we'll be safer.' He stopped.

After a silence, the sergeant said 'yes, sir.'

'Very well. We'll need a plan. I think the colonel who visited said something about the ridge being mined and wired. Do you know what that means?'

'Yes, sir.'

'Yes, sir.'

'Well, well. Go and have your breakfasts anyway, you two. I'll think about what we are going to do.'

The men left.

Polystom retrieved his case of brandy, and drank a long swig straight from the bottle. He settled into his chair with the bottle on his lap.

There was a *shush*ing sound from beyond the door. It was raining again. Polystom stared at the wall. He told himself that he was thinking what to do, but in fact his mind meandered.

The sound of a single gunshot banged through the air. Polystom hurried out of his dugout and along the trench, hurrying through the rain with a sick feeling in his gut. He knew what the noise signified. His feet slid unsteadily on the mud at the floor of the trench. Black was draining from a charred corpse in inky rivulets. One of the corpses they had laid there from the night before. Now it was leaking like oil from a faulty auto-engine.

Polystom had to exert his will to lift his eyes. He stepped on briskly. Past the men, each arrayed on one side of the trench or other. At least the rain had stopped. At the far end of the trench he ducked and stepped inside the lieutenants' dugout.

Stet had shot himself.

Polystom drew his breath deep into his lungs. Horrible. Why would he do such a thing? Unable to endure the pain? Unprepared to face the humiliation of going on with his life facially disfigured? Polystom didn't know him well enough to guess. But his chair was upended, his body still sitting on it with his back on the floor and his knees up in the air. His arm was limp along the ground, the pistol still in his grip. Grimacing, Polystom stepped closer, peering down at the mess of the man's face. The old wound was still there, its black-red patchwork tinged with pale green, like the edge of cut ham, along the lines of the exit hole. Despairing, perhaps crazed with pain, Lieutenant Stetrus had put the barrel of his pistol into his mouth and shot himself. The bullet had emerged from his left temple, a thistle-like ring of spiked flesh around a dark red centre marking the place. Stom, his stomach going queasy inside him, tried mentally to plot the path the bullet must have taken: up through the palate of the mouth, parting the wrinkles there and cutting up into the flesh, chopping through sinus bone, liquidising the left eye – Stom could see it still in its socket, black as a cherry – nicking a portion of the frontal lobe and finally bursting out through the bone at the side of the head.

He stood up and called out into the trench. 'Sergeant? Anybody?'

Faces at the door. 'Sir?'

'Come in here please. Lieutenant Stet has – the lieutenant has –'

Two men, awkward as tramps in a stylish sitting room, stepped into the dugout. 'We heard the shot sir.'

Now that these men were in the space, Polystom wondered why he had called them in. He had half a mind to tell them move the body, but now that he came to think of it there seemed little point in that. Why not leave the two lieutenants in this dugout space, turn it into their tomb? This was as good a place as any. Better that than have them cluttering up the trench. The nearer of the two soldiers was leaning forward a little, craning his head to get a better look at the fallen body. This struck Polystom as inappropriate.

'Alright,' he said, trying to sound sharp. 'There's no need for you, actually. You'd better get back out, back on guard duty.'

Sheepishly, the two men left.

Polystom stood for a few minutes more. He felt that he ought to do something, to mark the death of these two men of good family. But the only thing that occurred to him was to take Stet's pistol. The lieutenant would, obviously, have no further need for it. And Polystom was missing a pistol. The traditional thing would be to assemble a dossier, accounts of his life, to memorialise him. To hold a funeral. Polystom realised he knew next to nothing about his lieutenant – about either of them. None of that civilised marking of a death was appropriate here.

He hunkered down to uncurl the dead man's hand from the butt of the gun. Stet's corpse shuddered, and a faint, rasping noise came from its throat.

Polystom stood straight up.

For a moment he just stood, frozen. Then he called through the door again. 'Back in here! Back in here please!'

From outside: 'Sir?'

'Come in here please. Right away.'

The muddy, sheepish soldier stepped back in through the door. 'Sir?'

'The lieutenant is – is not dead.'

The body groaned, shifted a little.

'Well,' said Polystom. He was sweating. The day was heating up rapidly. 'Well, what shall we do?'

'I don't know, sir.'

'Well – lift him up. Go on, lift him up.'

A second fellow came into the dugout, and between the two of them Stet was raised up, still on his chair, and then lifted out of it and carried over to his bunk. As they laid him down his breath seemed to catch, whistling in the hole in his throat. His breast shuddered, and his pistol fell from his fingers.

Polystom ducked and picked it up.

'Now,' he said, feeling awkward. 'That'll do for now. I suppose he'll need medical attention. Is there anybody in the platoon who would be able to help?'

Nothing but blank looks.

'Alright,' he said. 'That'll be all.'

When the men were gone, Polystom stood, looking over the pistol in his hands, turning it over and over.

To put a bullet in your own head.

The figure on the bunk – Stet – seemed to be gasping a little. Polystom took a chair and dragged it over to the side of the bunk, accidentally banging it against the charred legs of Sof's body as he did so. He started to apologise to the supine body, stopped himself, feeling foolish.

Sitting brought him closer to Stet's level. His one seeing eye swivelled, turned, spun up into his skull and came back down again. It was barely visible amongst the puffed flesh.

'Stet,' said Polystom, not knowing what to say. 'You've made a bit of a mess of yourself, I'm afraid.'

The eye seemed to settle on him momently, but then went on restlessly.

The superstitious – and, he rebuked himself immediately, idiotic – sense came over Polystom that it was impossible to die on this world. Impossible to die, no matter how hard you tried to. He had seen the ghost of his wife. Stet had been shot twice in the head, the two trajectories crossing X-fashion through his face, and *still* he was alive. But it was a stupid notion. Sof, on the floor, was undeniably dead. The bodies lining the trench outside were clearly dead. Polystom turned the pistol over in his hands again, the thought nagging him that Stet had intended this gun to end his life. I am, Polystom thought ruefully to himself, so little a soldier that I have no idea whether suicide is regarded as an honourable or dishonourable action for a serving officer. Perhaps Stet's roving eye expected him, his captain, to finish

229

the job for him? He hefted the gun in his right hand, aimed the barrel at Stet's one good eyes, toying with the notion of stopping the man's misery right away. Stet's eye rested briefly on the gun, but continued its rolling and rolling. His other eye, black-balled, seemed motionless.

And then, again, shouting from outside. From a hot silence bothered only by the buzzing of insects, the air was filled by the whining of falling shells, the spitting of rifles, the noises of shells detonating.

Stom hurried outside. They were, it seemed, coming up both sides at once. He ran from trench-side to trench-side, from west to east and back, leaning over and firing his pistol. Stet's pistol, rather. Figures appeared as if from the mud itself, rearing up and scurrying forwards. The enemy had positioned two cannon in the western dip and was now firing upon the trench, despite the fact that their own men were at that moment assaulting it. 'Tell the gun crew!' yelled Polystom. 'Have them fire upon those cannon!'

'They caught it, sir,' said one soldier, between firing his rifle. 'The enemy came,' *crac*, 'out of the ground. That,' *crac*, 'was the first we knew of it,' *crac*, 'the shouts of the gun crew dying.'

These enemy seemed to have no sense of personal danger. They reared up on the very edge of the trench, silhouetting themselves against the sky. Polystom shot one such figure, and watched as it jerked backwards and fell away. Another appeared almost immediately behind him. Stom was too stunned, or startled, or his brain was not working for some reason or other, and he didn't raise his pistol. One of his men shot this figure down with his rifle.

And then, as soon as it had started, it was over. Putting his face over the lip of the trench, Polystom could see the surviving enemy troops running and hopping over the mud, down into the shelter in the valley.

Polystom's heart was pumping so hard he could hear it in his ears.

There were nine of them now; one officer and eight men. The gun was still operational, but none of the survivors knew how to fire it.

These men were all servants, Polystom knew. But he preferred to think of them as men, as real people. It somehow made it easier. He brought out his last two bottles of brandy and – to the uneasy astonishment of the soldiers – insisted that everybody have a drink. Polystom took one glass, and the other was passed nervously from hand to hand. The liquor gleamed inside him, but the uncertain, unhappy looks on the faces of the men unnerved him a little.

It was hotter by the minute. The clouds had broken up and dispersed and the disturbingly fat sun thrust its heat upon them. Polystom was sweating, a prickly tickle of dots over his chest and back. 'Health!' he called, to the men, tipping his glass into his mouth.

Insects grumbled through the hot air: thumbsized blueflies; slender day-flies like floating splinters, and silver-skinned air-ants whose wing-noise seemed to swirl up a semitone, down a semitone, up again, down, in hypnotic rhythm. The mud, too, was speaking, with odd popping and muttering noises as the sunlight dried it out. Looking over the rim of the trench it was possible to see the surface of the land paling and cracking.

'Sergeant,' Polystom said to the man next to him. He still couldn't remember the fellow's name. That blank spot in his memory bothered him, gnat-like. Why couldn't he hold the name in his head? 'I'm sorry, man,' he said. 'What's your name, again?'

'Mero, sir.'

'Of course. Of course. Mero – how long have you been here?'

'Sir?' That distantly panicked expression came into the men's faces whenever Polystom asked them a question. It was starting to get on his nerves. They were comrades-in-arms, weren't they? 'Come along man,' he chivvied. 'Don't be shy. How long have you been here.'

'On the Mudworld?'

'Yes.'

'Less'n a year, sir.'

'Under Captain Parocles?'

'Yes sir.'

'Was he a good captain?'

'Sir?' Whites visible all around the man's pupil.

'I mean – did the men respect him? Did he have their respect?'

'Sir.'

'Did he . . . um, did he command well?'

'Sir.'

'He had a lieutenant?'

'Two sir, and a subaltern.'

Polystom stopped for a moment, trying to form up in his own head exactly what he was trying to get at. 'I suppose what I'm wondering,' he said, taking another swig of drink and watching the flies bounce swarmingly from corpse to corpse, 'what I'm wondering. Well, sergeant. Did you know that this is my first term of service on the Mudworld?'

'No, sir.'

'My first term of service anywhere, actually. Have another sip of brandy.'

'The cup . . .'

'Use mine.'

'Sir, I don't think . . .'

'Go on.'

The man gobbled at the lip of Polystom's glass. 'Thank you, sir.'

'I think what I'm asking you, what I'm wondering, is how typical this – this experience is of warfare. Now you've been in the army a year . . .'

'Three years, sir,' said the sergeant, emboldened by the booze to interrupt his superior.

'You said a year?'

'A year on the Mudworld, sir. But I've been in a couple of other engagements. It's a five-year term, service, for the ground troops, you see. I was considering renewing my term when the five years're up. Now I'm not sure I will.'

'No?'

'Not sure, sir.'

Polystom sipped again at his brandy, pleased that the barriers were coming down a little between himself and his man. 'Why's that?'

'This last year has not been . . . has been hard, sir.'

'So this is harder than usual service?'

The sergeant looked sheepishly at the floor, as if he were betraying somebody or something by saying so. 'Come on man,' Polystom chivvied him again. 'It sounds like you've had a fair bit of experience, fighting.'

'That I have, sir.'

'Whereas I don't have any. So if this seems hard to me – I mean, the last few days have been . . .' He petered out; filled the gap with another drink. The sergeant took the proffered cup, and drank more decorously than before.

'Well, sir,' he said, 'the way I see it is. I've seen some hard fighting before. When I joined up, sir, after the basic training we were taken off to sort out some trouble on Rhum. There was a compound in the mountains, there, where some servants had gone bad, killed their masters and so on. Well, it was difficult to get to, on account of the mountains and snow, and it was pretty well defended. That was some hard fighting: uphill, in the snow and cold, and precious little cover. There were plenty killed those first few days, and it was the shock of it, you know sir? My first experience of the killing and the dying. Training is all very well, but it's not the same. I remember that well. Then we had several months mopping up in the mountains, and we all grew to hate the cold, the nights especially. Frostbite, misery. Now, when we were told that we were coming here there were men in the platoon who were happy enough. At least it'll be warm, they said. Warm!' The sergeant flashed a grin. 'It's warm enough.'

Polystom realised that the man's name had again slipped from his mind. 'You mean, hard fighting?'

'I'll tell you sir,' said the sergeant. He looked at the floor. 'It's not that. Though it's sorrowful to see the captain – Captain Parocles, I mean – catch one, and we've had our numbers cut back pretty bad. But it's not that. I've known fights before where casualties fall as thick as this. It's not that.'

He stopped. 'So what is it?'

'It'll sound foolish to you, sir.'

'Tell me anyway.'

'It's this planet, sir.'

'Yes? What of it? The mud?'

'No sir.'

'What then?'

'The sense of it is, sir, amongst the men, that this world is haunted.'

For a moment Polystom didn't quite catch the word; then he felt a twitchy shiver run up his back and over the back of his head. Beeswing's mysterious expression; her lips forming the word, *hello*. 'What did you say?' he asked, a little too sharply.

'Haunted, sir. All the men agree on it.'

'But tell me what you mean by that.'

'Dead people, sir. We've all seen them. They come at odd moments.

Some of the men say that they get a good look at the people we're fighting, and they recognise some dead commander or dead person.'

'Dead?'

'Some who died a long while ago, some who died more recent, but here they are, walking over the mud, sitting in the trench below the wall smiling. Raising a rifle and aiming it at you. Dead people all around.'

Polystom felt a rushing sensation inside him, in his heart, as if the world were pouring through him. 'Have *you* seen the dead?' he asked. 'These dead, these – ghosts?'

'Yes sir, many times. Before I was in the army, sir, I worked on the estate of the horseman, Huperbolus. You heard of him? Famous equestrian trainer and rider, marvellous master, just marvellous. Anyway he died, fell off a horse on jumping practice, and his son took over the estate, and that's when I was offered the option of joining the army. No disrespect to his son who's a fine master, but I thought I'd rather not be around the estate with the old master dead. So I joined up. Now, Huperbolus was a distinctive-looking man, very tall, pure triangular nose. I know I saw him yesterday.'

'Yesterday?'

'In the first attack on the hogsback. Captain Parocles took us up to the base of the ridge before we were turned back, and that's where I saw him.'

'You're sure it was him.'

'Plain as daylight, sir. He came up out of the mud, smiling. There was no mistaking him. Ask any of the men, sir. They've all seen dead people.'

Polystom was close to saying something about his encounter with his dead wife, but something held him back. Battlefield intimacy was one thing, but this sergeant was, for all that, a servant, and Stom's mind rebelled against the idea of sharing details of his marriage with such a person. But ghosts! It was the plot of an opera, not real life.

He thought back to the night before, to Beeswing's appearance. He had not seen her on the battlefield; she had come to his door and peered inside.

Flies shuddered up through the air. The day was getting hotter and hotter.

'Sir!' called somebody from the far end of the trench. 'Sir!'

*

They had called him over because, inside the dugout, Stet had started moaning. It could be heard clearly from outside, a weirdly musical and pure line of sound. Polystom waved the men back, and stepped into the dugout. The stench was horrible.

'Stet,' he called, covering his own mouth against the smell. 'Stet, dear fellow. What's wrong?'

The figure of the lieutenant was shuddering on the bunk, the whine broken only when he sucked in breath, beginning again straight afterwards. Polystom sat in the chair beside the bed, looking down on the ruined figure of the man as if examining a scientific specimen through a microscope. He complained like a child. His body shook, as if feverish. Perhaps he *was* feverish. The wound on his right cheek was starting to look a little rotten.

'What's wrong, man?'

Only the wailing. Polystom wondered if the problem was one of water. Perhaps Stet was thirsty. The lieutenant's jacket was hanging from a pole by the entrance, and Polystom located the water bottle easily enough. Back at the bunk he offered it to Stet's shaking head, and when this got no response he held the man's mouth and poured the fluid in. The flesh felt as slick and cold as a fish. Stet's moaning stopped; he started choking, then swallowed deeply. The water gurgled at the gap in his throat, and dribbled down the sides of his neck. When Stom took the bottle away, Stet's hand lurched up and gripped his shoulder, until he poured more water down.

After a drink, Stet seemed calmer.

'I've some brandy,' Polystom said.

Did he shake his head at that? Or had his tremor returned? The head lurched from side to side for several moments, and then subsided.

Feeling awkward, Polystom didn't think he should leave his lieutenant's side. He sat for a while, looking around himself at the dugout. He ought to have Sof's burnt corpse moved out of here; it probably wasn't hygienic. Not that Stet would live much longer, he thought. But still. Or perhaps it would be better to have the men carry Stet down the trench to the other dugout? But he shied away from that idea. He couldn't quite rid himself of the thought that his own dugout was haunted. Like the sergeant had said. That the ghost of his dead wife lurked in that underground mud-cave. He looked at Stet, who appeared now to be sleeping.

Ghosts?

Did *ghosts* change the apprehension one felt about death? The lieutenant had hurried to embrace his own demise. Did he know that the planet was haunted? Did he hope to slip off his painful flesh in the expectation that he would return to the would in smiling, spectral form?

Outside again it was enormously hot. The men, some languidly in position along both lips of the trench, some lolling in the path of shadow underneath the eastern wall, looked dead themselves. Polystom stood for a while staring up into the violet sky. He half expected the noise of the colonel's plane: *Well done, captain, your men are relieved, the battle is over.* But nothing happened.

The heat drew out the buzz-stained silence, lengthened the hours.

He tapped a soldier on the shoulder. 'Any action down there?'

'No, sir.'

'Come with me: I want to have a look.'

Soldier first, captain after, they mounted the steps and huddled over to the burnt wreck of the northernmost gun. From there Polystom peered as far north as he could. The shouldered hunch of the mountain loomed, brown and white, just visible over the horizon. Mines and wire, the colonel had said, between this ridge, this prong of the mountain's base, and the mountain itself. He had no idea, although clearly a captain ought to know – no idea how to traverse mines and wire. Perhaps the sergeant would know.

Why were things so quiet?

Back in the trench Polystom drew the sergeant with him into his dugout. It was cooler, and the air did not stink the way the lieutenant's dugout did, but Polystom was uncomfortable, nonetheless. He turned round, and turned round again, like an arachnophobic checking for spiders, except that it wasn't spiders he was checking for.

'Sergeant,' he said, eventually.

'Sir.'

'Sergeant, my judgement is that we're pretty much understrength here.' He paused, maybe hoping that the sergeant would confirm his judgement, but the soldier stood passionless, expressionless. Waiting for commands. 'Look,' said Stom. 'If they attack again – when they attack again – I think it'll be best for us to withdraw. Strategically withdraw, you know. Along the ridge. Yes?'

'Sir.'

'Now, I know there's some wire, and some mines, along the ridge. Do you know how to deal with those?'

A fraction of a pause. 'No, sir.'

'Have you never encountered them?'

'Yes, sir. But I don't know how to deal with them.'

'Ah,' said Polystom, hoping that the colonel would fly in and relieve them, hoping that there would be no further attacks, hoping for any sort of release. 'Ah, well. I suppose we deal with that eventuality when it arrives. If it arrives.'

'Very good, sir.'

Polystom tipped his chin up, and the sergeant started turning towards the door. 'Oh, sergeant,' Stom said.

'Sir?'

'When you said . . . you know, earlier.'

'Sir?'

'About the haunting. About the ghosts. Is it, you know, generally known? Is it general knowledge?'

'Official? No sir. The men talk about it, of course, swap stories, that sort of thing. But not an official thing.'

'This whole war,' said Stom, waving vaguely with his right arm. 'It started as a servant insurrection, I suppose.'

'I suppose, sir.'

'What I'm trying to say,' said Stom, falteringly, 'is that – I don't know – do you think this planet was, ah, haunted before the war? Or is it haunted *because* of the war, you know?'

'I don't know sir.'

Polystom dismissed his man, and rustled through his box until he found his very last bottle of spirits. A wheat whisky from his homeworld. Would he ever see his homeworld again? He unstoppered the bottle and took a swig. A more disturbing question occurred to him. Say he died, here, in battle; say the enemy put a bullet through his very heart. Would he return as a ghost? Would he, like the villain from some second-rate opera, be condemned to walk this world for ever?

Behind him, a female voice. 'Stom?'

His face chilled; he felt the tiny hairs that lined his cheek bristle and move. It crossed his mind: it's as if my thinking it has summoned her up. He didn't want to turn around, but with the inevitability of a dream he knew he must.

Beeswing was at the door again. No, it wasn't Beeswing, but a young soldier. Polystom's heart hammered. 'What did you say?'

The soldier looks startled. 'Sir?'

'I said *what did you say?*'

'Nothing, sir.'

'Don't lie to me!'

'I said *sir*, sir,' squealed the soldier, his boyish voice rising even higher. For a moment Stom hovered on the edge of rage, then toppled back into rationality. He was breathing deeply. A stupid mis-understanding.

'Well,' he gasped. 'What is it?'

'It's the lieutenant, sir.'

Stom made his way along the trench again. The men seemed to have formed a near-superstitious fear of going into the lieutenant's dugout, but even from outside Stom could hear the whimpering of the injured man. 'What is it now?' he called, stepping through the entrance.

Lieutenant Stetrus's bashed face looked weirdly contorted, his one good eye bulging like a tongue in a cheek. He had pulled himself halfway into a sitting position in the bunk, and a doubled gasping sound was emerging from him, once from his mouth and once from the sagging hole in his throat. Stom faced him, caught his eye, followed its glance, and turned.

Beeswing was sitting, looking comfortable, in a chair behind the entrance.

Polystom didn't call out, didn't swear. The inside of his mouth felt like dried leather. He backed a step, and another. Then he stopped.

'You see her too?' he said, huskily, to the figure on the bed.

'Oh, of course he does,' said Beeswing. 'Are you Polystom?'

'I,' said Stom. 'I. I'll sit down.'

The seat by the bed was pressing at the backs of his knees. He sank into it. Should he call in the men from outside? What good would that do? He could, he thought with a vivid, sudden flash of inspiration, he could take out his revolver and shoot her straight away. But almost as soon as the inspiration came on him it drained away again. Shoot a ghost? Ridiculous!

What had she said? *Are you Polystom?*

'Don't you know me?' he said.

Beeswing frowned. Wrinkles appeared on her clear brow like ripples in a pond.

'I'm not sure,' she said. 'I think so. We were married?'

'Yes.'

'It's not clear. It's vague. Like a baldly written outline, not like the real thing at all.'

'This is extraordinary,' Stom muttered.

'Is it?' said Beeswing, with a more characteristic insouciance.

'Of course it is! You do know you're dead, don't you?'

'Dead?' she said. 'You mean – *you* are. If by dead, you mean not real, not alive. Or maybe you're right,' she said, her gaze wandering along the walls, past the lieutenant's half-unpacked boxes. 'Maybe I'm the one that's dead. It's not very nice in here.'

'No,' conceded Polystom. The shock of her appearance was dissolving itself into a series of tremors running up and down his arms and legs.

'What are you doing?' she asked, sharply.

'I'm having,' he said, as he unstoppered his bottle, 'a drink. I need a drink. This is most disconcerting.'

'If you were really married to me, once upon a time,' said Beeswing languidly, 'you might be pleased to see me again.'

'To see the dead?' he snapped, emboldened a little by the drink. 'To see a ghost?'

'Am I a ghost?' said Beeswing, examining the back of her hand, as if the answer were written there. 'How strange.'

'You were always strange,' he muttered. 'Why are you bothering us now? What is it about this world, that the dead don't stay where they should be, but come bothering the living? Is it the war? Did the big guns wake you?'

Beeswing was looking intently at him as he said all this. 'I don't understand any of that,' she said. 'Or very little. It's clearly unpleasant for you to see a ghost.'

'Of course!'

'If that's so, then it's equally unpleasant for us to see you. Don't you think it works both ways? Don't you think you are as uncanny for us as we are for you?'

Polystom hadn't considered it in that light before. He took another long swig from his bottle, scowling as it burned its way down the back of his throat. Ghosts scared by the living, eh. People terrified by ghostly apparitions, ghosts scared by living apparitions. It went round his head. The alcohol made the heat worse, but it dampened the sense of stink in the oven-like dugout.

'Well,' he said. 'This is something.'

'Well,' she echoed.

'You came to see me before.'

'Last night,' she said. 'It was tricky, then. It's easier now. It's a sort of knack, you know.'

'Really,' he said. 'Haunting, a knack. If you say so.' He laughed, briefly, abruptly.

'Why are you laughing?' she asked.

'To be holding a conversation, like this, with my dead wife! I don't know, it seemed funny somehow.' Polystom swivelled in his chair, and looked at Stet. The lieutenant had calmed himself since his captain's entrance, had lain down again, and was now breathing heavily but steadily.

'Funny,' said Beeswing, distantly.

There was a pause. Had they run out of things to say already?

'So,' said Stom, with slightly forced conversational effort. 'What is it like being dead?'

'Like being alive,' said Beeswing, distractedly. 'Only less so. We haven't really got time to chat, you know.'

The fear, dormant for several minutes, leapt up again in Stom's chest. 'What do you mean?'

'How frightened you look!'

'I don't want to die,' he said. 'I think I should ask you to go and leave me in peace.'

'Your uncle,' said Beeswing's ghost. 'I think that's who he is. He wants to see you, to speak with you. Come along!'

'My uncle?' But that made sense too, to Polystom's slightly drink-furred brain. In the kingdom of the dead there would be promiscuous social interchange. In the kingdom of the dead corpse would tangle with corpse, ghost swap ectoplasmic wisp with ghost. Alive his uncle had never liked Beeswing, Polystom knew. But maybe everything changed after death.

'Oh,' she said, exhaling a sudden disappointment. 'Oh no. Another time.'

'What?' asked Stom. 'Am I saved? Have you decided not to drag me down into the lands of death today?'

'Silly!' she said. 'It's not that. Only I can hear the rain starting again. And I can hear the guns firing, which means you're under attack outside. No, my one-time husband,' she said, suddenly on her feet, somehow instantly by his side, bending over him so that her hair flopped down and brushed near his face with ticklish intensity. 'No I've not come to drag you down to death. That's not the arena in which your uncle wants to meet with you. In fact,' she added, whispering now, her lips touching the lobes of his ear, tingingly, 'if you die in this attack then it won't be *possible* to set up the meeting. Bye bye.'

'Sir! Sir!'

Shouts from outside the dugout.

Stom was alone, save only for the ruined body of Lieutenant Stet, who seemed now to be asleep.

Stom rushed through the door, and out into flashing silver strings of rain. Almost at once, like thunder and lightning, he heard the detonation of the shelling. His men, all eight of them, were leaning over the east side of the trench, their guns sounding and sounding. Stom, rushing, tried to stop, but the gooey, slippery new mud at the bottom of the trench wrongfooted him and he slipped down. Falling down.

'What about the west flank?' he bellowed, getting to his feet.

One of his men peeled away and slammed himself against the west side of the trench. 'Nothing down there, sir! They're massing in the east,' he said, tearing himself away, mud smeared down his front, and dashing against the east side again. 'Coming up!'

Stom took up position on the east, leaned as far over the trench as he could, and fired his pistol again and again. He fired, wildly, into the blurring of the rain, aiming at shadows and nothing, until all the bullets in his slot were discharged. His finger kept beckoning at the trigger, even though the mechanism could only cluck emptily like a hen.

A rank of figures swarmed up through the rain. They were going to reach the trench easily. The shots of his eight men were hardly dropping any of them. In an ecstasy of panic, Stom threw his pistol from him, dropped to the trench floor, searching for a rifle from one of the rotten corpses. drowning in the puddles there. He couldn't find anything.

'Men!' he bellowed, standing up. 'Sergeant! Up the west side, and to the gun. Now! Now!'

He scattered down the trench, slipping and kicking in the water, the rain tapping hard into his face. He was up the stairs and on top of the west side of the ridge before he realised that nobody was following him. Maybe they hadn't heard his orders. 'Hey,' he bellowed at the backs of the men, now a little below him. 'Hey!' Trying to make his voice carry over the clatter of the rainstorm. 'This way! Sergeant! Sergeant!' What was the man's name? 'We're retreating up the ridge, a tactical retreat.'

The enemy swept up the far side. He could see several of them taking aim at him – exposed, above the level of the trench. One went onto a knee to steady his rifle. Another simply hoisted the weapon to his shoulder and fired. A bullet whistled past him. Another hit the mud at his feet.

Polystom had just been talking to his dead wife.

Everything was pressing upon him, terrifying, overwhelming.

I can hear the rain starting again, Beeswing had said. He had felt her lips, her dead lips, against the skin of his ear.

He turned, ducked, and ran as fast as he could towards the wreck of the gun, expecting at every step to feel the kick of a bullet in his back. The agony of that.

At the blackened metal of the gun, he swung himself about, taking cover. He could see the little sparky flames from his troop's rifles, and just about make out the mass of enemy soldiers, individual bodies collapsing, others pressing on. But it was all misty, a kinematic image not properly focused.

His breath was dense, loud in his ears.

He turned again, ducked forward, and hurried out of cover, running northward along the hogsback ridge.

[sixth leaf]

He struggled through the mud for more than an hour, as the noise of battle retreated behind him, until he collapsed panting into a puddle-bottomed shellhole. The rain had ceased, and up in the sky snaggle-edged clouds broke and reformed against a deep mauve background. For a long time Polystom simply sat in the hole, until his breathing was under control. He thought about what he had done. For several minutes he peered over the edge of the crater, the direction from which he had come. He could just make out the asterisk of the ruined cannon, on the horizon, but he could see nothing more, and no sound carried. Were they still fighting? Maybe they were all dead. All his men, dead. He slid back to the bottom of the crater, his feet splashing into the warm brown water. Would they come back now, as ghosts, like Beeswing, like Cleonicles? Beeswing had said *your uncle wants to see you, to speak with you.* The more he thought about it, the more his breathing hurried. He turned and turned, half expecting to see the ghosts of his dead men rearing up from the mud to accuse him. You abandoned us. You deserted us.

The sun appeared from behind a cloud, and sunlight was every-where, turning the puddle into glowing copper.

Polystom slitted his eyes against the glare. Somebody was in the crater with him, indistinct in the wash of light. And, with a shudder, the sunlight drained to grey as another cloud passed before the sun.

There were three of them. Beeswing and two others. Polystom did not recognise the others.

'You startle me,' he said, scrabbling halfway up the crater wall. 'You frighten me.' His heart was beating palpably in his chest. He reached for his pistol before he remembered he had already discarded it.

'Husband,' said Beeswing. 'Husband.' It wasn't clear whether she was addressing him, or explaining his relationship to the other dead people present. Polystom looked more closely at them. One was a tall, black-haired man, thin save for a balloon-shaped pot belly. Were all the imperfections of flesh carried into the afterlife? The other was a short woman of indeterminate age, with the curiously glazed polished skin of the dead. 'You're all three of you dead,' Polystom said to them. 'You all are.'

'We're all dead,' agreed Beeswing, as if placating a child.

The two figures, one on each side, said nothing.

'What is it you want with me?'

'Personally,' said Beeswing, who – somehow – had zipped through the air in an instant and was now sitting in the mud at his side. 'Personally I don't want anything from you.' Polystom noticed that the mud was marking the pale grey of her trousers, blotching onto the hem of her grey shift. Did the dead go about dressed? Did they have to wash their clothes?

'You need to go further north,' Beeswing was saying.

'North?'

'To the mountain. Not all the way, necessarily, I don't know. It *really* isn't clear.' She seemed momentarily cross, but the emotion faded as soon as it appeared.

'What are you talking about?'

'Your uncle. He can't make it out here to meet you.'

'I need to go further north to meet my uncle?'

'Yes yes yes,' hurriedly, impatiently.

'Why?'

'Ask him,' she said, dreamy now. 'I don't know.'

'Those two,' said Polystom, indicating the two. 'Who are they?'

'Nobody you know,' said Beeswing, standing between them again. 'Nobody you *knew*, I should say – although, as I mentioned before, from our perspective it is *you* who are not real, you know.'

'It's creepy,' said Polystom. 'Dead people appearing all over the place.'

'Oh, we're all around you,' Beeswing replied. Her voice was smaller now, reducing, as if she were retreating from him, although simultaneously she was standing clearly in front of him, and in fact seemed to be growing, swelling. 'All the time, all around you. You take us for granted. Like the air,' she added, putting her head back to stare at the grey sky, 'like the air, that only sometimes condenses itself into clouds, but which is generally perfectly invisible, and which is purer and purer the further away you go, until it is almost invisible, with only the slightest,' (very faint, as if she were an enormous distance away, and yet she was still right there), 'purple in the immensity.'

'Death has changed you, Beeswing,' Polystom said. 'You were never like this when you were alive.' But he was alone in the crater. With a sense of anticlimax, the air shivered into swathes and swathes of warm drizzle.

Polystom trudged further northward, berating himself as he went for doing so. Following a ghost's instructions, deserting his post, all his men dead, this was nothing less than madness. The drizzle came and went, interspersed with occasional periods of bright sunshine that made his uniform smoke moistly, clouds steaming off him like pollen. Then the sun would hide again, and the rain would start drifting down again.

Another hour's slow progress and he was hungry. He was also thirsty, which surprised and infuriated him, amongst all this water. If he stood with his head back and his mouth agape the drizzle did wet his lips and tongue, but he didn't seem to get enough inside to count as a really satisfying drink. There were puddles all about him, but he could not bring himself to drink out of any of them: they were all a shitty brown colour. In some of the them oddments of humanity were visible: a leg sticking up like a post, bodies that appeared to be wearing inflated lifejackets that bobbed in the pools, although the lifejackets were just uniforms, their material sealed with mud and the gases collected underneath those layers noxious even from a distance. At one stage the rain intensified, and thunder rumbled in the sky, but a jittery Polystom mistook the noise for ordnance and dived into a shellhole for cover. At the bottom of the hole was a great pile of shoes, half in and half out of the puddle of accumulated water. It bothered Polystom that somebody had dumped so many good shoes, until, looking closer, he realised that every single one of them still contained its owner's foot. He tried to imagine how so many feet could have been blown off at once, but the more he thought about it the more alarmed and disturbed he became.

He hurried on. It must have been mid-afternoon, although the cloud cover made it difficult to judge. He saw one huddled group of people, away to the west of the ridge, bent double under the downpour. He could not tell whether they were enemy troops or friendly, but he did not seek to attract their attention.

The ridge was more or less deserted, with only the scattered fragments of men and machinery to indicate that it had ever been contested. Polystom found himself wondering why he and his men had been detailed to defend the far end of the ridge, and what had stopped the enemy simply coming up onto it further to the north. Then, shockingly, the rainstorm became heavier and heavier, drumming colossally down onto the earth, and Polystom had to bend practically in two. He felt like a nail that the sky wanted to hammer into the earth.

He took shelter behind the lip of a large crater waiting until the rainstorm lessened its severity. Below him three or four bodies – it was hard to tell how many complete bodies the tangle of mutilation added up to – gripped at one another like drowning swimmers. If anything, the rain was even heavier now. Polystom tried to shift position, to shuffle along the edge of the crater, but the slipperiness of the surface and the force from above betrayed him. He slid, thrashing, kicking out at the bodies below him. They, too, launched into a slide, their limbs jerked into ersatz life in a grotesque orgy of dead fumbling and twisting. Polystom could not stop his descent, and went splashing into the mini-lake at the bottom. The water was all around him, up his noise, in his mouth. He waved his arms, with the fear of drowning fiercely in him, knocking aside logs, or whatever obstructions they were that floated and bumped into him.

His head broke the surface, although the air was almost as wet as the lake. It was hard to keep above water with the weight of his boots, but with a few enormous splashes he felt the slope of the crater's wall under his feet. It was tricky gaining purchase. He tried levering himself out of the water, but the mud was too slippery. After a deal of effort he worked himself round to a place where a slight ledge underpinned his feet, and there he stopped until he had regained his breath.

Eventually the rain stopped. The sun came out.

It was nearly an hour's labour to work a way up the side of the crater; each handhold, each stepping point, had to be scooped out of the mud. At the top Polystom lay on his back, looking up at the purple-and-white sky.

*

Increasingly hungry, he marched further north. He tried to think through the reasons his uncle might want to speak to him. What should he say to him? Would the dead man want to know what had been done to avenge his murder? Would he know? Those two men you executed, they were not the ones who killed me. What could Polystom say to such a thing? I know, Uncle. It was done for show; to encourage the others. Tell me, Uncle, do *you* know who it was who murdered you?

'I don't,' said Cleonicles. 'I have no memory of that at all. I know it happened, but only because of, what would you say, a sentence? A few words?'

Fatigue completely filled Polystom now, and he was feeling slightly feverish. Probably shouldn't have ingested the water from that shell-hole. Probably not clean. Still, what could he have done? It had been beyond his control. He fixed his eye straight ahead. The mountain was much larger, and the ridge much wider, more corrugated. I will, Polystom told himself, I will walk as far as that hillock, and there I will rest.

'Good idea,' said Cleonicles.

But with his very next step, Polystom felt a savage pain in his left shin, and he tumbled forward. He was face down in the mud. His legs were up in the air, pushing his head down. He tried to push himself up with his arms, but that intensified the sharp pain in his legs. He was making hoarse little noises with his throat, as suggestive of exhaustion and exasperation as pain. Looking behind, he could see that he had walked blindly into a shin-level stretch of barbed wire: that in tumbling forward he had caught his flesh on the metal thorns. With surges of hot pain he twisted a little to one side, and managed to disengage his legs from the barbs, and pull himself round. His shins ached enormously. Stupid of him! Stupid, stupid, stupid.

He got to his feet with difficulty, and turned north. Now that he actually looked, he could see banks and banks of wire, like petrified heather, parallel to and intersecting his path. He limped onward another twenty yards or so, zigzagging around where the wire was laid. A crater marked the place where a shell had punched a hole in the stuff, and Polystom slipped into this, the weariness coming up through his body in waves. He lay on his back, and slid down, until his feet hit the water. But this was a small crater, and the puddle at the bottom was no more than a foot deep.

He lay for a while, gathering his strength, whilst the pain throbbed through his legs. 'Have you,' he said to the figure beside him, 'been with me for a while?'

'A while, yes.'

'Walking beside me?'

'Yes.'

Polystom shook his head. 'I'm so tired,' he said. 'I can't take much more.'

'If I were you,' said Cleonicles, 'I'd rest here for a bit.'

Polystom turned his head. 'Is Beeswing with us?'

'Beeswing,' said the ghost of Cleonicles, as if trying the word out. 'Beeswing. Now, is that your wife?'

'Yes. Don't you know?'

'It's there somewhere, one of those vague little memories. You must understand, it's not the sort of thing that is central to my . . . well, what would you call it? My being. My mind. It's a bit of background description, as far as my character is concerned. It's not prominent in my mind.'

Polystom wasn't following this. He drifted into a dazed sleep.

He was woken by rain on his face. His legs still throbbed with pain.

'Awake?' asked Cleonicles.

Polystom pulled himself into a sitting position, rubbing the rainwater over his face to wake a little more. 'Uncle,' he said. 'You're the ghost of my uncle.'

'Ghost,' said Cleonicles. 'Yes.'

'This world is madness,' said Polystom, wearily. 'The war, that's madness. Ghosts, death, mud, suffering.'

'So, *you* are my nephew,' said Cleonicles, as if realising the fact for the first time.

'Beeswing was like this,' Polystom said, a little sulkily. 'It's as if death bleaches out your memory. Don't you *remember* me, Uncle? All the talks we had? You lived on the moon of Enting, and I used to fly up to you in my biplane to stay with you.'

'Of course, of course. But it's one thing to know a fact, something written down, and another to actually encounter it.'

'I'm hungry,' said Polystom. 'I wish I had some food.'

Cleonicles didn't say anything to this.

The rain faded from the air. The surface of the pond at the base of the crater went from stucco to plaster-smooth.

'Do you know,' said Polystom, 'that I haven't had a cup of coffee in a week? Even more than food, I think I'd like a cup of coffee.'

Cleonicles didn't say anything to this either.

'So,' said Polystom, turning to the ghost a little. 'Here I am on this mud-world, having a jolly conversation with my murdered uncle. What would you like, Uncle? Revenge? Beeswing, the ghost of Beeswing, I should say, told me that you wanted to talk to me.'

'Indeed I do,' said Cleonicles.

He looked simultaneously as old as, and much younger than Polystom remembered him: his features were as pronounced as the old-man Cleonicles, his eyes as sunken, his nose as beaky; yet his skin had the curiously smooth, bland texture that all the ghosts he had seen shared. And yet here he was, eerily substantial.

'I've myself to blame as much as anybody. A spider caught in my own web. The maker snagged in his creation.'

'I don't understand.'

'Let me explain. I do know you, but not with any great intensity. You'll pardon if I seem a little distant? I mean, a little more distant than I used to be?'

Polystom shrugged. 'You are dead, after all.'

'Dead,' said the ghost. 'Yes. You know what's in the mountain, do you?'

The bulk of it reared over the opposite lip of the crater. 'Military Command told me,' Polystom said, 'that there was a gigantic Computational Device. They told me to tell nobody about it. I wonder if that interdiction included dead people? Am I disobeying my orders by talking to you about it, you ghost?'

'I – which is to say, Cleonicles – built it. Not alone, of course. But I was instrumental in designing it. What's crucial, you see, is that there are four major seams of a crystal material, created by the folds of geological activity. This fact, combined with the heat differential under the ground and the abundance of solar energy this close to the sun, made the site ideal. You notice,' said Cleonicles, smiling slyly, 'how much more fluent I am with that sort of discourse?'

'Indeed.'

'All *that* sort of stuff is loaded up very centrally in me. Other stuff, the emotional history and so on, is more difficult to retrieve.'

'Whatever you say, Uncle.'

'More important than the building of this enormous processor, this enormous Computational Device, was the *writing* of it. This was where I played the most important role of all. We tinkered, for a few months, with writing into the circuitry of the Device models of reality. Versions, do you see? We'd write in the basic rules, first of all: physics and the like. Then we'd add on detail and layer, modelling a number of things. We produced a very interesting model of the atmosphere on Kaspian, trying to model weather. We discovered that it was possible to produce similar weather patterns, but very hard to predict precisely the way the actual weather might go. We could start with the same initial parameters, and the model would diverge from reality. Or,' Cleonicles chuckled, 'reality diverged from the model. Do you see?'

'Not really, Uncle.'

'Well, let me try to explain further. I used my influence to take charge of a very large project, a very large instance of Computational Modelling. I wanted to write into the circuits of the device an entire system, like ours in many ways, but different in crucial respects. You know, I suppose, that I was fascinated for a long time with the possibilities of vacuum physics? Many scientists disagreed with me, about the practicalities of the discipline – they denied that there could be such a thing as "vacuum" except under very particular experimental conditions. But certain observations of mine lead me to the conclusion that outside our own System there exists not only vacuum, but that this vacuum is dotted with stars.'

'I remember many conversations on this subject, Uncle.'

'Do you? I can't say I do. But anyway. I used the Computational Device to write into existence such a System. I started from the base up. I wrote in a star, burning in vacuum, about the same size as our star; and around it I placed a number of planets. I wanted life on these planets, so around each of them I placed a breathable atmosphere. But in between the worlds I wrote in nothingness. It was fascinating to see what happened. It's all about a balance of forces: gravity on the one hand, and the dispersing pressure gradient on the other. As had been predicted by some, the vacuum initially pulled the atmosphere clean away from the smaller planets. So then I designed much larger, denser planets, with gravity ten times what it is on Kaspian, and this had the opposite effect; the too-strong gravity compressed the atmosphere into liquid and solid forms. I tried getting the balance exactly right, but it was so precariously balanced that no atmosphere could be retained. And then – because, you see, it is possible to vary the rate at which time passes in this simulation – I let a few thousand years pass. In the system in which I started out, there were a number of rocky airless worlds, and a burning sun: over a few thousands of years this star emitted so much matter in the normal course of its functioning, emitted so much gas, that the System-sized sphere of vacuum filled up. I had started with something radically different from our own cosmos, and it swiftly reverted to our reality. Of course, the gases were not breathable, and my model planets remained lifeless, but I seemed to have defeated my own theories about the possibility of a vacuum universe beyond the boundaries of our own space.'

'But you did not give up on your ideas?'

'No,' said Cleonicles. 'No, I did not. It took me a month or so, but I came up with a workable model. Now, I had to fiddle the physics a little. And the System I created looks very different from our own cosmos. To begin with, I had to make the sun burn only through nuclear fusion; there's none of the conventional "burning" that happens in a real sun where the surface ionises and oxidises. So I wrote a sun, a little bigger than the real one, and it refused to ignite. I tried again, bigger still, and again it refused to ignite. I was left with several large globes of gaseous-state liquid. Eventually I did manage to make a burning sun, but only by accumulating so much matter – a ridiculous amount, actually, something equivalent to all the mass of our System compressed into a gaseous-state liquid ball. The sheer weight of it, compressed, the sheer *gravity* of so much matter broke apart atoms at the heart of the thing, and the heat began radiating. With such a large sun, I had to place the planets much further away, or they would have been cooked. So I designed an absolutely enormous System, thousands of times bigger than the real one. This solved a number of problems: for example, it didn't fill up with gas the way ours has. I put the failed suns I'd tinkered with into orbit, and then added a few iron-cored worlds. But the trouble I had fixing the equations so that these could have an atmosphere! My first few attempts at it failed completely. Then I put in an outer world, and some moons to the larger planets, and there the temperatures were so low – so far from the sun, you see, and without the friction of orbiting in a medium such as happens in the real System – that the atmospheres simply froze. That at least gave me enough tensile strength in the material to resist sheer vacuum evaporation.'

'Uncle . . .' said Polystom.

'Then I tried making a world, smaller than Kaspian-sized: I was trying to recreate my moon, although on a slightly larger scale. But most of the atmosphere bled away into the vacuum. You must understand that all through this process I was adjusting certain parameters, increasing the viscosity of the gas, sharpening the gravitational incline, that sort of thing. So not all the atmosphere vanished, but it was too thin and cold for life. I called this planet *War*, because it was so hard on life.'

'Uncle, may I just . . . ?'

'I tried again, with a proper-sized world. But here the parameters were overstated, a little. I added in a mysterious "glue" force to hold the atmosphere in place. But I was too successful: the atmosphere congealed, as it were. And because this world was in a closer orbit it became far too hot – hundreds and hundreds of degrees, raging fires hot enough to melt lead. I called this world *Lust*, for that reason.'

Polystom put his hands together; there seemed to be no stopping and no interrupting this ghost of his uncle.

'Finally I got it right: a similarly Kaspian-sized world to Lust, but further away from the sun, and with the "glue" force at a lesser level. Here, out of all the worlds I was writing, was one in which life could exist comfortably. This planet I named *The World*. Now, having learned the tweaks that nature needed to create breathable atmosphere worlds in vacuum, I could have erased the files I had written so far and started again – made a wholly new cosmos with six worlds, like ours, and put life on each. But I decided not to do that. There were two reasons for this: firstly, because my sun was so much larger than the real sun, it was necessary to put the planets considerably further away: to have the six worlds realistic distances apart, so that people could travel easily between them, would have arrayed them far too close together – collisions and mass death would have been inevitable. The only alternative was to space them much more widely, which made most of the worlds too cold. But the second reason was that, looking over what I had written, I was quite pleased with the variety of worlds, nine of them, big and small, boiling and frozen. There was that aesthetic element to the composition. I seem to remember – it's in my memory somewhere – that you admire poetry. Perhaps you can understand the appeal of aesthetics?'

'Oh,' said Polystom. 'Indeed.'

'So I arranged my nine worlds, in their enormous vacuum orbits, around my monstrous nuclear star. I sketched out a cosmos surrounding this system on a similarly vast scale – billions upon billions by multi-billions of miles. I became quite caught up in the sublimity of the infinite, I remember. An enormous number of stars, most of them no more than a few lines of code. I'm afraid, actually, there are some inconsistencies in that – the inhabitants of the System are starting to find them out. But I had no idea they would become so advanced as to be able to determine them. The stars were really my whim, intended only as a background.'

'Inhabitants?'

'Oh yes, I wrote in inhabitants. Why else construct the System? This was the rationale of the whole experiment, in fact: to model populations, to discover the laws that underpinned human interaction. It's hard to use the actual world as the basis of your observation. Our community of worlds is so stratified, so static, that human behaviour is tightly restricted. But what would it be like if several populations of millions of human beings interacted without these restraints? What patterns would emerge? The military were involved, closely, of course, from the very beginning. They hoped that the Computational Device would enable them to develop better tactics. Servant insurrection, after all, is a form of free, random human behaviour. The Counts in the military hoped that my model of such behaviour would give them insights into why some insurrections are easily crushed, and others linger on for years. The whole thing was an *enor*mous success. Much more successful than I had ever dared hope.'

'How so?' Polystom asked, drawn into his dead uncle's narrative despite himself.

'Oh, it all functioned so smoothly! Really. I could be quite proud of myself. In the first instance the research goals were fairly large scale. I wrote in about forty fully realised characters, individuals; and then I sketched in populations of thousands and hundreds of thousands – not fully functioning, free-will individuals like the forty, but much simpler characters who obeyed this algorithm or that. I created a core civilisation, modelled closely on the antique civilisation of Kaspian in fact, located in a small geographical area of many islands clustered around a sea. About forty individuals, with complex consciousness algorithms, and the ability to reproduce these with certain variations blended genetics and environment. That was the complicated part. Then several thousand background people. And, layer on layer, I wrote in a few other civilisations. I sketched in various tribes and peoples, some here, some there. None of them were real in any sense. Then in another location – all this was within a few thousand miles of the core civilisation – I tried a little experiment. I wrote one "real" character and made the rest of the population ciphers, basic algorithms. That didn't really work, I have to concede. The individual (I made him the ruler naturally) developed mental pathologies. It was as if he sensed that none of the people around him were real people, started believing himself the only genuine creature in the world, thought of himself as a god and so on. It meant that he regarded his population as absolutely dispensable, and acted in inappropriate ways: sending them into war after war for instance; having them give up their lives to devote to building him massive monuments and so on. But that's a by-the-way. All the land around a certain expanse of sea – modelled in part on the Middenstead, although much sunnier – all the land around this sea was populated. Then I sketched in populations on the other continents, but these were holding patterns; there were no real people in them. And the other planets? Well, most of the other planets in this system were all lifeless, all but one. That was easy, just a few basic algorithms for physics and chemistry.'

'And then?'

'Then we set the Computational Device running. I wanted to see how the populations developed, how they interacted when left to their own devices. And you need to understand, my dear fellow, that in a machine so large computing time is an extremely rapid thing. We initially set the parameters at one day of ours to one year inside the Device. So for every Kaspian-standard day that passed in the real world, a year passed for my made-up people. We watched, we observed, we analysed the data. It was fascinating: we saw whole cultures rise and fall, wars, dynastic struggles, populations fluctuate. Several of my simulated people were based on famous philosophers of our own, although, at this stage, in a very rough way. We were amazed by how responsive the person-algorithms were; advances in thought and science, although at a primitive level, were definitely made inside the simulation. They actually worked these things out for themselves.'

'How wonderful!' said Polystom. 'Like an epic poem.'

'Very much like that, indeed. It ran at that rate for six years, a little more than six years. Six and a half – of *our* years, you understand. In the written world of the Device thousands of years passed. Great empires rose, and fell. The focus of events shifted away from the original civilisation, the one we had originally written, which was a surprise in itself. Minor cultures grew and took centre stage, without our prompting, and the original civilisation withered and faded. We added more "real" characters, more algorithms with free will and problem-solving abilities, more "agent" characters as we called them. It was fascinating and absorbing. Then came the great change.'

'Change?'

'I had been involved with the programme for over eight years. It had transformed our understanding of population dynamics. Rather ironic, in fact. One of the initial reasons we set up the experiment was to help us understand servant insurrection. But we became so absorbed in the imitation world we had created that we ignored what was happening under our nose. The servants of Aelop rose up – an extraordinary, concerted uprising. Unlike anything in the history of the System. And Aelop began its transformation into the Mudworld.'

'Was the Computational Device implicated in the uprising?'

'Oh probably, Polystom, probably. It siphoned off considerable resources, which made the lives of the servants more unpleasant. And it dazzled us – *dazzled* us – so that we weren't paying proper attention to our own estates. There was even a theory that some servants had somehow obtained access to lesser sub-systems of the Computational Device itself, and used its analytic power to coordinate their activities. Well, that's all history now. Anyway, war broke out, and that changed everything.'

'I was told,' said Stom, 'that the Computational Device was essential to the war effort.'

'Our imaginary world, the one in the simulation, had seen more wars than you would believe. That was one of the things we discovered: without the restraints of custom and order that we are used to in the real world, humanity is an astoundingly quarrelsome race. It has an enormous appetite for war. Generals and Counts learnt new tactics from the written people of the Device: several "agent" characters had occupied positions of superiority in their armies, and they came up with a variety of brilliant novelties in the art of war. Of course, it's possible that the insurrectionists were somehow able to access these same data.'

It was drizzling again, the surface of the pool stippled with restlessly shifting constellations of icing-drops. The rain bounced from the head and shoulders of the ghost Cleonicles, as if it were a real and material being.

'It was decided,' he said, 'to change the parameters of the simulation. Our written computational world had reached undreamt-of levels of complexity. In order to be able to study it more efficiently, we decided to slow the relative passage of time inside the System. From one year passing to every day here, we changed the coding so that one and a half years passed in the System for every *month* that passed in our world. Three written weeks for every real day. It brought incredible levels of complexity to light, complexity that had lain buried under the onward rush of the data. And we made one other change, the most significant of all, perhaps.'

'What was that?'

'We introduced real people into the simulation.'

Polystom wiped the rainwater away from his face. 'Real people?'

'It was my idea. This is why I talk of irony, caught in my own web! When I had written the algorithms for the first "agent" characters, I had sketched them fairly roughly, or based them on famous historical figures. But they were a little crude. Many of them functioned well enough – better than well, indeed. But sometimes there were problems. Several of these characters seemed, oddly, to sense that they were more *real* than the people around them. There was a much higher incidence of insanity, schizophrenia, amongst the agents than we had written in for the population at large. Several of them founded religions – would you believe it? The general population was written to follow the prevailing belief systems, but these individuals (there were a couple of them) genuinely believed that they were gods, or that they talked to gods. Thus, I suppose, they explained to themselves their own sense that they were special. These new religions swept through our simulation.'

'You were never a religious man, uncle.'

'So I understand. It annoyed me, I know, the prevalence and variety of religious belief inside the simulation. But the decision to introduce real people into the simulation was not mine alone. It was thought that real people as "agent" characters would make the simulation more realistic, and that we would learn more from it. We took the funeral dossiers of a number of people: we collected bundles of them, or copied them, soon after the funeral oration was made. They're wonderful raw material, funeral dossiers, particularly if they are not skimped in the writing. When a next-of-kin assembles a very detailed dossier, when the deceased has properly attended to the matter when alive, then we have almost an entire life already written. So I, and some others, transferred various of these dossiers into Computational Device coding. Dozens to begin with; then hundreds. The more detailed the dossier, the more "real" the person.'

Cleonicles stopped, looking at the rain falling around him. 'Eventually I withdrew from the project. But I was very assiduous, throughout the rest of my life – thirty years, or more – in assembling the data for my own dossier. I kept it in a fat folder with a C on the front. And after my death, after my murder, they transferred me into the simulation. I am in one sense the most real person in it, because my dossier was the fullest. I was certainly the one with the greatest self-awareness, the greatest understanding of the artificiality of the environment. Or that's what I thought. I thought of it as artificial. It's . . . complex. It's all suddenly got very complicated.'

He stopped. He seemed to be in a little pain. 'Uncle?' said Polystom. 'Are you alright?'

'It was a revolution. The introduction of real people into the System, I mean. This is about five centuries ago. Five hundred of the simulated years, I mean. A little more. Thirty of *our* years. We broadened the parameters of the world: certain populations that had been largely static, without agent characters, were written up in greater detail and agents introduced. And the real people acted in ways new to this world, acted in ways that the earlier, the original, agents hadn't. They were much more inquisitive about it. As far as they knew, of course, it was the *only* world. None of them had the self-awareness I was just talking about. They grew up in the simulated world, and they accepted it as real, they didn't know of anything different. Nevertheless, a high proportion of them became scientists, artists. There was an explosion of intellectual activity. Each of these algorithm-people spawned similar algorithms, that was part of the programming; agent-characters gave birth to agent-characters. And these in turn carried the restless, questing spirit into the world. One consequence was that a great many of these new agents felt the urge to explore the globe. They went on lengthy, dangerous voyages to all corners of it – we needed to revise the world with increasing frequency, to add detail and verisimilitude to parts of the globe that had been functioning, before this, on a sort of automatic pilot. So many areas of the world I had just sketched in, now agents decided they wanted to visit these places, so we had to go back and fill them in much more convincingly. It was hard work: inventing whole cultures, providing background detail – you see, it wasn't enough simply to flesh out a new population in some southern hemisphere or distant latitude with agent characters of their own, although of course we did that. But we also needed to invent these cultures' histories: to write the ruins of their past. I'm afraid we weren't as inventive as we might have been – for example, with several of these cultures we scattered ruined pyramids in their wildernesses, really because I couldn't think of anything else. But we were working fast.

'It became harder and harder to ensure consistency; and hardest of all when these simulated people approached a level of technological sophistication consonant with our own. I'll give you an example of what I mean. In my original parameters for the System, you remember I mentioned I created a planet called War?'

'Yes.'

'Well, it was an early piece of writing, and its atmosphere was very thin. It was a cold world, barren. But nonetheless, at that early stage, I had toyed with the idea of several inhabited worlds – it's what I was used to, after all, in the real world. So I sketched in some basic Computational

Patterns for this world. I made it mostly desert, but gave it two ice caps of water. Then I toyed with the idea of a great system of canals, by which the population brought this water from the poles to the cold deserts of the central latitudes. There was a very crude sort of culture, kings and princesses and so on: but I wrote no "agent" characters for this world, nobody with any free will. As with all such background populations, they simply bubbled along, innovating nothing. To be honest, I got so caught up with the events on *The World* that I more or less forgot about this other planet. Its deserts were red, and it was just visible from the World as a red dot in the sky. Anyway, long after I had left the project, one of the agent characters began examining this world, War, with the benefit of a telescope. He was a scientist, you see. He studied it, saw the canals, mapped them out, published his research. There was a great deal of interest in what he saw. It brought the distant planet into the remit of the simulation. And the writers who were working on it were faced with the necessity of inventing this entire new civilisation – of filling in all the detail in its history, and of writing agent characters for it. Who knew but that one day our simulated people might not go there? But the writers were too busy to do all this. They couldn't really be bothered. So – do you know what they did?'

'What did they do?'

'They changed the core code! It boggled me when I heard it, I don't mind telling you. They rewrote the whole of the planet War so that there was no indigenous population, no cities, no ruins, no canals, nothing at all. Amazing! They wrote in some hasty physics algorithms, and left the world cold and dead and barren. They even changed my water poles to poles of frozen carbon dioxide. Imagine! They couldn't change what the agent character had written and published back on the World, though, not without erasing the entire programme. But they were in too much hurry, too harassed, to really care. If truth be told, there are thousands of suchlike inconsistencies. So, in one decade a respected scientist observes through a telescope and reports canals; and in a later decade new scientists look with more powerful telescopes and see no canals at all. Naturally they rubbish the earlier scientist. One thing that keeps the whole system running is that its simulated inhabitants possess a sort of *will to consistency*; they ignore things that don't fit with their accepted world-view. Anyway, that's a little off the point. Where was I?'

'I'm not sure. Real people in the programme, I think.'

'Ah,' said Cleonicles. 'Real people.'

'What has happened more recently,' said Cleonicles, 'is that the simulation has become *more* complex and *more* sophisticated than the real world. Can you imagine it? In a sense, it's more real, now, than we are.'

'How could that be?'

'Well, well. One example is technology. Technological levels in the real world, our world – your world, I should say – have remained more or less constant for centuries now. There are good reasons for that, in fact. A tool is developed, be it a fork or a flying machine, and it does a certain job. There's no point in inventing a tool to do a job nobody needs, and once a machine does the job then it does the job. We're a conservative people, nephew. But it has not been like that in the Computational Device.'

'No?'

'Oh no, indeed not. Change built on change. The rate of change accelerated. The simulated population discovered and invented, they developed, many of the aspects of civilisation with which we are familiar in the real world. And then they superseded us.'

'Superseded.'

'Certainly they did! They developed propeller-driven flying machines, just like ours, ten or eleven years ago. Our years, I mean. But then they refined and enhanced their invention; they made bigger flying machines, faster ones. They fought wars with them. They invented new engines for them, engines that sucked in air, ignited it and ejected it explosively behind. Our military, the real military I mean, have been trying to duplicate the technology, but it's hard. When *we* built similar machines in the real world they would mostly blow up and kill the test pilots. The same thing happened in the simulation – only they didn't seem to mind. They are profligate of life. They invented bigger, faster cars.' He shook his head. 'When I first laid down the System, I did not believe that they would ever travel from world to world. To travel through vacuum? The difficulties would surely be insurmountable. But they achieved it – can you believe that? These Computational Device imitation-people built air-filled containers, fired them with explosives, and travelled the enormous

260

distances I had written into their cosmos. They went from the World to their moon – nothing like my beloved moon, nephew, although with some of the same features. But an airless, grey wasteland. Nonetheless they went there, for no other reason than they had the technological capability to do it! It was instructive, and awful, to watch. And there are two other things I must tell you, before my lengthy lecture draws to a close. Do I bore you?'

'Not at all, Uncle,' said Polystom.

'Two more things. Two more developments in the World of the simulation. I had withdrawn from the project long before, of course; I was living on the moon of Enting. But I was in constant communication with the military. I was convinced, you see, that the insurrectionists on the Mudworld, here, had somehow tapped into the simulation. They adapted and improved themselves, fought as no insurrectionists had fought before. For thirty years, forty, however long it has been. But more than this, I began to suspect their presence in the simulation. Somehow, I don't know how. Before we introduced real people into the simulation there had been insurrections against simulated social order, of course, as there are in the real world. And like the real world they had been small-scale affairs. And even after real people were introduced, social stability was retained. But suddenly, in the simulation, the world was full of revolutions. Imagine! Whole nations rebelled against their leaders, their ruling families. Higher orders were butchered in great numbers. In *all* portions of the globe, uprising followed upris-ing. The whole World went mad for revolutions. Some of these rebellions were crushed, but many were successful, and on a huge scale.'

'You suspect the intervention of the insurrectionists from the Mudworld in the simulation?'

'Indeed I do. I think they somehow infiltrated the Computational Device itself. The military, in particular, were worried: they had come to see the simulation as predictive, you understand, of real events. Although there's little actual evidence of that. But I think the real insurrectionists have introduced some strange code into the pro-gramme, turning people into revolutionaries. I don't see how you explain it otherwise, the sudden mania for revolution.'

He stopped. The rain was falling more softly now.

'And the second thing?' Polystom prompted him. 'You said there was a second thing, the thing that rounded off your lecture?'

'Ah,' said Cleonicles. 'The most important thing of all. The most important thing.'

'We did not anticipate it. We did not realise that it could happen. In retrospect this was naïve of us. But the inhabitants of the simulation developed Computational Devices of their own. This changed everything.'

'A Computational Device inside the Computational Device?'

'Well, yes. Wheels within wheels, eh? They were tinkering with the principles of computation fifteen years ago, or more. Our years, I mean. But it wasn't until a few years ago that they perfected it. And, again, they took it further. They found more efficient, and much smaller, methods of binary analysis than valves and crystals. Suddenly, in a month or so of our time, the world of the simulation was overrun with Devices. Almost everybody possessed them. Devices much larger in capacity than even ours were created.'

'I don't see,' said Polystom, slowly, 'how the machine could contain a bigger machine.'

Cleonicles merely smiled. 'A good point, I suppose,' he said. 'Oh, the philosophical abyss that has opened up since that happened! It's less a matter of size, I think, than efficiency. Or something like that. Certainly, the interaction between actual computer and simulated computer has, somehow, changed the fundamentals of the programme. It's not exactly clear how. The military continued to put in the algorithms of real people, but they were no longer accepted. Instead of fitting into a preset childhood package, which allowed the characters to be born into the simulation, to develop within the system absorbing its influence as they grew . . . instead of that, the programme refused to accept the new input. Refused! The new "agent" algorithms wandered, fully formed, ghostly, in the other world. Or in this world. And not really present in either.'

'Is that what happened to you?'

'Indeed. Well, no, my situation was rather different. My dossier was turned into code in a much more detailed way. The scientists who put me there were hoping, I think, that I would address the problem, whatever the problem was. Take the example of your wife: Beeswing. I took her dossier at the funeral, and wrote it up into code myself, trying to find ways of getting around the blockage, whatever the blockage was. I failed. Beeswing is also caught in this odd liminal state.'

'I don't understand,' said Polystom. 'Is she dead? Isn't she a ghost?'

'Yes,' said Cleonicles, with a blank face. 'I think so. I think she is. Understand the transformation that has taken place, in me for instance. Nothing of the man you knew of Cleonicles, that is to say, nothing *essential*, is present in me. I was constructed after his death, out of a dossier of his memoirs and various other accounts. I remember everything that Cleonicles put in that dossier.'

'A strange sort of ghost,' said Polystom. 'More a poem than a ghost.'

Clouds parted, and a frying sunshine fell onto everything. It was mid-afternoon, or thereabouts; steam oozed out of Polystom's sodden clothing. The ghostly Cleonicles, although his form had intercepted the falling rain, seem to have absorbed none of the water. He sat, clean as a wax figure.

'What do you want me to do, Uncle?' Polystom asked. 'I don't understand why you've come to me.'

'I want you to go to the mountain,' said Cleonicles. He was standing now, although Polystom could not remember him having actually gone through the process of getting to his feet. He was standing on the far side of the pool, his arm outstretched, pointing. 'To the mountain!' he called.

'Why there?'

'Go to the Device. It needs to be rewritten. The whole programme has gone very wrong. I can tell you how to do it.'

'Me? Why me?'

His uncle was, oddly, at his side again, sitting in the sunlit mud beside the little brown pool. 'I've tried talking to the scientists and the technicians inside there – of course, I can appear in there. Naturally. But they won't acknowledge me. I don't know, to be truthful, if they can't see me, or *won't* see me. But I can't get through to them, whichever way it is. I suspect they *can* see me, you know. There's a sort of harassed look that comes over some of their faces when I harangue them. But they don't respond. And I have gotten angry, actually. It's very difficult for me, practically difficult, but I've physically interacted on occasion, pushed them and so on. They just sit on the floor with their hair ruffled and astonished looks on their faces. Perhaps they think they've had a fit of some sort. A gust of wind. I don't know.'

'The men, the ordinary soldiers, know about you all.'

'Of course they do! They have those virtues of common sense that the top brass necessarily lack.'

'So,' said Polystom, weighing the idea. 'You want me to go into the Device?'

'There are control rooms, and a large bank, like a sort of four-shelved piano, at which the primary programmes are written and put-in. Once you're there, you'll see what I mean. Then I can guide you. We need to rewrite the whole simulation!'

'I couldn't *reach* anybody else,' Cleonicles was saying. They were walking now. Perhaps Polystom was a little feverish because he couldn't remember starting the walk; he had no memory of clamber-ing out of the crater, yet here he was, picking his way awkwardly between the strewn lines of barbed wire. 'I couldn't get through to anybody else; then I met the agent, the ghost, of your wife. Beeswing. Because *you* had written her dossier, and because *I* had revised it when I was still alive – and because neither of us knew very much about her origins and childhood, she was a different sort of ghost to the rest. Her personality is mostly constructed around you; so she knew about you. And I knew that you had gathered a troop of soldiers and were on the world.'

'Why did she have to come and get me though? Why couldn't you come yourself?'

'I'm tied to the Device, to the mountain. I'm not sure why. I think it has something to do with this peculiar interaction of Computational Device and the Computational-Device-within-the-Device. It's set up resonances in the programming logic, the substratum of the logic of the written experience within the machine, that are very hard to predict, to understand. I think my close association with the Device has become, in a way, literalised in the logic of my algorithm, with the result that I cannot move too far from the *actual* machine in the *actual* world.'

'I don't understand.'

'It doesn't matter. Beeswing, however, *could* appear to you fairly easily – again, perhaps because the logic of her algorithm was closely allied to you. She's not really Beeswing at all, in fact. She's your perspective of Beeswing. So I asked her to go fetch you – to persuade you to come close enough to the Computation core of the Device for me to be able to pop out and say hello.'

He smiled.

Polystom stopped. There was a stretch of barbed wire before him that ran right down both flanks of the ridge. 'How do I go on from here?' he asked.

Cleonicles, the ghost, frowned, lines puckering into his brow like tic-tac-toe. 'Can you go down and round?'

'The flanks are mined. I'd be blown to shreds.'

'Perhaps you can go over? Or – or dig your way under?'

'I'm hungry, tired,' said Polystom, dropping to the ground with his legs before him. 'This is too much.'

'I don't understand how things like poems,' said Polystom, after ruminating for a while, 'how things like poems can haunt the real world. If you're written into the, what are they, the *pages*, so to speak, of this great Computational Machine, then how do you find yourself outside the machine with me?'

'That's the most interesting question of all,' said Cleonicles. 'I'll not pretend I can answer it straight away. But, observe: this situation has only come to pass since the simulation has developed cognate or even superior computational abilities of its own. It has something to do with the interaction of these two systems – perhaps that interaction enhanced the respective ability to realise the agents many times over? Perhaps some complex of energy and ordering, of power and computational, bodies forth myself, Beeswing, all the rest. The Device, in the mountain, does use an enormous amount of power. It's something along these lines, I'm certain. Or perhaps you'd prefer to think that we're actually ghosts? Spirits from the dead?'

'Poems walking around,' Polystom repeated, with a degree of stubbornness. 'In the world.'

'The important thing is that we must rewrite the simulation.'

'And this will help?'

'I believe so. I believe it will liberate all of the ghosts.'

'What will you do?'

'The culture of the simulation has advanced too far. If, as I believe, it is their own computational power that has brought this terrible situation into being, then we must rewrite the simulation to do away with that power.'

'Simply write-out their simulated Computational Devices?'

'Not *simply* write them out, no, no. I said that the simulation absorbs a surprising degree of self-contradiction, but there are limits. No, there are more elegant ways of solving the problem. These civilisations, inside the device, are enormously belligerent, as I said. They have invented some extremely powerful weapons of destruction. It would be an afternoon's work for me, for you with me guiding you, to have some of these devices malfunction, attack an enemy, such that the enemy retaliates. In a day, one of our days, their culture would be smashed back into primitiveness.'

'You'll write-in a war?'

'Yes. Write-in the collapse of their civilisation. I'm convinced that it will end the interference pattern, the destructive interference pattern of their own independent advances, their own computational skills.'

'Won't millions die?'

'I daresay.'

'Bad news for them,' Polystom observed.

'Well, quite,' said Cleonicles. 'But they're not real, now, are they?'

'As real as you,' said Stom, with a spiteful emphasis. 'I'm sure they feel real. I'm sure, from their point of view, they feel very real indeed.'

'They *may* very well feel that,' said Cleonicles, levelly. 'But that doesn't make it true, now, does it.'

After a pause, Stom asked: 'what happens to *you* when you write-in this mass destruction for the simulation? I mean, what actually happens, for you and Beeswing and the others like you? You say this will liberate the ghosts – what does that mean? Will you cease to be?'

'I hardly think,' said Cleonicles, smiling, 'that I'd be planning such a course of action if *that* were to be the result. No, I assume what will happen is that our "agent" algorithms will be inserted into the simulation in the usual way. Which is to say, what used to be the usual way before the onset of the problem. I suppose I'll be "born" some-where, have to grow to adulthood inside the simulation, and so on. It'll be preferable to wandering these wastelands for goodness knows how long,' he added, with an unconvincing smile. 'Believe you me.'

*

On Cleonicles' instruction, Polystom took off his jacket and spread it over the nearest wire. Then he tried gripping the strands of biting steel, his hands cushioned by the fabric. It took several goes before he got purchase. He tried pulling the wire, shaking it (with the vague idea that he might set off mines further along its length and blow holes in it), but the thing was simply too heavy and massive. He couldn't move it. Then he tried to recover his jacket, to find that it was gripped ferociously by the barbs. It didn't matter. The afternoon was very hot. He was better off without the damn thing.

'Try climbing over the wire,' urged the ghost. 'Use your jacket as a way of passage.'

But Polystom didn't like the look of that. The jacket stretched only halfway over the metal brambles, and an intimidating stretch of barbs glinted in the sunlight.

'Can't you move the wire out of the way for me?' he asked his dead uncle. 'You're dead, after all. It can't hurt you.'

'I don't really interact with this world in that way.'

'You don't? But you're speaking to me. I saw the rain bounce off your shoulders.'

'You didn't, not really. You saw my programme, my writing-essence, adapt to the environment by adding rain. The rain in the air was real, but the rain bouncing off my shoulders was not. And yes I can talk to you; and I have been able, on occasion, to affect things more materially. But not very well, not without great effort. It's a matter of the algorithm that describes me; it functions only on the boundary of materiality – you can see me and hear me, but I can't move the wire for you.'

'It's hopeless,' Stom said. 'It's hopeless. And even if I could go on, there would be more wire. Wire and mines.'

'Now, now,' said the ghost of his uncle. 'That sounds like the counsel of despair.'

'And if I did reach the mountain, how could I possibly persuade the authorities there to allow me to rewrite the patterns inside the Computational Device? It's madness to think of it! What would I tell them? That the ghost of my dead uncle told me to do it?'

The light thickened and greyed around him, as a new raft of clouds slid in front of the sun. These clouds were black as plums, threatening renewed downpour. The change in the quality of the light was extraordinarily pronounced: from bright sunshine to an almost submarine gloom. It took a second for Polystom's eyes to adjust to the duskiness, and when he looked around for his uncle he found himself amongst a crowd of silent figures. They had appeared from nowhere, every one of them a foot or more taller than Polystom, all dressed in dark clothes, their skin looking grey in the dimness of the light. They stood all around him, distributed evenly amongst the wire, the craters, but every one of them was turned to face him, Polystom, faces like grey sunflowers aimed at the sun. Their silent attention was thrillingly upsetting.

'Uncle?' Stom said; but Cleonicles seemed even more startled by the arrival of the ghosts than he was.

And then, from nowhere, the land to the west exploded, the air shattering with noise, a cliff-face of brown hurled up by the explosions and atomising into a locust-cloud of mud-clods, swarming brown through the air as Polystom, half knocked-over and half diving for cover, put his face into the mud.

There were half a dozen more detonations, each one making the earth tremble beneath Polystom like palsy. He wrapped his arms about his head. A heavy rain of mud clattered against his back. More explosions. Something jagged into his arm, by his shoulder; a bullet? Shrapnel?

Polystom waited minutes after the last of the explosions, the wound in his shoulder burning all the while, before he considered it safe enough to sit up. A shard of wire, with three barbs upon it, had stuck itself into his flesh. It had not gone deep, and the end that had inserted itself into his flesh was barb-free, so that Polystom was able to pull it clear. His shirt wore a rosette of blood on its arm, but the bleeding dried up quickly.

Only after he had pulled the wire free did Polystom look around him. Cleonicles was gone. The eerie crowd of motionless, grey figures was no more. Away to the west, the ground was newly cratered, up and down like a monumental sculpture of an ocean stormscape. All around him were gathered mud-coloured men, all of them carrying weapons of one sort or another.

Polystom had fallen into the hands of the enemy.

His heart lurched and pounded. They were about to kill him. To kill him. One of them lifted a hand, closed it to a fist, holding it around the level of his shoulder. And then, with a ridiculous sense of relief, Stom saw the ghost of his dead wife making her way through the crowd.

[seventh leaf]

The insurrectionists tied his hands behind him, and marched him for several hours westwards, down the broken landscape of the west ridge and into the valley. 'Beeswing?' he called. 'Beeswing?'

'Hello again,' she said, at his shoulder.

'Are you with these people?'

'Indeed I am.'

'Wife, please tell me that they're not going to execute me. Please. I couldn't bear that.' Under the power of these servants, Polystom couldn't help think of the flayed man, the ghastly individual who had haunted his dreams.

'Couldn't bear it,' said Beeswing distantly. 'Excuse me, I have to go.' She tripped off, away, out of sight.

They marched in silence along the valley, Polystom sobbing openly; footsore, hungry, thirsty, his shoulder throbbing with pain, and fear chewing at his insides like toothache. The strands of muscle bunched together like balls of red wool, just below the comforting cloth of the skin. The flayed man grasping at his ankles. The servant had caught him at last.

They had come from the Mudworld, those two who had been executed. Perhaps they had been the colleagues of these dour, dirt-covered soldiers. Had they followed the news? Polystom tried, with an increasing sense of desperation, to remember the occasion. It had been widely reported; that had been half the point of it. Had reports showed him sitting on the pedestal, observing the execution? Had these reports reached the Mudworld? Of course they had, he told himself. Of course they had. How had he appeared, on those reports? He had – surely – worn a face of elegantly repressed distress. He had thought it a barbarous, unnecessary manner of death. He had only attended because the military insisted. But would these insurrectionists under-stand that? Could they be made to understand it?

They stopped for ten minutes in a shell-crater as a heavy storm rolled through the sky. Thorns of water bristled in ever-changing patterns on the surface of the pond. Polystom watched the patterns in a sort of ecstasy of fear. Then the sky cleared, and they were off again.

They pushed him, and he tumbled forward into a trench, landing awkwardly and winding himself. Gasping, tears in his eyes, they hauled him upright and threw him into a dark dugout. The door was shut behind him.

He wriggled round, his arms still tied behind him, and managed to get himself sitting against the wall. Eventually the blackness resolved itself into a grainy greyness, the thread-thin Π of light from the edges of the shut door seeping illumination through. The walls and floor were mud. There was no furniture.

'Hello again,' said Beeswing. Of course she had appeared from nowhere, through the closed door. Polystom could just about make out the shape of her, uncertain in outline in the darkness. She moved, her shadowy silhouette passing in front of him. Then she was on the other side.

'Beeswing,' said Polystom. 'You've got to help me.'

'They took you,' said Beeswing, in her singsong voice, 'on my suggestion. They're not much given to taking prisoners, you see. They tried it, as a tactic, decades ago, in the early years of the war – or so they told me, when I suggested taking you. Said it had never done them any good in the past.'

'Beeswing . . .'

'But I talked them round.'

'They listen to you?'

'It's a funny thing,' she said. 'They do. They seem to regard the ghosts as a sort of supernatural talisman. Something like that. Some of us have convinced them that we're on the same side. There's little we can do, as ghosts, you know,' she added with a bubbling chuckle, 'except pop up out of strange places and frighten the soldiers. But we are privy, some of us, to important information. That counts for something.'

'This is all madness,' sobbed Polystom. 'I shouldn't be here. I'm a poet, not a soldier. I never intended those men to be executed, certainly not in the manner they were. Please tell them, Beeswing, please tell them. It wasn't my choice.'

'What on earth are you talking about?'

'Please, wife, please,' Polystom whined. 'Please, please.'

It took him several long moments to realize he was alone.

Polystom was in the dugout for days, or weeks, or a day: it was impossible to gauge the passing of time. He was brought a hunk of bread and some water in a can. In the seconds that the door was open, and bright sunshine spilling in from outside, the bread looked blotchy with mould; but in the greyness that followed the door being shut he was able to tell himself that he had been dazzled, that the bread was fine, and he ate it all down and drank the warm water.

'I never meant to be a soldier,' he told the ghost of his wife. 'Do you know why I think I volunteered?'

'Tell me.'

'It was because my uncle was killed, you know.'

'That happened after my death,' Beeswing reminded him. 'That wasn't in my dossier. I've heard something about it subsequently – and of course, spoken to your uncle personally. But, you know, *he* doesn't remember his own death except in a secondhand manner, because that wasn't in *his* dossier. Anyway, go on: you were saying?'

'I think I volunteered out of guilt.'

'Guilt?'

'My uncle was assassinated, and I didn't feel anything. Can you believe that? I was numb to it. I knew, in my brain, that it was a terrible thing that had happened, but I didn't *feel* it, in my heart. Do you know what I mean?'

'Having neither heart nor brain,' said Beeswing, 'it'd take me an effort of imagination.'

'It was all blank,' said Polystom. He was lying on his back, his captors having removed his bindings. 'I felt nothing. Eventually I felt guilty that I felt nothing. And because I felt guilty, empty, nothing; and because I was surrounded by all these military men who seemed so purposeful and assured; and because my uncle had been involved, in some mysterious way that I didn't understand, in the war on the Mudworld. Because of all this I thought to myself that a glorious military commission would make things better, somehow.' He coughed. 'So I volunteered. What a fool I have been. I don't belong here.'

'I *certainly* don't belong here,' said Beeswing.

273

'Cleonicles, his ghost, said that if the Computational Device could be rewritten . . .'

'I know all about that,' said Beeswing, cutting him off. 'That's a bit misguided.'

'Misguided?'

'Oh yes. Doesn't go nearly far enough. The people here, well now. They're keen to see the whole machine destroyed.'

'Destroyed?'

'I told them you could help. That's why you're still alive.'

'Destroyed?' said Polystom again. 'But that's insanity. What about the simulated world in there? Whole civilizations! You, yourself – and all the other ghosts like you. You only exist because you were written-in to that imaginary cosmos. How could you destroy it? You'd be destroying yourself!'

'Well,' said Beeswing, her voice very close. 'Let me tell you about that.'

'Cleonicles told you,' came the ghost's voice in the darkness, 'that he personally wrote-in an entire world, into the switches, crystals and valves of the Computational Device. He did that?'

'He did.'

'He explained it to me in similar terms,' said Beeswing.

There was a silence. Polystom was acutely aware of the grey shape, to his left, of his wife. It was hard to believe she wasn't real, a material presence. If he reached out, would he touch her skin? Could he slip the shift from her shoulders? Or would his hand go through her body like slipping through cold water?

'He told you,' she went on, her voice as light as it had ever been in life. 'He told you that some years ago, *their* years, the simulations inside the Computational Device invented Computational Devices of their own?'

'Yes.'

'That these Devices are more powerful, faster, more capable, than our own Devices?'

'I told him,' said Polystom, 'that it seemed, what would you say, *counter*-intuitive to me. But he said it was a question of efficiency rather than actual capacity. Or something like that.'

'It's not like that at all,' said Beewsing. She moved her head. The darker shadow that was her hair moved a fraction later. 'It's not like that at all.'

'What do you mean?'

'Well I'll tell you. How can I put it? This way: which would you say is more likely? That our Computational Device, here in the mountain, has invented the whole cosmos of which we've been talking? Or that *their* Computational Device, invented *this* cosmos?'

'Well that's just ridiculous,' said Stom, immediately.

'Why ridiculous?'

'Obviously, it is. I know I'm real.'

'So do I. Yet you'd describe me as a piece of writing, rather than anything else. But if I feel real, under those circumstances, why might you not feel yourself to be real too?'

Polystom thought about it. 'Our cosmos predates theirs,' he pointed out. 'My uncle invented it, for one thing.'

'Their cosmos,' said Beeswing, 'predates either of us. It's been around longer than we've been alive. That's all we know. Assume your uncle is a programme: may be he's been programmed to tell you that he invented the other cosmos. Perhaps everything around us was invented, say, thirty years ago.'

Polystom shook his head, a meaningless gesture in the dark. He saw what Beeswing was trying to say, he could see the slippery-smooth logic of the statement, but nonetheless his soul rejected it as non-sensical. As sophistry. He couldn't refute it rationally, he saw: any statement he brought up to counter it could be explained away. Nonetheless he *felt* its wrongness. He felt, in his gut, the real-ness of his own existence. This other realm, which he knew only through descriptions from his dead-uncle, sounded far too outlandish – vacuum throughout the System? A constant state of war? Worldwide revolutions? It did not have the smack of reality.

'If I kick a stone, on this world,' said Polystom, 'I feel it as a stone. It's not a piece of writing, it's actually, really, a stone.'

'Of course you'd say that,' said Beeswing. 'It feels that way to you because that's how it's been written.'

'This is nonsense.'

'It isn't.'

'By your own logic,' said Polystom, 'it could be either way. Any argument you make about the *unreality* of our world, could be made with equal relevance about the unreality of this other place, this vacuum-cosmos. And vice versa: any argument you make about the reality of *that* world, you can make with equal validity about this world, our world.'

'Well that's a very interesting point,' agreed Beeswing. 'I can see the force of that argument. What can we do, then, except set the two cosmoses side by side and see which is the more likely? The more plausible? Can we agree, you and I, in his dark hole, that we should believe in the more *plausible* of the two?'

'Well,' said Polystom, uncertainly. 'I don't know.'

'I can't see any other path.'

'If you like,' said Stom. 'But our world is much, *much* more "plausible" than that other, the cosmos Cleonicles described to me.'

'Why so?'

'Of course it is! A massive swollen sun? Millions of miles of emptiness and vacuum between the worlds? It beggars belief.'

'I think,' said Beeswing with an infuriating catch of smugness in her voice, 'that actually what you are saying is that you, personally, are more familiar with this world than the other. That's all. If you'd grown up in the other cosmos, you'd consider the things you mentioned normal, and would consider our System outlandish.'

'Don't be absurd.'

'Let us,' said Beeswing, her shadowy presence moving in front of Stom to take up a position on his right side. 'Let us be rational about it. In what respects is this other world *less* plausible than ours?'

'It has no stability, according to Cleonicles. Thousands of years of constant fighting and war? Such a civilisation would have destroyed itself. And yet, on the contrary, rather than smashing itself to atoms this civilisation is supposed to have developed with staggering rapidity to staggering levels of technical sophistication? How can this have happened? It's nonsense.'

'Agreed,' said Beeswing. 'That's hard to understand.'

'And it's a *vacuum* cosmos,' said Polystom with heat. 'Because my uncle had a strange obsession with the idea! So he invented this System with emptiness between its worlds. Scientific opinion in *our* System is adamant that such a world is an impossibility, but my uncle made it anyway, for his own reasons. He told me he had to fiddle the physics, to make it happen. It could never occur naturally! The vacuum would suck away all the atmosphere from any world – it would be barren.'

'Agreed, again,' said Beeswing. 'That's two good points.'

'There's a *hundred* points,' insisted Polystom, although he couldn't think of any more at that moment. 'It's absurd. And there's nothing illogical about our System, the real System. It's entirely self-consistent – which, Cleonicles told me, wasn't the case with the simulated System either.'

'Very well,' said Beeswing. 'But I'm not sure I share your belief in the inherent stability of our model of reality. If we grew up in a System with vacuum between the worlds, bizarre as that sounds to us – but perhaps if we grew up in such a world, then we would regard our System, with its interplanetary atmosphere, as outlandish and strange. The friction of worlds circulating through the air would slow everything down, and the worlds would all spiral in towards the centre.'

'Nonsense. The air is orbiting, just as the worlds are.'

'Possibly. And maybe that explains why our worlds are so close together,' Beeswing mused. 'But we have other considerations. If *ours* is the real world, then we could write-in characters in the other realm. But if that's the case, then what am I doing here? I'm dead, I died.'

'You were written into the Computational Device,' said Polystom. 'Using your dossier.'

'Let's say I accept that; that I'm constructed, not real. What we two are trying to determine is – who wrote me in? Was it somebody in *this* system? Or somebody in the other?'

'Obviously, somebody in this System.'

'Then what am I doing *here*?'

Polystom was silent. He saw what she meant.

'If I'm *here*,' she went on, 'I must have been written from the other place. If I were written from *this* place, I wouldn't be here, I'd be there.'

'I asked Cleonicles about that,' said Stom.

'And?'

'I can't remember exactly how he explained it. He said that the Computational Device in the simulation set up – something – I can't remember the phrase he used. But he had an explanation for it.'

'It seems to me,' said Beeswing, in the darkness, 'that the fact there are ghosts on the Mudworld implies that the Mudworld isn't real. That's one point.'

'Well,' said Polystom uncertainly. 'Well, I'm not sure.'

'The other point,' said Beeswing, 'the other point is the fact, which your uncle concedes, as quickly as anybody, the fact that this other System is more advanced than we are. How can that be? The Computational Device supposedly inside our own Computational Device – how can that be better than its parent machine? How can this invented society be more advanced than the society that invented it? To me, the gradient should run the other way. Don't you think?'

Polystom was silent for a while. 'That's two points on both sides.'

'To me,' came Beeswing's voice, 'the arguments are stronger on my side than yours.'

'Well,' said Polystom, his aching body and weary head flaring up in a display of petty irritation, 'well, to me it seems exactly the other way about.'

'Well,' said Beeswing.

'Well,' said Polystom.

They sat in silence, in the darkness, for a while.

'Suppose you tell me,' said Polystom. 'Tell me the way *you* think it is. Suppose you give me your version of events.'

'I think,' said Beeswing, her voice steady and mellow, 'that there is a civilisation out there, outside us. I think that civilisation developed Computational Devices, and that one of these Devices has been given over to an elaborate simulation. I think somebody in that other world wrote our System into being; he, or she, wrote a complex set of Computational algorithms that modelled our cosmos, our worlds, our population. I can believe, as Cleonicles said, only he meant it the other way around, that most of the people in this world are varieties of computational automata, that they follow their preprogrammed pattern and that is all. And I can believe that a small proportion of the population is written differently, with algorithms that mimic consciousness, so that those individuals feel themselves to be real, they operate in a problem-solving, free-will manner. Who knows why they would construct such a thing? For study, or pleasure, I don't know. I think that it's probably based on aspects of the root-culture, that various aspects of the written-world are copied from paradigms in the real world, out there. I think that when we were written, we were given the illusion of a lengthy and detailed historical past. But

I'm not sure I believe that we actually *have* a past. For all I know, the entire simulation was constructed, past and all, thirty of our years ago. Maybe less. I also think that from time to time they change things. I think that they've written this war, on the Mudworld, into being: for whatever reason. Education or entertainment, I don't know.'

'But who could find entertainment in any of this?' Polystom said bitterly.

'I agree, it's hard to understand the attraction of it, it's all pain and death here. But I think that the "ghosts", of whom I am one, have been written-in to leaven this aspect of the simulation. That's why I'm here. The back-story, all the stuff told to you by Cleonicles, has only been introduced to help iron out the inconsistencies in the programme that would otherwise bewilder the free agents within it. But, actually, *you*, Polystom, are precisely as unreal as I. We both come from the same source: from the Computational writers in this other place.'

There was a lengthy silence, after Beeswing had completed this speech. Eventually Polystom stirred.

'I think we haven't moved on,' he said. 'We're in the same position we were before. Either of these versions of reality could be correct. They are each equally plausible.'

'There's a test we can make.'

'Which is?'

Beeswing's voice sounded very close, in Polystom's ear. 'We can destroy the Computational Device.'

'Back to that?'

'If we destroy the Device, then – assuming your uncle is correct – the whole of this *other* cosmos disappears with it. Yes? And all the ghosts on the Mudworld disappear too. Do you agree?'

'Yes,' said Polystom.

'If I – and your dead uncle – if *we* only exist because we were written into the Computational Device inside the mountain, then when that machine is destroyed we will disappear. But if the Device is destroyed *and we are still here* – then there will be only one explanation. It could only mean that our existence does not depend upon the Device in the mountain, but on something else. Something outside our world.'

'And this is why you want to blow the thing up?'

'Yes.' Her voice sounded very pure.

'Did you tell all this to your insurrectionist friends?'

'Goodness, no.' There was the sound of laughter in the dark. Beeswing's ghost seemed to be moving around the space. 'That would not be appropriate at all. Tell them that none of them were real? They'd simply ignore me. No, they want the Computational Device destroyed because they believe that the Forces of Authority depend upon it. They believe that with the Device gone, they'll soon enough be able to win the war here on the Mudworld. But the *why* doesn't matter so much. What matters is testing the theorem.'

'You make it sound very abstract.'

'Don't you want to know? To know the truth?'

'I don't know anything at all,' said Polystom. 'I'm a little confused, I think. And tired. Very tired.'

'Then sleep,' said Beeswing. 'And be grateful that your writers have written-in the release of sleep for you. Sleep is a particularly lovesome thing.'

'Do you,' said Polystom, rolling onto his side and slotting his elbow under his head as a pillow. 'Do you sleep?'

'I'm a ghost,' came his dead wife's voice in the dark. 'Ghosts don't sleep. Surely you know that?'

Over two weeks Polystom is brought round. He spends every day with the ghost of his wife; and, later on, he spends some time with the leaders of this particular insurrectionist troop. They are a taciturn group of men and women, the women almost indistinguishable from the men in mire. Although he only gleans fragmented aspects of their story, he has the sense that they have been fighting blood-and-bone, tooth-and-nail, for a very long time: fighting for very survival, fighting with the determined work-ethic that had once defined them as servants. They do not talk much. Some of them are old, in their forties, fifties, one old woman so crumpled with age-wrinkles that she might have been ninety except for her sprightly, murderous physical energy and agility. Others of them are young: twenty, fifteen, it's hard to tell. They eat and sleep in common, and their command structure appears to shift in ways that Polystom finds hard to follow. On the third day they bring him out of the dugout, and allow him to eat with them. On the sixth day their position comes under attack from aerial bombardment, and they dig themselves deeper under the earth. Later that same day there is a ground assault, which they repel with grim, silent, collective action. During this assault Polystom cowers at the base of the trench, every explosion and every gunshot like an electrical jolt to his nervous system. He has come to hate, very deeply, the unexpected violence of this Mudworld war.

Once the attack is repelled, the troop pulls back, up the flank of a hill and into a network of tiny tunnels. Polystom clambers through this claustrophobic network for hours, a soldier in front of him and one behind. He weeps as he crawls, with exhaustion and fear. Eventually they reach a groined-out chamber, fifteen yards high and twice as long. There are other enemy soldiers here, and the two groups spend two days in the darkness, lit with electric torches. From time to time the walls tremble and the earth around them rumbles, a dyspeptic sound on a huge scale. But no disaster befalls, and nothing else happens. On the third day they exit this room, and make their way along another tunnel, soon appearing in the open air. From here the troops split, one party heading south, and Polystom's original captors moving north up the valley.

The troop of insurrectionists seem to regard Beeswing as a talismanic figure. They rarely speak to Polystom, and he comes to realise that, as a representative of the ruling class, they despise him on principle. But they chat with the ghost-woman all the time. Do they ponder how she came to be here? Do they have any comprehension of the situation, of the philosophical double-bind of the two Computational Devices? They give no indication, if so. Perhaps they don't care.

'I've told them that you're prepared to work with them,' Beeswing says to him. 'To help them destroy the Computational Device. Please tell me that you are.'

'I am.'

And he is: the longer he spends with these people, the more he admires them. Perhaps it has something to do with the surly disregard they use on him. Subconsciously, perhaps, he wishes to ingratiate himself with them. Or perhaps he is seduced by the sheer uncomplaining effort that their lives are. Like the men on the skinframe, back on the moon of Enting, a million years ago, it seems to him, there's a ferocious authenticity about their mode of life. They labour and labour at the business of making war; they put all their strenuous efforts of work in that business. Beside them, Polystom feels himself to be insubstantial, to be as unreal as Beeswing would argue he is. He sees the life he used to live as frothy; wealth, poetry, nothingness. Here, in the soil, amongst death and pain, is real human will, real experience, real existence. And every tossed-aside remark in his direction makes him glow. When they share their food with him he feels like a patted dog. His inner being twists a little in self-disgust; but more and more he feels that these people, these authentic human beings, are his rightful superiors.

It does not happen instantly, but as day follows day his sense of his own worth crumbles; he is a miserable creature, sickly, cowardly, pathetic. The only thing to which he can cling is the worth of his captors. Their strength. Their courage; unshowy, genuine. Their superiority to him.

One evening he is waiting impatiently, hungry, for the group holding him to give him some food. A youngster brings in a satchel in which are several round loaves, going blue in patches but still plump and appetising. Stom fidgets in his corner as the soldiers tear gobbets of bread from the loaves and eat them, laughing occasionally and slapping one another's shoulders. Finally he steps towards them, reaches out to help himself to some bread, as they are doing. Hardly looking at him, one of the group pushes a fist at him, catches him hard on the side of the head. As Stom rolls on the floor whimpering and crawls back to his corner the group's laughter increases in intensity. Polystom slumps himself in a coign of the dugout, rubbing the side of his head and staring at them. They make a perfect circle, of which he is not part. He resents them, hates the hurt they have so casually caused him; and at the same time, he admires them. They are so much more stronger and perfect than he. It is clear – he understands this now, realises that he has understood it for a while – it is clear that he deserved to be cuffed around the head. It was impertinent of him to approach them. Later that evening somebody brings him two raw potatoes, and even though he has to scrape away portions of slimy blackness from both before eating them, he is extraordinarily grateful. He gabbles his gratitude, between gobfuls of food, thank you, thank you. And he means it. He feels, in a small way, that he has been accepted into the group. He feels he belongs, even as a minion. He cannot remember when he last had the sense of belonging.

'We'll assemble a force,' says the old woman, who adopts the position of leader more often than anybody else. Her face is like a relief map of the terrain, her wrinkles cut deeply into her skin, yet her eyes seem to Polystom more alive than anybody he knew in his former life. 'Close to the southern entrance to the Machine. You know it?'

'No,' he confesses.

'Don't matter. We'll turn you loose there, and you go inside. You're a captain, aren't you?'

'Yes.'

'They'll let you inside, won't they?'

'I think they will.' He is eager as a puppy that she is talking to him. Talking directly to him!

'Two things,' says the old woman, gruffly. 'Go up to the big gun, dug in over the entrance. You need to disable it.'

'How?' Polystom's voice is nervous; he is unwilling to admit his ignorance of military matters. He doesn't want the old woman to think less of him. But there's no getting around it. He just doesn't know.

'Shoot the gun crew. Put a grenade in the chamber and get out of there.' The old woman is utterly matter-of-fact. 'Then you need to raise hell inside the Machine itself. Run about, shooting, making noise. When we see the cannon go up, we'll launch an assault.'

'I understand.'

And he does; or he thinks he does. He's in a kind of dream. Every evening he talks with Beeswing. She is a different Beeswing from the live one he married. She is eloquent, filled with knowledge, and even with moments of poetry. Of the water, beading on the tight stretch of taurpaulin pulled to make an awning and shelter from the rain: 'like seeds, don't you think?' Something promises spectacular growth on this world, if only the growing season could blossom uninterrupted. Something between Polystom and his dead wife, if not physical then perhaps spiritual. 'Have you noticed?' she asks him, one red-purple sunset. 'There's a kind of grain to the mud, like wood. Maybe it's the way it slides.'

And as the weeks pass, he comes to see that her version of reality has its own beauty. The logic of it, taut and perfectly proportioned as an acorn in its cap. Everything around him, he tells himself one midday, imaginary. Everything here, the *being*ness of everything, is actually a sort of writing, conjured into being by one of the people from the other world, the world outside the world. The sluggish pliability of the clay; the weave of fabric in his shirt; the exact pattern of red jags and splotches of his dried blood on his sleeve. None of it real. He feels a light-headedness. It may be merely the diet of mouldy bread and occasional broths of impossible-to-determine meats, together with brackish water – but it feels like philosophy. It washes through him, just the idea of it. And although he can't quite surrender his own sense of reality, his visceral belief in the mud and the cloth and his own blood, nonetheless there's a part of him that joys in pretending that he does. What if Beeswing is right? The prison of reality is loosened, and that's somehow a glorious prospect. The people he sees around him, the misery and the suffering, it all vanishes as the reality vanishes. Those weren't real people he saw flayed alive on the skin-frame: they were just algorithms. Their pain was just the addition of a few lines of writing, not real pain. All his men, the men he had seen killed, shot and blown apart – none of them were real. Their deaths weren't real. He is liberated from the sense of guilt and despair, because none of it *actually* happened. The boots he found when he was going up the ridge – for a time those boots, each carrying their passenger severed feet, those boots had preyed on his mind. It was so grotesque. But now it was alright. They weren't real feet: no *real* people had to suffer that violent amputation. Almost all the people he sees are not real. Perhaps only a few dozen out of the whole population of the system. Maybe once or twice some of those people, those 'agents' get caught up in the teeth and cogs of the system, and maybe they suffer. But the *weight* of suffering is lifted. It is epitomised for Polystom by the flayed man. For months that figure had haunted his dreams. But Beeswing's version of events frees him from the nightmare. The skinless figure no longer drifted through his dreams; because he had never been real. Lines of code, not flesh and blood – the fact that the flesh and blood, so prominently displayed, had appeared real was simply a function of the expertise of the code-writer.

The world around him acquires a mystic transparency to Polystom's eyes.

They move up the valley until the mountain looms over them, and then they dig into well-concealed hide-holes. Polystom, hunched against the wall, leans toward the figure of his wife at his side.

'What's her name? The old woman?' he asks, sotto voce. She is the leader, it is clear; but more. She is a hero, a great person, a sort of queen. It is important to him that he know her name.

The space is busy with insurrectionist soldiers: some eating, some cleaning their weapons. No matter how dirty their written-not-real bodies and clothing get, these soldiers are scrupulous about keeping their written-not-real rifles clean.

Polystom could almost will himself into the belief: Beeswing's world was like religion, an act of faith.

'She's called Alea.'

'She's the leader?' he murmurs, almost awestruck.

'They try not to orchestrate it in quite that manner,' said Beeswing. 'But yes.'

'She told me what to do.'

'And?'

'Go up there. Get into the gun emplacement and kill all the people there. That's what she said, "shoot the gun crew". Isn't that cold-blooded?'

'War,' says Beeswing.

There is a silence.

'A question,' says Polystom. 'When you were alive . . .'

'When I was alive,' repeats Beeswing.

'When we were married, and you were alive, did you . . . love me?'

'I did,' says Beeswing, looking directly into his eyes. 'I loved you. We were different, you and I, but I loved you, for your poetic soul. Mind you,' she adds, looking at him more strangely, 'you're not talking to the Beeswing you married, are you now. If *you're* right, then you're talking to a being that your uncle wrote, based on the dossier you assembled – for none of my own notes, assuming I made any (and I don't even know that) were part of the dossier. And if that's the case, then what else would you expect me to say? You wrote me, of course I love you. On the other hand,' she said, leaning back, 'if *I'm* right, then we are both written, written by some creature in the vacuum-surrounded world outside our world.'

'And if that's the case,' says Polystom, seizing on the idea, 'then this person, he or she, would surely write you – as ghost – as an extension of the person you had been when you were alive?'

'Possibly,' concedes Beeswing.

*

285

It is another reason to believe in her version of reality rather than his. In his version, the Beeswing he married is fundamentally unknowable, locked away on the other side of death, and this Beeswing he is talking to is nothing but a self-serving fiction of his own concoction. But in *her* version, this Beeswing is the real one.

In *her* version she loved him.

She loves him.

The weight is so strongly on that side of things that he can almost feel it. Like a physical pressure. Everyone, he realises as he stretches on the floor to sleep, is a ghost. I'm a ghost myself. All around us, all walking breathing ghosts. The spectres are truly everywhere yet invisible, like the air.

The next day comes, and they give him a pistol, standing warily round him as if they expect him immediately to start shooting at them with it. That, he realises with a start, is what one of them would do if the positions were reversed. But he is enamoured of them all, of this crude vital life they lead, of the insubstantial figure of his wife. He loves all of them. He loves them so much that there are tears in his eyes. For their heroic struggle, the unstinting, unselfish persever-ance of it, the *reality* of it. When he thinks what they have endured! – not merely them, but *all* servants, everybody – his wife, Beeswing, what *she* had to endure – when he thinks of it, he cannot hold back the tears. He is so profoundly grateful to them: that they are labouring at this work, this rebellion, that they have the strength for that. Grateful that they have accepted him, even in so small a capacity. Grateful that his wife has said the words she never said when she was alive.

There are tears in his eyes as he leaves them, and strikes out alone at the foot of the mountain. There are tears in his eyes as he makes his way up the cloddy ridge, his pistol in a belt at his side, his hands up. The sentries are suspicious of him, but they yield to his automatic habit of command. 'Captain Polystom,' he tells them. And the rifles aimed at his gut; the pistol taken away from him; walked through to a mess-hall – properly built, with stone floor and plastered walls – where a colonel is having breakfast. He fetches another officer, somebody who recognises Polystom, and is, in fact, related to him distantly. There's a deal of embracing and several slugs of cherry-wine. As the alcohol washes down his throat, and starts to blur his perceptions, he thinks to himself *this isn't real, is it – not real wine, not a real sensation.* The colonel, indignant with the sentries, retrieves Polystom's pistol, and Polystom smiles and smiles as he slips it into his belt again. Another colonel, and then a general – honoured to meet the nephew of the great inventor, is his own drawled testimony – come along to join the drinks, to debrief the newcomer. Hilarity. More wine. Toasts, to the Princeling. And, says the general, to the Steward of Enting. It takes Stom a moment to realise they are toasting him. Then the conversation wandering into more military matters. Tell us your story, my dear man. I got separated from my platoon, Polystom says, thinking but not adding, *my various examples of Computational Programming that appeared to me as people.* We retrieved them weeks ago, beams the General. Half a dozen men, and an officer too – Lieutenant Stetrus. Stet? Alive? A trifle drunk with written-not-real wine Polystom is suspiciously over-enthusiastic at the news. Eyes narrow, fractionally, around the table. But he carries it off, his relief seems so genuine. I thought he was dead. He was certainly injured, concedes the general, he was fairly shot up. Head wounds, they're nasty. But he's off the world now, being cared for in a top-rate Berthing military hospital. I thought he was dead, repeats Polystom, noticing albeit thorough a haze, the attitudes around him. Or I would have gone back for them. Ah, says the general. Ah, say the colonels. What would be marvellous, says Polystom, reaching for the bottle, would be a tour of this splendid facility. A tour around the marvellous corridors of the marvellous Computation Device. Now, says the general, freezing more than a little. Let's not get ahead of ourselves. We do need, my dear fellow, to plot out where you've been for the last two weeks. More than two, in fact.

Polystom, frozen in the act of reaching for the bottle, looks around him. There are smiles on the faces, but that fact doesn't conceal the suspicion. He senses the good humour of the moment slipping away. Have you seen any ghosts? he asks. The dead? They're all around us, you know. I've had several fascinating conversations with them.

He can see from their expressions that he's gone too far. Well, says the general, opening his mouth only a little and drawing the syllable out. But Polystom never finds out what he was about to say, because he pulls his pistol out of his belt and fires a bullet into the man's forehead. No, he reminds himself as his heart hammers and the general topples backward on his chair, not a man, a piece of writing in the shape of a man. Only writing in the shape of a man.

The colonels are all on their feet: all three of them. But only one has the presence of mind to be reaching for his own pistol. Polystom's mind is suddenly sharp, the alcohol distilled away by the adrenalin, and he takes a moment to aim his pistol properly and shoots that one in the chest. The colonel sprawls back dramatically, but the blood that showers out with surprising force is not real blood. It feels real, feels warm as pee on the face, but it's not. One of the other two colonels is scrabbling with the button-down-flap on his holster. The other is dashing towards the door. Polystom, not thinking consciously, shoots the second first, knocking a red dent out of his back so that he tumbles straight down. Then his eyes meet those of the one remaining colonel. The pistol is not in the other man's hands. He lurches to the left, ducking down, trying to get under the table for cover, but Polystom is too fast for him. Too fast for him. A properly-written person, a person with *agency*, facing an unreal, a mere shadow, it is no contest.

There are shouts in the corridor, footsteps, so Polystom steps through the back into the little kitchen. A servant is standing there, upright, frozen, and Polystom ignores him, stepping through into the storeroom, and out of that into a service corridor. This leads down to the sunlight, and Stom steps into the imitation sunlight and breathes in a lungful of imitation air. He can see for many miles from this vantage point.

He can see the cannon away to the left; its barrel enormous like a roll of carpet. It is hedged about with slabs of metal, but a little path runs along the slope, with lengths of wood embedded into the mud to ease passage. Polystom trots along this, greets the sentry at the doorway to the gun emplacement cheerily. Sir, you alright? says the sentry, nervous. The general sent me along, says Polystom, trying to remember the name of the general he had just killed. Sent me along. There's blood on your face, sir, says the sentry. Polystom lurches forward, as if drunk, as if tripped or slipped in the mud, and pushes himself up against the young fellow. He can see his face enlarged by proximity, confused and terrified. But it's an easy thing, from this position, to hold the barrel of his rifle with his left hand, to prevent the sentry from lowering it or aiming it, whilst bringing out his pistol with his right. He feels the heat of the discharge as he shoots it point-blank into the sentry's stomach: a sudden spurt of heat, not unpleasant. Then a spreading sense of wetness, warm again. Polystom steps back, lifts the gun and fires again. Through the door without looking back, swept along on the on-rolling motion of events now. The space inside, cluttered with metal shapes and stacked shells, contains only two people. They are sitting on boxes, using another box as a table, cards fanned out before them, more in their hands. They are both staring, wide-eyed, at the doorway, one half-turned at the waist. Polystom thinks of the insurrectionist commander. Shoot the gun crew she had said. Shoot the gun crew. The pistol is hot in his hand now, toasty with use. He shoots, misses, shoots again as they simply sit there, stupid and wooden men. Shoots again, shoots again, until their blood is dashed over the wall behind. Then he is fishing the grenade from his underpants, where it has nestled all this time like a third weighty bollock. It takes him a moment to determine how to swing the heavy doorway of the cannon's breach open, to pull the fuse cable of the grenade, to place it carefully inside the cavity, and to push the circular doorway closed – not all the way shut (he had been told), leave a sliver. Then it's away, away, mustn't hang around, stepping briskly back through the doorway (ducking so as not to crack his head), past the body of the sentry, none of them real, none of them real in the slightest. He's twenty yards up the path, and almost back inside the service tunnel, when he hears the explosion behind him. Turning he sees a banner of smoke curling out of the sighting windows, and a second thread coming out of the barrel. And, moments after that, in the valley at the foot of the mountain he hears the appallingly realistic-sounding crashes of shellfire, the shouts of men. He can even see, distantly, the swarming soldiers drawing closer. But he mustn't loiter here. It's almost time. Soon enough the insurrectionists would over-run the Computational Device and destroy it. That would be the moment of truth. That would resolve the difficult philosophical problem.

And then he would know whether his wife truly loved him or not.

[A note on the leaves.]

The text of *Polystom* is preserved upon thirty numbered leaves, most of which survive in a reasonable state of repair. Each leaf is a narrow strip of pseudo-paper, no more than twenty-six characters to a line, although some leaves are as many as forty or fifty feet long. They were stored rolled tightly and tied about. Some decay is evident at the outer range of some of these leaves, whilst others are pristine. The numbering does not seem entirely logical or consistent, but has been largely followed in this edition except in such cases where confusion might result from the numbered order, and small corrections have been introduced.

Editorial interventions have been made on the principle of non-intrusiveness, although occasional headnotes have proved unavoidable. The current edition draws heavily, of course, on the work of Professor the Lord Barnaby, to whom all Polystom scholars owe an incalculable debt, both for his *Polystom: a Variorum Edition* (University of London Press, 2019) and his monograph *Entropy and the Polystomic Manuscripts* (Everyman, 2017). The following quotation from the latter work is quoted by gracious permission of the author, and remains copyright to Earl Barnaby and his electronic estate:

Given two universe, one 'real' and one 'programmed' from within the logic of physics of the other, it can be very difficult to determine grounds upon which one is to be preferred to the other. As Polystom and his dead wife discuss in leaf 28c [this ed. Book 3, leaf 7], evidence for the 'reality' of each in turn can be presented with equal apparent validity. The two key pieces of evidence, it seems to many experts, are, on the one hand, the appearance of the software 'ghost' programmes of specific individuals in the Polystomic world rather than the other – and, on the other hand, the implausibility of 'vacuum' in any naturally occurring cosmos. On this latter point, my own experiences are perhaps relevant. I have been in a high-flying airliner, in which the compartment is pressurised to two thirds of an atmosphere and the air outside at considerably lower pressure. On this particular occasion a rear porthole shattered, and the explosive decompression that followed – even though the air outside was not vacuum, but merely 'low pressure' – was terrifying to behold. The pressure gradient between sea level and vacuum is much more pronounced than this, and on a cosmic scale these two pressure differentials are essentially next to one another.

On the other hand, as is argued in leaf 28c, there are inconsistencies in the internal coherence of the Polystomic world: it is hard to see, for instance, how programmes written into the mainframe of a computer could manifest themselves outside that computer. The debate is moot.

But there is one benchmark, one absolute, that will help us gauge relative merits, something more universal, even, than gravity (for there are places in the universe called black holes inside which even gravity ceases to become constant): and that absolute is entropy. Let us thumbnail our definition of entropy as 'the tendency of pattern and order to degrade over time'. Then we may examine the extent to which the transmission of text from one cosmos to the other can be thought of as entropic. Because in the subordinate cosmos, a limited system controlled by the superordinate cosmos, entropy will be a minor consideration; whereas in the superordinate cosmos it is a major. Hence a text passed from up, as it were, from the model to the reality will be intact; whereas data passed from the reality to the model will tend to degrade. Think of it this way: if you enter data into your computer there is a high chance of error, whereas if you download data from your computer you expect it to emerge from the databanks exactly as recorded there. If text passes from the subordinate to the superordinate world (from model to reality) we would not expect there to be any degradation to the data of that text; but if the passage is the other way – from reality to model – then there is a chance that a degree of degradation will occur.

Few scholars have been so even-handed. On one side there is the case made, polemically, by Gampson in his *Presentation, representation and power: a Foucauldian reading of the Polystom manuscripts* (University of Woking Press, 1999) which has attracted many followers. 'Most people take the presence of *interplanetary vacuum* for granted, just as they assume that "gravity" is somehow "enough" to keep the violent Brownian bubblings of our atmosphere in place on our world. Even when physicists talk of the upper level of the atmosphere – where gases "boil into space" – they do so without noting how enormous the spherical area is over which this loss continually takes place, and without explaining what mechanism replaces the leaking atmosphere. Such people – not to mince words – are cretins.' Professor Gampson's implication is clear: for him the Polystom universe is the real one, and 'our' universe a poorly constructed computer model.

Other scholars have been equally intemperate on the other side. Gampson's great rival, Hibson, insists that 'any assertion of the ultimate "realty" of the Polystom universe represents a sort of intellectual imbecility, ignoring as it does the manifold impossibilities of that universe: most notably the absurdly reduced size of the solar system, the consequent proximity of large gravitational bodies, the friction of large bodies orbiting a sun through a medium howsoever rarified etc.' Gampson's only reply to Hibson on this point is to assert that 'just as the larger spheres orbit the sun, so do the smaller spheres of atmospheric molecules; everything is in orbital motion at once, and friction, accordingly, is minimal.' Hibson's second major objection to the cosmos (that the air pressure at ground level on any world in a solar system of interplanetary gravity would crush living things with its weight) is dismissed by Gampson with particular contempt:

Take a point x, *at a geostationary orbital position above the Earth. Imagine a column of air reaching from ground level to* x; *such a quantity of air would indeed be very much heavier than that found in our world, and would weigh horribly upon the person standing underneath it. But imagine the same column extended, as it would be in the Polystom cosmos, as far out again, to* 2x *(and, indeed, further still, but let us simplify the model). As with the hypothesised Clarke space-elevator cable, the weight of the quantity of air from* x *to* 2x, *moving away from the world under centrifugal orbital effects, would in practice* counteract *the weight of the quantity of air from ground to* x, *and the net air pressure at sea level would in fact be less than is the case on Earth. In fact, and because we are not dealing with a rigid structure like a space-elevator cable, we cannot think of a vertical column of air over every person. Instead we must imagine very long, spiral trailing areas of air, in which the cumulative weight of all the individual molecules of air does not press directly downwards, but instead acts via a complex pattern of shearing forces and diagonal partial-pressures. Calculations suggest that air pressure under these circumstances, at sea level on any rotating body with gravity g, would be slightly* less than one bar. *To suggest otherwise, as some slapdash scholars have done – scholars of whom one must say, in certain cases, that they really ought to have known better – is to be guilty of solecisms that would embarrass a schoolchild.*

Interested readers may consult the extensive bibliography on the subject to be found at www.polystom.com.

[Acknowledgments]

I'd like to thank the following people for help and support during the writing of this novel: Simon Spanton for the economical excellence of his editorial work, as well as for his friendship; Malcolm Edwards; Malcolm Dixon, who read the manuscript; Steve Calcutt; Roger Levy; James Lovegrove; Bob Eaglestone, who disagreed with the physics of the Polystom world. Most of all, I would like to thank my wife Rachel, who read the manuscript and made many helpful suggestions.

I would also like to acknowledge one very particular debt. Gillian Allnutt's exquisite collection of poetry *Lintel* (Bloodaxe, 2001) provided me with general inspiration for this novel, as well as specific quotation. Polystom's own readings of Phanicles' poetry are taken from three of Allnut's poems: 'turf', the opening of 'Tabitha and Lintel' and 'Annunciation'. These lines are quoted by kind permission of the author, and remain copyright to her.

This book is for Lily.